Love the Wine You're With

By

Brooke E. Wayne

Hearts & Flowers
Publishing

First Edition

ISBN-10: 069297752X
ISBN-13: 9780692977521

Title: Love the Wine You're With
Series: Vineyard Pleasures Series, #2
Author: Brooke E. Wayne
Publisher: Hearts and Flowers Publishing
Epigraphs: Public Domain, http://www.brainyquote.com
Cover Photo: Shuttershock

Description: Sprinkle an emotionally unavailable woman, a lovelorn man, and some delicious chemistry into the middle of wine country then candy coat it with a whole lotta passion when a friends-with-benefits arrangement turns a vacation into an unexpected journey.

Category: Women's Fiction, Contemporary Romantic Comedy, Contemporary Romance

I dedicate this novel to Joel, my husband.
Your crazy ideas and loving support
are what brought this novel to life.
You are my happily-ever-after.

Chapter One

"And so it is, that both the Devil and the angelic Spirit present us with objects of desire to awaken our power of choice."
~Rumi

Blanca

Maxine Novaline tightened her grip on Chase L'Angevin's hand as if, without holding onto him, she would topple magnetically into Julien L'Angevin's arms. The closer Julien, her boyfriend's cousin, came to them, the harder she squeezed. He embodied sexuality the way a seductive flute of champagne knew that with one sweet taste you'd give into its pleasure and consume every last drop.

At least that's how Maxie had painted that hot mess leering at Blanca Grazia, who stood on the other side of her bestie, second-guessing whether their whole scheme was really such a good idea after all.

It was as if Julien knew Maxie was trying to fling Blanca at him on purpose.

"Bait," Maxie had called Blanca the night before, when they were concocting their plan of diversion to lure Julien away from trying to mess up her relationship with Chase again.

"He's way hotter in person even if he is a dick-face."

Blanca mock-laughed at her own joke, trying to lighten the mood as all three of them watched Julien maneuver through the bustling courtyard.

The only sight of said hottie Blanca had gotten a glimpse of was a picture Maxie had posted on Facebook a couple months ago … Maxie's cornflower blue eyes glazed over with inexplicable joy … Julien's luscious lips plastered to her cheek … and a medieval Parisian village sprawling out behind them.

Quite the scandal.

But, it wasn't entirely Maxie's fault. *When in France, right?*

Maxie offered Blanca a nervous giggle, but Chase only cleared his throat—his eyes panning the mass of revelers at his egocentric birthday gig. He always hosted it on the last Saturday of October disguised as his annual Halloween party.

I love her boyfriend to death. But narcissistic much?

It was such a huge event that his cousin had even flown in for all the way from Champagne—the city, not the drink. Although, the L'Angevins quietly bottled the bubbly on that side of the world, unlike Chase's parents' estate, Angel of the Vine Winery, which was the adult Disneyland of Napa Valley, California. And, at the moment, where every twenty-something within a thirty-mile radius was rockin' some kind of peek-a-boob costume, while writhing to the beat the DJ kept spinning from his makeshift platform.

Chase, who was actually born on All Saint's Day, had Maxie's burgeoning feels all to himself, but for some lame reason, Maxie thought she needed Blanca to keep the peace between those two *stunads* (idiots) in the event Julien tried something shady like he'd done when he had met Maxie a couple months ago.

Over summer, Blanca and Maxie had spent some time in Paris together before Blanca had to head back to the states, leaving Maxie to continue her vacation all alone. Maxie and Chase had just called it quits on trying to date, but Maxie had been having second thoughts. Chase wouldn't answer her texts, so Maxie took a detour to Champagne with hopes of meeting some of Chase's extended family members at the French L'Angevin estate. She thought she might be able to get one of them to convince Chase he should at least let her apologize to him for some mistakes she'd made. And, the next thing Blanca knew, her bestie had found herself fending off Julien's manipulative advances.

Julien's need to seek revenge on Chase by vamping on Maxie, like he had every other girl Chase had taken an interest in, had caused some serious trouble. And, it had nothing to do with Maxie and everything to do with a two-year-old feud between the cousins over an artist that pretty boy, Julien, was going to propose to ... until Julien had walked in on Chase, stripped down to his birthday suit, while he let her *sketch* him in her private studio.

Sketch? Yeah, right. Pft.

The story they had both told Maxie was that, after Julien walked in on them in the middle of their so-called art session, his would-be fiancé went cray-cray and fled to Italy without so much as a proper goodbye, leaving those two numb nuts to fight over nothing in the wake of her departure.

Normally, Blanca was all about minding her own business on that kind of train wreck of a story, but, when Maxie became the object of the cousins' ongoing game of tug-of-war, Blanca felt the need to step it up for her BFF and keep that sexy beast entertained just in case he was still up to no good.

Julien, who was now giving the threesome a full-blown Cheshire grin the closer he came to them, was more pathetic than an actual threat. Maxie had explained the situation to Blanca last night, and she understood she had a job to do, on account of Chase being a raging lunatic when the slightest whiff of jealousy crept up in him.

Once my CEU workshops are over, remind me to never, ever abandon my BFF in a foreign country again. The girl is a chaos magnet when I'm not around to keep things under control.

Maxie was the kind of girl that guys climbed all over each other to get to with her big boobs, big ass, and a waist you could cinch a napkin ring around—a living Barbie Doll—with no clue how hot she was. Chase was only her third partner-slash-boyfriend. He would probably be her last, too. They'd been inseparable once they'd returned to the states by the way they'd been acting all emoji-heart-eyed for each other after Chase showed up in Champagne and put Julien in his place.

Ironically, he came to drag Maxie back to America to deal with even more trouble she'd inadvertently caused at home with Chase's family. That dude sure knew how to play the hero, and Maxie ate it up like a bucket of Nutella. *Inside jokie joke.*

Blanca, on the other hand, had an aversion to true love.

Her one-and-only boyfriend broke her heart five years ago when he popped the question on her, then, snatched his ring back before she even had a chance to get the damn thing sized. Ever since, she'd decided to live her love life to the fullest—sans any actual love. Commitment was not her style. Not even close. Besides, helping out her bestie by distracting that fine piece of lily-white, French ass had its short-term perks.

Maxie had described Julien to her as being salty, rugged, and a danger to the stability of whatever it was the happy couple had blossoming between them. *Insert finger, proceed to gag.* Whether Blanca hit it off with Julien and created their own kind of happily-ever-after before the night came to an end or not was just a potential bonus to their plan to keep him busy all night.

The first thing, scratch that, the second thing Blanca noticed about Julien was how spot on Maxie had been about the unique color of his eyes—faded tropical sea glass bleached by the sun.

Lordie.

His thick, sandy blond hair that hung in waves at his squared jaw line, which was in dire need of a trim, offered just enough contrast to make them practically glow. Even the mottled hues of tangerine and goldenrod that filtered through the twilight couldn't dim those angelic peeps that seemed to tug at her for attention. And, thank God, because that horrendous prosthetic schlong bobbing around off the end of his nose was almost too much to handle.

Two pointy, red horns protruded from the top of Blanca's head in a place where a halo would never be at home. The vibrant, gradient blue hue in her waist-length ombre was all that could be seen tucked up in a giant sock bun—her whiskey brown roots barely even noticeable. She ran her hands up along her slender hips, inconspicuously nudging the ruched fabric of her red dress, revealing another inch or two of her lean legs.

Maxie might have had ginormous boobs to flaunt, but Blanca's legs were her best asset in gaining a man's attention—that and her eyes—an exotic gift from her Mediterranean-American mother and straight-up Italian father—jade green. Although, it wasn't her eyes that she was hoping would detour Julien's attention away from her bestie and back over to her.

"*Bonsoir, mademoiselle,* Maxine." Julien extended his hand out to Maxie as he greeted all of them with an exaggerated head bob—his full lips spreading out in a conspicuous grin, while that sex-shop-reject *thingy* on his face kept tempo with the music enveloping them.

"Hi, Julien. It's, uh, it's nice to see you again." Maxie placed her hand in his, and he pressed the back of it to his lips, making sure to cut his glance over to Chase for a reaction.

"All right, Cyrano de Bergerac, that's enough," Chase said, as Maxie tugged her hand back. "Julien, I'd like you to meet Max's best friend and roommate, Blanca."

His eyes shifted from Maxie's to Chase's then finally landed on Blanca, as if intentionally avoiding acknowledging her at first for whatever hidden agenda he might be brewing behind that sinister smolder.

Challenge accepted.

"It is a pleasure to make your acquaintance." He reached up and tipped his feathered hat. Then, he bowed his head quickly with a wobbly-nosed nod, detonating laughter from all three of them.

"*Bonsoir,* Julien. *C'est un plaisir de me rencontrer, vous verrez bientôt* (Good evening. It *is* a pleasure to meet me, as you'll soon see)."

"*Ah, vous parler un peu de Français* (Ah, you speak some French). *Bien. Bien.* I see I am going to have to disguise my endless chatter to my cousin about you two beauties with another language then, *non?*"

Julien panned Maxie's Cinderella costume—from her Swedish blonde French twist to the endless panels of baby blue tulle enveloping her from her neckline to her ankles. Two princess-worthy, clear resin shoes peeked out underneath her gown. Ever since they'd left Blanca's house twenty minutes earlier, Maxie had been whining about those shoes killing her arches.

That dress was a Halloween get-up Maxie *just had to wear* to match Chase instead of Blanca. They'd always worn coordinating costumes as the dynamic duo—good versus evil angels—*you know, the ones parked on your shoulders when moral decisions needed to be made. But, noooo.* Chase won that round of tug-of-war, and Blanca was left looking devilishly delicious without her sidekick sweetie to pull off their long-standing joke. *Grr.*

"Go right ahead, but Blanca speaks four languages fluently and will have French mastered in a couple more months." Maxie slapped her on the shoulder in an attempt to push her forward towards Julien, causing the enormous, black, feathered wings anchored by a harness strapped her shoulders to bounce up and down as if she were about to take flight.

Julien reared his head back. "Ah, now that is interesting, and what languages do you speak?"

"All the Romance Languages," Maxie interjected just as Blanca parted her lips to reply.

Chase made a garbled sound and tugged at the baby blue satin ascot around his neck.

Blanca cocked her head and squeezed her eyes shut in annoyance. "Maxie."

"Sorry. Go ahead, Blanca. Tell him about—"

"—I've got this," Blanca growled through clinched teeth.

Julien's smile dimmed as he panned all of them. "I see you ladies are empty-handed. Is Prince Charming here letting you down, as usual? May I grab some drinks for you? I hear the bartender has a blood-red cocktail called The Monster Mash with jellied eyes floating around in it."

"I'd love to see that." Blanca quirked up the corner of her mouth and hooked her arm through the crook of Julien's elbow, dragging him backwards a couple of paces before he turned around. They both shot a quick glance over their shoulders at a disgruntled Chase and beaming Maxie.

Blanca squeezed his arm as she held onto him. "I owe you one, Jules."

"What's that?" Julien asked, raking her with his luminous eyes briefly as they distanced themselves from the Disney cake toppers.

That's right buddy. Feast on all this wicked sexy.

"I love her to death. We've been inseparable since high school, but sometimes I need a breather, especially when Chase is around. They're kind of unnerving when they're together."

"Trust me, I understand, but I can see why. Love does peculiar things to some people."

"Love? Oh, I don't know about any of that. They only just started spending every waking hour together since Wednesday. Up until then, they were just weekenders. She hasn't started tossing the L-word around yet."

Julien furrowed his brow for a moment. "Why Wednesday?"

"I just closed on a house about fifteen minutes from here, and Maxie is my roommate. We haven't even finished unpacking yet because she's always with your cousin."

"Ah, your first home?"

"No, second." Blanca's voice rose high above the rumble of the music as the crowd swallowed them up the closer they came to the bar—her wings brushing into the other guests left and right.

"You both lived in Sacramento, *non?*"

"Our whole lives," Blanca groaned, nudging her way through a cluster-freak of zombies.

Julien wrapped his warm hand around hers and stepped in front of her, allowing her to trail behind him safely—a coy smile tickling her lips as she took the opportunity to thread her fingers through his.

They slipped between two Grady Twins drenched in glittery, red stains, who instantly recognized Julien and tugged at him to play with them *like last year.* He shrugged them off and mumbled something polite as Blanca tipped her nose at them in passing.

Sorry, girls, Dick-face de Bergerac is taken tonight.

"I hope you don't mind," Julien began, shouting at her over his shoulder, "but I have to ask. Did they set you up?"

"I willingly volunteered to keep you distracted. Maxie hasn't shut up about you since Chase confirmed that you were still flying in for his party. You'd think she had a crush on you, if she hadn't told me you were also as shady as shit. You're an easy sell, though."

Julien turned completely around and stopped them—the end of his prosthetic nose almost touching hers as he peered down at her petite frame, still much shorter than him despite her four-inch stilettos.

He squeezed her hand. "I was referring to you moving here just a stone's throw to my cousin's home."

"Oh, gotcha." A faint tinge of embarrassment washed over her for a split second then evaporated.

He turned and began to move forward again in the direction of the bar.

Blanca cleared her throat and continued to ramble as loud as she could above the music at the back of Julien's plumed-hat-wearing head. "Yep. I had to quit my job. The salon I worked at in Sacramento lost its lease. Maxie suggested I look into working at one of the resort spas here, so I did. I even cashed out the equity in my condo and bought a house here in Napa Valley, so I wouldn't have to commute. We haven't even finished unpacking, yet, and I start my new job at the end of next week."

"And Maxie gets to come along for the ride," Julien scoffed, looking over his shoulder at her, then smiled as if to himself. "Lucky bastard."

"As long as she pays me rent, they can think they got one over on me all they want." Blanca offered a sly smile in return.

He stopped pulling her along and scammed on her once more. "So, you were, ehm, saying something about me being ... what was it?"

"Shady. As. Shit." She pinched her fingers together and flicked the long, rubbery whatchamacallit dangling in her face. "And, from what I can tell, in need of some decent company tonight."

Or indecent. Take your pick, pretty boy.

He glanced over at the Grady Twins who were hanging all over some pathetic loser in a Where's Waldo get-up then focused his attention back to her, fighting off a laugh. He tipped his feathered hat in the direction of the bar and pulled her with him again. "All right, Max's best friend, I'm all yours."

"Don't say things you don't mean," she purred, as they sidled up to the bar.

Julien grabbed two of the bloodied drinks off a tray on the countertop that did, in fact, have horrid eyeballs ogling up at them.

"Follow me." Julien nodded towards the other side of the courtyard where the largest of the buildings housed the main offices.

He led the way through the crowd again as Blanca barely kept up with him. They skirted around the huge fountain in the middle of the courtyard that was illuminated in lime green. The light created an eerie glow over the winged angel poised for flight in the center of it. Curling ribbons of water churned all around the creature in a fury, muffling the drone of a wordless song that hung in the cool breeze.

As they neared the perimeter of the crowd, Julien slowed his pace and handed Blanca her drink. They sidestepped two enormous metallic trees, several of which were staggered around the courtyard, all decked out in crystal leaves that pulsed to the music in an LED display of shimmering autumnal colors. They finally arrived in front of the large, double-doors leading into the building.

"I figure we could enjoy our drinks in private. " His French accent thickened for a second. "Catch me up on this plan Chase hatched for me. Although, I must say, Blanca, you are an intriguing sidekick to our lovely Maxine, and I would've taken an interest in getting to know you, nonetheless." He went to swing the door open, but it only trembled in its place, rattling off a warning not to intrude.

"Well, that stinks." Blanca sucked her teeth. "I get that you must think there's some big Chase-induced scheme going on here, but really, there isn't much of a story to tell. Maxie asked me to distract you from getting on your cousin's nerves. She said you had a way of using her to get at him."

"Is that so?" he scoffed, throwing back his drink in a few swift gulps and turning his back to the door. "Ehm, what if we try the wine cave?" He snatched her hand up in his and tugged her along towards the side of the hill, sloshing her drink over the rim of her glass.

"Jeez, what's the rush? I'm just supposed to wow you with my witty banter. I'm not sure we're on the same page here, buddy." She pulled back on him, trying to steady herself as she teetered in her stilettos—the stone pathway not exactly high-fashion friendly.

What the hell have I gotten myself into?

He let go of her hand and spun around. Blanca stumbled backwards a few feet, and Julien lunged forward, trying to wrap his arms around her to keep her from falling down. Her massive wings only complicated his efforts, though, and she toppled forward into his arms. She grabbed onto his ruffled shirt with one hand while most of the contents of her glass in her other hand went flying off to the side.

He slipped his hands around her waist and pulled her upright against his massive body. "I've got you, *mon chéri.* We don't need any more lawsuits complicating matters for my aunt and uncle."

"Whoa. Now that was a low blow. You know, it's not her fault. Maxie had no idea her ex-boyfriend was suing Chase's family over her accident until he threw it in her face when she was hanging out with you in France." Blanca found her footing and wrestled out of his arms—her cocktail nothing but a couple of jellied eyeballs looking up at her from the bottom of her glass. *Blech.* "Besides, she settled it. Settled it for nothing, if you ask me."

She handed the glass to Julien.

"A half-a-million is *not* nothing." He stacked her glass with his and fished out an eyeball, tossing it up and catching it in his mouth.

Blanca perched her hands on her hips and stared him down—or up—the dude was at least six-feet-tall to her tiny five-six frame, four-inch stilettos included, of course. "She didn't get a half-a-million. She had the insurance company reduce the settlement to $10,000, and she's given Chase's parents so much dirt on that douchebag ex of hers, they should be thrilled that the fool who knocked Maxie down the stairs is only getting a chump-change payoff for his lawsuit."

"I suppose Chase did mention something to me about it last night on the way back from the airport, but I was half-asleep with jetlag. He's such a bore sometimes. You, on the other hand, have me all kinds of interested." He reached out and took her hand in his then led her down the walkway in the dark as if the topic at hand no longer mattered to him.

Wow, this guy is slick.

"Care to elaborate?"

"I tell you what. We call a truce, and I won't kill my cousin for *using you* to keep me away from his girlfriend. This annual party of his is always crawling with opportunities. I don't need him to offer me a—what did you call yourself—a distraction? I am shocked he'd—they'd—bother to con you into wasting your time with me."

"Wow. Okay. So, you really are into her? I thought you were just messing with Chase's head." She tried to release his hand, but he only gripped hers tighter.

"She is wonderful—"

"Yes. Yes, she is. She is also off-limits."

"So, I've been told."

"And your angle here?" She lifted up their knotted hands to his face as they continued down the pathway towards the wine cave that had become lined with golf carts attached to narrow flatbed trailers.

"I have been known to hold hands with the devil on occasion."

Chapter two

"So the darkness shall be the light, and the stillness the dancing."
~T. S. Eliot

Julien
The massive, wooden doors leading into the wine cave were propped open, and two employees dressed as angels stood on either side of the entrance handing out blacklight wands and flashlights to a crowd of noisy drunks, otherwise known as Chase's friends.

So much for privacy.

Julien let out a disappointed grunt. "I guess there's a tour of some sort going on in the caverns."

"That sounds fun."

Fun? I could think of infinitely more entertaining things to do at the moment than whatever Chase has rigged inside there. "All right, then."

He released her hand and exchanged a few words, as well as the empty glasses, with the workers for a set of the lights and rattled off a quick thank you in French.

"We follow the neon markers." He handed a blacklight wand to his half-pint sidekick and kept the flashlight for himself. "Apparently, the alcove my uncle stores the LED trees in has been converted into a haunted something or other."

"Don't worry, Jules. I'll protect you."

Jules? Adorable. Who is this woman?

"You, ehm, scare easily, *non*?" He motioned for her to enter.

"I'm only terrified of things I can't control."

"You like being the master of your domain, then? " he teased, as they stepped inside the welcoming room of the cave. A handful of wrought iron bistro chairs and wine barrels were scattered about with a myriad of guests loitering around, making far too much noise for his liking.

He stepped in front of her and knelt down. "Hop on, *s'il vous plaît* (please)?"

"You want me to ride you?"

Julien grinned to himself. *Perhaps.*

"I want to get this over with, and those sexy, *petit* shoes of yours are only slowing us down."

"I can't."

"*Oui, vous pouvez* (Yes, you can)."

"My skirt."

He straightened up, tucked the flashlight into his waistband, and turned to face her. "Then we'll have to—" And in one swift movement, he swooped her into his arms being careful of her wings.

She let out a tiny laugh as she tossed her head back. "And, here I thought you weren't capable of sweeping a girl off her feet."

"Ready for some reckless abandonment?" He peered down the broad tunnel ahead of them that was illuminated by the partygoer's roving flashlights.

"I'm all yours."

Ah, we shall see, my devilish distraction.

With those inviting words, Julien plunged forward in a mad rush, skirting around superheroes, a band of pirates, some mermaids, and even a Rubic's Cube, as they passed several roped-off alcoves until they came to the chamber that hosted the haunted tour. Instead of putting his tiny, giggling vixen down, he just cradled her tighter, slipping around a small, yet obnoxiously loud, group of banshees in front of them.

"We are supposed to follow the footprints with the blacklight," he said.

"Are you planning on carrying me through this whole obstacle course?"

He dipped his knees down and then lunged up, getting her airborne out of his arms by a half a foot. She squealed as he caught her in his arms again.

"What are you doing?"

"I wanted to see if you could fly. It would be much quicker, you know, if you could carry me."

She tipped her head back and laughed. "What if I just take off my shoes?"

"You want to start undressing for me. Very well, then." He set her down again and tugged the flashlight out of his waistband.

Blanca laughed at Julien's unreserved wit, handing him her blacklight. Then she yanked her stilettos off and hooked her finger through the heel straps. "There. Happy now?"

Julien made a show of perusing the room above her head. "Where did that little imp go?" Then, he flicked on the small flashlight and shined it on her. "Oh, there she is."

She raised her arm to shield her eyes. "Ha-ha, very funny. I might be small, but I'm larger than life, once you get to know me."

"If that's a challenge, then I accept." He handed her the blacklight. "Since, you're so much closer to the ground than me, you be on the lookout for neon footprints."

She snapped the blacklight on and revealed neon red splatters appearing beneath their feet. "On second thought," she moaned, holding up her heels.

"Fine, if you must. Put your shoes back on. I'll just take it slow with you."

"Lesson number one in getting to know me, dick-face," she began, slipping her heels back on her feet and giving him a look that could kill a lovelorn man outright. "I don't believe in taking things slowly ... or seriously especially when it comes to you."

Well, well. I think I may have met my match.

* * *

After dodging goblins and ghosts, coffins erupting in hissing vampires, and even a crime scene that was so tacky it made B-list movies look fantastic, Julien finally emerged from the wine cave with Blanca. She was still in a fit of giggles from having to fend off Julien's attempts to offer her up as a tribute for passage to every ghoulish monster that groped at them in the dark for the past hour.

He suggested that they hunt down Chase for a set of keys that would gain them access to the main building, and finally found him on the dance floor with Max, twirling her around like the princess she was. Lost in their own world of rainbows and sunshine, Chase didn't hesitate to embrace Julien briefly, and ask if he'd been enjoying Blanca's company.

Julien swayed under the weight of Chase's arm. "She beats the hell out of spending the evening with the two of you."

"I'm going to grab a drink," Blanca said, snagging Max's hand and leading her away from them.

As Chase watched the girls melt into the crowd again, Julien waved his hand in front of his cousin's face. "You *really are* falling in love, *oui?*"

"Deeper and deeper every damn day."

"Nice. She has you dribbling poetic devices now. So that's it, then. I guess I wish you both all the luck in the world. She's going to need it. I can't say I would have pegged you for a giddy blonde, but, then again, I've never known you to be this happy. She suits you, I suppose."

"And you … you need another drink, *maintenant* (right now)."

Chase pulled away from his cousin and trailed after the two women.

And, you can't let her away from you for one minute. Pathetic.

Julien didn't desire Max, per say, he only wanted what his cousin shared with her—their absurd yearning for one another that both repulsed him and filled him with raw envy. Granted, he'd been completely intrigued by her when they'd met over summer. Why wouldn't he be? Her joy was almost contagious, and he was in dire need of a little dose of sunshine. She was liquid gold to him, but his heart never crossed the line when he realized his cousin wanted to mend his broken relationship with her.

Julien turned around and scoped the crowd surrounding him. He recognized several people and nodded as some of the guests acknowledged him. It amused Julien that he'd come all the way to the United States for yet another reason to celebrate Chase's many successes. Less than two years separated the cousins in age, but Julien was an old soul. It aged him even more to see Chase living his life to the fullest, including falling in love with an amazing woman.

Ah, yes, the bittersweet fruit of the vine makes such a succulent, desirable grape when crushed into a delectable drop of wine.

Blanca emerged from the crowd holding two deep purple martinis. "This one's called a Black Orchid."

He took the drink from her and tasted it. "I might need a few of these."

"Not having a good time, are you?" She brushed against him with one of her wings.

"I am having the time of my life, thanks to you," he drawled, faking a perfect American accent.

Blanca smiled between sips of her cocktail. "Damn right you are. Did you snag Chase's keys?"

Just as he was about to head through the crowd to hunt his cousin down, Chase emerged with Max, both holding some kind of fruity concoction that looked like a summer sunset.

"I'll ask if you're sure you are up for it," Chase said to Max as they approached them. "So, when these two lovely ladies return from their writer's retreat, Max would like all of us to take a hot air balloon ride before you head home next weekend. We could make a double date of it and grab dinner in town. You are staying the whole week, aren't you Julien?"

"Ehm, sure. I'll be around." He nodded, threw back his martini, and then glanced over at Blanca who shrugged at him.

"Yeah, sure, why not?" she added, finishing off her own drink.

Blanca took Julien's glass out of his hand and headed over to a table on the perimeter of the crowd where empty glasses were accumulating quicker than the staff could clear them.

He watched her as she returned—her lean hips swaying like a pendulum as those giant wings batted the air.

She really does have a certain charm about her.

"Could I get the keys to the main building from you?"

"I guess so," Chase replied, fishing out a set of keys from his pants pocket. "What do you need in the office?"

"Nothing."

Just give me the damn keys. All I want is to distance myself from all this noise and give you both an out with having to spend any time with me.

"Oh, then why—"

"I'd like some privacy. I can't exactly take my, ehm, my *date* to the house with your parents two doors down from the guest room, and your place with all the windows—well, I'd rather make use of the ballroom."

Max bowed her head—a faint blush igniting her pale cheeks. "So, you two really have hit it off tonight. I knew you would."

Julien could care less if he misled them … or not. One thing he did know for certain—he'd rather be alone with his naughty, little devil and her infectious laughter than waste another minute drowning in whatever the hell the DJ was spewing out of the speakers.

"Blanca's wonderful," he smirked, as she stepped up beside him.

"Yes. I'm adorable, and, as long as we're all talking about me while I'm not present, what else have you decided?" She quirked the corner of her mouth up, pursing her lips, and glared at Chase and Max.

Chase tossed the keys over to Julien. "I was just telling Julien that once you both return from your writer's retreat, we'd like to grab a hot air balloon tour of the valley and have dinner together."

"Now that sounds terrifying. I'm in. Jules, you scared of heights?"

"No."

"Then our answer is yes."

This little firecracker is too cute. "We'll be going now."

"Ciao," Blanca quipped, thrumming her fingers in the air above her head as Julien tugged her away from them.

* * *

Blanca

Despite Chase's efforts at creating something spooky in the wine cave with cool props and actors, the empty ballroom in the dark was way more terrifying. Blanca had been in there before for a tour when it was a madhouse of tipsy wine connoisseurs, but it carried a different vibe then. At the moment, it reeked of something out of *The Shining,* and she thought about those two girls on the dance floor from earlier that Julien probably knew all too well and wondered if they drew their costume inspiration from that creepy place.

Faint moonlight streamed in along the line of the ceiling through long, skinny windows high above them, barely offering any kind of visibility. They weaved around some overstuffed chairs, bumping into a couple of tables here and there, exciting a small lamp in a musical chime as its tiny, crystal strands jingled together. Julien let out an exhausted moan as he plopped down on a black velvet couch, smacking the seat next to him for Blanca to join him.

She remained standing and turned her back to him. "Could you help me with my wings?"

"Of course," he said, rising up behind her.

He fidgeted with the tiny snaps on the harness, popping each one apart until the wings separated. She slipped her arms through the plastic straps that were around her shoulders, freeing herself of the cumbersome wings, which she set on the ground at her heels.

Julien took his hat off and tossed it behind him then fell back on the couch. "I think I'll ditch the schnoz," he huffed, tugging and peeling at the base of the prosthetic until it finally detached, leaving his nose and cheeks flushed with a deep red. He tossed it over his shoulder to join his hat somewhere in the dark.

"Much better," Blanca remarked, squinting to see what he looked like without that heinous flobby-jeeby dangling from his face as she sat down next to him.

Hot, definitely smokin' hot, ladies.

She reached over to the silver marbled end table and tugged on the lamp's chain, snapping it on. A gentle glow emanated from it, enveloping them in a tiny halo of soft pink that filtered through its lacy shade.

Julien slumped down and tipped his head back on the couch. "Ah, some peace and quiet. I hope you don't mind."

"Not at all," Blanca cooed, warming up to the eerie serenity of the grand ballroom as she settled in closer to him. "I bet you're really feeling the time change right about now."

"You know me so well." He turned his head to her and reached out for her hand and cradled it in his own. It was a gentle, almost caring gesture as though he had known *her* for years. "What was Chase saying about a retreat?"

"Oh, yeah, that. Maxie starts working for your uncle in a few weeks, so we decided we would do this novel-writing-basics workshop we discovered on a forum. It's a full day of classes at a hotel in the Bay Area, and it's on the beach, so we're making it a mini vacation before we both get swamped by work."

She pulled his hand into her lap and began playing with his fingers thoughtlessly.

"Ehm. You lost me. None of that made any sense. What job could my uncle possibly want her to do around here?"

"She'll be spouting famous poetry and short stories while taking small groups on a private tour and serving up some flagship wine."

No kidding? Hmm. Keep your friends close and your enemies closer?" He squeezed both of her hands that fit perfectly into his singular palm.

"Exactly, but Maxie doesn't believe me that your aunt and uncle might be faking their enthusiasm over her."

"And, what does any of that have to do with writing a novel?"

"I guess it got her all hot and bothered to write again like she used to when we were in high school. We both joined NaNoWriMo and challenged each other to finish writing a manuscript by December."

"Nano rhymo? What the hell does rhyming have to do with one billion parts? Or a novel, for that matter?"

Blanca erupted in laughter. "No, silly! National Novel Writing Month. It's an annual event people from all over do together. You write a little over sixteen hundred words a day, and, by the end of the month, you have a fifty-thousand-word manuscript to work with."

"Ah, *oui, oui.*" He shook his head *no.* "So, if this new job has Max inspired to write, what's in it for you? What is driving you to write?"

She cocked an eyebrow at him. "I love an interesting challenge."

"Now *that* makes sense."

She scrunched up her shoulders and took a deep breath then released it with a little whine. "My shoulders are killing me. Those wings were heavier than my backpack ever was in high school."

He pulled his hand away from hers and raked his fingers through his thick hair that fell in wavy chunks around his squared jawline. "High school was how long ago?"

"I look a lot younger than I am."

"And that is?"

"Twenty-five."

Maxie had already filled Blanca in that she'd met Julien in August on his thirtieth birthday. It was kind of endearing that it mattered to him how old, or actually, how young he thought she could be. Their age difference made *no difference* to her at all. What, with him just visiting Chase then eventually sulking his moody way back to France by next weekend? *Meh.* It was nothing in the whole scheme of things.

In fact, it was borderline TMI for her taste, but she already had a hunch she wasn't going to need to go into her whole memorized rant about being emotionally unavailable if they *really hit it off* at some point that week. He seemed like he may have that one, teeny characteristic in common with her.

That, and having the hots for some peace and quiet.

"You are definitely right about that. You look like you graduated yesterday." He smiled more to himself than at her and sat up with an exhausted grunt. "Here," he added, motioning for her to turn around. "What if I do you first, then you do me?"

"Aw, you say the most romantic things, baby."

"I'm not as fluent in other languages as you are, but it might sound sexier if I said it in French." He dug his fingers and thumbs into her tight muscles as her head fell forward with a moan. "Or not. Sounds like I'm doing just fine with my hands."

She couldn't help but laugh. "I'm only conversationally fluent in several languages, with the exception of Italian, but Maxie can think I'm an expert linguist if she wants to."

"It's kind of odd for an American to be multilingual. You are American, *oui*? You do have an exotic look about you."

"I'm half Italian and half everything else east of Italy on my ma's side, but they've been in America for several generations. Learning languages is just a hobby of mine. It pairs well with my lust for traveling. I use more Italian American slang if anything. My Italian grandparents first settled in Philly then moved to San Francisco when my pop was a teenager. I consider myself a *Californian*."

"If you were wearing sneakers and smacking gum, I might believe you."

She smiled at his joke then let out another groan as he dug into her shoulders again. "That feels so good. Thank you."

"You're welcome," he whispered, nuzzling his nose against the base of her neck.

"Mmm. Nice," she sighed. "I wanted to be a Linguistics teacher once, but my life took a different turn, and I haven't looked back since. I'm a hair stylist. A damn good one, too. I really love what I do."

"I can see that about you." His fluid words fell softly on her skin in a warm caress.

"I do think your French drawl is ridiculously sexy, though."

"You do? Well, then, I'll have to keep talking your ear off all night."

"Or not."

Too soon?

A small stretch of silence hung between them as he continued to knead her bare shoulders—his fingertips curling around her delicate neck every now and then.

"Your turn." She twisted around until they were face to face.

She looked at him for a moment—her eyes darting between his lips and his eyes. "Your poor nose. Does it sting?"

"A kiss might make it feel better."

There you are, you big, sexy, French, beast of a man. I knew you'd come around eventually. "I'm sure a kiss would make all kinds of things feel better."

She smiled and leaned in, dodging his lips at the last second and planting her kiss on the tip of his nose. He grinned and wrapped his hand around the back of her neck, pressing his forehead to hers.

"You really did turn out to be a pleasant surprise tonight, Blanca."

The night's only just begun.

"Oh, is that so, Jules?"

He closed the space between their lips, kissing her slowly, softly, as though he wanted to savor the way she tasted. Her lips parted, and his tongue slid between hers, while his fingertips trailed from the nape of her neck down along her spine, pausing at the zipper on her dress. He opened his eyes and peered at her with heavy lids as his other fingertips found their way along her cheek, beckoning a faint smile from her lips.

He whispered her name as if to assure himself of her then thumped the end of her nose with his finger.

What the?

"Did you just boop me?"

"Is that what you California girls are calling it these days?"

Chapter three

"Writers are a little below clowns and a little above trained seals."
~John Steinbeck

Blanca

After sitting in on five hours of workshops ranging from *Plot Mapping Basics for Contemporary Romance* to *Polishing an MC's Arc in a Duel POV*, Blanca and Maxie were about done with the whole, 'Hey, let's both write novels next month—it'll be fun,' routine before they were even ready to start.

Feeling an overwhelming urge to vacate the sterile hotel premises, they ditched the scheduled meet-and-greet luncheon and opted to head to an eccentric coffee house that they'd read all about on Yelp. It was near 17-Mile Drive along Highway 1 and was only about ten miles off the beaten path in a hiccup of a town called Sea Sprite. Based on all the reviewers' pictures, it looked like it practically sat on top of the waves, and, if writerly inspiration was calling, that joint seemed like it could have a freakin' megaphone.

A soft rain sprinkled down on them as they hurried through the door of Fa*brew*licious Coffee & Tea and scoped out a place to sit. It hummed with so much eclectic, coastal ambiance, that they had to take a moment to soak it all in before they tossed their backpacks on one of two black leather couches to their left—the only place in the coffee shop to sit, as far as they could see. A set of matching chairs, two on either side of the ends of the coffee table, were occupied, and an entire replica of that same seating area to their right was also packed with others.

A half a dozen tables and chairs littered the area in front of each of the cozy, mock living rooms near the baristas' station along a solid brick wall, but, sheesh, if this hangout wasn't so big, it'd probably need bouncers to help with crowd control. Even a steady stream of cars lined up outside the windows to their right waiting their turn in the drive-thru.

If the driftwood accents and the contemporary art hanging everywhere wasn't enough to make Maxie and Blanca squee with delight, the entire left side of the building was all glass with a bar counter and wooden stools running along it. Customers occupied each stool while others just stood around, all facing, *drum roll please,* the raging sea.

Beyond the busy deck, cluttered with picnic tables tented with umbrellas quivering in the wind, the waves rolled in. They crashed down upon the mocha-colored sand, bursting into a foamy display of all things craggy and wonderful. A literal writer's paradise.

"I'll grab us our drinks. What are you in the mood for?" Maxie offered.

"Something hot, sweet, and loaded with enough caffeine to snap me out of the gawdawful trance those classes put me in."

"Oh, come on. The classes weren't *that* bad."

"They weren't that good either." Blanca slumped down on the couch next to their backpacks and mustered up a smile. "All righty, surprise me with something I could only get in a coffee house like this."

"You got it." Maxie headed over to the counter in the back under the overhang and eyed the chalkboards along a brick wall while striking up a conversation with a flannel-wearing barista that had more facial hair than Santa Claus.

Blanca pulled out her laptop, some materials, and settled in. They had taken copious notes in journals on as much as they could and had even brought a couple of *Prompt Me* workbooks with all kinds of graphic organizers, prompt starters, and worksheets for them to outline their novels with, just so that their friendly month-long competition would be a cinch.

Or not.

Blanca let out an exhausted exhale and surveyed the place, offering up a half-hearted smile at the men and women sitting around her in their comfy niche.

Well, well. What do we have here?

If inspiration to write a romance were a religion, she'd found its heaven.

This coffee house had more sexy, diverse, casual warm bodies swarming about in a cloud of laughter than Sunset Boulevard the night before the Oscars. Every unique and gorgeous twenty-to-thirty-something person west of the San Andreas Fault, decided to all have coffee at the same time that afternoon right smack dab there in coffee house heaven.

Blanca threaded her fingers through her loose hair, fluffing up her blue ombre, suddenly aware that she was being scoped on by one, two, five, nine, a dozen, holy schnikes, way more hot guys than she was capable of handling without some caffeine to help her wakey-wakey and get her flirt on.

She snatched up one of their *Prompt Me* workbooks she had set out on the coffee table in front of her and buried her nose in it, regrouping her wayward thoughts, as she waited for her bestie to return.

Within a few minutes, she was sipping on a frothy, dark chocolate something-or-other with a hint of almond and black cherry that had at least three shots of espresso in it, pointing out to Maxie which prompt they should use to wrap their stories around.

"'Her mischievous grin deepened as she opened her hand to reveal …'" Blanca read aloud, as Maxie peered at the options on the page.

"'A ring!'"

"Really? What about, 'A note from a secret admirer?'"

"No. I like, 'A ring.'"

"I know you'd like a ring, but the two of you haven't even said your *I love yous* yet."

Maxie clucked her tongue. "At least I'm trying to go about this relationship with my head on straight this time, so you can credit me that. By the way, I'm still waiting for you to fess up about Saturday night with Julien."

"I told you. He fell asleep."

"After ..."

"After we talked for a while."

"Nah. I still don't believe you. When do you *not* dish on your sexcapades."

That word garnered a quick, stunned glance her way from the half-a-dozen wanna-be models sitting near them on the chairs and other couch across from them.

"Sexcapades?" she repeated a teeny bit louder than Maxie had, offering a humored laugh. "That's new. Let's just stick with my word, sexploration. It sounds less glittery, and, like I said, *nothing* happened. I mean, we kissed—we kissed a lot—but as far as me worrying about having to see him again after we all go on our dreamy, little hot air balloon ride in a couple days, I'm all good."

Maxie just blinked at her.

"So, anywho, are we still agreeing to use the same prompt, or what?"

"Let's do the same starter but go with our own option. I like, 'A ring.' You keep your secret admirer. I still want to share the main character's name, though."

Blanca took a long sip of the best mocha in the whole world. "Just remember I came up with Rayne."

"I knew the coast would get to you. You're like a shark nomming on chum in all this rain. I'm surprised you didn't demand we sit out on that deck. I bet it has a heck of a view." The lilt in Maxie's voice was almost deadly.

"Oh, we'll be going out there to see the view before we leave. I just need to warm up first."

"Speaking of *bets,*" Maxie added.

"Yasss?"

"What's the wager, assuming we both finish our rough drafts by December?"

Blanca pursed her glossy lips in pensive thought. "So, let me get things straight. We're betting on who writes the better book based on the same story prompt, and, we're also calling our main characters Rayne in honor of the best weather ever, but, as of a few seconds ago, we opted to go different directions with our plots."

"Sounds about right. Oh, and we want to call our books *Stormy with a Chance of Rayne.*"

"No, *Come Rayne or Shine,*" Maxie insisted.

"We have to do different titles to go with our different plots. Problem solved," Blanca decided.

Maxie nodded. "Fine, but here's the deal. The only way we can prove who wrote the better book is to publish it digitally. We put them up on Amazon and wait. It's free. Whoever gets the most positive reviews in a certain time frame, like, say about a month, wins the bet. I've been watching YouTube on how to upload a book."

"Fine. Whatever you want, but I'd hate to do all this work for nothing. I mean if my book's going to conquer your book, I want to be rewarded big time for my trouble when I win."

"That's so not going to happen. Be prepared to pay up," Maxie countered with a genuine smile. "How about the loser pays for a legit boutique publishing package, and we just pull the winning book off the market, revamp it with all the bells and whistles, then republish again?"

"A *what* package?"

"A small company you pay to republish it with swag and an advertising budget, and we find a company that uses a legit editor to clean up the manuscript. If the book is doing well to begin with anyway, then let's kick it up a notch and back it up."

"I have no idea what swag has to do with writing unless your character's lover is a total stud, but whatever. Sure. You're on. You handle all the technical stuff on Amazon, and I'll kick back and wait for the win." Blanca set the workbook down and thrust her hand out in front of Maxie who shook it, beaming like she'd already won.

And, she probably would. What the hell do I know or care about writing a novel besides what I learned today, but whatever floats my BFF's boat. I'm just having fun.

Just then, the soft rain pattering outside shifted, and a deluge poured from the gray sky, driving all the gorgeous people hanging outside back in through the double doors. An even louder murmur filled the building after a huge clap of thunder cracked, rattling the glass paneled wall that loomed at least twenty feet up to the ceiling on the left side of the building.

In a matter of seconds, a tiny, old man spitting out Italian cuss words came stomping down the stairs that ran along the right side of the building. The overhang in the baristas' station was most-likely an office or two. He leaned over the counter and shouted something to the drive-thru operator, partially obscured by the staircase, then spun on his heels and parked his hands on his hips still rattling off Italian words as he surveyed the scene.

Blanca started laughing. "Ooh, he's got a mouth on him. Didn't one of the Yelp posts say a hobbit named Fabrizio owned this place?"

They watched the old man assess the growing crowd then go around the counter on the other end and park himself in the middle of the baristas who were casually churning out drinks. He smacked the one barista with the gnarly facial hair on the back of the head, who immediately scrounged for something behind the counter then produced a net and proceeded to stuff his beard in it as best he could.

As the crowd grew thicker, a handsome man who looked about twice their age took the liberty of wedging himself between Blanca and Maxie on the couch, grabbing Blanca's backpack off the seat and setting it on the polished concrete floor.

"Hey, don't touch my stuff," Blanca snapped, dragging her backpack over to the other side of her high heel boots.

"Sorry, sweetheart." He stretched his arms out and draped them across the back of the couch. "There's just nowhere else to sit."

Blanca had an overwhelming urge to punch him in the throat but refrained. Maxie leaned forward, wide-eyed and looking like she was ready to bolt for the door, so Blanca downed the rest of her dark chocolate, cherry-almond mocha and stood up, hoisting her backpack over her shoulder. "I think I'd like to check out that view now, girly-girl. Let's stop hogging the couch and give someone who might be interested in this old man's cooties a chance to sit with him."

"Creeper," Maxie whispered, as she gathered up their workbooks and crammed them in her backpack.

She followed Blanca over to the glass doors leading out to the deck, and they pitched their disposable cups in the recycle bin off to the side. No one was outside anymore, and rightfully so. The brewing weather looked like something out of a movie—a ridiculously romantic movie—and the stormy climax was about to unfold.

They stared through the water-speckled glass at the torrid sea as it clamored up to the shore in the distance—the weathered slats of the fence creaking and moaning in protest of the wind.

"We definitely have to make our setting in a beach town like this," Maxie said.

"I'll do whatever you do, as long as it's raining on every single page." Blanca bounced her eyebrows and motioned over her shoulder at the buzzing crowd. "I'm about done with all this noise. Let's get back to the hotel and get this vacation over with. We are definitely coming back to Sea Sprite again someday, though. This beach town rocks."

Chapter four

"Love is an irresistible desire to be irresistibly desired."
~Robert Frost

Julien

"I'm going to make you start unpacking everything you touch if you don't keep your hands to yourself," Blanca warned Julien, as he set the stack of books he had just pulled out of a cardboard box down on the granite countertop in the kitchen.

Keep my hands to myself? What is this foreign command you speak of?

"Not there," Blanca groaned, rushing around Chase to scoop up her books.

"Where would you like me to put them?" He blocked her from the books and wrestled them back into his arms.

"I haven't assembled my Ikea bookshelf yet, so stick them back in the box, please."

"I can put it together for you, if you like?"

"Thanks for offering, but I'm fine." Her voice seemed strained with politeness.

Maybe I should start touching all her things and give myself something to do besides stand around and wait for this dreadful day to come to an end.

Julien wandered out of the kitchen ignoring the fact that Chase seemed to be uncomfortable in Blanca and Max's new home.

"That looks like Montmartre," Julien said to no one in particular, walking over to a detailed sketch of Max that hung in a frame on the living room wall.

Chase jumped up off the couch and wedged himself between Julien and the picture. "Hey, why don't you make yourself useful and see what you can do to help Blanca with?"

"I was just kidding about unpacking everything you touch, Julien. Don't touch anything. I have a system going here that I don't need either of you to mess up."

What? No 'Jules'? We've regressed so quickly.

"Is your system to keep everything packed until you're ready to move again?" Julien cracked a smile at her, as he turned away from Chase and walked around a few boxes to the dining room.

"You're like a caged animal," Blanca quipped and trailed after him.

Julien peered into her empty hutch that ran along the side of one wall, glancing at his reflection in the mirror backing.

I look like a shadow of myself ... like someone who's been dead for ... for two years.

He turned his back to his reflection.

Maxie finally appeared from down the hall, and Julien sidestepped around her without a word to use the restroom before they headed out. He could hear them mumbling something about him through the bathroom door. No doubt mulling over what to do with him.

He emerged a few minutes later inspecting a bright pink silicon apparatus that had one large and two small cutouts on one end, which he had found in a drawer. "I have to ask," he started, as he walked up to Blanca.

"Give me that!" She snatched it from his hands. "Stop snooping."

"What is it, or should I not ask? Something tells me you wouldn't be the least bit embarrassed if I knew."

She scrunched her adorable ski slope nose at him. "It's a lip plumper."

He peered at her lips—the top one a delicate, bow-shaped line, the bottom—thick and protruding. An urge to tug on it with his teeth welled up in him.

"Stop staring at me. I only use it for special occasions."

A dirty thought slid past his mind. "Show me."

A mischievous smile quirked up the corner of her mouth.

Chase and Max watched them with mildly amused grins while Chase helped Max put on her cardigan.

"Sure. Come here." She crushed the device in her palm and reached up, placing the open end over his mouth, creating a vacuum suction as she unclenched her hand.

Now what?

He rolled his eyes in mock exaggeration as his lips pulsed and tingled.

Max started giggling as a devilish smile spread across Blanca's face. "Just a few more seconds," she said, then popped the device off his mouth.

"How do I look?" He tossed his unkempt hair back and puckered up.

Everyone burst into laughter.

"Like you might be of some use to me later on, after all," Blanca replied, eyeing his full mouth.

Chase clapped his hands together then ushered Max to the front door. "Okay, everybody, let's get out of here. We're going to be late for our hot air balloon ride."

* * *

No one seemed to be able to keep a straight face when looking at Julien while they were all nestled inside the compartments of the giant basket, awaiting takeoff on the ride of their lives.

A thrill Julien wasn't in the mood for but played along with anyway.

He ran his tongue along his fat lower lip, creased down the middle like a big ass crack, which drew Blanca's attention away from the doting couple who were tangled up in each other's arms just a couple of feet away. Despite that firecracker of a woman next to him, all he wanted to do was cut to dinner and wrap up his trip to America—his first of three connecting flights leaving tomorrow morning out of SMF.

The hot air balloon staggered off its ropes and began to rise high up in the air. Julien watched as Blanca looked over the edge, clinging to the rim of the basket for stability in her high heels. His eyes traveled the length of her lean legs, wrapped in a short, black skirt that clung to her slender hips. She had an endearing finesse about her like she was fully aware of every part of her thin, toned body and knew damn well that every square inch of it demanded his attention.

"Don't you know that Halloween is over?" He moved next to her and tugged on a curly lock of her blue hair.

Blanca smiled at his joke but didn't turn to look at him. "Says the boy who looks like he made out with a vacuum."

"*Touché.*"

I probably should have taken a look at my mouth before leaving her house.

Julien slipped his arm around Blanca's shoulders and peered over the edge at endless, delineated rows of grapes. "I don't suppose you're too embarrassed to be seen with me in public? We could tell them we have other plans and hide ourselves away at the compound while the lovebirds continue to celebrate Chase all by themselves?"

"Compound?" Blanca giggled. "Angel of the Vine Winery is one of the finest vineyards in all of Napa Valley. It's where romance meets adventure," she crooned, as she waved her hand in front of her at the sprawling valley below.

Romance? Adventure? Absolutely, but not here.

"If you think this view is impressive, you should come to Reims. I could show you—"

"Come see you in France?" Blanca tipped her head up and stared at him. "Why would I do that?"

"To see the countryside. You told me the other night that you loved to travel, and you never ventured past Paris over summer. You could stay with me. I have—"

"I can't." She looked away, but he reached down and tilted her face up towards him again, then looped a fluttering curl behind her ear.

It only took about three seconds before she pulled away and doubled over with laughter.

"What? *Je ne comprends pas* (I don't understand)?"

"Your lips," she gasped with laughter. "They are hysterical. You're going to ruin my mascara." She fluttered her hands in front of her eyes, trying to stave off tears.

Chase and Max glanced over their shoulders at them for a second then turned around again.

Julien slid his fingers into Blanca's hair—her infectious laughter only making him want to ravage her mouth even more. He leaned over to taste her lips again. Instead of protesting, she took the opportunity to nip at his bottom lip playfully before he covered her mouth and slid his tongue over hers—a soft moan rising up to meet his ears.

He relished in a few minutes of passion, tangling his tongue around hers, savoring the intimacy he'd been longing for from a beautiful woman for far too long. It didn't matter to him that they were sharing the hot air balloon ride with three others.

The pilot in the middle of the crammed basket pulled a lever then fueled the balloon to rise even higher.

"I guess we could ditch them," she offered with a hint of mischief in her eyes, as she pulled away to catch her breath.

"What are you two scheming?" Chase interrupted.

"You really don't want us around for dinner, do you?" Blanca twisted in Julien's arms and faced her best friend. Julien took the opportunity to loop his arms around the little vixen's shoulders protectively.

Chase and Max looked them over, no doubt coming to all kinds of conclusions that Julien could care less about. For the first time, he saw the two of them as a united force now. His impulse to corrupt their relationship felt detached and discarded like an anchor hacked off and abandoned to the sea. Julien's dispute with his cousin over his ex-girlfriend, a woman he had morphed into some kind of mythical goddess who had stripped him of his heart and pride, was now nothing more than a painful memory he longed to forget.

Julien did yearn to love again. He thought often of how much he wanted to find someone to love and marry and to have children someday. Those wants only intensified as he watched with detached wonder at Chase and Max embracing one another.

Julien didn't realize until he'd uttered an agreeing, "*Oui*," to whatever plans Blanca had rattled off to Max and Chase, that he had become lost in his reverie of a perfect life. All he knew was that he was on board with whatever it was they had all been prattling on about.

Blanca swiveled around in Julien's arms and pressed her cheek against his chest, sliding her hands around his waist and sighing as she gazed out in the distance. Whatever *it* was they had all settled on made it easy for him to not only feel at ease, but also revel in the unreserved attention Blanca Grazia, a practical mystery to him, was giving so freely.

A mystery he felt a sudden impulse for wanting to solve.

* * *

Blanca

Blanca had to assume the abrupt shift in Julien's mood from mopey to chipper had something to do with the fact she had made good use of his voluptuous lips from the moment they'd gotten back to her home.

She had pulled together some honeydew melon wedges wrapped in prosciutto and dressed some sliced tomatoes and mozzarella with a drizzle of olive oil and torn-up basil leaves for them to share. Blanca even insisted on feeding him the juicy melon bites herself—stepping up her A-game with some shameless flirting.

They cracked open some Private Reserve Pinot Noir and took turns sipping the wine straight from the bottle while hanging out together on the couch. She'd blamed the need to share the bottle on not having unpacked her wine glasses yet, but she knew which box they were in. She just wanted to see if she could get Julien riled up about breaking wine etiquette while mouthing the same rim with a sensual back-and-forth playfulness.

Julien's new, placid contentment to go along with whatever she wanted straddled on him either becoming a total lunatic or worse, a complete bore since he dropped the whole Curious George routine from earlier.

A freakin' gorgeous, wanna-climb-you-like-a-tree bore, but, yeah, snooze-fest all the way,

Speaking of straddling ...

Let's just get it out in the open already and go from there. Women can be as, what's the right word ... Primal? Too derogatory?

Wanton? Too turn-of-the-century romanticized?

Horny? Too tacky and a tad bit direct?

Sexually piqued? ... as men.

Meh. We'll go with that one for now.

Blanca was not a slut. Or a whore. Or a hoe-bag. Or loose. Or frivolous. Or even a skank. Or any other heinous moniker society could try to slap on her because she wasn't a dude getting his high-fives on when she walked away with dignity after a night—or late afternoon—of sexual satisfaction.

On the other hand, that scrawny beotch that Maxie's last boyfriend cheated on her with that he met at the gym, now there's an example of a skank.

You never, ever come between a committed couple no matter how bad their relationship looks, or you deserve ... All. The. Bad. Words.

One thing Blanca always made clear was, when the situation would arise *(pun intended),* she was not and never would be emotionally available should her partner care to make their encounter anything other than a heart-pounding good time meant only to be lived in the moment. She rarely hooked up with strangers, she never consented to being anybody's bootie call, and she would rather die than engage in any kind of sexploration if it didn't involve all the safe-sex precautions known to the human species.

Blanca had a feeling—and not just an emotional one—that Julien was up for about anything she suggested doing. Including her.

What, with him flying back to France the next morning, he'd need to head back to Chase's estate soon, foregoing her need to explain how he wasn't permitted to spend the night. Besides, the likelihood of there being any future awkward encounters between them were slim to none for a while. She had a knack for being able to friend-zone a former tryst with all the class in the world should any of her ex-lovers ever work their way back into her life somehow. And she could pretty much guarantee she wouldn't be seeing Julien until next fall, if at all.

Her bestie, on the other hand, was all kinds of chaste, and shy, and inexperience, all rolled into a pin-up body with no clue how to even wield that kind of sexy. Maxie was a long-term relationship hopper, because, God forbid she ever permit herself to have a little fun every once in a while without any strings attached (*you know, commitment, cough-cough*), but anyway, who was she to judge?

Speaking of God … and judging … and forbidding … a healthy dose of heavenly guilt, thanks to Blanca's religious upbringing, used to loiter around after a whole lotta partaking of the naughty during the months that followed after her ex broke off their engagement. But, the operative word in that little confession was *used to.*

Blanca had found her balance. She never misled or mistreated her partners, and she demanded the same of them. She wasn't opposed to falling in love, just not any time soon, and she couldn't wrap her head around Maxie's inability to separate the two. Love was love, and sex was sex. Neither mutually exclusive as far as she was concerned.

Having cleared the air about her intentions while straddling Julien's lap and spoon-feeding him some pineapple sorbet straight from the pint, it seemed an audible reply of consent wasn't even necessary on Julien's part. He just took the spoon and pint from Blanca, set them down on the coffee table, and slid his hands underneath her thighs—her mini skirt bunching up around her waist—and stood up prompting Blanca to wrap her legs around him and link her ankles together below his rounded ass.

She nipped at his lips breathing out tiny moans as he headed down the hall with her.

"Not that one," she mumbled, as his hand grappled for a doorknob.

"Sorry, Max's room?"

She reared her head back, smirking at him for bringing up Maxie in the heat of their intimate moment. "No, my Zen Den."

He pressed her back against the hall wall and kissed her with an edge of aggression, erasing any irk she thought she might have gotten. "You may need to visit your Zen Den after I'm done blowing your mind."

Now, there's the not-so-boring-after-all guy I knew you could be.

"You'll want to prove that to me two doors down on the right."

After a few staggering steps and lots of heavy breathing, Julien nudged her bedroom door open, backing in and whirling her around, then collapsing on top of her on the end of the bed. She writhed under him, managing to wiggle out of her top as she kissed him, leaving her in nothing but her bunched up skirt and a matching black lace bra and barely-there thong that left nothing to the imagination.

Julien became all hands and grunts and tugs reluctantly pulling away from her lips as he'd managed to yank off his shirt, kick off his shoes, and get at least one leg out of his jeans. He slid his hands down her smooth legs and gripped her ankles, guiding them over his shoulders as he knelt down at the end of the bed.

His fingers toyed with the ankle strap on her stiletto. "We're keeping these on, *oui*?"

"Oh, you're a heels kind of guy, are you?"

He slid his palm along her heart-shaped calf. "You alone could give me a foot fetish because of these shoes."

"Really? Hmm. If you like these heels, you should see my private reserve."

"*Que voulez-vous dire, mon petit plaisir* (What do you mean, my little pleasure)?" He pursed his plump lips in an enduring attempt to smile.

Hello, sexy mouth.

She reared up on her elbows—her flexing abs causing him to involuntarily groan as his eyes roamed all over the honey glow of her body.

"I mean every woman should own at least one pair of heels only meant to be worn when dangling over the shoulders of her lover," she purred.

She was sexy like that.

Chapter five

"No distance of place or lapse of time can lessen the friendship of those who are thoroughly persuaded of each other's worth."
~Robert Southey

Julien

Grand-mère Mimi settled into her rocking chair as Julien draped a hand-painted patchwork quilt over her lap. It was a quilt that her students had presented to her as a gift on her last day of teaching two years earlier. They'd given it to her shortly after Julien's grand-père had passed, and only days after Millicent Devereaux—or rather, Millie—had packed her bags and stormed out of his life.

Millie had been his Grand-mère Mimi's favorite protégé, but all she had inadvertently gifted his grandmother with upon departing were a handful of nude sketches of Chase she had abandoned all over her studio floor. The painful memory of the night that Julien had walked in on his soon-to-be fiancé with his cousin drifted through his mind. It was a memory he found impossible to forget. His grand-maman had hung those nudes up in her living room for all to gaze upon, or rather, *stare at.* Little badges of honor and disgrace. Millie's talent, astonishing. Oh, the detail she had put into them. And the horror.

Julien collapsed onto the couch that resided below those infuriating sketches after a long day of running errands in Reims. He had worked diligently all week at the L'Angevin main offices, making up for lost time the week before on his trip to America. He sighed and looked up behind him at the wall of defeat, then bowed his head in his hands and hunched over.

"You are troubled by something?" Her quiet voice held a tone that already knew his answer.

"You referring to Chase's junk hanging over my head drawn by the love of my life?"

"*Ma maison n'a pas de déchets* (My house does not have junk in it)!"

Julien hid his smile, dragging his hands down his face then folding them behind his head as he leaned back. "Can I get you any tea?"

"*Je vais bein* (I am fine)." She raised an eyebrow and *tsk'd* at him. "You were saying something about Chase and that girl, Max, you introduced me to on your birthday. You enjoyed her friend's company on your journey to America, *oui?*"

Every second. Blanca's incredible.

"*Oui*, I enjoyed her, ehm, company."

"You must have because you talk with her each day on the telephone since you returned."

"She's halfway across the world in case you were trying to make a point."

"Chase and Max, they are happy, *non*? You do not want the same?"

"Of course I want them to be happy."

"I was referring to *your* happiness."

Here we go again.

"Millie took it with her when she left."

"*Non, non.* She was only a fleeting moment in your life meant to teach."

"What lesson? To never trust, to never—"

"*Calme, mon doux Julien.* (Quiet, my sweet Julien.) She taught you to feel, but love does not leave."

"I tried to stop her."

"I meant you. She is, eh, she cannot be the keeper of your heart forever. Only the one who departed after loving enough. You are the one who left love behind by not moving forward to a new love." Her trembling voice was almost a breathless whisper. "*Amore,* Julien."

If you only knew how much I want to love again.

"I know what I need to do, grand-maman. Millie means nothing to me now."

Absolutely nothing.

"Ah, but you are chained by your bitterness. You must forgive yourself as you have forgiven Chase. He meant no harm. Your cousin, he is so proud, and she, she saw his beauty. Millie watched him long before you knew." She motioned to the sketches above his head outlining every curve of Chase's chiseled body—a product of working out like a lunatic. Julien, while thick and muscular in his own right, did not fine-tune every single muscle in an attempt to rival Adonis himself the way his cousin had.

"Wait. *Knew* what?"

"He could no longer keep her away."

Julien leaned forward and bowed his head—his heart emptying out the contents of its deepest fear of whether they had slept together or not. A question Chase emphatically answered with a resounding *no,* but it never seemed to satisfy Julien.

Grand-mère Mimi began to rock in her chair—the subtle creaking back and forth always the soundtrack to her stories. "She reminds me of when I danced at the Moulin Rouge. In 1956, I believe it was, your grand-papa, he came to the revue three days in a row, and he never took his eyes from Claire, and she, oh, she flaunted her feathers like a peacock. The flattery he must have felt."

Julien peered up at her. "*Je ne comprends pas* (I don't understand). Who is Claire?" His brow furrowed with concern as her stories of the past were often mingled with frustration in remembering all the details because of her waning health.

"The woman your grand-père thought he was coming to see. I knew he was meant for me, and, on the fourth day, I was the one who truly opened his eyes. So it was with you and Chase. He would have been her lover, but only for a time, and you would have moved on, but sometimes Synchronicity, she plays tricks on us. Millicent ran away from both of you before you could let go and before Chase could fall for her completely."

"You don't think they—"

"Were lovers? *Non,* but her lips would search out his with every kiss that she could steal from him right in front of you, but you never seemed to notice her attempts to seduce him. I knew Millicent wanted to draw Chase by the way she spoke of his lines. I wanted her to explore her talent beyond my models, but I did not think she would be so bold or Chase so foolish to consent to these beautiful nudes." She waved her crooked fingers at all the drawings above Julien.

"Why did you never tell me you knew what she was trying to do?"

"There was nothing to tell. Not yet. I did not think she would hurt you so deeply. You were not the only one she left broken."

"Chase?"

She lifted her hands to her heart. "*Moi. Moi.* She left without a word, my wild girl. Millicent was an untamed mare, so much like me in my youth. She wanted it all. You. Chase. Her career ahead of her. She flaunted her talent and beauty like Claire."

"And we both played the fool."

"Let the past go, and find a lover you deserve. She was never going to accept your proposal. She only wanted to hear the words. Oh, sweet Julien, open your eyes."

"She did not want to marry me? I wh— Never mind. It does not matter."

"*Oui.* It does not matter anymore. Once your eyes are open to love again, you must then open your one true love's eyes *to you.* Oh, your grand-père, if he were here, he could tell you better than I can."

She began to tear up as a smile trembled at her lips.

Julien rose from the couch and approached her. "Grand-maman, you need to rest. It is so late. Let me help you to bed."

He leaned over, and she wrapped her frail arms around his neck. He lifted her onto her feet and steadied her, then looped her arm in his. As she made her way to her bedroom, she began to hum a song—a song that spoke of lasting love—a song that he hadn't heard since she used to sing it to him as a child, and the tune began to fill his heart with hope again.

When Julien left his grand-maman's house and walked over to his own, he gazed up at the sky at the countless stars, like pinpricks in the black velvet of night. He thought of the life he'd once dreamt of—a life full of children's laughter and a wife he could smother with affection. He even dusted off the memory of wanting his own line of L'Angevin wine, and, by the time he crawled into bed, he began to plot his future—a journey he'd lost sight of but suddenly felt every detail within.

* * *

Blanca

The evil thumping heartbeat of the cursor taunted Blanca with each pulse, mocking her measly one thousand seven hundred and twenty-something words, which was basically less than seven pages of blah, blah, rain, blah.

"Yes! Yes! Yes! I've just hit fifty thousand!"

"Get a room already." Blanca snapped her laptop shut, parked her elbows on the dining room table and fisted her hair as her head hung in agony. *Ugh.* "I mean, congratulations."

"Thank you." Maxie accepted the compliment and continued to peck away at her keyboard with her feet kicked up on the coffee table in the living room. "But, I'm not even close to being done. It's a good thing we've still got a little over a week left of NaNoWriMo."

"Yeah, about that. I'm just going to come right out and say it. There's no way I'll be done with my novel by the end of November."

"Why not? You've been working on it every day."

I've been hiding in my Zen Den napping every day and letting you think I've been working on it.

"I just need some more time."

"Do you want to extend our bet?"

Uh. Nope. "Sure."

"Let me see what you've got so far. Maybe, I can help you." Maxie got up and started walking over to her.

Blanca popped her head up and waved her hands in front of her. "No, no. I'm good. I have a lot of editing to do first. I can't have the girl with the English degree seeing my first draft before I even reread it at least once."

"Fine." She perched her hands on her tiny waist and cocked her head to one side. "Will you at least glance over my story once I'm done and help me fine tune it before we self-publish them?"

"I'd love to."

"*And?*" She scooped her pale blonde waves over one of her shoulders.

"*Aaaannnnddd,* I'll let you look over my novel, too, but only after I'm completely done. I have to change a few things first, but, like I said, I need way more time to finish it than just another week."

"Sounds fair. How about we plan to launch our challenge by Christmas? That gives us another month to polish our manuscripts, then get them up on Amazon."

"Christmas? Okay. Christmas it is. Ho, ho, humbug."

"Speaking of hoes," Maxie added, as she sank back onto the couch again. "What's up with you and Chase's cousin?"

Blanca grinned back at her BFF. "Hey, mind your own business."

Yes, it's true. Julien had become her friend.

Turns out, he's kinda cool.

Three weeks and dozens of texts and phone calls later, they'd managed to maintain a casual, flirtatious banter that suited her just fine considering they were literally continents away from each other.

Thank God for international provisions in my cellular plan!

"Yeah, right." Maxie smirked at her then resumed typing.

"I think I'm going to tuck myself away in my woman cave and get my tranquility on, so I can get over my sudden writer's block."

"Did you want to skip Midnight Bounce House Yoga later?"

"I do, if that's okay? I'm just not in the mood anymore." Since the end of summer, they both hit up random yoga classes each week trying out whatever the latest craze was together. If it sounded ridiculous and fun, they were all in.

Tonight? No thank you very much.

"All righty, girl." Maxie blew her a sweet kiss and wave goodbye, as Blanca grabbed her MacBook Air laptop and the workbooks she'd meticulously filled in.

Her workbooks contained as much romantic dribble as she could garner from as many romantic comedies that she could watch on Netflix late at night. After giving customers hairstyle makeovers all day at Beauty Defined Day Spa, her new place of work, she'd snuggle up with a movie and her cell phone buddy, Jules.

Blanca thrived on arguing with him about the ridiculousness of needing a happily-ever-after in a romance novel. He was always quick to offer up a Shakespearean-style tragic ending, leaving her craving more of his mild-mannered, quick wit. A side effect to their one-time tryst she hadn't bargained for, but enthusiastically accepted, even so.

Once inside the spare bedroom, Blanca locked the door, sidestepped her yoga mat, and dropped everything onto the powder blue chaise lounge below the window along the back wall. While Blanca emphatically referred to her safe space as her Zen Den, it was really more of a coastal-themed retreat where she could stretch, tone, breathe, and dream of where she would travel to next. A giant Old World map sprawled out on one wall, marked with tiny red hearts on the glass frame, pegging each of the locations she had ventured to over the last four summers.

Her wanderlust began as soon as she had graduated with her Cosmetologist certificate. Once she realized she had to earn continuing education units to maintain her credentials, she opted to travel far and wide to workshops. Most of them were in Western Europe where she racked up way more CEUs than she would ever need, while learning the latest techniques in hair trends.

Her previous salon consistently ranked number one in the yearly Best of Sacramento issue of Sacramento Magazine, and she always got a shout-out as their best stylist. But her glory days were gone. She had to start over with a new client list and climb the ranks all over again at her new job. The itch to bolt and go discover an rainstorm to twirl around in nagged at her subconscious as the weight of being a nobody at work on top of letting herself down about her stupid novel-writing skills messed with her peace of mind.

She plugged in her Himalayan salt rock lamp that sat on the corner of a small, white desk so only the warm, amber glow of the light was all that enveloped her. She pushed play on a CD player that teetered on a metal plant stand next to a mound of oversized, royal blue and taupe pillows. The soft sounds of her rain soundtrack emanated throughout her stormy, beach-inspired, sacred room of privacy as she leaned back against all the fluffy decadence.

Feeling the brunt of losing before the NaNoWriMo competition with Maxie was even over, she let out a defeated sigh. Their competitive nature sometimes dominated their friendship more than anything else. She didn't mind. In fact, she perpetuated it more than her BFF did. But this round of betting had become more than she could handle.

She looked down at the shimmering words Spiritual Gangster on her black workout tank top and rolled her eyes then reluctantly motioned the Father, Son, and Holy Spirit cross over her chest, slamming her eyes shut.

Breathe in. Breathe out. Breath in. Breathe out.

A couple minutes later, she pulled up Julien's phone number and sent him a quick text.

Blanca: *Hey, you, wake up. I'm stuck.*

A few seconds later, the ellipses marks on her cell began to thrum.

Julien: *Impossible. I can fit you into*
my pocket. How could you possibly
get stuck in something?
Blanca: *Lol! I knew I could count*
on you to make me smile.
Now, make me write!
Julien: *What's in it for me?*

Blanca: *Lol! No, really. HELP!!!*
Julien: *I'm calling you. And not because I want to help.*

Her screen went back to the home page, and, within seconds, her iPhone rang.

"I just want to hear that mellifluous voice of yours. It does things to me merely reading texts on my cellular cannot."

"You really are too much, you know that?"

"I thought I was *just right,* Goldie Locks."

"Ooh, good one." Blanca had transformed her whiskey brown to blue ombre into a caramel blonde ombre with less roots, which he'd seen the last time they FaceTimed each other a couple days before.

"Can I look at you?"

"There's not much to see right now, but sure." She stabbed at the FaceTime button on her screen, and, within seconds, Julien's tranquil beach glass gaze was peering through her tortured soul.

"Aw, there she is. I never get tired of looking into those mossy eyes of yours."

"How very ... gross. I'm like mildew on a rock. Fabulous." She pouted then batted her jade green eyes at him.

"How can I help you this morning, or rather, tonight on your end? Shouldn't you be asleep?"

"There's no way I can go to bed right now. I just pushed back my due date on my romance novel by another month. I have to win, Jules, but I'm so far from being done. Help me!"

"How much have you written so far?"

"I'm too embarrassed to say."

"Wrong answer." He looked like he was walking and a burst of pale light suddenly washed over his face.

"Did you just go outside?"

"I did. Don't change the subject."

"Fine. Less than two thousand words."

"Definitely start over."

"Thanks." Her flat tone evoked an unappreciated laugh from him.

"I mean it. Start from the beginning again. Forget trying to be funny. Forget trying to be romantic. Just start telling Rayne's story. The rest will fall into place."

"Easier said than done."

He paused for a moment lost in thought as she watched his brow furrow in concentration.

Damn, he gives good face.

"She's in a cabin. It's the dead of winter. There's a knock on the door—"

"I'm not writing erotica."

He laughed and slid his fingers through his messy, bedhead hair, dragging loose, dark blond strands away from his face. "What inspires you?"

"Traveling, languages, the ocean, rain—"

"Is that rain I hear now, or are you frying bacon?"

Blanca erupted into giggles as she sat up. She reached over and turned off her soundtrack. "Better?"

"I'm always better when I'm talking face to face with you."

"You say the sappiest, I mean, the sweetest things. Hey, wanna write my book for me?"

"You just call me when you need inspiration to write a love scene."

She shook her head, still grinning from ear to ear.

Nope. Nada. Never again. Friend-zoned from here on out. That's how I roll.

Blanca bounced her eyebrows at him. "So, Rayne's opening the door, then what?"

"If traveling and learning new languages turn you on, why don't you send her on a worldly adventure? Or, better yet, what if you write your novel *in* another language?"

"Hmm. That might be interesting."

Then, I could avoid Maxie trying to read it in case it stinks.

"Could you write it in French?"

"Probably not. I could try to write it in Italian, but I better just stick with English."

"Fair enough. Why not try to write about one of your experiences while traveling? You must have some moments you could capture or some places you've seen that stirred your heart. Throw a love story in the middle of something that was real for you, and don't worry about writing something lighthearted like Max."

Blanca let Julien's words sink in, nodding ferociously for a second then flashing him the biggest smile she could muster. "I think I know just the story. Thank you so much. What would I do without you, Jules? I totally owe you one."

"I'm holding you to that."

They looked at each other in silence for a minute, then his attention shifted to something in the distance.

"Whatcha lookin' at?"

A faint smile played upon his lips. "The sun is beginning to rise."

Chapter Six

"Wherever you go, go with all your heart."
~Confucius

Blanca

A handful of days later, Blanca was already nearing the twenty-five thousand mark on her word count after being holed up at her parents' house in Sacramento for the start of the holiday season. Thanksgiving came and went and so did the Friday, Saturday, and Sunday following it as she lost track of time while on vacation thanks to having absolutely zero clients booked.

Yep, that's bad. Financially, emotionally, you name it. Not good.

Blanca's determination to be the winner in their novel-writing bet drove her into self-induced insomnia. She filled what little downtime she gave herself with brief naps between shots of espresso and texted her favorite muse in the world nonstop, her just-a-friend, Julien.

Blanca wrote about an experience she'd had in Rome two summers ago when an elderly man had talked her ear off all afternoon over a shared meal, recounting Italian fairytales. Her favorite tale had been Giambattista Basile's, "The Three Enchanted Princes." A story she tweaked into something modern as it took on a life of its own.

All the credit went to Julien who fueled her imagination with creative suggestions about the romantic thread in the story before he headed into Reims each morning. She focused her retelling on the prince who had been transformed into a dolphin, but she ditched the merman notion for more feminine elements all spliced into a story-within-a-story narrative.

When Blanca came home Sunday night, Maxie had just returned from Chase's cabin, which was nestled on the hillside at the L'Angevin's estate. She was all smiles and sunshine, bursting at the seams with what Blanca could only imagine was a secret she was dying to spill.

"You better not be done with your manuscript already," Blanca warned, stretching her legs out on her chaise lounge in the Zen Den and unfolding her laptop to begin another chapter.

Maxie leaned against the threshold. "Even better."

"What?" She paired her flat tone with an eye roll.

"I told Chase that I love him."

"And?"

"He said it first."

"You said it in return because he said it first?"

"No, I meant it. I love him. I looooove Chase L'Angevin. He's the—"

"Don't say it."

"One."

"Dammit, Maxie. You've only been exclusive for, what, three months, if that? Just because he's the best boyfriend you've had so far, it doesn't mean you've found the one."

"What if I have? What if we're meant to be together forever? He gets me, Blanca. I might not be as experienced as you are in *relations,* but I do know a thing or two about *relationships,* and we are in love."

Blanca pulled her eyes away from Maxie and stared at her computer screen. "Fine. Congratulations."

I would die for that girl, but some days I swear I could kill her.

"That's it?" She crossed the room and sat on the end of the chaise lounge. "You're not going to keep lecturing me on my bad judgment or on how I think it's love, but it's really only an infatuation, and he's just using me?"

"He's not using you."

"Then, say something."

Blanca let out a strained sigh and closed her laptop. She folded her hands on top of it and contemplated her next words then looked her bestie in the eyes. "We both have had poor judgment. We both have mistaken infatuation for love. We both have been used. *I* just have a way of learning from my mistakes."

"Chase is not a mistake."

"I guess time will tell, won't it?"

"Why do you hate him so much?"

"Oh, please. You know I don't hate him. I think he's great. In fact, I can honestly say I think he's damn near perfect, which is why I worry about you."

"Why? I'm not good enough for him?"

"No!" She reached out and batted Maxie's shoulder. "I'm just worried that, if things between the two of you run out of steam, you're going to be so heartbroken I won't know how to fix you. You're moving so fast with this guy. I have to worry."

"I get that your life revolves around maintaining damage control in my life, but really, this time, I've got it."

"Now what?"

"That's it. We're in love. Just thought you should know."

Blanca mustered up a smile. "Like I said, congratulations."

Maxie reached out and patted Blanca's fuzzy, pajama-covered thigh. "Goodnight."

"Goodnight," Blanca replied, cracking her laptop open again.

Dammit.

* * *

"If this thing craps on me, I'm suing them." Blanca squealed, as a baby goat balanced itself on her arched back while she posed in the downward dog. "I'm not kidding, ahh!"

Maxie curled over onto her side, laughing so hard at the double entendre that she started to snort.

"No! Help! This isn't fun anymore. Not the hair. Not the hair!"

A handler rushed over and scooped up the animal on Blanca's back that had started gnawing on her ponytail.

Another kid came up to Maxie and perched on top of her hip as she writhed in fits of laughter. "They're so cute!"

Blanca hopped up and tugged down her neon green tank top that read, 'In My Defense, She Left Me Unsupervised'. Its neon pink counterpart rounding out Maxie's chest with, 'She Made Me Do It'. Their friendship steadfast and strong in a let's-wear-a-pair-of-our-coordinating-workout-clothes-today kind of way, despite Maxie's non-stop absence from home now that Chase and her were in love and all.

Blech. Blag. Blut. (This is me hurling right now, in case you were wondering.)

Blanca almost didn't mind the extra down time without her roomie around. She filled it with writing, writing, and more writing. She was nearing the finish line just like Maxie had already done.

Work had picked up the pace with Christmas around the corner, but another inadvertent, paycheck-free vacation, always spent at her nonna's house in San Francisco, was on its way. Only a couple of customers had booked appointments with her a few days before the holiday, but that was all. It still irked her that the only BFF time Maxie had for her anymore was when they were doing something that Chase couldn't tag along for. Yoga was all theirs, but only because he was more of an iron-pumping kind of guy.

Blanca sat back down again and twisted into the lotus pose. "This class looked way more organized in the YouTube videos."

"Just get your Instagram and Facebook pics already." Maxie reached over and scooped the baby goat teetering on her hip into her arms and sat up. "Aw. Can we keep it?"

A bleating kid flopped down in Blanca's lap for a cuddle, and she *eeped* a genuine laugh as she pulled her cell phone out of her waistband and took some selfies and pics of Maxie snuggling with all the cuteness. "Okay, maybe we can steal just one when the instructor isn't looking."

Of all the wacky yoga classes they'd attended together in the last few months, Baby Goat Yoga topped the silliest so far. They barely got an actual yoga workout in even though the instructor conducted the class like business as usual. Their abs, though, were going to feel it for sure later on with all the laughing.

When the session ended, and they hugged their new farm-friends goodbye, Blanca made Maxie swear they'd try Nap Yoga next. Apparently, a studio not too far from them in one of the spa resorts, attendees could log in some sleep. Except, naptime consisted of dozing on special air mattresses shaped like clouds as dry ice simulated a heavenly atmosphere all while being serenaded by a recorded choir of angelic voices.

You know you want in on that action, too, don't cha?

As soon as Maxie eased into Blanca's car, her cell chimed an incoming text right on cue.

"Let me guess, Chase knows the second you're out of class, so he's—"

"Oh, no!" Maxie cut her off. "His grandma died." Her thumb furiously pecked away at her iPhone screen.

Blanca bowed her head and motioned a cross over her chest. "I'm sorry. Tell him I'm so sorry. I know Julien says their whole family is really close."

Maxie's phone rang, and she answered it as Blanca started backing out of the parking lot. The muffled conversation on Chase's end left Maxie nodding a lot and saying *yes,* at least four times as they headed home. When Maxie eventually reached over and squeezed Blanca's shoulder while she drove, Blanca realized she had been included as the third wheel in whatever plans the two lovebirds had just concocted.

Always a freakin' threesome. Ugh.

Once Maxie finished her conversation with Chase, Blanca's iPhone began to buzz in the console. "It's Julien. Do you want me to reply?"

"Sure."

Maxie picked up the phone and texted Julien then put it back in the console. "Done."

"Your reply was entirely too long, girly-girl. What did you say?" Her eyes shifted from the road to her friend for a split second.

"I told him you were driving."

"That's it?"

"And, that you were really sorry about his grandma passing away."

"Okay, good. Thanks."

"And," Maxie continued—her voice lowering an octave.

Rut-roh.

"Aaannnd?"

"Yes."

"Yes, what?"

"Yes, you'll come to France with us for the funeral. He said you were the only one who could put a smile on his face right now."

Blanca could feel the sheepish grin on Maxie's face as she kept her eyes on the road. "Wipe that smirk off your face right now. We're just friends."

"I know."

"Okay, then."

"Okay, you're coming? He also said you owe him one."

I suppose he has inspired me to write, and I've never been outside of Paris before. "Is there a catch?"

"I don't think so. Unless you count that you're helping Chase and me by keeping him preoccupied."

Blanca's jaw flexed as she gritted her teeth. "I'd be giving you a side-eye glare right now if I wasn't driving."

"I know, I know. Just friends. Got it." Maxie made air quotes around the operative words.

But they were true in every sense. Julien was just a friend. A great friend. Why couldn't that be enough? They broke the ice over a mutual sexual interest and then settled into their permanent roles. The long distance made that possible where she'd otherwise have just moved on.

She was loyal like that.

Seeing him again, face to face, would only solidify our friendship. It had to.

"The funeral is next week. Chase wants to arrive the day before.

Then, we'll have the whole week afterwards to explore that region of France. You know you want to," Maxie continued.

I do, dammit. I loved that country.

Blanca drew in a deep breath then let it out. "Fine. It looks like we're going to France for Christmas."

Chapter Seven

"The real voyage of discovery consists not in seeking new landscapes, but in having new eyes."
~Marcel Proust

Julien

Dimitri, Julien's papa, raked his fingers through his stark white hair. He shuffled paperwork around and glanced half-heartedly at the information before him while he sat at his desk. "*Bien,*" he exhaled, then gathered up the assorted documents, ranging from the death announcement to the funeral arrangements of his mother.

Julien rocked on his heels with his hands stuffed into his pants pockets while he stood at his papa's shoulder. "Lillie will bring the urn to the cathedral, and Colette confirmed with the caterer this afternoon. I am still working with Victoria on all the minor details of the gathering afterward, but everything else is in place at the hall. We are expecting close to four hundred in attendance at the cathedral, and we have planned for at least another hundred to arrive at the, ehm, celebration."

His two older, fraternal twin sisters and his younger sister were maestros when it came to event planning, if planning a funeral could be called an event. Madeleine "Mimi" Lilliette L'Angevin had made quite a name for herself as an artist over the course of her life, and her passing had become headline news.

"*Merci.*" His papa turned around and offered him a weak smile as he handed the documents back to Julien. "What would I do without you or the girls? *Je vous prise tous* (I treasure you all)."

"*Nous avons tous perdu un morceau de nous. Elle vivra cependant dans nos cœurs.* (We have all lost a piece of us. She will live on, though, in our hearts)."

A smile crept across his papa's face. "And on every bottle of wine and champagne from France to America."

"And in all our houses." Julien joined in the laughter—a needed reprieve from the sorrow they felt in her death.

Mimi's paintings, thousands of them over the years, not only hung in a handful of art museums and galleries all over France, her work also graced the labels of all the L'Angevin bottles. They also decorated every family member's home the way thrown confetti always found a way of settling into every possible crevice it could reach.

"Her name was on the lips of everyone the last time I was in the city. The world is mourning with us. The ceremony will be a beautiful celebration of her many accomplishments, I assure you," Julien concluded, squeezing his papa's shoulder and bidding him *adieu.*

"*Bonne nuit* (goodnight)," his papa replied.

Julien had set aside his dealings with the potential bottling of a Blanc de Blanc Champagne he had been in negotiations with for the last week in order to help his sisters orchestrate everything. A Chardonnay grape producer had offered him a personal batch that would be coming off its second fermentation cycle within the next four months for a ridiculous amount of money. He was more than willing to pay whatever the cost, though, just to spearhead his vision of labeling his own brand—one of his dreams fast transforming into a reality in the wake of his Grand-mère Mimi's death.

Living in the moment had become Julien's anthem, just as Blanca would always say, and pursuing all his ambitions his priority second to ensuring his grand-maman's funeral would be nothing short of spectacular.

Julien left his parents' home, crossing over the expansive lot to his own, wanting nothing more than to put an end to another long day and prepare for Chase and Max, his aunt and uncle, and Blanca to arrive on the property the next day.

The L'Angevin estate consisted of three homes and a storage building of sorts all encircling a large driveway. His parents inhabited the biggest of the homes and his grand-mère the smallest, all of which were perched on the top of a hill overlooking acres of vines. Most of his relatives that were flying in or taking the train intended on staying in Reims, including Chase's two older brothers and their wives. Chase's parents, on the other hand, had claimed grand-maman's home, leaving him with the awkward position of having Chase and Max take up one of his guestrooms, when all he wanted was for Blanca to stay with him by herself.

Julien knew Chase would be fawning all over his girlfriend, and, while Blanca had gone overboard on her chronic declaration of their friends-only status, he still had every intention of revisiting their romantic chemistry while she visited.

How could I not? Our chemistry was undeniable, and, if our time again were fleeting, she would see the need.

It had been several months since he'd felt a woman beneath him before Blanca had offered her affection so freely, and the notion of taking up dating again hadn't settled well with his soul quite yet. Their intimacy had reawakened him to passion, and he couldn't, or rather, he wouldn't allow her to use her non-committal status as an excuse to forego a week of relentless and somewhat necessary lovemaking. Not when she had complained the other day that she hadn't been with anyone else since she'd moved to Napa, as if she could evoke pity out of him about how dried-up the dating pool in the valley had been.

Try the French countryside. It may as well be the Sahara.

As unconventional as it seemed for Julien to be pining away at the thought of seeing Blanca again amidst so much grief, she had become a sort of balm to his apathetic heart. Her clever, pithy rants had become his favorite pastime when they spoke first thing in the morning. Due to the time difference, he also gloated in knowing that he simultaneously tucked her into bed during their conversations as it was nighttime on her end of the world.

And, as a result, he had inadvertently become possessive of her in a purposeful way.

Over the last two years, Julien had grown stagnant—forgetting to hope, to plan, and to expect more from his dull life. But, the more Blanca claimed to need him as her muse for writing that quirky romance novel, the more purpose-driven he had felt in appeasing his adorable, little American *friend.*

* * *

Blanca

"Your story was amazeballs."

"Ew," Maxie retorted.

"No, really. Total awesomesauce," Blanca chided, elbowing Maxie as they weaved through the Reims-Champagne Airport, dragging their suitcases while Chase followed behind them weighted down with everyone's carry-on bags.

"Your novel was great, too."

"Great?" *Pft.*

The besties had spent the entire travel time on their three connecting flights from the US to Paris then their tourist-filled puddle jumper from Paris to Reims-Champagne Airport reading each other's NaNoWriMo book babies. Maxie had come in at eighty thousand five hundred thirty-two words to Blanca's seventy-one thousand forty-seven words.

"No, really. I liked it. You stuck with our prompt and still managed to blend in a fantasy with it," Maxie added.

"Fairytale."

"Exactly. That's great." Maxie stepped onto the escalator and turned around to face Blanca behind her. "Now, reread mine, and do me the honor of a thorough critique."

"You trust me to rummage through your novel to make it better? I barely figured out how to pull mine out of my brain. If it wasn't for your cuz," Blanca looked up over her shoulder at Chase who pressed his full lips into a frown while snapping a rubber band off his wrist and twisting his thick, golden brown curls into a messy man bun. "I'm just sayin', Jules was my biggest cheerleader, that's all."

Maxie continued on, "I'm proud of you. Of us. We did it. I just want to make sure when my book hits the market it's the best possible version of itself before you pay up on our debt and a boutique publishing company gets its hands on my winner. Were there any inconsistencies? How was my character development? Was Rayne's arc evident? If I had left out the part where the—"

"Whoa, hold up. I don't speak *that* language. You're good to go, and so am I. We've dragged this competition on long enough. We put them up for free then pull the plug after thirty days and decide the winner based on whatever reviews come in. That's it. Then, I'm out. You know all about the formatting stuff, so why don't you just get us rollin', and let the countdown begin."

Maxie flipped around and stepped off the escalator. "I still get two weeks to polish mine," she huffed over her shoulder. "And we can only do five days for free then we have to price them, and they'll also be stuck on Amazon for three whole months. We can save a lot of money if we just use Amazon's ASIN numbers instead of buying ISBNs, but it's wiser to just get them and be done. We definitely want to pay for copyrights, though."

Blanca stared at her like the third head Maxie had just sprouted asked for mathematical directions to another galaxy.

"Like I said, you deal with all of it. I'll just cut you a check," Blanca retorted, as she fell in step with her. "Don't you want to be done with this whole bet already? Christmas is literally days away, and we have to start planning our New Year's resolutions competition."

"Fine."

"Fine."

Chase crossed in front of the women to shield them from an outpouring of eager vacationers scurrying through two automated doors that had whooshed open and blasted them with freezing cold air. "Follow me, ladies. Julien just texted his location."

They walked in silence as they weaved around tourists of all nationalities. Blanca soaked in the diversity and half-heartedly discerned the different languages she heard in passing, picking up a phrase here and there as the Christmas spirit thrived among the bustling crowd.

In the distance, Julien leaned against the trunk of his car with his arms folded across his broad pecs. He was dressed in a dark blue cable knit sweater and gray slacks like he'd just come from a semi-formal event even though the sun had only been up for about an hour. He tilted his head to the side, and his blond hair fell in large, unkempt waves covering half of his face. Neither a smile nor a frown played upon his full lips, but the subtle wrinkles at the corner of his eye betrayed his excitement in seeing all of them.

He looked so beautiful … beautiful and sad.

Maybe, heartbroken might be a better word.

Blanca's footsteps fell into a slower pace as she inspected him. It was one thing to know in the recesses of her memory that she had seen … and touched … and, let's just come right out and be blunt … liked all of his bits and parts. But it was an entirely other matter when she had him trapped in her iPhone as nothing but an extreme close-up of sea-glass-bleached-by-the-sun eyes with a wicked grin that could seduce her outright. Except that she was impervious to his moves thanks to their lack of continental proximity.

But, seeing him again face to face sent an unexpected and entirely unwelcome zing of feels to *her* bits and parts, and an overwhelming urge to turn around and hop the next flight out kicked her in the chest right where she felt the biggest zing of all.

The gravity of the moment rushed up on all of them as Julien reached out to Chase first. Both men embraced one another, planting kisses on each other's cheeks and breathing out their condolences over the loss of their grandmother.

They had grown up together at Julien's family's estate. Chase, though American-born, had spent almost all his summers living in Champagne with Julien and his family, which was just a short walk across the driveway to his grandmother's home, according to Chase's explanation during one of their flights.

Julien pulled back from his cousin and faced Maxie, gripping both her shoulders and tugging her into a stoic kiss that barely grazed her cheek. When he finally turned to Blanca, his expression shifted to a curious eagerness that bordered on desperation, and her pulse decided to skyrocket.

What the?

"I am so pleased you've come to see me, to see my home. I wish it were under better circumstances." Julien cupped Blanca's face with his ice-cold palms and leaned down to kiss her cheek, catching the corner of her mouth causing her breath to hitch out loud.

As Blanca searched for a reply, Julien turned and opened the trunk and, with Chase's help, jigsaw puzzled the suitcases and duffel bags into his car while Maxie shuffled Blanca into the back seat with her.

Blanca crossed one leg over the other and started bouncing it back and forth.

"Are you okay?" Maxie patted Blanca's white jeans-clad leg. "You're going to stab one of these guys in the back with that spiked heel on your boot if you don't calm down. What gives?"

"Nothing. Everything. I probably shouldn't have come."

"Why? Julien obviously wants you here. He only asked you every day for the last week if you're still coming, and you even cancelled appointments for him. You can't back out now. Besides, it's Christmas. It's our duty to spread some joy up in these guys."

Spreading definitely leads to joy.

"I just don't want him to get the wrong idea. I'm only here to see more of France. I didn't think—" she lowered her voice to a whisper as Julien and Chase walked around the sides of the car. "I'd ever see him again, or, if I ever did, it would be like a whole year from now at another one of Chase's parties or after our routine chit-chat eventually lost its steam."

"So what? You talk to him all the time. What's the big deal?"

"He's just a friend. I don't regret fooling around when we met, but I can't be more than that now."

Maxie chuckled and shook her head. "No one's asking you to."

Tell that to my heart.

Julien and Chase got into the car, slamming their creaky doors and continuing their conversation in French as Julien fired up the engine and pulled away from the airport. Maxie shrugged at Blanca and leaned in, expecting a translation.

Blanca listened for a seconds, tugging her fingers out of her black leather gloves. "The funeral is tomorrow afternoon with a huge gathering afterward, and it's going to be packed," she whispered. "We're also the last to show up. Almost everyone's here in the city. They're, uh, he's offering, no wait, he said you guys should stay with Chase's parents at his grandma's house because of all the drama he caused the last time you three were under one roof." *Hmph.* "Which he's still sorry about," she added, under her breath. Then, her eyes flew open, and she swatted Julien's shoulder with her gloves. "Hey, where am I supposed to stay?"

"With me," Julien replied, then continued his conversation with Chase.

"Hellllo? Don't I have any say in this decision?"

"You can stay in one of my parents' guestrooms. I'm sure they won't mind, but wouldn't you rather keep me company? You spend all your nights with me on FaceTime as it is."

He's got me there.

Blanca leaned in and whispered into Maxie's ear to ensure they couldn't hear her. "If things get weird staying with Chase's parents, I'll fake a meltdown and get us into a hotel, and if Julien gets all grabby hands on me while I'm staying with him, I'll, eh, I guess I'll just see how it goes."

Damn, I'm weak.

"Atta girl."

"Shut it."

Chase twisted around in his seat. "What are you two scheming now?"

"Nothing," they both exclaimed at the same time.

Chapter Eight

"Pleasure is none, if not diversified."
~John Donne

Blanca

Julien helped Blanca out of her black, double-breasted peacoat and hung it on the coat rack in the entrance of his parents' home. Between his overly doting behavior and Chase's sudden urge to Super Glue himself to Maxie, Blanca didn't know what to do with herself. So, she just went along with everything happening to and around her until she could figure out how to get a grip on those pesky, intrusive feels she suddenly had for her *friend* Julien.

Speaking of around, she panned the home and noted that her new house could probably fit inside any one of the rooms tucked away behind the looming arches radiating out from the rotunda they all stood in. A wrought iron chandelier dangled above them like something out of an antiquated castle, but the home itself was surprisingly light and bright. Or maybe that was all the shimmering white lights framing every windowsill, threshold, and banister in plain view.

She spied an office to her left, then a hallway that stretched on forever. In front of her, a living room pulled at her attention with a massive, unlit Christmas tree adorned with all kinds of shiny ornaments. Julien nudged her towards the living room, pressing the small of her back with his hand, igniting another zing of excitement she fought to contain. *Gah!*

On her far right, Blanca saw a dining room that opened to a kitchen that she could tell was tucked away off to the side by the light pouring into the dining room from it. She also saw a smaller sitting room immediately to the right of the front door that had a small, unlit Christmas tree on a table in front of the window. She'd spied that cute, little tree when they ascended the brick steps up to the enormous rancher house a few minutes earlier.

The French end of the L'Angevin empire must reek of money, or history, or a history of money because that house, *err,* mansion, oozed all over the top of a hill that had more vines zigzagging everywhere than Napa Valley as a whole. And, to add to the rusty-colored-roof and sky-high-ceiling charm of the place, it had tiny, boxy house babies encompassing it across a huge driveway, just like Chase had mentioned. The first one, a modest rancher, belonged to Julien's grandmother, a two-story home near it belonged to Julien, and finally the last structure she was told was basically a storage unit—the fanciest storage unit she'd ever seen, though.

"They'll be here any minute," Julien replied to Maxie.

Blanca snapped out of her stupor and focused on the tail end of their conversation as she sat on the couch next to Julien. He looped his arm around her shoulders the moment she leaned back prompting her to spring forward and stand up again because that itchy, achy, tingly zing started nipping at her heart again. They all halted their conversation and stared at her with curious frowns.

"I, uh, need to use the bathroom." What she really needed was some air.

"Down the hall, third door on the right," Chase replied.

"Thanks." Blanca rushed out of the living room, disregarding any embarrassment associated with her sudden and dramatic urge to *pee.*

All she could think of once she locked the bathroom door behind her was how magnificent Julien's life must be.

And how lonely.

No wonder he wants me around. I really am his friend.

Everything about Champagne whispered of peace and tranquility. Decisions could probably wait. Cares, who needed them? Wants? Whatever—whenever. And, she understood Julien, and even Chase, just a little bit more, and her ah-ha moment made it a tad bit easier to consider lightening up and embracing the week ahead, arms wide-open.

Blanca rationalized that she needed to try on a different attitude than the one she'd been smacked with the second she had seen Julien in all his mouth-watering glory leaning against the trunk of his car. She knew she'd regain control of her emotions if she'd just chill out and give into being yet another luxury in that man's to-die-for lackadaisical life for all of one week.

Cut me some slack. I need a big word to describe what's going on in my guts right now.

Blanca chose to decide that she had simply mistaken suddenly having the feels for Julien beyond friendship for all that delicious, French ambiance she actually craved. He was just part of the surrounding package.

Her wanderlust was only getting the best of her, she resolved, and it finally made perfect sense to include him in her consumption of all things jaw-droppingly gorgeous about France. Her heart was just playing tricks on her. Friends can be lovers, too, when there's a definite expiration date just like before. Right?

Meh. Works for me.

She was crazy like that.

Blanca exited the bathroom feeling like she had gotten a grip on her perspective about risking nothing to have a little extended vay-cay fun, except on the day of the funeral, of course. She noted that everyone had gathered in the rotunda again to greet Julien's parents who had just arrived.

Time to bone-up on my French.

Julien's mother, a voluptuous beauty with silver hair coiled into a half updo, reached out to Blanca first, gripping her hands in a tight squeeze. "Welcome, welcome. I am Monique, and this is Dimitri. You must be Blanca. We have heard so many wonderful things about you."

"Merci de nous avoir permis de vous joindre à vous. Nous sommes désolé pour votre perte (Thank you for allowing us to join you. We are sorry for your loss)," Blanca replied, then gave Julien a side-eye and leaned into his mother. "What kinds of things?"

"He says you are friends, *non?*"

Friends? Friends. "Oui."

Julien's mother released her hands with an even tighter squeeze. "Your French is lovely. You have been to our country before?"

"She was with Max in Paris over summer," Julien interjected.

"I travel all over Europe every chance I get," Blanca grinned, as Julien's father leaned down and planted several kisses on both of her cheeks while still holding one of Maxie's hands.

And here, I thought my relatives were the model family for extreme affection.

"Welcome," Dimitri said, releasing Maxie's hand and dragging his fingers through his hair the way she'd seen Julien do a few times.

"Are you settled in? Have you eaten breakfast? *Aimeriez vous du café* (Would you like some coffee)?" Monique asked, shimmying out of her long, red coat and looping it next to Maxie and Blanca's garments on the coat rack. "Chase, your parents are at grand-mère's settling in and will be over soon for breakfast. I expect everyone to join us, *s'il vous plaît?*"

"Actually, I would like to get our luggage put away, too," he replied, snatching up the ladies' coats and handing Blanca's to Julien.

"I understand you are not staying with Julien? I thought—" Dimitri asked, as his wife turned and headed down the hallway.

"*Tsk. Tsk.* Don't ask, love. They are still recovering from Julien's darker side the last time Chase visited," she shrilled over her shoulder.

"Maman!"

"I see that it's all worked out for the best now, though," Dimitri replied, stretching his arms out in the air as if he were embracing all four of them at once.

Not awkward. Not awkward at all.

"And, on that note, let's all go see my aunt and uncle, shall we?" Julien smirked, as he helped Blanca back into her coat.

The four of them left the house and headed over to grand-mère Mimi's place—Julien seizing an opportunity to grab Blanca by the hand.

Again with the touchy-feely?

Once through the door—a simple kitchen to their left, a formal dining room and hallway to their right, and ahead of them a large living room with Chase's parents slumped on the couch murmuring something to each other at the sight of all of them—Blanca felt an urge to reciprocate some of Julien's clinginess and threaded her fingers through his. Her eyes darted everywhere. She captured a mental snapshot of the paintings and sketches littering every square inch of all the walls as Julien glanced down at her and flashed an amused smile, giving her hand a little squeeze.

They stepped into the living room behind Maxie and Chase, and Blanca finally noticed the infamous sketches of her BFF's boyfriend in all his—*holy mother of*—hung glory. The largest and most explicit in its detail was parked center stage over the couch surrounded by smaller sketches, including a few that were of a couple in, ehem, *intimate* positions. Blanca may have forgotten for a split second how to keep moving forward as she looked, no scratch that, gawked at *it—them*—the *sketches.* Yeah.

Julien released Blanca's hand and continued to head over to his aunt and uncle for the usual kisses while Maxie pulled away from Chase and sidled up next to her whispering something under her breath.

"Nice job, Maxie. Maybe, he is a keeper." *And, hello granny? Why on earth would you want to decorate your home with your grandson's—* "What?"

Maxie crossed her arms and gritted her teeth. "I said, stop staring at those sketches of my boyfriend."

Chase followed Blanca's line of sight then bowed his head as Julien turned around and addressed everyone in the living room. "I think we can all agree, now that grand-mère has passed away, that it's time for these sketches to go, as well, *non? Si'l vous plaît?* Chase, do you want to keep them or—"

His snapped his head up. "I'll put them in storage."

"I've always thought they were a bit *forward,*" Chase's mother grumbled, looking up behind her at the pictures of her naked son.

"You mean *upward,* dear." His father interjected, causing a nervous burst of laughter to ricochet through the tension in the room.

And, on that cue, Chase stretched over between his parents and reached up, unhooking the wires from their hinges and stacking the assorted smaller frames together on the coffee table face—*err, flobby-jeebies*—down. Then, he took down the largest sketch and leaned the frame against the end of the couch. "I can't believe she insisted on keeping them on display for so long."

"Pity you were never around to enjoy seeing them as much as me." Julien's smile had a unique glow to it, like he'd won something in watching Chase dismantle his shame. It was as if something manifesting itself had just come to a screeching halt because the evidence had finally been put to rest with the family's matriarch.

"It doesn't surprise me," Chase's father snickered. "It's great to see you again, Blanca."

"It's nice to see you both, too," she replied. "I wish it were under better circumstances."

"Thank you," Chase's mother nodded. "Julien could use the company." Her eyes drifted over Maxie and Chase as they embraced each other in an obnoxious, look-at-us-we're-so-in-love hug.

"We're staying with you," Chase announced to his parents.

"We understand—of course," they replied in unison, as their gaze shifted over to Julien who crossed over to Blanca and grabbed her hand in his again as if to stake his own claim on some public display of affection.

Dude?

***

Julien

Julien grabbed Blanca's suitcase and duffel bag from the trunk of his car and ushered her over to his place while Chase and Max snatched up their luggage and headed back to the other house.

"I have a guest room upstairs."

And one downstairs, as well, but you don't need to know that.

"My own room? Thanks." Blanca grumbled, as she panned his home once they entered it.

Julien kept things fairly clean and simple. His walls, much like everyone else's in the family, dripped with grand-mère's artwork, but he preferred only landscapes over any portraits or sketches of anything. His modest, black leather furniture with red throw pillows and such added a more masculine presence in the living room on their left, unlike the dining room just past the staircase and hallway on their right.

Ah, the dining room. I wonder what Blanca will think of me when she discovers it?

Julien's mother had redecorated the dining alcove for him with a shabby chic look, she'd called it, one afternoon while he was in America. She'd done it just to get on his nerves, assuming he'd need punishing over something or other when returning from spending a week with Chase.

Passive aggressive antics were a badge of honor among L'Angevin women, if you hadn't caught on yet.

Julien's office, which was across from the dining room, as well as the kitchen at the back end of the house, on the other hand, stood out sleek and modern—culinary interests running deep among the L'Angevin men.

He watched as Blanca's eyes danced over everything then motioned for her to go up the stairs. "After you, *mademoiselle.*"

"Such the gentleman. Have you forgotten who you're dealing with?"

Ah, there's my beloved flirt. I was wondering where you were hiding.

"Oh, I know exactly what I'm getting myself into with you," he replied, trailing behind her with a smile.

Once she reached the top of the stairs, she looked over the banister down to the entryway and part of the living room below then made her way towards a hallway in the opposite direction.

"Keep going. Second door on the left. The first door is my room, and the door across from yours is your own bathroom."

Her eyes raked the room as though she couldn't take it all in quickly enough. "This is really nice. Very French. I have to come right out and say it, though, I'm a little surprised you want me to stay here."

Julien set Blanca's suitcase on top of the hope chest at the end of the four-poster bed then put her duffel bag on top of the mirrored dresser. "I couldn't have you staying with Chase and Max."

"No. I mean *here* … in the guestroom," she replied, pointing down at the carpet with both fingers.

"Oh."

"Oh?"

"Ooooh." *This is too easy.* "You can, ehm, stay in my room with me, if you like. I would love it, actually."

"Don't say love."

He threw his hands up. "Of course, right, ehm, I mean, I wasn't sure what to expect—not that I was expecting anything—I just wanted to see you again. In person, that is. No pressure. You're only here for a week, *non?*"

"Exactly."

Before Julien could gather his thoughts and come up with something clever to say to convince Blanca that their friendship would in no way be jeopardized by their physical interactions over the next few days, whether he meant it or not, she lunged at him, fisting his sweater and pulling him down into a passionate kiss.

Chapter Nine

"The journey of a thousand miles begins with one step."
~Lao Tzu

Julien

Julien slipped his fingers into Blanca's thick hair as she released his sweater and looped her arms over his shoulders. Everything about her felt warm and inviting. He slid his tongue around hers tasting her like he'd been starved for weeks and had finally found his nourishment in her. Blanca's responsive moans nearly did him in. She parted from his hungry lips only long enough to wrestle out of her blouse and fling it to the ground. He had his sweater and pants off before she lunged at him again, and they caressed and groped their way over to the edge of the bed.

"I didn't think we'd see each other again. At least not for a while," Julien cooed, running his hands along her slender waist.

"Me neither. Not this soon anyway," she mumbled back, capturing his lips again as she eased up onto the bed.

Julien bowed over her, leaning Blanca back as he nipped at her neck savoring the feel of her skin against his.

"One week. That's it. Then we go back to—"

"Shh. *Oui,* my little nymph." Julien replied, covering her mouth with his again.

* * *

Julien wrestled his pants back on and tossed Blanca her silky, polka dot bra in Christmas red that matched her panties and solid red blouse that lay crumpled at her feet. "So sexy."

She snatched it out of the air. "Thanks."

Julien cracked the bedroom door open. "We'll be right down," he shouted out to Chase and Max who had let themselves in.

Julien rushed back over to the side of the bed and slipped his feet into his loafers as he watched Blanca. She had been trying to see her image in the mirrored dresser top in order to smooth her hair down, but her duffel bag blocked her view. An Italian cuss word rolled off her tongue as she turned around to face him. "You like red?"

"Very much so. Especially on you."

Blanca scooped her blouse up off the floor and slid her arms through the long sleeves. "What else do you like?"

Julien wanted to say, *you,* but knew that if he did she'd probably clam up again and start with the whole, *let's just go back to being friends* routine he'd been so accustomed to every time he suggested they seek out some intimate relief with one another on the phone. "I like that every shoe you own could double as a weapon."

Her fingers moved quickly over the buttons of her blouse. "Unlike those old-man slippers you like to call shoes."

"They happen to be very comfortable."

"Shoes aren't meant to be comfortable—"

"Let me guess, they are just meant to add height?"

Blanca couldn't help but laugh, and the sound of it flooded Julien's heart with satisfaction. That fiery, little devil had him questioning everything he thought he was sure of in their lopsided so-called *friendship* up until about seven minutes ago.

He wanted more. In fact, he wanted it all. Her laughter, her kisses, her trust, ... perhaps even her heart, if he could just wrestle it away from her.

Mission impossible.

Julien waited until Blanca tugged her boots back on then grabbed her hand and pulled her behind him in a rush towards the stairs. They could see Chase and Max below from the narrow overhang, and Blanca abruptly dropped his hand.

"Are you all right?" he asked, pulling her aside, out of view from the overhang.

"Yes, I'm fine. I just need to explain things to Maxie first before she gets all cuckoo on me and starts to plan our wedding, or worse, accuses me of using you," she replied, though her eyes held an element of panic in them.

"I understand," *Not really.* "But, you've reciprocated my affection all morning long in front of her."

"Just let me figure out—I mean, let me fill her in, one more time, just to be sure." She searched out his eyes. "You're okay with this?"

"Absolutely," he nodded, dragging his fingers through his wild, helpless hair.

"I could back off and just go ahead and stay in the guestroom if I'm asking too much."

"Asking too much? *Je ne comprends pas* (I don't understand). What did you ask to begin with?"

Blanca bowed her head. "I want to live life to the fullest while I'm on this vacation, and that includes us adding some *benefits* to our friendship."

"Benefits?" A small laugh escaped him. "I suppose that is one way to look at it. But, *oui,* I am, ehm, more than happy to help you on your journey."

"Journey? Right. Journey. Holiday. Sure. That's what vacations are called in Europe." She glanced up at him then looked down at her boots again and whispered as if to herself. "Look at me. I'm on a journey."

And, so am I, my little firecracker.

Julien couldn't help but swell with ambition to make every second of her journey matter as long as that journey led straight to him.

* * *

Once they descended the stairs, Max and Blanca drifted into the living room to talk, and Chase headed for the kitchen with Julien trailing behind him.

"Are the two of you going to be comfortable with your parents at grand-maman's? *Est-ce-qu'ils ont pardonné complètement* Max (Have they forgiven Max completely)?" Julien asked, as he leaned over the black and gold granite countertop.

Chase grabbed the kettle from the stove and filled it with water then lit a burner and placed the kettle over it. "I have to assume so. I just witnessed my father cry on Max's shoulder over Grand-mère Mimi. I think they finally see, now, all the wonderful qualities in Max that I love. It's so hard to believe grand-maman is gone."

"*Oui. Il y a trou dans mon coeur* (Yes. There is a hole in my heart)."

They stood in silence for a few moments, allowing their grief to run its course.

"And Blanca's comfortable staying here with you?" Chase began again, as he spooned a layer of ground coffee beans from a canister on the counter into a large French press.

"She seems quite comfortable." *Until you two showed up.*

"Are *you* comfortable with her here? I know you invited her, but—"

"But nothing. I enjoy her company."

"I have no doubt you do. She's an amazing person, but, she is also the complete opposite of Max in a lot of ways."

"And your point is?"

Chase took a deep breath and locked eyes with him. "She can't give you what you need."

Oh, but I beg to differ.

"And, what, exactly, is it you think I need?"

"Love."

"Love is all I need?" he purred in a sing-songy American accent.

"Just don't expect too much. She's only here for the week. It's one thing to talk to each other every night—"

Julien narrowed his eyes in annoyance as the kettle began to whistle.

Chase grabbed the kettle and poured the boiling water into the French press. "Max mentioned it. She said the two of you are always talking. She's got this crazy idea that you and—well, my point is, I hope some day you find what you're looking for. I just don't think you're going to find it in Blanca. The two of you aren't even living in the same country."

Julien considered Chase's words, and he concluded that his cousin did have a valid point in all that rhetoric.

* * *

Blanca

"So, then she told me she couldn't be more happy that I'm here with Chase. I swear she almost started crying, too." Maxie's cornflower blue eyes sparkled with enchantment.

"I hate to say it, but I guess I was wrong about them. About all of them. Chase really does make you happy, doesn't he?"

"I'm happy with or without him. Chase just makes me complete."

"Ew. Okay. Don't go all Hallmark card on me right now. You're only at the *I love you* and *his parents don't hate me anymore* stage in your relationship. Let it ride for a while. Please?"

"Fine. And what's your status with Julien?"

"Okay, so here's the deal. Don't get all wishful thinking on us, but I'm expanding the definition of my friendship with him to include sex—lots and lots of *hot sex* for the next few days. A girl has to stay warm, you know. It's cold up in here," she joked, hoping Maxie got her gist. The last thing she needed was for her bestie to start prattling on about how wonderful they were together, because *together,* they were not.

Maxie's cheeks began to blush, and she pressed her lips together as if holding back a squee.

"Go ahead. Get it out of your system."

Maxie quietly applauded—her hands furiously batting the air as she grinned ear to ear. "I'll mind my own business, but I have to know something. Why are you breaking all your rules? You're not setting him up to get his heart crushed at the end of the week, are you? He knows you don't do relationships, right? Especially long-distance ones."

"He gets it. I'm going full-French immersion this week, and he knows he's part of the course. Everything will be fine."

I think?

Chase and Julien entered the living room, both holding cups of coffee for the ladies.

"Cream and sugar," Chase quipped.

"Thank God," Blanca breathed, taking hers from Julien. "Where have you been all my life, you big, steamy stud?"

"In Champagne mostly," he teased.

"I was talking to the java," she deadpanned.

"Of course you were."

Chase sat down next to Maxie on the loveseat while Julien nestled in on the far end of the couch opposite of where Blanca was, obviously giving her some space he must've thought she needed. She didn't mean to be so hands-off coming down the stairs when they'd clearly been all hands-on only moments before Maxie and Chase showed up and ruined their frenzied reunion.

Blanca hoped he understood her intentions even as she was trying to sort all the details out herself. One thing she knew for certain was she didn't want Maxie seeing something that wasn't there and hoped her pathetic explanation was enough to appease her BFF, so she could carry on with her plans to keep ravishing Julien every chance she got.

Blanca was diving in head first and wasn't going to come up for air until she'd completely immersed herself in everything Champagne had to offer including Julien, her new, smokin' hot, French lover.

She was resourceful like that.

"Do you have any plans after tomorrow?" Chase asked Julien.

"Plans are your department. I was just going to toss my little, devilish sidekick here into the car and go."

"Just go?" Maxie repeated.

"*Oui.*" He tipped his mug to his lips, satisfied with his answer.

"I think that might be the best plan I've ever heard of," Blanca added, cupping her mug for warmth as the chilled winter stillness that permeated Julien's home sent a shiver through her silken blouse.

"One thing I know is that she loves an adventure, so I plan on giving her one." He slid her a side eye, which she reciprocated with smug delight.

Damn right you are. Adventures in French Sexploration, Chapter One.

Blanca smirked at Maxie, who was all aglow with silent pride. She shook her head at her BFF as if to warn her to wipe those happily-ever-after hopes about Julien out of her mind.

"Are you cold?" Julien asked. "I'll bring you a blanket."

He rose and left the living room before she had a chance to say, *yasss.*

Maxie nestled closer to Chase, tucking her head into the crook of his arm he had draped over her shoulders. "I'm game for anything."

"I like the sound of that," Chase replied.

"Aren't you two going to be a little weirded out at the thought of getting it on with your parents down the hall?"

"We're going to find a hotel after Christmas," Maxie replied.

"That's three whole days from now. You sure you can go that long, big boy?"

Chase shook his head and smiled. "We can always stay here in the downstairs guestroom."

"*Downstairs* guestroom?"

Heh, that sneaky bastard.

Julien entered the living room and draped a blanket over Blanca's lap. "I would start a fire," he began, motioning to the fireplace angled in the corner of the room, "but my maman is expecting us for breakfast soon."

"We came by to get you, actually. She said she put some pastries out and tossed a couple of store-bought quiche in the oven. She wanted me to stress the store-bought part," Chase explained, holding back a laugh.

Julien groaned and stood up. "Damn. I was going to make quiche for everyone, but I had some business to wrap up in the city this morning. Let's go then."

"I'll grab my coat." Blanca downed the rest of her drink then set the mug on the coffee table and scurried to her feet, twirling the blanket around her shoulders.

Julien watched her with mild amusement. "We need to buy you a scarf and a hat while you're here. A coat and gloves are not enough."

Blanca nodded as she edged past him on her way back upstairs. "I'd love to go shopping in town with you," she called out over her shoulder.

"You'll have to get her a beret to go with her French excursion," Maxie interjected with a laugh.

"*Oui*! *Oui*!" Blanca called out behind her. "I also insist on helping you make a bunch of quiche later," she added, as she disappeared up the staircase.

Chapter ten

"We are each of us angels with only one wing, and we can only fly by embracing one another."
~Luciano De Crescenzo

Julien

"Wake up, sleeping beauty," Julien whispered into Blanca's ear, as he brushed her caramel-colored locks away from her face.

One moment Julien had gone to the kitchen to pour Blanca another cup of coffee after watching her down at least three of them at his parents' house over breakfast, and the next he'd found her curled up on her side under the blanket he'd grabbed from upstairs for her when they had come back home. She hadn't even budged when he'd tugged her boots off as jet lag had managed to knock her out for most of the day.

"If you don't try to wake up now, you won't sleep at all tonight, and tomorrow is going to be a very busy day. Blanca?" He brushed the back of his hand along her cheek, letting his fingertip graze her lower lip—so full and inviting.

To see Blanca again, face to face, to be able to touch her skin and hold her in his arms once more, thrilled him. Though their intimacy back in the United States had only revolved around quenching a primal need, it reignited Julien's determination to pursue welcoming a woman in his life, perhaps even the woman before him if their circumstances weren't so impossible to resolve.

His Grand-mère Mimi—Chase—they both spoke of love ... of *amore* ... seeing through his stoic charade. Just looking at Blanca and what their friendship had rooted in him with his urge to tend to all her needs, he knew he had to determine if she could fill that void in his heart—if she could be his true love someday.

Their chemistry was undeniable—their friendship, a solid core anyone in an actual relationship could only hope for. Why couldn't they give in to falling in love? Why should their lack of proximity be allowed to get in the way?

Julien's days being numbered, he surmised that, since Blanca was so eager to throw her heart at his country, she might be willing to stay indefinitely if he could only intercept that eager heart of hers long enough for them to both figure those answers out.

Blanca parted her eyes, and a smile spread across her face. "Hey, you." She reached up and cupped his face for a few seconds. "I just can't get enough of your eyes. *And your couch, apparently.* How long have I been asleep?"

"All day, beautiful. Everyone has already eaten an early dinner. I made a plate for you. Max fell asleep, as well. The time difference is going to be easier to overcome if you can stay awake until later tonight."

"I'll try my best." She sat up and grabbed her boots off the tiled floor. "Do you mind if I take a shower?"

"You don't have to ask. My home is your home."

She looked around, considering his comment—her luminous, jade green eyes flaring with mischief, twisting his emotions into a tangle of delicious lust.

"Mine," she nodded then she stood up and slinked by him, poking a finger into his chest. "Also mine, too, but only for the week."

We'll see about that.

* * *

Blanca

Several minutes later, Blanca sauntered into the kitchen in socks wearing a black unzipped hoodie and matching yoga pants. She had a bright blue t-shirt on with black glittery lettering. Her wet hair was scrunched into cascading waves down her back.

Julien panned the saying on her clothes with an inquisitive smile then removed her plate of food from the warming tray in the oven and placed it on a golden charger plate for her. *"It's not you. It's your eyebrows?"*

"It's an American thing." Blanca waved his interest away with the flick of her wrist and picked up her dinner and the bundle of silverware he'd also put out for her. "So you made the quiche without me?" She thrust her bottom lip out and surveyed the messy mixing bowls and flour-covered counter beneath a half-a-dozen unbaked pies that Julien started shoveling into the hot oven.

"I am sorry I didn't have the heart to wake you."

"What else can we bake?"

"You really want to bake something with me?"

"I want to do All. The. Things. With you." She bounced her eyebrows at him and headed to the dining room for a better look around than the quick rubberneck stare she'd just given the space.

"Which one of these things is not like the other?" she sang out, as she perused the cluttered alcove.

It oozed with mason jars, mismatched pastel and floral print fabrics, as well as lots of shiny whozits, whatzits, and thing-a-ma-bobs that were nailed to the walls and filling up a glass hutch along another wall.

"A gift from my mother," Julien grumbled, watching her through the butler's pantry connecting the two rooms. "Perhaps while you're here, you can help me redecorate."

Blanca sat down at the table and breathed in the savory fragrances of her food. "I'm totally into that idea, but I'm also making you get a Christmas tree, too. Thought you should know. So, what are we baking?"

Julien pressed his lips together and *hmmed*. "The oven is going to be tied up for a while, but we could make beignets."

She loaded her fork full of mixed vegetables and a slice of filet mignon. "Ooh, fried dough. I'm in."

"Beignets it is."

"Thank you for dinner. I'm starving."

"I should've gotten you up sooner. You might find it difficult to sleep tonight."

She grinned at him around a mouthful of food. "Feel free to wear me out later."

I'm not even kidding.

He leaned against the threshold, folding his arms over his chest, smiling. "I'll do my best."

So will I, my sexy, French lover.

She continued eating her meal as he disappeared out of view through the butler's pantry, running water and clanking dishes as he cleaned up.

When Blanca finished her dinner, she gathered her double plates and silverware and brought them to Julien. He had all the ingredients needed to make their beignets on the countertop awaiting her.

He took one last peek at his quiche in the oven. "My maman can reheat them in the mornings while my aunt and uncle are here. Do you like to cook?"

She shrugged. "I've been known to make a killer stromboli from time to time."

"You'll have to make something for me, too, *oui*?" He offered her a warm smile as he stepped up next to her in front of all the ingredients. "First, we need to make the dough then let it rise. This is going to be a slow process. You have patience, *non*? Baking requires time."

"Then let's hurry up and get started," she teased, nudging his shoulder.

"First, we need to mix together some water, sugar, and yeast and let them sit while we prep the other items."

Blanca wielded the whisk in front of her while he measured things out into a small bowl then offered it to her to stir together.

"Now, we mix some evaporated milk, a pinch of salt, and the eggs together." Again, he measured the items out into another, larger bowl and stepped aside for her to stir the batter around.

"Is the *evaporated* milk your secret ingredient?" she asked, lavishing in every little detail of the process, while her tummy tingled with excitement.

"You're onto me." He took the whisk from her and set it down. "Now we wait."

"Now?"

"The yeast needs a few more minutes to completely activate."

Blanca looked him up and down. "When was the last time you made beignets?"

"It's been a while. I do plan on making some desserts for Christmas. We are a family that loves to eat."

"My family is the same way, especially when all my relatives come together. I'm used to working with pizza dough—not this sticky stuff you made."

Heh. Sticky stuff. Maaan, my mind's in the gutter tonight.

"You will have to make me something this week, *oui?*"

"Sure, if you want."

"I want," Julien smiled, finally pouring the yeast mixture into the bowl with the batter. He grabbed a container and popped the lid off then measured out a few scoops of flour, and finally added a dollop of shortening from a can. "Now comes the *exciting* part. Toss some flour onto the countertop for me, *si'l vous plaît?*"

Blanca scooped a little bit out of the container and sprinkled it over the granite surface. Then she watched as Julien pulled the lump of dough out of the bowl and set it down then scooped up another handful of flour and dusted the top of the oozing mound. He snatched up a bottle of vegetable oil and drizzled it around the bowl, coating the sides then he maneuvered behind her and covered her hands with his.

He began kneading the dough, squishing it through their fingers, igniting giggles from her.

Sexy in a playful kind of way. Cute. I could get used to this. Err, or not.

No, not going to get used to this. Live in the moment ... live in the moment ... live in the ...

Julien dipped his head down to her ear, sending shivers along her spine. "You are having fun, *non?*"

Ooh, I definitely need this moment to last for a while, though.

She leaned back into him and tilted her head to the side. "I am definitely having fun."

He let go of her hands.

No, wait. I'm not done yet.

"Remember what I said about patience?"

Oh, so we're going to be like that now?

"Vaguely."

Julien pulled the dough into a tight ball and dropped it into the oiled bowl then covered it with a cloth and set it on a shelf in the refrigerator. "We have to let it rest for a couple of hours while I rotate the quiche and wrap them up to take them over to my parents in the morning."

Oh, that makes sense.

Blanca crossed over to the sink and washed her hands then Julien washed up after her.

"Can *we* rest for a couple of hours, too?"

"You're not allowed to sleep just yet, or the jet lag will have you wide awake all night."

She slipped her arms around his waist and peered up at him. "Two whole hours? That seems like more than enough time to finish what we started this morning. Don't you think?"

"You have me thinking all kinds of things," he replied, dipping down to taste her lips.

Yasss!

* * *

Two hours later, with Julien's quiches baked, wrapped, and tucked away in the refrigerator, they returned to the kitchen together one more time to finish what they had started. Blanca stood next to Julien, engulfed in one of his long-sleeve undershirts and her yoga pants she had on earlier, awaiting his instructions.

Julien wore nothing but a pair of sweats thanks to Blanca having swiped his shirt before running out of the bedroom. He looked every bit the sexy beast that he'd proven himself to be yet again, as he threaded his fingers through his wet hair and breathed out a laugh. "Now, where were we?"

Blanca, barely coming up to his chest, rose up on her tippy toes and pulled him into a quick kiss. "Beignets. Now."

"All right. Let's do this."

Julien lit a burner under a skillet and asked Blanca to fill it with oil. Then he sank a thermometer on the side of it. "We need to cut up pieces next."

He tugged the puffy ball of dough out of its bowl and pulled it apart into several smaller sections. Then, he rolled out long ropes onto the counter. "Here," he handed her a pizza cutter. "Run this through the dough and make bite-sized pieces while I prep the powdered sugar."

Blanca obeyed his instructions quietly, raking her eyes over his body while she wrestled with the woozy intoxication of post-coital bliss.

That man had her all kinds of crazy, lavishing her with more affection than she'd ever been used to between the sheets. His kisses—countless, his hands—forever roving. Julien was by far the best lover she'd ever known—not that she meant to compare—but he definitely took his time to explore her body, unlike their last two passionate encounters they'd had, which had been more detached and frenzied than the lackadaisical—*there's that pesky, big word again*—love-making, *I mean, lust-making*—they'd just delved into like a real couple.

A real couple? Holy, schnikes. That kind of thinking has got to stop.

"Now all we need to do is drop the balls into the oil and pull them out when they are golden brown."

"Drop the balls," she repeated, laughing off his expression as she mentally swatted down a flurry of butterflies that took flight in her gut.

Blanca eased a few of the dough balls into the sizzling oil and stared at the mounds bobbing around, fully aware of Julien's half-naked body right next to her. His soft, sweet, soapy-smelling, warm flesh only moments ago had been wet and sliding against hers in the shower. When the French desserts had turned the perfect hue, he scooped them out of the oil with a wire basket ladle onto a plate and handed her a sifter full of powdered sugar.

Blanca sprinkled the sugar over the beignets. "I can't wait to try these!"

"What if we play a little game," Julien began, repeating the process with the rest of the morsels of dough. "What if I feed them to you, but for every bite, you have to tell me something about you I don't already know."

She dusted another layer of powdered sugar on the second batch of beignets while her insides did a little, tickly flip-flop again.

Quit! He's just trying to be a gentleman to counterbalance our physical actions.

"Can I just offer up random facts, or do I have to answer specific questions?"

"I don't want you to feel uncomfortable. I know you keep to yourself about your past, but if you want me to make your journey the greatest it can be then some direction as to what would make you the most happy would be nice, *non?*"

He pulled a plate from the cupboard and piled a small mountain of the pastry puffs onto it, waving the deliciousness in front of her nose as he exited the kitchen. She gave into the temptation and followed behind him as he marched up the stairs with her at his heels.

"And, what's in it for me with this game of yours?"

"Dessert."

Julien walked into his bedroom, which Blanca hadn't seen yet, and he sat down on the end of his full-sized bed while she hesitated at the threshold. It was a modest-sized master bedroom compared to the guestroom next door that she occupied. Her eyes ricocheted around the room. Walls and bedding—gray—leather chair and table—black—overall decor—covered in landscapes. Neat? *Nope.* His dresser top was cluttered with manly junk, and dirty laundry trickled along the floor out of the bathroom door.

"This is definitely you."

She noticed that the myriad of paintings on the walls, depicting French city streets, were glistening in the rain. "I love these paintings. Rain looks good on everything."

She finally settled her sights on him as she realized he was watching her assess his own private domain—her mostly naked, French, beast-of-a-man, balancing their homemade heaven-on-a-plate in one hand wearing a *caught-ya-lookin'* sexy grin.

Sigh. Big sigh. Huuuge.

She almost blushed. "I'll answer your questions as long as you give up something about yourself with each bite, too."

"Fair enough." He patted the comforter beside him. "Come."

So far, every time.

She fought a sudden chill—the temperature much cooler upstairs than downstairs—as she crawled up on the squeaky bed and crossed her legs as she faced him.

"Would you like some tea to warm you?"

"Question number one? *Oui.*" She smiled and tipped her nose at the plate of scrumptiousness in his hand. "Now, feed me."

"Ah, I see how it is, *très bien* (very well)." He picked up a golden morsel and dangled it in front of her. Her tongue darted out, and she caught a little bit of the powdered sugar on it. His eyes widened, and he leaned over and covered her mouth with his, parting her lips with his tongue to taste the sweetness. She gave into his spontaneous affection and pulled him into a deeper kiss, twirling her tongue around his, slowly savoring his taste mingled with the sugar.

He nearly tipped the plate of beignets in his hand as he adjusted himself closer to her, curling his long legs up on the bed.

She pulled away from his kiss and giggled. "Don't you dare drop any of those beignets. Why don't you get us some hot tea, and I'll find my blanket."

"All right," he said, sliding off the bed. "I have a fireplace to warm my house, but no central air, like in America, for heat or to cool things off." He paused in the threshold and looked down. "I want you to lay with me tonight. I can keep you warm. Besides, your sheets are dirty, *non?* You said earlier you were surprised I set you up in the guest room. It was only out of respect for our friendship, but we are, as you say, friends with benefits, now, *oui?*" He looked up and flashed her a quick smile.

Blanca weighed his reasoning. She couldn't just come right out and say that it had been years since she'd shared a bed with a man to actually sleep *in*, not *with*. Her comments earlier had been in the heat of the moment, but, before she had a chance to go ahead and agree, Julien stepped away from the door, humming a little tune, as if he knew he didn't need her to audibly say, *oui*.

* * *

"If I take even one more bite, I'm going to burst."

"But, I am not done asking you questions," Julien cooed, sliding a thumb pressed with sugar along his tongue. "Just one more."

"Fine," Blanca agreed, figuring what's the point in resisting. He'd managed to drag out details in her about all her favorite cities she'd traveled to, including how her wanderlust had begun with her first trip to Italy. She'd only been a teenager when she went to visit a multitude of distant relatives one year.

Blanca had even confessed to the reason behind her career choice of being a stylist over becoming a Linguist. She *did*, however, leave out the teensy part about how heartbroken she'd been after having her fiancé dump her without any clue that the break-up was even coming. The heartache had been what prompted her to drop out of junior college her second year and enroll in Cosmetology school.

Blanca had decided to just laugh her sad, short story version off as having been a poor dating choice in the first place, opting to blame her childish delusions about what real love should've felt like as the reason for its failure. She wasn't about to get into the whole men suck, and love isn't real rant, especially when she knew deep down that love was real. She just didn't want to have anything to do with it for at least another decade—maybe even longer considering the wounds her asshole ex had carved into her heart hadn't even come close to healing yet.

When Blanca's heart was steeled and impervious to breaking, she'd try commitment again, until then, she was living for the moment all the way. And that's all Jules, her temporary French lover, needed to know.

Julien's own sob story about *almost* proposing to his ex had been what prompted Blanca to finally leak her mini version about being proposed to and then dumped when she was only twenty-years-old.

Julien, the poor sap, had hired a string quartet to play on the street corner next to the restaurant he'd always take his then girlfriend to after they'd do the horizontal rendezvous at her art studio in Reims. Julien's romantic side had even gotten the best of him with the presentation of the engagement ring. He'd left the three-carat diamond to dangle on the end of the cellist's bow from a ribbon he'd stolen from his girlfriend's hair on their first date as a keepsake—a ring he'd abandoned along with his hope in ever finding true love again.

Julien had gone to his girlfriend's studio to surprise her that night with the intention to bring her out to the street corner on their way to their restaurant but ended up stumbling upon an even bigger surprise, walking in on her with Chase in her studio … naked.

Blanca questioned Julien about forgiving her for luring his cousin to pose for nudes. Whether he'd forgiven Chase or not, she'd figure that out on her own. His explanation that his hardened heart was better left undisturbed was all the answer he was willing to give for either of them. Something about acceptance over forgiveness mattering more to him now.

Personally, I'd wanna kill the beotch, but that's just me.

Blanca had begun to feel a unique kinship with Julien after their intimate conversation about their shattered hopes and dreams of finding everlasting love. Normally, the whole sharing and caring thing never breached her friendship with Maxie, let alone crossed over to someone she'd slept with. But, somehow it all felt right with Julien. What, with two horrid people undeserving of their love lurking around in their pasts, they kind of earned their heart-to-heart intimacy.

Blanca blamed it on destiny that their lives had collided at the perfect time for them to bring each other a little reprieve on their emotional journeys moving forward. They had the next few days to frolic in some shameless passion, and Blanca was sure their friendship could only grow stronger from it in the end.

"So bring it. What's your final question?" Blanca traced small circles with her fingertips on her stomach, reliving the sensation where Julien had licked some sugar off her tummy, as she lay stretched out beside him. His t-shirt she'd stolen from him was still bunched up around her ribs.

"If you could live anywhere in the world, where would it be?" He turned on his side to face her, propping his head up on his hand—the small bed moaning under his weight.

"That would depend on how long I had to commit to living there."

He reared up and parted his lips to say something, then reeled his thoughts back in and waited for her reply.

All righty, down boy.

Blanca studied Julien's gorgeous face, appreciating all that she'd reluctantly discovered about the man, succumbing to the temptation to simply tell him what he wanted to hear, so she could finally call it a night and get some sleep knowing she'd make him so happy with her holiday-induced answer.

"France," she concluded, unleashing his joy.

Why not? It might actually be half true. Everything about France right now is freakin' awesome.

* * *

Julien was all arms, and legs, and breath, and warm fuzzies—*Or was that all the leg hair?*—when they finally crawled into bed together. He took up most of the mattress and left Blanca with no other choice than to cuddle. And cuddle she did.

Within seconds, she had her leg slung over his hip, while the other one wiggled its way underneath his thigh. And, with her head on his bicep as a pillow, Blanca closed her eyes and fell into a deep sleep, convinced that no matter what they did together for the rest of the week, Julien deserved to have as much fun as her doing All. Of. The. Things.

Chapter Eleven

"Grief can be the garden of compassion. If you keep your heart open through everything, your pain can become your greatest ally in your life's search for love and wisdom."
~Rumi

Julien

Whether it was out of respect for the somberness of the event or to stave off any questions Julien might be asked by his multitude of relatives watching him, Blanca had decided to keep her physical contact with him to a minimum at the funeral. Though, she sought him out in passing. She stole secretive glances with him and brushed her fingertips along the back of his hand, each a way of supporting him through it all.

Those caring sides of Blanca made Julien's heart succumb even more with each and every glance. She was intrigue itself, and he wanted more. He hated having to explain to her the night before that he'd been the source of all scandals among his relatives thanks to his ex and his cousin.

Julien had let jealousy and foolishness get the best of him a couple of years ago. He had lured as many of Chase's dates, girlfriends, trysts, and whatnot away from his cousin as he could out of spite for a while. But no amount of wallowing in shame and repenting for his classless way of handling such a nasty break-up could undo his extended family's need to continue to meddle in his love affairs.

Finding Julien someone to replace his ex had become the new

mission among the L'Angevin brood as of summer. They were all ready and willing to marry him off to Max last August when she showed up at his thirtieth birthday bash looking to talk with anyone related to Chase. Of course, Julien had paraded Max around at his celebration knowing how it razzed Chase who kept calling and texting him about her during the party. A few days later, Chase even boarded an airplane, showing up to stake his claim on her though they'd broken up. It was just as well. Julien's infatuation with Max could've taken a turn for something real if they'd been around each other much longer. Max was and continued to be a lovely woman in his eyes. Though, nothing more.

Those aggressive antics of Julien's were behind him now.

Blanca, no doubt, had a target on her back. After warning her about it, she opted to wear it with pride much to Julien's surprise. She fed his soul with the hidden affection that it yearned for to get through the funeral.

* * *

Madeleine "Mimi" Lilliette L'Angevin lived an extraordinary life. From her childhood in Paris, to her 1956 stint as a cancan girl at the Moulin Rouge in homage of her mother, a 1930s dancer, to the decades she'd spent painting while living in Montmartre, she'd showered the world with her craft. In her latter days, as a teacher, she had seeded the desire to express one's love of painting in the students she'd taken under her wing.

A beloved wife and mother to five children, grandmother to nineteen, and Godmother to all, her legacy would live on in everyone's hearts as a cherished angel finally brought home by God.

The memorial service included a full Mass, the context of which Blanca knew quite well as she sat on the opposite end of a long pew away from Julien. He found it heart-warming to watch her quietly guide her best friend through the religious motions of the Mass, ensuring they both fit in as everyone including the priest spoke French. He wasn't sure if Blanca's minimal fluency skills were enough for her to completely comprehend all that was going on around her, but he wasn't worried about her feeling as if she didn't fit in. In fact, she seemed to be going out of her way to make sure he was the one feeling comfortable and comforted.

When the service ended, Julien sought out Blanca amid so many family and friends, as well as others he'd never seen before from his grand-mère's many walks of life. The hundreds of people who had crowded the cathedral spilled out into the foyer all at once sweeping Blanca up with them.

As soon as Julien reached for his iPhone to call her, Blanca and Max emerged from behind Chase's two older brothers, Burke and Cory, who had carved a path in the flow of people for the ladies. They all walked towards him, along with their wives Hannah and Amber, who had apparently made their acquaintances at some point during the service.

Julien's heavy heart bloomed with deep emotion at the sight of Blanca's sympathetic smile as she stepped up to him—Max continuing on straight to Chase. One of Blanca's fingers found its way around one of his in an inconspicuous union as they shuffled outdoors into the brisk, winter air. Careful to keep their affection from public display, they stared straight forward as they were caught up in the shuffle of bodies exiting the foyer to go outside.

"You will be joining us in the limousine for the processional," Julien finally spoke, as they descended the dozens of steps in front of the ancient building. "There will be no burial. The urn is going home with some of my relatives for a while. The celebration is only a few miles away at a community hall."

"Are all these people going to be there?"

"Likely even more. You can see now why I needed you. You are my calm in the storm, Blanca." He dipped down and pressed his lips to her temple in a flash.

Within seconds, family members pulled Julien in all directions wishing to express their condolences as Blanca distanced herself. He greeted them, exchanged heartfelt words, kissed several cheeks, and threw pleading glances at Blanca, receiving a constant, caring smile from her in return. Several minutes passed before he was able to break free from socializing and rush his precious minion around the corner.

The processional of limousines ran the length of an entire block. Chase and Max, as well as his other cousins and their wives had all found their way to their designated vehicle. Burke, the oldest among the cousins, threw the door open to their limousine and motioned for both of them to climb inside.

Though only a short distance away, it took almost thirty minutes for them to finally roll up to the recreational hall. It gave Julien plenty of time to explain to his cousins and their wives along the way to the gathering how he had met Blanca in October while in America visiting Chase and that she'd become an invaluable friend to him.

He also added that their friendship had many layers, none of which were anyone's business, and, if any of them happened to notice their fondness for each other, to just ignore it. After which, he took it upon himself to bury his nose in Blanca's neck and kiss her below her earlobe to prove his point.

"The last thing I need to deal with right now is being ridiculed for bringing a date to grand-maman's funeral."

He'd had enough of being the subject of all the gossip among the L'Angevin clan—the pathetic one with the broken heart—and wanted nothing more than to delve into Blanca's affection without any questions from his extended family. Especially since he harbored some jealousy over the way Chase and Max were able to dote all over one another in front of everybody.

"No judgment here," Burke laughed, draping his arm around his wife's shoulders as they waited their turn to pile out of the limousine.

"We're just living in the moment while I'm visiting," Blanca added, squeezing Julien's thigh. "I don't want him to have to deal with anybody asking him about me any more than he does."

"Understood," Cory, Chase's oldest brother, replied as his wife nodded.

Chase and Max just kept quiet, exchanging a silent argument by the look in their eyes.

Mind your own business, Chase. I've got my emotions in check.

Internally, Julien's awkwardness only heightened as he contemplated Blanca's reasoning. He wasn't sure anymore if he wanted her going home and snapping back into friendship mode on him when everything about her was fast becoming all he could ever want.

And so much more.

The warning Chase had given him the day before echoed in his mind, and he abruptly dealt with it by pulling Blanca into another kiss just before she wrestled free with a giggle and climbed out of the vehicle behind Max.

You'll see. You'll all see, eventually. If we're meant to be together, then love will find a way.

* * *

The community hall teemed with chatter. It had been decorated in hundreds of white and red poinsettias and about as many easels displaying Grand-mère Mimi's portraits of family members. It felt as much like a Christmas party as it did a celebration of someone's lifelong achievements. The mood had shifted from somber to reverent instantly.

They all snaked around the circular tables to a more private corner marked off for them that held an impressive view of all the guests in attendance. Julien's fraternal twin sisters, Lillie and Colette, and their husbands and children already took up several seats at the far end of one of the long, rectangular tables reserved for the immediate family. Cory, Burke, Hannah, and Amber found places to sit at the other end, prompting Cory to breathe out a complaint about having to leave his own children behind in San Francisco with Amber's parents as they took their seats.

Ah, family. To have my own little ones to miss ... someday.

The middle of the table had plenty of empty chairs, so Chase and

Max walked around the length of it to sit across from Blanca and Julien who kept their backs to the main room.

"May I get you something to eat?" Julien asked, as he and Chase rose up from their chairs almost as quickly as they had sat down.

"Sure, thank you," Blanca replied, eyeing him with a sweet smile.

Chase jogged around the end of the table again after exchanging a few words with Max, and then the men headed to where the refreshments and wine were being served, buffet-style, in yet another chamber of the enormous recreational building.

As Julien piled several savory and sweet delectable bites onto a single plate for Blanca to share with him, Victoria, Julien's younger sister, crept up beside him.

"You're right, she is so beautiful," she whispered in his ear—her sea green eyes dancing with excitement.

He cracked a prideful smile as he poured two glasses of L'Angevin Petit Sirah. "Isn't, she?"

He had opened up to his sister about befriending Blanca one night when Victoria had come by to visit. He had no choice. Several texts about whether or not Blanca's main character in her novel should have a natural hair color or go with something plucked off a rainbow came pinging through his cell in rapid fire, piquing Victoria's interest as to what all the commotion was about.

By the time Julien had wrestled his iPhone out of his baby sister's clutches, she'd read most of their texts. She managed to pry a confession out of him about that one afternoon on his trip to America he'd spent with Blanca being *more than friends* and how that encounter had inspired the momentum for their continued communication. Victoria was also the first to know when Blanca had agreed to come to France.

Julien grinned with pride. "Have you had a chance to meet her?"

His sister looked around at the sea of black-clothed bodies. "Not officially. You'll do me the honor? She is, like, eh, she is enjoying herself, considering, *non?*"

Chase leaned past Julien. "What are you two whispering about?"

"Julien's *friend,*" Victoria teased.

"Careful, he might throw you over his shoulder and toss you out of here if you tease him, Tori."

"*Non,* Tori can say anything she likes, as long as she says it quietly," Julien replied, staring his baby sister down with a smirk. "You are alone? No suitors from the university accompanying you?"

Only three years younger than Julien, Victoria was still earning her Doctorate in Archeology, and she was never without a gentleman she'd met in the program hanging off her arm. She carried herself like the world was at her beck and call, and men were her favorite accessory.

"*Non, non.* I think it would be too depressing."

"True," he replied. "The very reason why I find Blanca's company so inviting—she is my new definition of happiness."

"Of course, she is." Victoria snickered again.

"Come by our table and meet her soon," Julien insisted, concluding his conversation with Victoria when someone called out to his sister to join them.

"I wouldn't miss meeting her for the world. Good on you," she replied wide-eyed and smiling, then stepped away in a rush.

"I take it she knows more than she should?" Chase teased, gathering up his food and drinks.

"She's known about Blanca for a few months now. I'm guessing by the end of today, everyone will have something to say about me bringing a woman to grand-maman's funeral. At least Christmas Eve will only include our immediate families."

"Just don't get caught up in everybody's congratulations when you know she's leaving soon," Chase warned.

Julien set his jaw and nodded. "Thank you for the reminder, but I've got this under control."

"Just looking out for you," Chase retorted, shaking his head.

Julien balanced the two glasses of wine in one hand and held the plate of hors d'oeuvres in the other as he followed Chase back to their table. When he settled in next to Blanca, she slid her hand along his thigh under the table and gave it a gentle pat, thanking him for the wine and hors d'oeuvres, assuring him once again that she was there for him.

"Would it be awkward if I expected you to feed me little bites as long as we're sharing the same plate?" she jested, nudging his shoulder.

He nearly gagged on a sip of his wine with restrained laughter. "Now that would be a spectacle."

"There's my smile," she cooed with satisfaction, as she pinched off a piece of cheese and popped it in her mouth. "So, I overheard your sisters arguing that you're trying to branch out from the family business, but your father doesn't know. What's that all about?"

He peered down the end of the table at his older sisters then bowed his head, resolving to not bother addressing Lillie and Colette about gossiping.

Blanca continued to wait for an answer, so he leaned over and shared the simplest one he could think of. "I want my own brand."

"Branding is a big deal right now. Who do you see yourself as in the public eye?"

"I, ehm, I am not following. *Je ne comprends pas* (I don't understand)."

She cocked her head to the side. "What do you want your brand to be?"

Chase, who was seated directly across from Julien, butted in. "You're branching off? What's going on Julien? You can't step out on the family brand. Look what my brothers did to my father!"

"Clearly, I have no clue what's going down with you two, but carry on." Blanca waved at them then folded her hands under her chin and peered back and forth between the gentlemen. "No, really. I'd like to watch the two of you go at it. Maybe even do it again later but shirtless with swords. What do you think, Maxie?"

Max nodded, pressing her lips together to keep from laughing out loud.

Julien flashed Blanca a quick smile, masking the rage creeping up in him spawned by his cousin. "Right now, all I've been planning to do is label a batch of Blanc de Blanc I purchased that will be ready to bottle in a few months. I am not abandoning my papa. I am merely trying to be distinct."

"Oh, gotcha. A label kind of brand. Whoa, I was way off," Blanca interjected.

Chase reared back in his seat and rested his arm on the back of Max's chair. "You want to slap your personal brand on some bottles and call it your own? Take pride in a cuvée you had nothing to do with through the whole process?"

Blanca and Max grew quiet and held their tongues as Julien leaned back in his seat, crossing his arms as he stared up at the ceiling. It was as if the answers to those scathing questions were floating above him like a storm cloud getting ready to burst.

He leveled his eyes with his cousin's. "When you put it like that, I guess I'm just wasting my time. All I wanted was to have something of my own. It was only a starting point."

I need to begin living my life again somehow.

Julien could sense Blanca beginning to posture against Chase, and he almost wished she would unleash some of her over protective rage on his cousin.

Chase slid his thumb along Max's shoulders as she sat still, blushing with obvious discomfort. "You shouldn't be so eager to want everything handed to you so easily."

Julien and Chase glared at each other in silence—the two of them just exchanging bitter stares until Chase bowed his head and gave in. "Forgive me. As long as you are not foregoing your responsibilities with your sisters to maintain the L'Angevin good fortune here in France, then I wish you well, but you shouldn't be meddling in someone else's grapes."

"Neither should you."

Chapter twelve

"In literature as in love, we are astonished at what is chosen by others."
~Andre Maurois

Blanca

It took at least an hour of small talk to get Julien and Chase to totally chill-the-freak out and go back to being amicable again. Blanca determined to get to the bottom of their squabble over non-L'Angevin grapes later when she had Julien all to herself. Whatever it was Julien was trying to do that Chase was so vehemently against, Blanca felt a sense of urgency to side with Julien and cheer him on.

The hall had thinned out to less than a hundred people by the time Victoria had made her way to meet Blanca, introducing herself with a friendly hug, unlike the standard death-grip shoulder squeeze she'd been getting used to among the L'Angevins.

Not to mention the kissing. Lots and lots of kissing.

Left cheek, right cheek, left cheek, right...

No wonder Julien had gotten increasingly more affectionate as the evening dwindled away. He even looped his arm over Blanca's shoulders as they meandered around chatting with the remaining guests and threaded his fingers through hers while they sauntered from easel to easel while admiring his grandmother's artwork.

Either his spat with Chase changed his mind about worrying what his relatives thought of her being there with him—the curious American he suddenly couldn't keep his hands off—or he must've felt the need to compete with all the pseudo-making out she'd done with half the people in the room. Of course, he had to tell off a half-a-dozen nosy relatives the clingier he got, but she didn't mind.

Jealous Julien is a sexy Julien. Ooh, la, la.

Speaking of sexy. His sister, Victoria, was a living work of art. All legs. Straight, strawberry blonde hair. Eyes just as tropical and mesmerizing as her brother's.

Even Maxie went all girl-crush on her when the two of them reminisced about meeting over summer at Julien's birthday party.

"You two have been writing books, my brother tells me?"

"He did, did he?" Blanca replied, giving Julien a little nudge.

"We both wrote a book," Maxie clarified.

"It was not easy. Let me tell ya," Blanca continued. "Maxie and I bet each other that we could write a novel, and we did. We are going to self-publish them and see who wrote the better story based on who gets the most positive reviews."

"The loser—that would be Blanca here—has to pay for a publishing package that includes an actual editor to clean up the winning manuscript for a better publication launch," Maxie teased.

"That is absolutely wonderful! I take it you both like to compete just like Julien and Chase, *non?*"

Maxie slapped Chase on the back. "Are they competitive? I hadn't noticed."

"That's because I'm always winning," Chase retorted.

Julien buried his nose in Blanca's ear as he pulled her into his side. "When are you going to let me finally read that story of ours?"

"Oh, so it's *ours* now?" she whispered back.

He wagged his eyebrows at her. "I may have only helped you with locations and hair color choices, but, that book, darling, is ours. You're owning-up on being my comfort as pay back for all the inspiration I've given you. You wouldn't even be here with me if we hadn't made that *book baby* together."

Blanca let out such a sharp laugh that it garnered some turned heads around them. "Book baby? That's awesome. You've been eavesdropping on my conversations with Maxie, haven't you? You can read our bouncing baby book whenever you want. I brought my laptop, so I'll email it to you when we get ho—get back, back to your house."

Again with the staking-a-claim routine. Rawr.

Victoria gave Julien a funny look, like she was in on their intimate arrangement. Then a child skipped up to her and tugged on her hand, telling her in French that her mommy said it was time for all of them to leave.

"I guess it is my time to say goodbye. I will see you all on Christmas Eve. *Bonne fin de journée* (Have a good evening)."

Everybody said goodbye to Victoria, then Julien grumbled to Chase something about the forty-five minute drive back home, both agreeing that it was time to leave, as well.

As they exited the hall in search of their limousine to take them back to the cathedral where Julien still had his car parked, a woman emerged from under one of the ornate arches lining the corridor. She stepped in their path, causing Julien to come to a standstill and Chase to bump into the back of him.

"Millicent?" Julien's hand went limp in Blanca's.

"*Bonsoir,* Julien—Chase." She didn't even bother acknowledging Blanca and Maxie.

Oh, hell no.

She stepped up even closer to him. "I wanted to pay my respects. I was at the service. I—"

"Thank you for coming. Now, if you'll excuse us." Julien reclaimed Blanca's hand and tried to step around his ex.

The woman shot Blanca a pleading look.

Oh, now you're acknowledging me?

Millie struck Blanca as odd. *Pretty*. But, not quite right.

Her eyes were the color of cloudy ice. Void of distinction. Her flesh, the color of an onion-skinned page out of a centuries-old book—thin, translucent—the blue veins distinct beneath its fragile surface. Her blunt, angular haircut was a deep auburn, save for the gray at her temples that framed her delicate face.

Let me repeat that.

Gray. At. Her. Temples.

Like, old-lady gray.

Because, my friends—

Millicent Devereaux was ...old.

If Julien had Blanca beat by five years, Millie had Julien beat by another five, maybe even ten.

What the hell?

"I owe you an apology. *Si'l vous plait* (please)? And you, as well, Chase," she added, tipping her head to the side to see around Julien to Chase, who had, at that point, maneuvered Maxie behind him so that they were all in an awkward row lined up in front of the woman.

Julien squared his shoulders—the tension in his grip closing tighter on Blanca's hand and nodded, providing his ex with an in.

Millie craned her neck to peer at all of them—her vapid eyes widening as she searched their faces—the silence only marked by Julien's heavy breathing through his nose.

You've got this. Be strong.

A torrent of French poured from her mouth so fast Blanca could barely make out any of the words. Something about *foolishness* and *guilt* and *temptation* and *lust* and *smothering*, or was it *smoldering*? No matter. It became apparent Millie was coming clean about the disaster she had wreaked a couple of years ago. Her confession was enough to cause Chase to step up next to Julien on his other side and both of them to loosen up a little.

Then, another long stretch of silence draped itself over all of them again.

Maxie appeared at Blanca's side and linked arms with her, so that they all inadvertently formed a human wall.

A badass battlefront.

Millie bowed her head, and a pathetic laugh escaped her. "I see you have both found good company. I am Millicent—*Millie.*"

Her introduction seemed too little too late, but Blanca went ahead and opted to be polite. "Hello, Millie. I'm Blanca, and this is Maxie."

"Oh, you are American." She turned her attention back onto Julien. "You are not in France any longer? I wondered if you had finally made something of yourself."

Ouch. Not cool, cougar.

Blanca was about to unleash some rude all over the late-thirty-something-year-old granny, but Julien came to his own defense instead.

"*Non.* I am not in America. I am still right where you left me. You, on the other hand, ran away, to—where was it—Italy?"

Millie offered an apologetic smile. "I meant no offense. *Oui,* but I was only in Florence for a few months then I moved to Nice. I have my own gallery there for my sketches, but I have made a name for myself creating art installations now. I have several all over Paris. *Madame* Mimi would be proud."

"Julien's making a name for himself now, too," Blanca blurted out, unable to contain her overprotective urges.

She was feisty like that.

"Is that so, Julien? What are you up to now?"

"He's creating his own brand." The words tumbled out of Blanca in a rush before Julien had finished clearing his throat.

"A Blanc de Blanc," Chase interjected.

Julien shifted on his feet, searching the corridor for the words escaping him. Blanca pulled their laced fingers up to her lips and kissed the back of his hand, hoping to impart some confidence in him as she postured on the woman.

Millie peered at him. "And what should I search for? You will not be using the family name?"

"Of course, I will use L'Angevin. Proudly! My vin will, ehm, will be marketed with a secondary moniker." He looked at Blanca, who looked up at him with a mischievous grin. "My line of L'Angevin's Blanc de *Blanca* will be sold as a novelty. Unique and playful, just like its inspiration."

"Blanc de *Blanca,*" Millie repeated as if tasting the words while her eyes raked Blanca from head to toe—a hint of amusement and disgust playing on her glossy lips.

"We are all very proud of him," Chase added, smacking Julien on the back. "Now, if you'll pardon all of us, we need to head out."

"I understand." She leaned forward as if to exchange kisses with Julien, but he reared back on her, prompting her to recoil.

Atta boy.

"*Adieu,*" Millie muttered, then nodded once and walked away before either of the men could say goodbye ... again.

Chapter Thirteen

"Though she be but little, she is fierce."
~William Shakespeare

Julien

Blanca shook her *petit cul serré* (tight, little ass) at Julien knowing damn well his eyes were glued to it when she barely bent her knees and slumped over, letting all that thick caramel-colored hair topple to the floor.

"Rag doll," she groaned, prompting Maxie to assume the same position.

"We've died and gone to heaven," Chase quipped, sitting on the couch with Julien.

The ladies had moved the coffee table out of the way in Julien's living room, covering the tiled floor with blankets and creating a decent place for them to challenge one another to a game of Champagne Shot Yoga.

They wore coordinating red and green graphic tees. The shirts had both with Naughty and Nice printed on them, but only one of the ladies had the Nice box checked, and the other had Naughty checked.

You could probably guess who was wearing which shirt.

The gentlemen obliged the ladies by serving up shots of Champagne each time they performed a yoga position. If there were to be any actual competitive outcome to this whole event, clearly the winners were going to be Julien and Chase.

Julien held out the two shot glasses, and Chase poured the golden liquid and then they handed them off to the beauties once Max called out, "Break."

After downing their sixth shot, they both twisted into something called an *eagle,* though neither of them could stand on one foot long enough, what with all the giggling, for Max to consider the pose held to call out for a break again.

"I give up," Blanca laughed, tumbling to the floor. "Let's finish with a Cat and Cow."

The men just exchanged amused glances. They watched the two women get down on all fours and arch their backs then bow them up, intermittently.

My God, this is the best day of my life.

An involuntary moan escaped Chase.

"Indeed," Julien sighed.

"Okay, that's enough. Break," Max snickered.

"But we were having so much fun," Julien taunted them, pouring the ladies one last shot.

Blanca took the drink from him and examined it for a moment. "So, Blanc de Blanca, huh?"

"I'd apologize, but it's actually growing on me. I think I'm onto something. I could make the label appeal to the young, modern woman."

Blanca arched an eyebrow and cocked her head at him. "Yeah, no twenty-something is going to grab a bottle of Champagne over some other kind of wine at a liquor store then head to a friend's house for movie night. You'd definitely have your work cut out for you, but I'll support you one-hundred percent."

With that adamant declaration, Blanca turned and flashed Chase a smug grin then downed her shot.

"I think we're going to head back to our place. I'm pretty tired," Max declared, taking the shot glass from Blanca and handing it to Julien along with hers. "Thanks for letting us invade your living room."

"Anytime. It was our pleasure," Julien replied, putting the glasses next to the bottle of Champagne on an end table.

Julien saw Chase and her to the front door.

"Let's catch a train ride out in time to be there by sunset," Chase commented, referring to a conversation they'd concluded while the ladies had been busy in Julien's office before they decided it was time to do some yoga.

Chase gripped Julien's shoulder in a partial hug—a rarity between them, but, after their lengthy talk earlier about Millie, the act was compliant to their official truce.

All it took was a little heart to heart between the cousins.

While Blanca and Max had been in Julien's office on his computer researching royalty free pictures to use for covers for their novels, Chase and he sat on the back porch in the cold discussing the past. Chase had finally admitted his attraction to Millie as Julien listened in silence. Chase's curiosity and fascination with her, when Julien had first started dating her almost four years ago, led to his weakness in succumbing to her plea for him to undress and pose for her.

And Chase confessed that he knew damn well that his decision had been wrong from the start.

Julien was only twenty-six—Chase, a mere twenty-four, when Millicent Devereaux, their Grand-mère Mimi's favorite art student—pranced into their lives. She was the redheaded blonde with eyes like white-hot flames and the personality of a troubled artist.

Millie, at nearly thirty-four-years-old back then, had a demanding presence about her that, not only ensnared the attention of everyone in the art class, it had seduced Julien outright from the moment they had met. Their first meeting had ended in a first kiss together. Their first date had ended in a first night together. Their first fight had ended in a first breakup together.

And then they'd get together again.

Passion drove her every move, and Julien, so eager to please the older woman who spell-bound him, clamored after her in the wake of her lust for life—one moment being the center of her world, the next, the blame for all of her dissatisfaction.

As Julien confessed to feeling nothing but contempt at seeing Millicent again, Chase confessed to his role in their final breakup. Chase admitted to having been caught up in her seductive flirtations but never imagined she'd fully act on what he thought was exactly that, *an act.* He had explained to Julien out on the back porch how he'd been lured to her studio under the pretense that she had wanted to show him what she'd been working on as her first gallery piece. When he had arrived, she had begged him to let her draw him in the nude to add to her collection. He even admitted to indulging in the guilty pleasure of being in the spotlight of her attention, wanting for himself what she had so freely given to Julien.

Julien finally understood that Chase, in a moment of weakness, fell into Millie's seductive snare just like he had done in the beginning as his cousin detailed the account of that night's events. Details Julien had only guessed at for two years.

Naked, vulnerable, Millie had lavished Chase with compliments about his muscular body as she sketched him, all the while prattling on about how much more she had loved Julien's broader shoulders, softer flesh, smoother skin, reducing Chase to petty jealousy, challenging him to prove he was worthy of her lust.

Julien had finally seen Millie through his grand-maman's eyes—wild and untamable, a troubled soul, predatory towards what she wanted at any cost. Chase had expressed his deepest regret in not walking out of her studio that night the moment he had realized her intentions were to humiliate him.

Chase's confessions had been enough to finally close that door on Julien's heart. Coming face to face with the woman earlier that evening had only reaffirmed that he'd truly let her go. His heart had emptied out of her and not even a bittersweet memory had remained.

And just like that, Julien and Chase had finally put an end to their feud.

"Sounds like a plan," Julien replied, cupping Chase's hand on his shoulder briefly before nodding in agreement as they stood in the threshold.

"And what plan would that be?" Blanca asked, as she gathered the blankets up off the floor.

Julien closed the door once Chase and Max stepped out and then snatched up the bottle of Champagne and shot glasses Blanca had put on an end table.

"We're going to Strasbourg." Julien headed to the kitchen. "We'll be walking for hours on cobblestone streets, so, as much as I hate to say it, you'll need to wear comfortable shoes and dress warm."

Blanca followed behind him into the kitchen. "What's in Strasbourg?"

Julien pulled a flute out of a cupboard and poured the rest of the Champagne into it for himself and downed it in one biting gulp. "Strasbourg, my naughty, little elf, is the Christmas Capital of the World."

* * *

Julien looked at Blanca's thick-heeled boots and shook his head with a smile as he approached her. "Here, one café au lait and croissant, darling."

He offered the treats to her after returning with Chase from a vendor outside of the TGV train in Reims. It seemed befitting that her graphic tank top that she'd crawled into bed wearing the night before had read, "Powered by Caffeine," because the two cups of coffee he had poured her that morning hadn't helped her shake off the grogginess she was still complaining about that afternoon.

Earlier, they'd spent some time shopping in Reims for a few cold weather essentials for Blanca and Max—hats and scarves—thick knitted ones that were identical save for their colors, one set red and one set blue. He was quickly realizing these two young ladies, as vastly different as they were in personality and appearance, were very much alike in many other ways and made sure everyone around them knew it. They really were *best friends forever*, as they consistently claimed.

"Thank you, thank you, thank you," Blanca cooed, wrapping her gloved hands around the hot cup. "I'm so cold!" Even though she had on her new red sock hat and scarf, she still quivered from the cold air.

Julien stretched his arm around her shoulders and pulled her into his side.

Right where I'd like to keep you indefinitely.

The gesture seemed to suit her because she stopped shivering, and, once she disposed of her empty cup and crumpled tissue paper, she latched onto his side again as if she knew it was where she belonged.

A few minutes later, they all boarded their train to Strasbourg, and, within three hours, they were walking through the historic part of the city towards what Julien insisted was going to be Blanca's absolute favorite part of her journey.

The sun had set leaving a deep plum color behind as heavy clouds mottled the sky, obscuring the stars from view. The closer all of them approached the bustling portion of the city where the festivities and vendors inhabited, the more excited Blanca became. A glow hung over the area from the multitude of twinkling lights. Even the sky-high cathedral, with all its ornate intricacies, played the part in creating a visually stunning Christmas wonderland.

They stopped to take a few pictures under an enormous, illuminated arch that exclaimed in bright green lights, "*Capitale de Noël.*" This was, indeed, the Christmas Capital of the World.

While other neighboring villages also had holiday markets bustling with tourists, that particular market meant the most to Julien. He hadn't missed a single year attending it up until a couple of years ago when the holiday season failed to bring him much joy. But, with Blanca in his life, her infectious laughter and playful affection had him falling deeper and deeper into his own fantasy landscape of hope.

Hope that, at the very least, she might consider extending her stay or returning to see him again soon because her journey thus far had been so satisfying for both of them. And hope that, at the very best, he would be able to transform their makeshift love affair into something more permanent if things continued their steadfast course.

Julien watched Blanca peer up at the village's enormous Christmas tree, lit in blue and adorned with giant white bows along with gold and silver ornaments. His heart swelled with pride as she turned and smiled at him—a silent thank you forming on her cherry red lips. She waved her hands about like a child as if she'd just stumbled upon Santa's village, lunging at him in a rush and planting a kiss on his lips.

"You weren't kidding about this being the best place on earth. How did I not know this event ever existed? How many years did you say the market has been happening?"

"We are approaching five-hundred years." He reached up and raked his thumb across his lips then inspected it for lipstick, but no impression had been left on them.

"Don't worry. It's kiss-proof stain. I'm fully prepared to pretend we're in lo—la la land together. You and me. The happy couple living it up in Strasbourg."

We are a happy couple—no need to pretend.

Her air quotes around her words *happy couple* only reaffirmed Julien's urgency to convince her to extend her stay with him longer. In his mind, they were already halfway to becoming something very real.

"I take it as a challenge to try to kiss you so much your lipstick could wear off."

"Challenge excepted, lover."

"Lover? I like the sound of that." He leaned down and placed a tender kiss on her cheek.

"For the week, right? I can call us that, can't I?"

"I am most definitely your lover. Tell the world, if you must." *... for the week, the month, all next year ...*

"I just might do that on my social media accounts once I post all my pics. Apologizes in advance if I selfie it up tonight with you. Come on," she exclaimed, grabbing Julien's hand and tugging him with her, plunging them both into a magical land of all things Christmas.

Chapter fourteen

"The soul should always stand ajar, ready to welcome the ecstatic experience."
~Emily Dickinson

Blanca
Chase and Maxie tried to keep up, as Blanca emerged into the crowd, looping her arm with Julien's to keep from getting separated as she bounced from one vendor's booth to the next like Tigger on a play date with Pooh.

Her eyes feasted on every item from the hand-carved ornaments to the delicately painted bulbs—or *bubbles,* as the French would say. Each item held its own kind of fascination as if she'd never seen so many shiny things before in her life.

"I wish I could buy one of everything," she exclaimed, shaking a snow globe. Blanca held it up for Julien and her to watch as the sparkling particles swirled about the tiny village inside that resembled the one they were in.

"I'm buying the globe for you," he insisted, pulling out a wad of euros and paying for it before she had a chance to protest.

In reality, she didn't want to tell him not to. The giddiness he had found in doing things for her had become one of his sexiest traits lately.

They crossed over to another booth, displaying all kinds of glass and porcelain trinkets. She eyed all the different nativities. The display was also filled with a multitude of miniature replica buildings just like the real ones that actually surrounded them—German in style, timber framed, and decked out in Christmas decorations.

One of the chalets towering above them had Santa's entire entourage of reindeer racing across the side of it. Another chalet they had passed moments before had human-sized white teddy bears tethered all over its facing, along with sheets of red ribbon that had bright red bubbles dangling from the ends of them.

Bubbles! Tee-hee.

Every booth they visited pulled Blanca deeper into the Christmas spirit as she crooned over all the minute details each of the crafts possessed. She finally gave in to embarking on Julien's shopping trip of a lifetime with plans to revamp his country-bumpkin dining nook, whether he was into the spree or not.

From the looks of him, though, she thought he might be.

Blanca had never seen Julien so happy, not that she had a vast reference of time to compare the moment to, but he did have a swagger about him that took her a little by surprise. His smile alone could've lit up the village all by itself, and what it did to her guts, with that achy itching and all, had been dismissed as part of the holiday excitement and nothing more.

Julien had bought two large, green canvas bags sporting that year's themed logo on them and had encouraged Blanca to fill them up with all the decorations she just had to have—all of which he insisted on paying for.

A set of reindeer and a Santa in a sleigh, as well as a dozen elves holding Christmas presents were the first thing to go in one of the bags. Some royal blue bubbles that were hand-painted with flogged snowflakes were the next delights. Even a nutcracker to go along with two small paper bags full of chestnuts and walnuts she'd snatched up were added to the other bag.

One booth that was selling angels made out of silver filigree entwining small crystal globes throughout the wings caught her eye, and, though pricy, Julien didn't hesitate to purchase one of them for her as a special gift.

"An angel for my devil. Let it be a reminder of me. Your Angel Wine lover," he said, tucking the delicate trinket into the bag he held.

"L'Angevin—*angel wine.* You guys lucked out on the sexiest name ever. No wonder all you boys became vintners. It was your destiny."

Julien peered at her, quirking the corner of his mouth up in an amused smirk. "Do you believe in destiny?"

"I don't know, maybe. I think it was destiny that I chose the career that I did. I wasn't meant to do what I thought I wanted to do. Taking a different path has allowed me to travel and delve into other languages and cultures that a different career choice might not have permitted. I love working for myself."

"*Très bon.* Beautiful answer." He leaned over and kissed her.

Blanca shifted on her feet.

Except, I'm going broke starting from scratch again at the new salon, but that's my problem not yours.

A wave of guilt suddenly washed over Blanca for a moment as she looked between their canvas bags bursting with expensive decorations she couldn't afford on her own.

Julien turned towards her again—his eyes clouded with deep thought. "I want to work for myself, too. I think it's honorable that you have followed your dreams."

Blanca shrugged off the gnawing ache in her tummy, worried she'd offend him more if she said they had to return all the goodies than if she just kept being grateful and received his generosity. "I mean, doing hair, is, you know, whatever, but I'd like to think that I'm talented at making people feel good about themselves. Like, when they leave the shop, they're so happy. It's more than just styling. I feel like I'm helping them find themselves, and that's the person everyone is going to be looking at."

Julien looked into her eyes—contemplative, focusing on her words. "I see."

Geez, I'm a mess. I need to get my finances in order when I get back home.

This whole pretending to be a couple and letting the alpha male treat me all the time thing is horrifying.

"Well, anywho, let's keep shopping, shall we?" Blanca swallowed her pride and let Julien feel good about himself by smothering her with gifts as he tugged her along to yet another vendor selling a multitude of delectable treats.

Let yourself love this moment as much as he does.

Julien bought them a couple of gingerbread men, and some marzipan candies shaped like dirty snowmen. Blanca added some sugar cookies that had frosting blobbed on them to make them look like wreathes with holly berries, as well as other unique, gooey, nutty nougats she'd probably only ever taste while in France.

Julien even found some hardened sugary candies in the shape of elves posing in various craft-making positions—holding saws and hammers—all of which he kept insisting he needed for the cakes he had to bake the next day. Between the two of them they'd bought enough Christmas decorations and candies to open their own candy shop.

Julien toted those heavy bags around proudly, gloating at how excited the whole experience had been for her all because of him. But the thing was Blanca could tell his own joyful meter was popping off the charts as they sauntered around together, side-by-side, dwelling in their own make-believe world of Christmas wonder.

And that brought Blanca the greatest joy of all.

* * *

The four of them bought some mulled red wine, spiced with cinnamon, cloves, and oranges and stood around a tall table, planning the rest of the night as they warmed themselves with their drinks.

"A chorus will be singing inside the cathedral in a little while, so we should make our way back over to it if you guys are interested," Chase said to Julien and Blanca.

"I'd love to hear a live performance," Blanca replied, between sips of her steaming wine.

"There's a live nativity not far from here. We could see that, too, before we head over. What do you think?" Chase added, looking back and forth between Maxie and Blanca.

"I'd love to see that, too," Blanca interjected again—Maxie adding a, "Yeah, baby!" to the conversation.

The men laughed at the ladies' obvious enthusiasm. Julien assured Blanca, "We'll stay as long as we need to. We're in no rush to get home."

"Good, then let's take the last train out of here back to Reims," Blanca decided, as she reached into one of the canvas bags at her feet and fished out a cellophane-wrapped lump of divinity.

Blanca tugged at the silky red ribbon, unwrapping the candy and offering everyone a bite. She took the liberty of dropping a small pinch of the fluffy white treat into Julien's mouth and relished in letting him do the same for her. The sweet, gooey morsel dissolved on her tongue, unleashing a few moans of pleasure out of her. She made all the sexy noises just so she could add some fuel to the look of embarrassment on Chase and Maxie's face as they stared at the two of them in horror fawning all over each other.

Sure, Julien and Blanca had gone from friends to lovers in the blink of an eye in front of them, but the context of their new *arrangement* was what mattered to her. She knew their days of playing the part of a happy couple were numbered, but she rested assured believing everything about their friendship would fall back into place naturally once an entire ocean popped up between them again. In the meantime, she wanted to squeeze out all the feels she could with him since he seemed to be enjoying it as much as her.

As long as we're on the topic of squeezing ...

Blanca slid her hands over Julien's rounded buns and gave them a solid clinch.

He jolted and let out a hearty laugh. Then, he pulled her into a sticky sweet kiss that lasted long enough to cause Chase and Maxie to mutter something about meeting them over at the live nativity display when Blanca and Julien were done putting on their own show.

As soon as they were alone together, Julien pulled away from Blanca.

For a split second, Blanca thought she might've offended Julien, but he searched and found her hands and cupped them in his, pressing them over his heart, anchoring his eyes to hers. "I have to tell you something, but I don't want you to flip out on me."

Her smile began to melt into a frown. "Saying that is not helping."

"Hey," he cooed, tipping his nose down to hers and offering her a quick kiss. "I just want you to know that I love, ehm, that I've loved being with you today. This might have been the best night of my life."

Blanca searched his face in wonder and curiosity, weighing whether she should give him a quick reminder of their agreement for both of their sakes—or just go ahead and tell the truth.

He rocked on his heels, stealing another gentle kiss as he waited for her response.

The words tumbled from her mouth slowly as if she were giving each of them permission to be heard. "I *l-loved* being with you, too, Jules. Tonight has definitely been the best night of my life, as well."

A moment of stillness hung in the air.

Even the crowd around them hushed for few seconds as if they'd all been eavesdropping on their awkward confession of loving each other's companionship.

But then a tiny snowflake drifted down between them, close enough that Blanca, without giving any thought to her actions, lunged out and caught it on her tongue. Julien, clearly unable to resist his primal urge to have that tongue all to himself again, lunged at *her.*

Julien's tongue, sugary sweet, slid over hers—warm and inviting. His fingers delved into her hair, knocking her sock hat off her head. It didn't deter him, though, from stealing a few more seconds of passion. He twirled his tongue around hers a few times before he revoked his delicious mouth and picked her hat up off the ground, thrusting it back down on top of her head all the way over her eyes.

"The longer you look at me with those gorgeous green eyes of yours, the longer it will take me to get over them when you go," he quipped.

"We always have FaceTime," she offered, peeking out from beneath the hat with a broad smile.

"That's like being offered a glass of water by someone you know is in possession of the best wine."

"Ooh, deep thoughts from a guy who's naming his wine after me, when the wine's already technically named after me."

"Whatever you say, darling. Or, would you rather I call you Pure Grace?"

"I'm not sure I'm capable of bringing the meaning of my name any justice."

"Maybe, I'll just call you Bubbles, instead."

She laughed so hard it drew the attention of others around her, more so than their random make-out sessions.

France was awesome like that.

When they finally caught up to Maxie and Chase at the nativity scene, the snowfall had increased, dusting everything in white. The village was truly magical, and Blanca began to bargain with herself that she needed to come again on vacation someday. As long as Julien didn't mind giving her a place to stay so she could afford it, she was already planning their next rendezvous.

As they all listened to an actor recite the story of Christ's birth in French, Blanca slipped in front of Julien, nudging him to wrap his arms around her to keep her warm. He didn't hesitate at all to pull her into him, resting his chin on top of the small, floppy pom-pom on the top of her sock hat. She enjoyed the comfort of his embrace as much as she enjoyed the performance as both stirred her heart.

A few more days of anything goes then I'll go. I can do this.

After several minutes, the four of them weaved their way through the thinning crowds, taking a detour to gaze at the canal that wound through Strasbourg. Then, in passing, they gawked down several narrow streets of the wood-framed buildings, so close together a car couldn't even pass through. Each narrow passage way had long cords of lights looping between the adjacent rooftops, creating a luminous canopy for pedestrians to stroll under.

"Hold up guys," Blanca screeched, stopping their momentum as they neared the cathedral. "I just need to do one more thing." She gave Julien a sinister, flirty smirk and then set her sights on what she *needed* to do so badly.

One passage way had gold and white tinseled angels that were blowing trumpets angling out from the rooftops. Between the angelic decorations, the canopy of shimmering lights seemed to be begging her to take a closer look. So, like the two lovers they were determined to be for all of one week, Blanca and Julien, in a silent agreement, took one final detour together.

They swung their knotted hands back and forth, practically skipping along that twinkling tunnel of Christmas love. If it weren't for the ten pound bags of Christmas crap each of them held in their other hands, they would have hurried along even faster. As it were, they *umphed* along—their laughter ringing out in the snow-covered stillness of the night.

She was fun like that.

* * *

Julien

As the snow continued to drift down in quiet whispering flakes outside the cathedral doors that were propped open, the increasingly cold air seeped in through Blanca's coat. The chill caused her to shiver as they stood among others near those doors. Julien curled his arms around her dainty shoulders and cradled her against him—her cheek resting against his heart.

Right where you belong.

A chorus of children sang hymns in French—their soprano voices flooding his heart with a yearning that could only be quenched by knowing Blanca's journey to Strasbourg's Christmas Market had also filled her heart with immeasurable joy like his.

Though, he made every effort to keep Blanca warm, she still continued to tremble as the night waned on. He let go of her and unbuttoned his coat, taking it off before she had a chance to realize the intent of his actions and stop him from going overboard on his chivalrous deeds. He draped the coat over her shoulders then pulled her into his arms again.

"You didn't have to—"

"Shh." He rocked her back and forth, ever so slightly, to the angelic music engulfing them. "I have to keep you warm."

"Because you're so hot," she teased.

I have to give you everything you want and need. You're mine.

"Like you." His body shook in silent laughter as she squeezed him even tighter, as if trying to impart her warmth to him now that his coat engulfed her from head to toe.

"Thank you for all these moments, Jules. I couldn't have imagined a more amazing experience than tonight. You really know how to make the most of my journey."

"*Je vous en prie, masi nour commençons à commencer notre voyage, mon amour.* (You're welcome, but we are just getting started on our journey, my love)."

Blanca lifted her chin and looked up at Julien, and that broad, comforting smile he saw as he gazed down at her was all he needed as a reply.

Chapter fifteen

"Friendship may, and often does, grow into love, but love never subsides into friendship."
~Lord Byron

Blanca

Blanca eased onto the loveseat wearing some cozy jammies, still chilled, but not to the bone like before once they came home.

Err… I mean came back ... to Julien's home ... not like I meant our home. Nope. Not that. God forbid I go that deep into my fantasy life here in France.

She had taken a scalding hot shower then dried her hair and flatironed it straight thanks to the handy plug converter she'd finally dug out of the bottom of her suitcase. Then, she had headed downstairs to hang with her lover at his request instead of collapse into bed like she wanted to.

Blanca curled her legs under her, settling in, and plaited her hair, fastening it with a hair tie then slung the thick braid over one shoulder.

Old-school mermaid hair in the morning? Yes, please.

Julien kept busy in the kitchen brewing something delicious for them to drink by the fire that crackled before her. Between the aroma of whatever it was he was making, paired with the fresh, three-foot tree he'd bought her right before departing Strasbourg that he'd set up in the middle of the dining room table, the Christmas ambiance was on maximum swoon.

He had moved the loveseat so that it was angled in front of the fireplace in the corner—the amber flames providing the only light in the living room enticing her to want to drift off to sleep as it was well after midnight.

The golden hues danced over Julien's smooth, pale skin, making him even more drop dead gorgeous, if that was even possible, as she watched him out of the corner of her eye. He approached her with a hot cup of something scrumptious that had a mound of whipped cream peeking out on top of it that made her perk right up.

"Please tell me this has a shot of booze in it—"

"Irish Cream," he interjected, as he sat next to her.

"Yasss! You are the best. Goodbye frostbite." She took the mug from him and brought it to her lips. "Is this hot chocolate?"

"*Oui.* I melt only the best chocolate with milk and cream. I even added some vanilla bean as it simmered this time. I know hot cocoa is childish, but it warms like nothing else."

"Especially with a little bit o' Irish luck swirled in," she teased, taking a sip. "Ahh. This is even better than your French pressed coffee you're probably running out of by now because of me."

"I will just buy more. You can have anything you want. What's mine is yours."

"Well now, that's very generous of you, but you've already gone overboard in spoiling me."

"Anything for you."

I'd say it's time to call it quits on the doting, but that killer smile you get when you do—

Blanca grinned back at him, snuggling into the warmth his drink brought to her mind, body, and soul. "So, what's the best chocolate then?"

"I use a particular brand of Belgium chocolate that has a hint of hazelnut in it. It melts very smoothly. We could use some to make cookies with it tomorrow, if you like, *non?*"

"Now you're talkin'. You must have a million things to do tomorrow, what with it being Christmas Eve."

"Ah, *oui*. I am in charge of desserts."

"Why does that not surprise me?"

"Thirteen different ones, actually. It is a French tradition we like to incorporate into our Christmas gathering. I am the one in the family who always prepares the desserts, *comme vous le savez* (as you know)," he drawled—his French accent growing thicker as the night carried on. "I also need to make enough *bûche de Noël* to feed about *vingt* (twenty)."

"The Yule log sponge cakes?"

"*Oui*," he nodded, setting his mug of half-slurped cocoa on an end table. "Ma mere, she will have real Yule logs burning in the *cheminée* (fireplace)."

"Sounds like a postcard perfect Christmas Eve to me. I shouldn't be keeping you up if you have all these things to do in the morning."

He turned towards her and tugged at her legs so they lay on top of his as he rested his own along the edge of the cushions, looking as though he wasn't about to budge.

"Ah, it's good for me to stay awake a little longer. We can sleep in together. Tomorrow, we have *Messe de Noël à minuit* (Midnight Christmas Mass). Then, everyone brings the food here for the *Réveillon* (Christmas meal). We will not sleep again until after sunrise."

"I'll help you with everything you need to bake tomorrow unless you think I'd just be in the way." Blanca finished the last swallow of her cocoa, and he took the mug from her, putting it next to his.

"But, ehm, I love having you in my way all the time." His fingers traced along the white snowflakes on the fuzzy fabric of her bright red jammies. "Is there anything in particular you'd like to do with our time while we stay up?"

"I've only got one thing of my mind."

He dragged his fingers though his thick hair and smiled—his eyes glued to hers. "Go on."

"Your nuts."

He looked down at his crotch. "Like I said, everything that's mine is yours."

She burst out laughing and sprung off the couch, paddling out of the living room in a rush only to return with the mini paper bag of chestnuts he'd bought at the Christmas market.

"I want to roast your nuts until they're so tender they melt in my mouth," she purred, emptying the sack on her seat cushion. "So, show me how to make your magical Christmas nuts."

Julien sat up and grabbed a stray chestnut that had rolled off the couch onto the tiled floor. "I'd love to show you how to tenderize the meat of my nuts."

Blanca laughed so deeply that she doubled over onto the floor. "*Ahh,* this floor is so hard!"

"Keep talking about my delicious nuts and the floor's not the only thing that's going to feel hard to you."

"Oh, and that's the next thing I'm going to make sure we do tonight."

* * *

Julien

"You picked me out the cutest Charlie Brown tree," Blanca said, peering at the Spruce tree on top of the dining room table that they had both wrestled with on the train ride earlier much to everyone's amusement. All the ornaments she'd unwrapped in preparation for the next day, even though technically it was already the day before Christmas by at least an hour or more, surrounded it.

"Charlie Brown? Isn't he that miserable kid who always has bad luck?" he called out, scooping up their discarded chestnut shell pieces off the end table in the living room and carrying them to the kitchen to throw them away.

"Things do work out for him, just not like he ever plans."

"Sounds like me."

"What is it you want that life's not handing over to you?"

A wife, lots of children, a name for myself. "I don't know," he called out.

"Well, you seem to know your way around planning for the holidays. But, if it's okay, I'll tackle redecorating this whole room for you in the morning. It's going to take me at least an hour just to pack up all this junk."

Junk! I love this woman.

He entered the dining room through the butler's pantry and leaned in the threshold and gazed at her. Hip cocked, jade eyes ablaze, her determination to right his maman's wrong amused him.

So damn irresistible. Why can't we just make what we have work?

Blanca's eyes raked the room with all its shabby chic clutter. "What was your mom thinking with all this frilly stuff?"

"That I probably deserved a punishment when I went to see Chase."

"Were you a bad boy, Jules?"

The tone of her voice washed over him with an open invitation for her to show him just how bad he could be.

"You tell me. As I recall, you were central to my visit," he retorted.

Blanca batted her eyes at him. "I think I might need a reminder."

Julien barreled at her, looping his arm around her waist. He hoisted her over his shoulder, carrying her to the base of the stairs as she squealed out that adorable sound he'd grown to love so much.

He set her down, and she raced up the stairs as he swatted at her *derrière.* "We can talk about how inappropriate I can be while we're in bed," he growled with laughter.

"Or you could just show me, unless the chit-chat involves narrating what you're about to do, my sexy *braggiol'*," she retorted, turning around to face him as he backed her into his bedroom.

"*Braciole*? Isn't that an Italian flank steak?"

She perused his clothes with a smirk. "It's slang for your sweet meat."

"Nice."

Julien yanked off his black sweater, taking the gray t-shirt he had underneath with it, and bowed over her as she shimmied up onto the bed. She pulled him into a kiss, wrapping her legs around the back of his thighs and causing him to collapse on top of her with an *umph.*

Once again, her hysterical laughing vibrated through him, enveloping him in waves of desire and need. She had become a necessity—her lilting voice, the sweet taste and fragrance of her honeyed skin, her exquisite, *petit* body—everything about her electrified him.

Julien hovered his lips above hers, pausing long enough to send her mouth crashing into his, eager to take what she wanted. Her tongue maneuvered around his with fierce determination—his heart thrashing in his chest as he rolled her over on top of him. She straddled him, rearing up, clinching his hips with her gorgeous, toned thighs. He slid his hands along her pajama pants, grabbing the fabric in his fists and groaning out his plead in wanting to yank them off her.

"What are you waiting for?" she mumbled against his lips.

He rolled her under him again and eased off the end of the creaking bed, tugging her pants down as he went, revealing a pair of lacy red panties. "There's my naughty girl."

Sweet mercy.

"A little something I picked up in Reims this afternoon."

"You mean yesterday afternoon," he teased, peppering her stomach with kisses along the edge of the delicate fabric.

Blanca parted her lips to reply but only a hurried gasp escaped her as he clinched the scrap of lace below her hipbone with his teeth and tugged her panties down with a growl.

Julien slid his hands underneath her, gripping her slender hips, lifting her up as he knelt down.

"What was that, darling?" he mumbled, spiraling into ecstasy along with her.

"I can't remember," she moaned right back at him.

* * *

"I can't even move. There's no way I can stay awake any longer," Blanca groaned—her body slumped over Julien's between his legs as he cradled her in his arms.

"You should sleep. I'll probably only stay up another hour or so."

She lifted her head to look at him. "Are you going down stairs?"

"*Non.*"

"You're just going to lay here under me and what?"

"Hold you."

And fall in love with you.

"You're such a sap, but I lo-*ike* that about you."

"I could read that novel I helped you with."

"You mean our book baby?" she snickered then yawned. "Actually, I'd still be trying to make Rayne get it on with a billionaire like every other romance novel on the market if you hadn't inspired me to write something original. Besides, I probably wouldn't have come, if I hadn't felt the need to return the favor and keep you company, so Maxie and Ch—" She yawned again. "Well, anyway. I'm here for you."

And you are here for me. So stay.

Blanca lifted herself off Julien and climbed over his thigh, sliding off the edge of the bed. She staggered out of the room and returned a few seconds later with her laptop. "Here you go. Have at it," she breathed, handing him her Macbook Air. "I can't even walk straight. What the hell did you do to me?"

"You enjoyed everything, *non?*" he asked, reaching his hand out to help her onto the bed with him.

She climbed onto the groaning bed and crawled under the covers. She curled up on her side with her back pressed against him, and he draped his arm along her silhouette. "Oh, I enjoyed everything. Two maybe three times over."

"*Bien.*" Julien held up the computer and examined its hard shell cover that had an image of the Eiffel Tower in the rain on it. "Were you wanting to go to Paris while you're here?"

She didn't reply.

"Blanca?" He peered over her shoulder—her eyes closed, her

breathing slow and deep. "*De beaux rêves, mon amour* (Sweet dreams, my love)," he whispered.

Julien opened her laptop and pulled up her documents in Word. He scrolled through the short list until he found her novel about Rayne, the mischievous imp of a character who he owed the whole world to and more. He was falling for Blanca, like an outpouring of rain, and every part of his life felt quenched by her inner beauty and grace.

Chapter Sixteen

"But he that dares not grasp the thorn should never crave the rose."
~Anne Brontë

Blanca

It really did take Blanca a whole hour to pack up all the do-dads in the dining room while Julien labored away in the kitchen like the hottest pastry chef in all of France.

Or at least that's how I'll always remember him.

As she decorated his walls, his hutch, his table, and their Christmas tree with all the ornaments and trinkets she had organized according to color and theme, Julien brought her nips of this and licks of that, feeding her little morsels of his masterpieces. He didn't think twice about slipping his thumb in her mouth or gliding his tongue along the corner of her lip to remove any sugary smudge he may have totally caused on purpose. Of course, she gloated in every second of his playfulness, returning his affection unreserved.

After several hours, and, eventually Blanca's side-by-side help, they both had managed to knock out thirteen-plus desserts for the *Réveillon.* Their first endeavors included baking mini pastries—glazed tarts in blackberry, apricot and plum, to be exact.

They also made a dozen each of some sugar, chocolate chunk, and oatmeal raisin cookies, which made the house smell like holiday heaven.

Julien even piped out some shortbread bars that Blanca dipped in dark, milk, and white chocolate, adding them to the cookie-palooza invading half of the counter space.

Julien also showed her how to create some colorful melt-in-your-mouth minty drops that, once they hardened in the refrigerator, looked like they belonged in a party favor bag at a bridal shower. He even created a red-and-white-swirled white chocolate bark that looked almost too pretty to eat.

While one batch of this baked and another batch of that cooled, they worked together to wrap little caramel toffee bites into tootsies with waxed paper. He had taught her how to make the caramel from scratch, too. Her favorite candy she'd helped him make, which reminded her of Christmases with her Nonna Alba in San Francisco, was a toffee brittle that had three kinds of crushed nuts in it.

Julien's grand finale were four sets of three types of Yule log cakes in vanilla raspberry crème, chocolate vanilla swirl, and good-ole-fashioned chocolate. They frosted all of them in white buttercream frosting, only pressing shredded coconut into the icing on the ones with the ribbon of raspberry jelly curling through them. Julien fashioned the tiny, hard-sugared figurine elves on top of the snow-covered logs as if they were hacking into them. Between all the treats they'd made and the ones they'd bought in Strasbourg the night before, Julien and Blanca had managed to fill twenty serving plates with all the different Christmas desserts.

Exhausted, and yet, a little buzzed with sugar from all the nibbling, Julien and Blanca headed across the lot to his parents' home along with Maxie and Chase who had come over to help carry all the dessert platters.

Maxie had kept in touch with Blanca all day, texting about all the crazy cooking going on at their place, just as Blanca had filled her in on all their fun in the kitchen. Maxie said they had spent all afternoon making several casserole dishes of ratatouille and boiling enough lobsters that the ocean had probably run out of the little creatures.

When they entered Julien's parents' home, the furniture in several rooms had been rearranged, and the dining room table had been fitted with extensions and converted into a buffet. Julien's mother, Monique, greeted them in the rotunda and asked everyone to put the dessert trays on either end of all the tables that had been set up in the living room, sitting room, and office.

"You could invite everybody in France to come over for dinner in this house," Blanca chided Julien, scanning all the tables draped in red tablecloths with golden runners adorned with pine cones and silk garlands of holly berries.

"We're always celebrating something inside or outside in the back," Julien replied, as he scanned the room then began to put the plates down on two of the tables, prompting Blanca to do the same across the room.

"If I could entertain everyone in Champagne, I would," Monique called out from the kitchen tucked away alongside the dining room. "Everyone in our immediate family will be joining us after church tonight, so that is close enough." Peels of laughter echoed from the kitchen.

I love that woman. I don't know her, but I love her.

Julien pulled Blanca aside in the sitting room while Chase and Maxie kept busy setting out cold dishes on one end of the buffet table. "You are comfortable with so many people, *oui?*"

"My family gigs can beat your family gatherings any day of the week." She thumped his nose.

"*Bien.*" He stole a quick kiss then led her back to the kitchen to help his mother with whatever else she needed.

By the time they were all headed out the door for the Midnight Christmas Mass at the Notre-Dame Cathedral of Reims, Julien's older cousin on his mother's side named Jean showed up. He volunteered to stay back and bring out the hot dishes and light the sternos canisters under all the warming trays, so everything would be ready when everyone returned from church.

Between the forty-five minutes to and from the L'Angevin estate and the hour-and-a-half at Mass, the anticipation of the night's meal had become epic in proportion to the rest of the French traditions. Everybody had something to say about the excitement of eating the Christmas meal together as a family.

A ginormous, happy, loving family just like hers.

Blanca was as eager to sample everything there was to eat, as Colette and Lillie's children were to skip eating altogether and hurrying off to bed.

Le Père Noël (Santa Claus) would be sneaking toys and treats in and around their shoes sometime in the next couple of hours. Julien and Blanca had even snuck something for each other under the tree that they'd both picked up in Strasbourg.

"You didn't have to," Blanca had purred a few minutes ago, bumping into his shoulder playfully as they had crouched before the Christmas tree, putting their gifts under it.

"I know. Neither did you, love," he had replied, nudging her back.

"I know."

As the young cousins were all tucked into the beds in the two spare bedrooms—their tummies full—the men lounged around in the living room talking about their current vintage while the women hung out in the kitchen portioning up the leftovers. Blanca and Maxie kept the coffee flowing for everyone, fitting right in with all the wives and sisters like they'd both known the L'Angevin families for years.

As Blanca approached Julien with a fresh cup of coffee, she couldn't help but notice his attention was glued to his cell phone, hardly engaging in any of the conversations surrounding him, and an annoying ping of pay-attention-to-me flared up in her.

"What's got you so intrigued?" Blanca asked, handing him the mug.

"You," he replied.

Nice try.

She pointed at his phone. "You haven't even blinked since I came out of the dining room to bring this coffee to you."

"I'm serious. *You.* I am almost done reading *our* book. I created a

PDF of your file and sent it to myself last night. I hope you don't mind that I used your email. It's easier to keep reading it on my cell phone than to cart around your laptop."

Huh? Oh, that's right.

"I don't care. I've got nothing to hide. I was just humoring you last night having you actually read that dang thing. You really like my story enough to actually read the whole thing?"

Wow. He really does think that lame book is our little bundle of joy. I guess it is, after all, the reason behind why I'm even here.

Julien reached up and threaded a lock of her hair behind her ear. "Honestly, I've never read a romance novel before, but, for your first crack at it, I am very impressed. You know I'm only jesting when I claim that it's ours. This cute, *petit* story is all you. I was only good for a tip or two, but I am in no way taking any actual credit for all your hard work."

Blanca bit her lower lip, trying to mask her apparent excitement that he approved of her story. Writing that novel had been one of the hardest challenges she had ever accepted from her bestie.

"Thank you, but if I'm going to be honest, the best part about the process was watching all those romcoms with you while we chatted on FaceTime," she muttered, as the other men carried on in French about the family business. "I'll let you get back to it."

Julien nodded, flashing her a lazy smile and roaming his eyes over her. "You are the most beautiful woman I've ever known. How did I get so lucky?"

Julien's words tumbled out in a quiet whisper so matter-of-fact like Blanca couldn't tell if he meant to say them to her or just to himself. A tinge of pink crept up on her cheeks as she drifted away towards the kitchen again.

He likes me. A lot. A lot. Aw.

Blanca paused halfway through the rotunda and turned around to look at Julien again—his wild, wavy hair, his cranberry colored sweater, his black slacks—he redefined gorgeous. She even wore a knit dress in a similar shade of cranberry just so they could coordinate. By the looks of things, they had transformed into an actual couple.

Rut-roh.

Julien had become more than her long-distance friend, more than her temporary French lover, more than the something-or-other she was too overwhelmed by to give an actual name to.

Blanca watched as one of Julien's nieces danced up to him and handed him a sugar cookie she had topped with a mountain of whipped cream. He took the cookie from her as she climbed onto his lap. He raked some of the whipped cream onto his fingertip and tapped her nose with it, evoking an innocent giggle. Then, he bit into the cookie as if it were the most delicious treat he'd ever eaten. His nurturing, fatherly charm radiated from him as the little girl hugged his neck then wiggled off his lap.

And, before Blanca could rationalize the tingling ache that welled up in her gut, a sudden deluge of panic washed over her, robbing her of her sense of independence and control over her heart.

Oh, my God. I love him. What have I done?

* * *

Later that morning as the sun rose above the tree-lined horizon, the children emptied their shoes of little gifts their mommies had tucked in them. Then, they tore into the presents their daddies had unloaded from the trunks of their cars all in the name of Père Noël.

Blanca couldn't help but reciprocate a more guarded kind of affection with Julien as she tried to wrangle her wayward heart. While everyone was gathered together in the living room, they opened the gifts they'd gotten each other and discovered they'd both picked up the same present to exchange while at the Christmas market—silver Champagne bottle charms. Julien had fastened hers onto a long chain necklace, creating an elegant gift for her that he proudly looped around her neck. Whereas, she'd clamped his charm onto an ornament of an elf so that the little guy held the bottle out in front of him like … *yep, a not-so-elegant gift.*

"A little reminder of when we met, *Cyrano*," she grinned, rearing back when he tried to kiss her between his bouts of laughter.

Blanca couldn't help it. She couldn't help but try to avoid his kisses and hugs. And, every time Julien's hand found hers or his fingers fidgeted with her hair, she'd make some lame excuse to see what Maxie was up to and scamper off to find her BFF. She even managed to tuck herself in a corner undisturbed for a whole hour, texting her brother in order to stay informed of her own relatives' gathering in the Bay Area that she was missing out on.

Julien's affection had become a siren, warning Blanca with each touch that her heart was days away from shattering when she had to say goodbye. And the worst part was, that day couldn't come soon enough. She had to get back to her own home, her own things, and her own life. She had broken her rules to keep the doors to her heart shut, and the painful consequence of heartache in ending something that never should've begun in the first place suddenly haunted her.

Blanca had avoided dealing with the new life she had started in Napa Valley long enough. If she expected to travel over summer again, indulging in her wanderlust wherever her whim would take her, she needed to get serious about her new job and start generating the funds. Eventually, the extra money she had been living off of from the equity in selling her condo would run out. She wasn't a success story in the city of Sacramento any longer. She was just a nobody in wine country, and that reality was not acceptable to her.

The last thing Blanca needed was to have to drag back the remnants of a broken heart from allowing herself to get too close to Julien. But it was happening. Like it or not.

She was screwed like that.

The laughter, the joy, the powerful bond of family Blanca had been flooded with by being around Julien was just like being around her own family. And her own family was all she needed, nothing more. Julien's life was his, not hers. Living out her Parisian fantasy since arriving had left her vulnerable, and real feelings of being in love with Julien had been born out of that experience.

Feelings she couldn't take home with her.

Feelings she didn't want getting in the way of her responsibilities to reestablish herself back at home.

Feelings she couldn't allow herself to explore.

Julien was not hers to keep. And losing herself to him, or to any man for that matter, was not an option until she'd found herself again.

Chapter Seventeen

"Unless you love someone, nothing else makes any sense."
~e. e. cummings

Julien

After sleeping in late the following morning, Julien and Chase took the ladies to their family's underground chalk caves. They wanted to show them where all the L'Angevin Champagne fermented. Most of the bottles rotated in mechanical equipment, churning the sediment on timers, but their Prestige Cuvées of Champagne rested in dusty bottles protruding by the hundreds on tented, adjustable wooden racks that had been in the family for decades.

An elderly man that had worked for the family for over thirty years turned all those bottles by hand adding to the authenticity and uniqueness that the L'Angevin brand brought to its products.

Julien kept Blanca tucked under his arm due to the frigid temperatures in the tunnels, despite her playful protests that he was smothering her. The tunnels were twenty-five feet underground providing the perfect, chilled environment for the fermentation process but could freeze his beautiful darling to death if she got her way and he let go of her.

"Does your riddler wear a monocle and carry a cane when he turns all the bottles?" Max teased Julien, sidling up next to him, while linked arm in arm with Chase.

Julien squinted at her quizzically until he realized her comic book reference to their elderly employee. He let out a hearty laugh that echoed in the broad tunnel. They were the only people deep down in the belly of the beast, as he liked to call it. Their riddler had the day off, given that it was Christmas Day. They normally kept their caverns closed to the general public anyway, only offering an occasional tour to buyers upon request interested in vending L'Angevin Champagnes.

"If you'll excuse us," Chase said, pulling Max away from Julien and down a different tunnel that protruded off to their left.

"Come back soon," Blanca blurted out to her best friend, flashing Julien a banal smile when he looked down at her tucked neatly under his wing.

"Am I keeping you warm enough, my love?"

"Yes," she replied, watching Max and Chase disappear around the corner.

"Is there anything more that I can do to comfort you?"

She squirmed under the weight of his arm, and he finally released her.

"You've already done too much." Her eyes danced around the tunnel, flitting from the racks to the walls, and up at the lighting tracks running along the high ceilings.

"These caves can get pretty eerie at night. Would you like to come back? As I recall, the haunted caves at Angel of the Vine were pretty amusing to you." He tucked his hands into the pockets of his coat to warm them, always forgetting his gloves wherever he went.

Blanca shook her head, searching the floor then leveling her eyes on him. "Julien, I can't—I can't thank you enough for sharing your Christmas with me and for entrusting me to be by your side through your grandmother's funeral."

Non, Jules?

Julien stepped up to Blanca, but she took a step back.

His heart seized inside of him instantly.

Not now. Not here. Not while we still have more time.

"But?" he replied—his eyes pleading for her to be kind in her response, knowing that she had been troubled by something since leaving his parents' home earlier that morning.

"I feel like we're getting too close."

"Too close? I thought you enjoyed our intimacy."

"I have, but I'm not talking about that. I mean us. You and me." She motioned between them. "This isn't a thing. I have to go home the day after tomorrow."

But, you'll come back to me. "I know."

"So, I can't—wait. What? You don't care that I'm leaving?"

"Of course I do." He stepped up to her again, only that time, she didn't budge. In fact, her gloved hands parked themselves on her hips like she was posturing for an epic battle of wills.

You're not going to make this easy on me, are you, my love?

Julien cleared his throat and continued. "I do care that you are leaving. It devastates me to even think about it." He tugged his hands out of his pockets and cupped her face. "But, I need to ask you something."

Blanca swallowed so hard he could hear the tiny gurgle in her throat—her hands flopping down to her sides. "What?"

"I think you should take care of whatever you need to do in America then turn around and come back home to me."

Blanca's lips parted but only a squeaky breath came out of her, so Julien continued. "Just hear me out, love."

"Stop calling me that." She covered his cold hands with her gloves and lowered them from her face, but, instead of letting them go, she only gripped them tighter.

Julien looked at their joined hands—her thumbs rubbing his knuckles to warm them like the caring person she was. "I don't mean to make you uncomfortable, ehm, but everything has been going so well with us."

"See. That right there. There is no *us.* There is you, and there is me, and all we've done is ruin our perfectly good friendship with real feelings while we've been pretending that we're together."

A jolt of heartache nearly knocked him over.

Pretending?

"How has that ruined things?" Julien withdrew his hands from hers and dragged his fingers through his hair before tucking them into his coat pockets again. "I thought being friends first is how most relationships that last begin."

"Our feelings are a fraud based on my fantasy that I could have it all for one week then walk away with no regrets, like a *stunad.*" Blanca's elevated voice must have frightened her because she recoiled from her own words and leaned in to whisper. "I can't give up my life in America to live out this fantasy with you in Champagne. The bubble will eventually burst."

As hard as Julien fought it, a smile crept over his face as he panned the thousands of Champagne bottles lining the perimeters of the tunnel behind Blanca in an overly exaggerated manner. She must have realized how befitting her analogy was because she also started laughing, covering her mouth to stifle it.

"Well, I don't mean to *burst your bubble,* but the truth is, this very real, very beautiful love story we have developed between us deserves a chance. At least consider returning again so that we can figure out how we will make this relationship work, *s'il vous plait* (please)?"

"You have to stop calling this a relationship," she sighed, blinking back tears as her smile began to fade. "I can't give you my heart, Julien. I'm emotionally unavailable. I screwed up letting myself get too close to you. I thought I could handle it, but I can't."

"I understand you've been hurt in the past, but that pain should not define who you are now. You need to give yourself permission to love again."

"I'm not ready for all the things you want in life, Julien. I have too many responsibilities to add an impossible relationship into the mix."

He shook his head and peered at her. "Impossible? Why? What kind of responsibilities?"

"Well, for one, I just bought a house. I also have to start all over again and build up a client list at work so I can afford my new house. It's time for me to face that reality. I do lo—love you, but I'm not *in love* with you. I can't give you what you want in return, and, from what I can tell, you want a family of your own like your sisters and cousins."

Julien looked down at his feet and scuffed the ground with his shoe. "It isn't far-fetched for me to want those things with you."

"Believe me, I tried to rationalize drawing out the fantasy of a life here with you by coming back whenever I could. I really did—"

He looked at her again—hope fluttering in his heart. "You thought about it, about us living here together?"

"Yes, but—but I would only be using you. I can't commit to you. Even if these feelings I have for you are real, they're uninvited, and they're not going to last. I'm sorry."

The anguish in Blanca's eyes grieved him. He wanted to pull her into arms again. Comfort her. Make her *see* that she was wrong.

And there it was—his grand-maman's warning. He knew he would have to wait while Blanca's attention was divided before she could truly *see*—see that he might be everything she ever wanted, if given a chance, the way he had begun to see her as someone who could possibly be the one he deserved.

Julien shifted on his feet and reached out to her, hesitating at first, until she stepped forward into his arms—tears spilling over in her eyes. "Oh, my sweet Blanca, please don't cry. I cannot stand to see that you're hurting."

"Aren't you mad at me?" Her words came out muffled against his chest.

"*Non.* How could I be upset with you for being afraid of what you feel?"

"I'd be pissed."

"I can't be angry at you when I am in the process of falling in love with you."

"You have to let me go, Julien."

"*Non.* I cannot do that for you."

She tilted her head up—his eyes locking onto hers as he continued. "You need to know something about me. You see, it doesn't matter to me how you feel about me or even how you've made me feel the last few days by bringing me so much joy when I could have been miserable. We *have* been living in a fantasy. You are right."

"I'm always right," she interjected as if to try to lighten the mood as Max's squee echoed through the tunnel they'd disappeared down, pulling her eyes away from Julien's stare.

He reached up and glided his thumb along the curve of her plump lower lip, drawing her attention back to him. "I want you to know that I am falling in love with you because of who you are with or without me. I am not floating around in some fantasy like you, hanging onto every compliment and gesture of affection you give me as if that's a reason to have genuine feelings for you."

"You're not? You don't like—wait. I'm so confused." She pulled away from him again, looking up at him with pleading eyes.

He gripped her hands in his and took a deep breath, then sighed as he rocked on his heels. "I love you, but I don't hinge my feelings on how you can so easily manipulate me into a flustered wad of passion with only a bat of your eyes. I see you. I see how wise you are and, ehm, how calculating and precise you can be with your decisions. I see that every choice you make is weighted on whether or not it will benefit others in your life. You care about other people more than anyone I have ever met. And, one day, I am going to be the one who spends his life cherishing every moment I get being the one who cares for you. I love *you.*"

Blanca blinked at him. And blinked again. Then parted her lips to speak but just groaned in frustration instead.

No point in holding back now. "I deserve your love."

"Not helping," she gulped.

"I don't care if you think you're not ready to fall in love with me—"

"But I'm not." She tugged her hands out of his and went straight for her hips in combat mode again.

Julien staggered backwards and smiled at her. "You will be."

"How can you not be totally mad at me right now? I'm breaking up with you. It's over."

He motioned to her with a flick of his wrist. "No, it's not. I know you too well."

"We've only been around each other for less than two weeks total. Ever."

"We've also talked to one another every single day for the last two months."

Blanca's eyes wandered to the ground. "Oh, yeah. There's that," she retorted, then looked back up at him. "I'm still leaving the day after tomorrow."

"I know."

"And I'm not coming back."

"Perhaps, not for a while."

Blanca stepped up to Julien again and tilted her head back to try to glare at him, only to come off looking even more adorable. "I'm serious. I'm breaking up with you."

"We were never really together, remember?"

"Dammit. Okay, fine. But I'm not kidding. I'm such a *gagoots* (moron). I hate that I have to feel like this."

"Like what? *In love?*"

"No!"

"Then tell me what it is you do feel?"

Blanca searched the space between them for a second then looked back up at him. "I feel ... I feel heartbroken. I let myself down. I let you down. I never should've ruined our friendship like this. I never should've crossed that line the first day I got here. I never should've convinced myself I could handle letting my guard down. I don't want to give up my life for you, Julien. I don't think I can ever give up my life for anyone. I just don't work that way. I'm sorry. I have to go home. I have to start over, and I can't be distracted by—"

"Blanca," Max shouted, as Chase and she appeared around a bend in the tunnel off to their side, swinging their hands together and laughing. "You have to come check this out."

She glanced over and called out, "Okay, we'll be there in a second," then looked up at Julien again giving him one last morsel of attention. "I really have loved my time with you here, and, as a friend, I do love you, too, but this regret I'm feeling is enough to make it all turn to hate if I don't get my crap pulled together back home where I belong. I have to let you go, Julien. These new feelings for you only break my heart because they don't belong inside of me. Please, don't make this any harder than it is. I really am sorry."

Blanca took a step backward and turned her attention to her best friend again, cutting Julien off from countering her as she blotted her cheeks with the sleeves of her coat.

You only need more time to see.

Blanca walked away, and Julien followed at her heels down the cavern until they met up with Chase and Max.

"I have to show you something. You're going to flip," Max said, linking her arm with Blanca's and dragging her ahead of the men, leaning in to whisper something into Blanca's ear that he could not hear.

Chase gave Julien a once over glare then shook his head, neither of them voicing their silent argument as they walked beside one another. Chase would, no doubt, seek him out later to remind him he had told him so about Blanca's inability to give Julien what he needed.

An argument he only needed more time to win.

It took a few minutes for everyone to reach the secret cove hidden behind a rack identified by a brand mark on one of the lower boards. They all had to duck down to get through the short tunnel, pitch black and icy cold, but, once the narrow space opened up, light from nearly thirty feet above poured out in a radiating prism upon them. A misty rain created a rainbow veil enveloping all of them in a natural chamber.

The small space, cluttered with large stones covered in pungent, velvety green moss and speckled with hundreds of glistening coins, barely fit all of them.

"Rain," Blanca breathed—a wistful smile replacing her frown. "This is amazing."

"We have a double-walled concrete perimeter around the opening for obvious safety reasons," Julien began, pointing upward. "Although, that still doesn't deter our nieces and nephews from hurling coins at the gaping hole in the earth when they're on the property. They like to pretend it's a wishing well. This end of the cave is near the warehouses where we store all our harvesting equipment."

Julien halted his rambling as he realized he was simply trying to fill the distance that was growing between Blanca and he with meaningless chatter. "Well, anyway, we'll, ehm, head back home after this."

"I think that is a great idea," Chase replied, as he embraced Max in a protective hug to keep her dry.

They all waited quietly—a trickling sound of water echoing in the stillness around them—as if someone or something had told them all to be still. As much as Julien yearned to reach out and steal a fleeting moment of affection from Blanca, he only watched her in silence. She was completely lost in her own world.

Blanca had tugged her gloves off and was cupping her hands out in front of her, trying to catch the droplets, but the soft rain only drifted about her in a faint, ethereal swirl overwhelming her in a shimmering, iridescent veil—intangible, mystic, only meant to be admired, not obtained.

Just like you, my love.

Julien knew that his time with Blanca would come eventually. He needed only to wait. Be like the mist. Tread so lightly his love for her would fully envelop her before she could lay hold to cast him away the next time they would meet again.

Chapter Eighteen

"One of the most beautiful qualities of true friendship is to understand and to be understood."
~Lucius Annaeus Seneca

Blanca

Awkward couldn't even come close to describing the whole vibe Blanca and Julien had caused among the four of them all evening as the couples, err, one couple and one flailing mishap, parted ways after a late dinner at Julien's parents' home.

I know. I know. I'm horrible. I get it.

Blanca had filled Maxie in on every single detail of what went down in the chalk tunnel. She even confessed to feeling like she was falling in love but backed up her statement with a truckload of all the fears that came with it. Surprisingly, Maxie didn't unleash her inner cheerleader on her and lecture her on embracing the idea of falling in love with Julien or tell her that sex and love were bound to collide and that she should just go for it. Instead, she only listened and nodded and hugged her ... a lot.

Like a true best friend should.

Maxine Novaline defined the expression Best. Friends. Forever. From the moment they had bonded over the last giant cookie that the cafeteria wench had been peddling on their first day of high school that they had both reached for, to the day Maxie had moved back into Blanca's condo last summer all snot-nosed and whining about her asshole ex-boyfriend, Bart Moore, they were always there for one another.

They had each other's backs like a two-members-only superheroes league.

When Blanca's fiancé had dumped her five years ago, and she had dropped out of college to avoid seeing the jerk, Maxie had been the one who had helped her redefine her ambitions and enroll in beauty school. When Maxie's first boyfriend of forever had told her that their relationship had run its course and marriage wasn't going to happen, Blanca had helped Maxie find her independence by getting her to move in with her and finish her English degree.

Their friendship had survived the silliest of spats, the craziest of adventures, and the hardest of heartaches. They were as much alike as they were different. One determined. The other demure. One, sporting a halo. The other, a couple of horns. But together, they'd always had each other's backs. Anyone who could take Blanca's rants, hold her own and fire back, then find themselves squeeing over coffee two minutes later was the ultimate best friend material.

When Maxie's world had fallen apart last summer because of her douchebag ex, it had been Blanca who had convinced her to move back into the condo with her a second time. When Blanca's career as a stylist in Sacramento had tanked because the salon was closing down, it had been Maxie who had convinced her she could reinvent herself again as the best stylist in Napa Valley.

The wine country had become home sweet home, for better or worse, for both of them.

Blanca's motherly instincts—protective and fierce, always on overdrive—sometimes drove Maxie nuts, but had never been unwelcome. And Maxie's moral rants—innocent and meek, always with the intent to protect and preserve Blanca's self-worth, had never been completely shunned.

They balanced each other out. The way any type of relationship should.

Once the tight hugging and the joint crying had stopped, Maxie offered her one simple statement. And that's all it took for Blanca to feel like she was doing the right thing. That it was okay to abandon her unwanted feelings for Julien.

And all her bestie did was quote Ralph Waldo Emerson. "We must be our own before we can be another's."

If Blanca didn't have her bestie, she didn't have anything at all. She just needed time to catch up to the white picket fence and the two-point-five kids. Could Julien be those things? Doubtfully. France was too far from her own family. The United States was too far from his. And trying to rationalize their continental conundrum made the room spin and her ears ring like a school bell. But, loving someone someday didn't seem like such a monstrous feat anymore. It seemed more like a new challenge, when she'd taken care of herself.

Just not anytime soon.

* * *

Julien was at his best being cordial to Blanca when she'd gathered her belongings out of his bedroom and settled into the one next door where her luggage was anyway.

Again, awkward. Times ten-billion.

He'd even told her he'd bring her a cup of his homemade cocoa with a shot of Irish Crème in it to help keep her warm while she slept since she no longer needed him.

Ouch.

And, why wouldn't he do something so awesome as that? Because he was wonderful, that's why. An honest-to-goodness gentleman. The kinder Julien was to Blanca, the more miserable her heart ached even though in her head she knew she had done what was best for both of them.

Funny how breakups are so unfair.

Except that they didn't really break up because they were never really together in the first place. At least that was what she kept telling herself as she slurped on his delicious, chocolaty drink while bundled up under several blankets he'd tucked neatly around her before saying goodnight, or actually, *bonne nuit,* because, you know, hot French guy and all.

When morning came and the sun began to crescent over the forest-rimmed horizon, Blanca searched and found Julien sitting outside. He was on his back porch in the freezing cold taking in the sunrise spilling over the fog-covered vines while nursing a steaming cup of coffee.

"May I join you?" Her words poured out of her in a trembling rush.

"Of course." He motioned to the chair next to him.

Blanca had lugged a blanket downstairs with her and had cocooned herself in it seconds before hopping outside so that when she flopped into the chair like a caterpillar trying to escape its chrysalis, Julien had no other choice than to laugh at her silly antics.

"Oh, this is quite a view," she breathed, as she wiggled into a cozy position while panning the vines bathed in golden, misty hues that jetted out before them.

"When we have our morning talks, I often sit here and enjoy the sunrise ... and you."

Dang. That hurts.

Blanca pursed her lips to the side. "I'm going to miss that about us." *Us?* "Our friendship, I mean."

Julien shifted in his chair and looked at her. "You can't take your friendship away from me, Blanca."

She looked over at him—his expression stern, sullen, and determined. *Why do you have to be so ... so ...* "Fine. Friends. But the thing is, Julien—"

"Please, call me Jules."

Good God. Kill me now.

"Okay, Juulleezz, the thing is I need to catch my breath when I get back home. Don't be mad if I don't answer your calls for a while."

That reply seemed to be good enough for him because his attention drifted back over to the rising sun again. They both just sat in silence. Only it wasn't really silent because all kinds of birds and bugs were cluttering their peace and quiet with noise.

After several minutes and lots of sighs from both of them, Julien turned to Blanca again, dragging his eyes up and down her mummified body with an amused smirk. "I have only one request."

"Okay, but if I don't like it, the answer is *no*."

"Hear me out. Last night, you said you needed to take care of things in your life first before you could share it with someone else, that you have to feel accomplished for you to be satisfied—"

"So? I'm only twenty-five. It could take me a really, really long time to get my life to where it needs to be before I even think of allowing myself to be vulnerable to love again?"

"Vulner?—ah, the ex. That's a reasonable defense."

"It really is."

"All I am asking is that you consider coming back to visit me. Take all the time you need—months if you have to—but give us a second chance to see if what we've begun is capable of becoming everlasting before I lose you to someone else."

"It may be years before I can say I'm ready for a commitment. You'll be dead of old age by then."

"Though lovers be lost, love shall not. And death shall have no dominion," he quoted.

"Shakespeare?"

"Dylan Thomas."

"Ah-ha. See, you need to find someone like Maxie. She's really doing great as a poetry spouting tour guide at your uncle's winery."

Gah! Not Maxie. No. Stay away from my bestie.

"I don't want someone like her. I want someone like you."

Someone like me. Someone? Who is this beotch? We need to talk.

For a hot minute a tinge of jealousy flared up in Blanca. But recognizing that she was capable of even getting jealous meant only one thing, she really did have to purge her heart of him if she was ever going to keep moving forward and redefine herself.

She groaned. "You may not think so after I'm gone. In fact, I bet you'll eventually forget all about me."

"Not if you come back to visit again someday. Please give me something to hope for."

Blanca's urge to care for Julien, to coddle his needs and wants, almost overcame her to tears. He deserved hope. He deserved joy. He deserved happiness. He deserved someone other than her.

Blanca came to the conclusion that she had hurt him deeply enough just by taking her love away and destroying their friends-with-benefits deal, so she decided she owed it to him to please him one more time.

She was giving like that.

"Okay, Jules. I'll see you again. I don't know when. I don't know where. I don't know much. But we will meet again. I promise."

"Thank you." He smiled at her as if she had promised him the world.

* * *

The rest of their day played out lazy and hushed even though Blanca had nervous knots in her stomach—and not the good kind. She spent way more time than she needed packing up what little she had brought, and Julien kept stopping by the threshold of her room, handing her items he'd wrapped carefully for her trip back to America. He'd made sure she would be taking home the Strasbourg replica snow globe, the exquisite filigree angel bedazzled in crystals, a hand-painted elf holding the letters j-o-y clumsily in his tiny arms, and, of course, some sugary treats for the long string of flights she'd have to endure.

Their conversations were as drab as the mood that swallowed them up. Julien's smile never reached his eyes, but his tone revealed nothing but tenderness. Blanca tried to be polite, scaling back the flirt, but everything out of her mouth sounded like a warning. She went from wanting him to be the happiest person in the world to making him the most miserable.

That night, when they murmured their goodnights to one another in the hall, Julien reached out and held Blanca's hand even though he could not bring his eyes to meet with hers. He only seemed to want to touch her, as though to feel her near him one more time. No words. Just a quiet moment. She gave into the emotionally explosive experience of wallowing in France with him one last time.

Then, she let him be the one to finally let her go.

* * *

Blanca had plenty of time to mourn over departing the land of Christmas magic and misery on all the flights home. She'd also had time to reread Maxie's novel again while Chase and her bestie canoodled in a nap together on their second connecting flight. She had only made some critical comments on the way Maxie had Rayne falling madly in love by the first chapter. She had pecked out a side note that insta-love was impossible in real life. She shot the marked up document back to Maxie in an email when they were biding their time in another airport before their second flight. She didn't even care if her BFF even bothered to reread her book and offer comments on how fabulous it was … or not. She could care less at that point.

The book was done.

The need for Julien was done.

The bet was coming to a close.

Time to move on.

At the airport in Reims, Blanca had given Julien a passionless goodbye peck before backing away from him—her heartstrings snapping with every step. The feel of his tender lips still tingled in a phantom reminder that she would likely never taste his kiss again.

But I have no choice.

Blanca had to scrape her reputation as a serious stylist off the bottom of the ocean and resuscitate her career again. She had to save enough money to travel again because, somewhere between New York and San Francisco, she'd definitively made up her mind to go back to her roots in Italy. Next summer, she had decided that for her next continuing education workshop, she would drown out her love of all things France with another round of wanderlust that hit closer to home in her heart.

* * *

Julien

Julien's thumb hovered over the send arrow on his iPhone, contemplating his text to Blanca. He wondered if she'd respond or push him away like she'd warned. A whole week had already passed, and each day weighed heavier than the next as he battled the emptiness she had left him with.

In the two months they had spent cultivating their friendship, Blanca's sudden absence in Julien's life was a resounding void, empty and desolate. He missed sharing his morning sunrises with her on FaceTime, as well as ached for all her random texts throughout the day. And, though they'd only spent a fragment of time together over Christmas, he missed her warm body curled around him each night to the point that insomnia threatened him the entire week he had spent without her.

Julien missed Blanca enough to know that his feelings weren't based on merely being caught up in a moment with her while she visited. He knew without a doubt that he couldn't bear to be without her. He might have even needed her. In fact, he knew for certain, he genuinely loved her.

He deleted his words again—words that begged her to reconnect—then started anew.

***Julien:** Hello stranger.*

Be stealth. Be simple. Be present. He pressed send and waited.

Within seconds, his text garnered a reply.

***Blanca:** We're not strangers yet.*

***Julien:** Yet?*

***Blanca:** Can't talk right now,*
in the middle of scraping out toe jam.

Julien: *Pairs well with belly button lint*
and a tart Chardonnay.

That was all Julien needed. That sassy pith he loved so much about her. He put his iPhone down and rolled onto his side, shutting his eyes to try to sleep.

Only checking in.

No need to type *good morning.*

No expected *text you later.*

Nothing.

Only planting a seed.

Baiting her playful banter of rejection with a little of his own.

It was a start.

Julien plotted to do it again in another week—just a quick, simple *hello*—then calculated how he could close the gap, one day at a time, until he had Blanca talking to him again every day.

* * *

It was nearly four weeks later, when Julien's plan revealed itself to be a success after a quick text asking how she had been doing.

Blanca: *I am freaking out-*
That's how I am!!!
Julien: *How can I help you?*
Blanca: *A time machine would*
do the trick then I can tell Maxie
hell no about writing that
stupid book
Julien: *What happened?*
Blanca: *U know how I said we knew*
jack squat about how
Amazon works and only got a
week to give our books away
FREE then had to set a price,
well at .99 for the last three weeks,
reviews r in ... not good, Jules,

not good
Julien: *How so? Please*
FaceTime with me?

...

Julien's heart leapt when his iPhone fluttered with an incoming call. He ran his fingers through his hair and answered it, instantly overcome by Blanca's beauty once again—her eyes aflame with rage, her plump lips pursed in frustration. How he had missed her quirky expressions so much.

"I suck at everything," she screeched. Her pitch jolted him with laughter. "It's not funny!"

"It can't be that bad, can it?" He reclined on his couch and relished in seeing her come to life again.

"One reviewer said my book was their favorite bedtime story because it made her fall asleep after the second page. Another one said my story was worthy of a good arse wiping. *Arse!* People in England even hate my book."

"It sounds like they're only trolling you. It only takes one to start a landslide of negative reviews. How did Max's book do?"

"Damn right they're all trolls. Little, hairy, nutsack trolls. She did great. Fourteen reviews to my three."

"Three? What did the last one say?"

"You don't even want to know. I also had to cough up almost two hundred dollars to pay for copyright fees and a social security number for my book that Maxie insisted we needed to have after all."

Julien waited for her to share the final insult with him, but she only stared off to the side. He could tell she was lying down on her mound of pillows in her Zen Den. "You mean the ISBN?"

"Bingo. That's the one."

"Max won the bet?"

"Maxie won the bet. Nothing but five-star reviews with several write-ups about how great her story was. I'll be sacrificing my next paycheck in a couple of weeks, so she can make her book even fancier with a legit boutique publisher. I, on the other hand, am the one-star queen. All of them. The last review said it deserved negative stars, and Amazon needs to stop letting imbeciles self-publish books."

Julien's smile faded—her rant no longer amusing him, as the pain in her expression burrowed through his heart like a hot blade. "I'm so sorry that you've been hurt by this experience. They are only strangers. Just ignore them. I thought your book was lovely. Sweet."

Blanca looked at him—her throat working down a lump. "Thank you."

"You can always revise it or send it to a professional editor—"

"Once I unpublish it, Amazon still owns my ass for a couple of months. I signed a stupid three-month contract. I don't even want to fix what's wrong with it and try again when I'm allowed to. I suck at writing. I suck at everything right now."

"Please, don't be unkind to yourself. You're an amazing writer with a creative imagination, and those reviewers are wrong about your skills. You don't suck badly at everything. I do recall you sucking quite nicely—"

"Julien, I can't. I can't go there with you. Not anymore."

He nodded then looked away from her, unwilling to let her see that her words stung him. "It is good to see you again. I had forgotten what you looked like."

Worth a shot. Bait her with rejection. Reel her in slowly...

She smiled through her furrowed brow—little creases forming between her eyebrows. "Sure, you have."

"I do need to get some rest. Things have been fairly busy around here." Julien glanced at her then looked away again, exaggerating a yawn that only triggered her to yawn back. "I'll text you again or call. I don't know. Whichever. I am going to have a proof of my new label ready soon. You would like to see it, *non?*"

"Blanc de Blanca? Wouldn't miss it for the world. *Ciao,* Jules."

"*Salut, mon ami* (Goodbye, my friend)."

Jules? Perfect.

Julien ended the call and thought about Blanca's situation. He had to help her. He had to show her how wonderful, how talented, and how successful she could be. He rose and went down the hall to his office across from the dining room. Sitting down at his desk, he pulled Blanca's novel up on his computer in the email he had sent himself to create the PDF and scrolled through the story, giving it a quick once-over.

Rayne, you tireless, troublemaker you. What the hell do I know about romance novels to make your story any better?

As Julien contemplated in what ways he could help Blanca with her book so that he could ease that burden of failure for her, he only drew a frustrating blank. He had to find a way to keep tethered to Blanca through that silly love story. It was the perfect *in.*

Earn her partnership.

Earn her love.

Begin their relationship again.

I'll start with hiring a decent editor first ....

* * *

Blanca

That wasn't nearly as horrifying as Blanca thought it was going to be, speaking to Julien, seeing those beach glass colored eyes again, listening to that thick accent—all of it still washing over her in waves of nostalgia. A month had almost passed since they'd seen one another. He'd been texting her here and there, sometimes a few days in a row, but nothing major.

No professions of love, no mention of a reunion, and no hint of any residual feels.

Just little questions about insignificant things. How's the weather, any rain? How's the hair biz, any celebrity customers? How's the lovebirds, any ring?

That one text last week about gave her a heart attack.

Rain? Never enough. Work? Fine—starting to have regulars. Maxie and Chase, or Masie, or Chax? It was getting harder and harder to tell them apart. They were practically joined at the hip. Twenty-four seven.

No ring, though. Thank God.

Their relationship was moving way too fast as it was, what with Maxie spending all her time at Angel of the Vine Winery working her Wine with Words tour five days a week. It had become a trending venue that other wineries around were catching onto, which was actually kinda cool.

Poetry never tasted so good. And romance so sweet.

But Blanca kept her distance from all things swoony, including accepting any offers to go on any dates. The wound of a broken heart still stung a little, even if Julien seemed to have already moved on like she wanted him to. Messing around with him had cured her of her need for so-called temporary companionship for a while.

She was done like that.

Chapter Nineteen

"False friends are like our shadow, keeping close to us while we walk in the sunshine, but leaving us the instant we cross into the shade."
~Christian Nestell Bovee

Blanca

When you're not in a relationship, and you don't want to be, Valentine's Day can be a beotch. Holed up at home, bunkered down in her Zen Den, and hell bent on surviving the night alone with pride, Blanca sprawled out on her yoga mat like a starfish, belly-up. Not exactly wallowing in a tranquil moment, but the sentiment would have to do.

Her rain CD belted out a storm as she sucked in a deep breath and let it out with a snarl. One minute Blanca had been planning on having strawberry margaritas with Maxie and Chase in town at a local hangout they'd promised to take her to, then, the next minute, Maxie was making all kinds of excuses about suddenly wanting to spend Valentine's Day alone with her main squeeze. Something about it being his idea since it was their first VD and that Blanca's emphatic stance against celebrating love was reason enough to exclude her.

Whatever.

It was bound to happen someday. Third wheel lobbed off, just like that.

Blanca slid her legs together and lifted one of them straight up—the lean muscles firm with tension. She rocked her heel, tipping her toes, focusing her thoughts as thunder and lightning tore through her tiny safe space. She alternated her legs, rocking and tipping, breathing and thinking.

I don't need a man to define me.

Exhale.

I don't need a job to be successful.

Inhale.

Although, my client list is getting longer. Yay me!

Exhale.

Blanca's tank top read, "One Year is Equal to 365 Opportunities." Sarcastic? Nope. Pithy? Depends. What kind of opportunities was she volleying for? She didn't know. All she did have nailed down were her two New Year's Resolutions—to be the most sought-after at Beauty Defined Day Spa and make enough money to travel for a week or so over summer back to Italy where she was fluent in the language and had relatives tucked in every nook and cranny. Adding anything else to her list might need more than three hundred sixty-five tries.

At least she'd won the New Year's bet she had made with Maxie to see who could survive the longest eating a raw vegan diet. Not that she could afford to lose any weight as thin as she was, but she did notice her eyes had brightened up a little bit.

Blanca's iPhone chirped an incoming text.

Julien. Why am I not surprised?

He seemed to have gotten into the habit of texting her while he ate an early lunch at one particular café in Reims during the weekdays. A new routine he had fallen into. "No harm, no foul," he'd claimed in texting her before. Their chat usually nothing more than exchanging descriptions on their food choices—hers always being a late night snack due to the nine-hour time difference.

Blanca lowered her leg and lifted up her cell, taking a peek at what he had said.

Huh? He'd just sent a picture: A fork loaded with lettuce leaves, a cherry tomato, and a red onion ring.

Odd.

Blanca: *Where's the big,*
meaty sandwich of the day?

Julien: *I'm taking some pointers from*
Chase - even bought some weights

Blanca: *What ever for?*
Ur muscular, defined but
still big and soft. You are perfect
just the way you are

Julien: *Speak for yourself, gorgeous.*

"I can't do this right now," she whined and put her phone down at her side. She sat up and crossed her legs, pulling her hands together into a praying pose, closing her eyes.

Namaste, dammit.

Another chirp fired off. Blanca snatched her iPhone up again and let out a sharp groan before checking his text.

Julien: *Sorry. Uncalled for. What's*
your snack tonight?

Blanca lifted her chin up and sighed—her frustration melting away with his kindness.

She got up off the floor and lay down on her chase lounge then texted him again.

Blanca: *I'm protesting all food*
and drinks tonight.

Julien: *Why?*

Blanca: *I was uninvited by CHAX*
to celebrate my awesome status
as perpetually single

Julien: *Who's he? Can I FaceTime you?*

Blanca: *NO*

Julien: *Don't YELL*

Blanca: *FINE!!!!! no*

Julien: *Chax?*

Blanca: *Chase + Max*

Julien: *Clever*

Blanca: *Thx*

Julien: You were all going out together?
Blanca: 'Were' being the operative word –
Three's a crowd on Valentine's Day
Julien: Ah, I see. I put that day behind
me yesterday
Blanca: Lucky you
Julien: Not really, I would've loved
to celebrate the day with someone
that I love

A pit opened up in Blanca's stomach, all gnarly and bleak like a monster within—or was that her hunger pangs just firing off a growl? Either way, she anticipated Julien continuing the thought with some snarky comment about them, you know, about the future they'd never have together, but he didn't send another text.

Ten whole minutes passed before she realized the conversation had come to an end. No *bonne fin de journée* (Have a good evening). No *vous parler bientôt* (Talk to you soon).

That was it.

Heh.

Blanca turned her soundtrack off and unplugged her Himalayan salt rock lamp then went to the kitchen. She rummaged around in the refrigerator, producing an apple and took her measly snack and her mopey butt to the living room to sulk and watch even more television like she had all evening long before ducking into her sanctuary to try to find some peace.

After she finished the apple, she took a picture of the core and sent it in a text to Julien. She couldn't help herself. She had to have the last word. *Sorta.*

She flicked the TV off of whatever infomercial she had zoned out to and went to bed not even bothering to change out of her workout clothes or even brush her teeth.

Happy freakin' Valentine's Day to me.

* * *

The following morning, Blanca was met with puppy-dog moans in her ears as Maxie nuzzled up against her side. "Wake up, wake up, wake up. Hmm, mmm, hmmmm. Come on, Blanca, get up. Hmm, mmm, hhhmm."

"Okay, fine. I'm up. What on earth do you want? It's like—." She grabbed her cell phone off the nightstand. "It's ten in the morn—*eck*. I have to get ready for work in an hour."

Maxie tugged on Blanca's arms and helped her into a sitting position halfway off the bed. "We need to talk."

"Coffee first?"

"I'll make the coffee. You go brush your teeth. Blech."

Blanca waved her hands at Maxie dismissively towards the door and stumbled to the bathroom to brush her teeth and splash cold water on her face.

When Blanca met up with her bestie in the kitchen, a cream and sugared coffee awaited her with a very bouncy, bubbly, and downright annoying Maxie sitting at the table in the breakfast nook.

"Okay, what gives?"

Maxie wiggled in her seat. "I have some good news and some bad news."

"If you tell me you got engaged, I will kill you. You can't jump into marriage with Chase this soon. Marriage is forever, girly-girl."

Maxie slow blinked then plastered on her fake smile—the one that looked all sweet and homey—but held a measurable amount of cutthroat behind her to-die-for, cornflower blue eyes.

"He didn't propose."

Whew. Almost had to wake up for that one.

"Well, don't be sad about it," Blanca said, tossing her hand at her. "That's a good thing. So tell me what's so bad."

Maxie softened a bit. "The good news is I don't want you to pay for a boutique publishing package for me. You're off the hook. I want to make some major changes to my manuscript, and then I'm going to pay for a serious editor to take a look at it. I might even consider pitching my book to an agent and forget going indie all together."

"Good for you," Blanca shrugged. "You win. I win. So what's the bad news?"

Maxie cleared her throat and looked down at her half drank cup of coffee. "I'm moving in with Chase."

Whaaaat!? "What?"

"I'm moving out."

Holy schnikes.

Blanca closed her eyes and pressed her lips together, breathing heavily through her nose. "And this little plan of yours was hatched last night?"

"We'd talked about it in France on our last night in the hotel, but, officially, Chase asked me last night."

"When?"

"Over drinks."

Blanca leveled her eyes with Maxie's. "No dumbass, *when* are you moving out?"

"I was going to say next weekend, but maybe I should change that to today."

"Fine."

"Fine."

They stared at each other for a few seconds then Maxie caved and rolled her eyes. "I thought you'd be pissed."

"You just moved out of Bart's house. Now, you're shacking up with another boyfriend. Just like that."

"Thank you. Thank you very much for throwing my past in my face."

"Your past? Bart wasn't ancient history, you know. That was, like, barely six months ago—"

"Seven!"

"Really?" Blanca set her mug down with a loud crack on the glass-top breakfast table. "I don't care if it was years ago or yesterday. You are rushing into ... into ... what?"

Maxie crossed her arms under her ample breasts that spilled out over the neckline of her pink sweater dress. She leaned back—one eyebrow cocked—with a smug grin on her face. "Go on. Tell me all about how I'm wrong to want to commit to someone. How being in love is a fool's game. Remind me again how I used to feel worthless and fat all because of my ex, and, what was it you called me? Oh yeah, *a dumbass,* for falling for a guy like him."

"Sorry." Blanca shriveled down to about the size of a pesky, buzzing gnat. A pissed-off gnat, but no less significant.

Maxie just continued. "Chase isn't perfect."

"His body is—" *Bzzzt.*

"Shut it."

Okay, now is probably a bad time to make a jokie. "Go on. You were putting me in my place." Blanca rolled her fingers at her to proceed with the tongue-lashing. *Bzzzt.*

"He's perfect for me. He respects me. He supports me. He cares about me. He cares about my family. He even cares about my friends." She motioned to Blanca with both hands then tented her fingertips on the table, very businesslike. "Someday, I am going to marry him. Probably. I hope. But, for now, we are taking it one step at a time, and that includes me moving in with him. I'm at the estate every day with work anyway."

"True," Blanca muttered, parking her hands under her thighs and looking out the bay windows at her backyard with all its tall weeds and unkempt lawn.

So much for being able to afford to hire a landscaper.

"Chase thinks the world of you, Blanca. He really does. He felt awful not including you last night, but he wanted to ask me to move in with him without you doing exactly what you're doing right now."

Blanca slid her gaze over to her bestie with guarded, squinty eyes. "So you're abandoning me next weekend?"

Maxie kept to her businesslike posturing. "You can keep the full month's rent. I'll even give you next month's if you need it."

Blanca's eyes flew open.

Ouch. Now, I'm a charity case.

Her BFF's big blue eyes begged to be let off the hook for screwing her financially when Maxie knew damn well she was in over her head with the new mortgage.

"I'll manage," Blanca lied.

"I'm sure you'll find a new roommate in no time."

"Yep." *Bzzt.*

"Okay. Well, I better let you get ready for work. Things are going good, right? You've been at the spa almost every day now."

"Just dandy." *Bzzt. Bzzt.*

"And we're still going to find crazy yoga classes to go to from time to time."

"Sure." *Bzzt.*

"Nothing is really going to change—that much."

Everything is about to change.

Blanca's heart began to race with anxiety. "Whatever you say."

"Okay, well, I have to head out. I have a tour that starts soon."

"Have a nice day." *Bzzzzzt.*

"You, too."

Maxie got up and grabbed her purse off the kitchen counter then left in a rush.

Blanca stayed put—her empty mug of coffee begging for a refill, her head all swooshy from the adrenalin rush of their fight, and her heart smashed to bits with what she knew was the end of an era in her life.

Chapter Twenty

"Everything is funny, as long as it's happening to somebody else."
~Will Rogers

Julien

When Julien texted Blanca a picture of a soufflé he had made, Blanca immediately replied with the flirtatious sarcasm he'd missed so much.

Blanca: *Pack it up and*
ship it pronto. I'm eating
ALL. THE. FOOD. Tonight!
Julien: *Valentine's Day end*
that bad, eh
Blanca: *The morning after*
was the worst!

That comment shocked Julien unexpectedly. His worst fear was that Blanca would attempt to erase all the memories of their intimate moments by creating new ones with other men—a fear he knew he had to overcome considering he had no claim to her.

He walked around the bar counter in the kitchen and proceeded down the hall to his office where he took a seat at his desk. She was upset about something, and his jealous speculations about her physical encounters with others had to be set aside. He had to make sure he was fully prepared to give her all the right responses necessary to meet her needs, no matter how much it might hurt to hear her reasons for being in turmoil over *the morning after*.

Here we go. God help me. Don't let her say no to seeing me.

Julien: *I'm FaceTiming you*

Before he even released the breath he had held, his iPhone buzzed with her call.

Thank you, God.

"Hi," she squeaked. Her eyes were bright emerald, rimmed in red as though she had been crying.

"Oh, darling. Tell me what's wrong." Not having seen her in such a long time then to see her so broken was almost unbearable.

She blotted her nose with a tissue as he waited. "Maxie is moving out."

"She is? What happened?"

"She fell in *looovvee*."

The wail that accompanied the word *love* made Julien wince and rear back. "It's going to be all right. People fall in love all the time. They've been in love for a while."

Blanca only offered him a lopsided smile as a response while her breath shuddered out of her.

Julien swallowed hard. "What can I do to help you?"

"Tell Chase to change his mind."

"I can't do that. Besides, they belong together more than any two people I've ever met."

Except us.

"I was kind of mean about it when Maxie told me she was leaving me."

"I'm sure she'll forgive you."

I did.

"I'm sorry that I'm bothering you with this. I just don't want to have to explain everything that's happened from start to finish to one of my other friends, you know? Women can turn on each other over the stupidest stuff when someone starts gossiping. I just need to vent to a neutral friend."

So, I'm friend-zoned again. It's a start.

"I understand. Say what you need to say to me. I know Max will always be your best friend. Are you going to find another roommate?"

"I have to. I can't afford this house by myself."

"I'm sure you'll find one easily." Julien watched as she looked around—the camera shaking as the view behind her changed from room to room until it looked like she was outside in the dark. "Where are you?"

"My back patio. The view sucks. No rolling hills of grapevines for me. I have weeds as tall as trees, though. This is my first backyard, and I'm not handling it very well."

Julien smiled at her. Even in tears, she could muster up some humor. He loved that about her. How she could always default to lightheartedness when he could clearly see that she was devastated by the news that Max had decided to take her relationship with his cousin to a whole new level.

"Blanca," he began again, drawing her wandering gaze back to him. "I'm sorry that Max is moving out, but she is still your best friend."

"And my worst enemy right now."

"Just get through this one day at a time." *Like me.* "She isn't abandoning you, she is only doing what is best for their relationship. She needs your support."

Julien could tell that Blanca was weighing his words with skepticism and maybe even a little bit of disgust, but he had to be straight with her. The love between Chase and Max deserved a fighting chance. He had migrated away from his petty jealousies to a place of respect for what they were trying to build between them.

"I guess I'm just going to have to learn the hard way how to take care of myself all over again. I did it once before."

"Come again? She's moved out on you before?"

"Yes. Everyone I care about always sticks it to me. Sometimes the ones I care about the most do it more than once."

Julien searched Blanca's countenance—her eyes unfocused, her face lost in the shadows of darkness outside. He wished he could hold her, kiss her, and comfort her with his love.

"There's something I want to show you that might cheer you up." Julien rose and went back into the kitchen and pulled a champagne bottle out of the cupboard and held the camera up to its label—shimmering metallic white embossed with sparkling blue snowflakes.

The words Blanc de Blanca scrolled across the label in silver script.

Her mouth dropped open. "Oh, look at that! Your label."

"*Our* label."

"It's beautiful."

"If you need anything, even if you only need some quiet company, I'm just a phone call away."

Blanca looked at him, angling the camera so that her entire face filled the screen on his phone—her exotic beauty overwhelming him with pangs of longing and desire. "Thanks, Jules. I think I've got this. I just have to be strong and keep moving forward."

"See, there's my … friend. Strong and independent."

She flashed him a sincere smile. "I'll talk to you later, Jules."

"*Bonne nuit.*"

"*Ciao.*"

* * *

Blanca

By Saint Patrick's Day, Blanca was on her third roommate, a lanky girl with armpit hair, which was fine—she didn't smell or anything—but she could've used a hipster make-over big time with the whole rat's nest entity she was cultivating on top of her head.

Either go full dreads or don't, but wear your hair like the crown of glory it should be.

Blanca's last two roomies were a whole other story. The first one had been a staunch businessman. Yes, *a man.* He had been the first person to answer the ad after it had been running for two whole weeks. She had to be non-discriminatory at that point needing rent money ASAP.

Day one, he had been way too pushy. He had wanted to convert the Zen Den into his office. He had even offered to pay a couple hundred more a month for the room once he had filled her home with a huge moving truck full of all his crap. He had been crowding them both out of her home with unusual furniture like an indoor hammock that had hung from the ceiling and a chair that looked like a sadistic torture device that doubled as a masseuse.

After Blanca had said *no*, a few days later, he had countered with trading rooms, claiming the master bedroom suited him better, and he needed the space for his rowing machine, that—*let me tell you ladies*—he probably never used because he was kind of beefy, and not in a sexy dad-bod kinda way. Again, he had offered her practically twice the rent, but she had given him another resounding *nope*.

So, then he had tried to come onto her the day after that. He'd tried to work his way into her bedroom after all with some awkward and obviously insincere sweet talk. When she had to knee him in the groin after he had grabbed her in the kitchen that morning and had planted a wet one on her mouth without a warning, he had told her he'd never date a broad who didn't appreciate getting to share all his expensive things.

So, that's what it's like to live with a guy? Screw that.

Roomie number two had been sweet. *Too sweet.* She had prefaced everything she said or did with an, *I'm sorry, but*, or an, *I don't mean to, but*, every single time. All Blanca had wanted to do was just scream at the top of her lungs, "Get a damn drink of water like a normal person—they're your glasses in the cupboard now, too!"

And Blanca kind of did just a teensy-weensy bit one morning when she had caught the little cutie pie trying to quench her thirst at the faucet like it was a drinking fountain, lapping up the stream of water as if she were a kid in the park. She had even mumbled something about needing to go buy her own cups, so she wouldn't be a burden.

The girl even *yes, ma'amed* Blanca at least a dozen times the day Blanca had finally reached her wit's end with the mousey girl and had told her it just wasn't going to work out. Of course, the poor thing had cried when she left, all apologies for having bothered her, which only made Blanca feel like the biggest turd in the world.

So enter roomie number three, Skyler. The hipster who grew up in Napa Valley. She wasn't much of a talker. Wasn't around most of the time. And periodically let it slip that her family was weird, even to her, like—lived in a giant tee-pee in their backyard while they were growing up, leaving the house to her brother and her to stay in—weird.

Skyler said she had learned how to cook when she was seven. Rabbit being her specialty. *Not vegan, I know. Go figure. But wild varmint, ew.* She also told Blanca that it was vital for both their reproductive systems to breathe in a little moonshine—the actual glow from the moon, not the booze—when She was full. *Good to know*. But, the fruit clearly didn't fall far from the weird tree with that one.

They were nearing the two-week mark on their happy-go-lucky cohabitation when Blanca started noticing little things that irked her. She had made it clear to Skyler that she was welcome to any and everything in the house, just to be respectful of her things, and, at some point, be willing to let her do something about the hairy scribble parked on the top of her head.

Skyler actually appreciated the makeover gesture and agreed to pay her a visit at the spa someday, claiming depression had gotten the best of her self-care. She said she'd gotten over the hump with the use of herbs but hadn't bothered dealing with her hair yet.

Legal herbs that she promised to only partake of outside on the back porch now and again.

Whatever.

To each her own when it came to coping with a mental illness.

She was cool like that.

Blanca wasn't into drugs of any kind and never wanted to be. The idea of opening her mind up, only to have something her nonna said could crawl out of hell and take up residence in that void, scared the beejeebies out of her. But, if California didn't care that her roomie toked up, why should she?

Just not in the house.

Nobody wants her new home to smell like sweaty ass.

Just sayin'.

What started irking Blanca was that every time she went into her Zen Den to chill out she'd notice subtle changes to the space, like her lamp was on the opposite side of the desk, and some of the slip covers on her pile of throw pillows were on inside out. The yoga mat even had little symbols penciled in on the four corners that looked like hieroglyphics. What infuriated her the most was her wall map with all the heart stickers identifying her travels. Skyler had started peeling them off and re-adhering them to the glass upside down.

What the freak?

On April Fool's Day, of all days, her roomie had finally shown up at Beauty Defined Day Spa for her makeover. Blanca tried to probe about the mysterious tweaks to her personal sanctuary while she began to untangle the girl's wild mane. Skyler said it was for her own good but wouldn't elaborate. She didn't have much else to say because she was all giggles and long wales of snorting laughter. Apparently, Skyler needed to light up before getting her hair done.

No cool showing up at my place of work wasted. It's the same as being drunk.

Blanca's talent for patience and an eye for detail took that girl's matted clump of straw-colored neglect and transformed it into shaggy, silken locks of metallic rose gold with chunky highlights in custom blended peach. Cell phones were videotaping and clicking away as Skyler went from a sorry sight of self-neglect to a glamorous representation of all that was hip, sexy, and laid-back in their generation.

By the time Blanca realized that her new roomie had been trying to hex her since moving in, Skyler had become both a blessing and a curse. The before and after photos and videos of the makeover that the other stylists had plastered all over their social media accounts that day had gone viral in the valley. Several of the pictures had also been added to the spa's website alongside the story of Skyler's battle with depression that she had given a formal interview about.

The fact that she was totally wasted and having the time of her life while getting her hair done wasn't a negative in eyes of the Beauty Defined Day Spa's owners. In fact, they thought it was a hoot and didn't mind capitalizing on all the attention their business was getting from the peculiar story.

A steady stream of new customers poured into the luxury spa every day in the week that followed and most of them insisted on having Blanca style their hair, including a celebrity. Julien was so tickled when she shared that tidbit over their text-talk meal together the day after it had happened. A mealtime routine she'd come to look forward to between them.

A country musician named Skeeter Dee that she'd never heard of before, because country music wasn't her forte, had even showed up with an entire posse of skinny boys in cowboy boots. They were in town for a concert, and they had caught wind of all the hoopla at the spa, so they had to see for themselves what it was all about. The singer was so taken with Blanca's beauty and sass, he invited her to join him on tour as his personal stylist, to which she said, "not in a million years," but the opportunity to travel and do hair simultaneously got her thinking of all kinds of crazy, wanderlust opportunities.

So that was how Skyler had been a blessing in Blanca's life.

The curse part, though, came the day after the cowboy had strolled into town. Blanca had to tell her new roomie to get out and take all her creepy juju with her after doing a quick internet search on all the symbols she'd found written in red lipstick liner along the baseboards in her dining room.

Apparently, or *not so apparently*, Skyler had been trying to harvest her soul.

I kid you not.

The day after Skyler moved out, Nonna Alba sent the family priest all the way from San Francisco to right what was wrong in Blanca's house. She had let it slip to her ma how bad things had been going in the roommate department, and the next thing you know, Father Seabridge was knocking on her door. A few Our Father's and some holy water sprinkles later, Blanca was perfectly content to live alone for the rest of her life if need be.

Chapter Twenty-One

"All the beautiful sentiments in the world weigh less than a single lovely action."
~James Russell Lowell

Julien

Julien sipped on some espresso as he sat alone at a bistro table outside of a café in Reims. He could barely make out Blanca's face as the bright morning sun glinted off his iPhone screen.

"My plan is to market that particular Blanc de Blanca over Christmas. It's a small batch. We'll vend it out of our tasting room in Épernay. It's not all that I want to do with my brand, but it's a beginning. I have other plans in the works. Believe it or not, Chase is really going out of his way to help me."

In more ways than this one.

"Chase, huh?" Blanca looked away from the camera. "So what's Chax up to these days, anyway?"

"They're doing well. I thought you were on good terms with Max, *non?*"

"We've only gone to three yoga classes together since she moved out. *Trios.* That's it. No lunch dates. No phone calls. She's only texted me twice in the last month. I've texted her at least a million times, maybe more, but all I get are crickets in return."

"Crickets?"

"You know, like you're outside at night, and it's so quiet that all you hear are their chirps. Like this." She held her cell out to what looked like a lawn studded with a few trees. It was too dark to distinguish. A faint sound of high-pitched, squeaky *thrumming* could be heard.

Must be the crickets.

"Don't give up on her. She still needs you in her life even if she's not as present as she used to be in yours."

Julien's heart twisted inside of him at his advice.

Like me, my love.

Blanca inhaled and let out her breath with a small whimper. "On a happier note, I'm making enough money at work to officially plan my summer trip."

"Italy, *oui*? Please, tell me Italy is still your destination."

"*Sì*! Get this. I applied to be an understudy for this famous Italian stylist a few weeks ago. He is leading up a team that will be working with a rookie fashion designer for her first, small-time runway show that's part of some graduate rites of passage with a fashion institute. I got the call this afternoon that I'm in. Just like that. Milan, baby!"

A throng of excitement welled up in Julien. She'd only be a quick flight away. "When?"

"I arrive the first week of July. I can only swing one week, including travel days, but I've never interned before. This is a whole new experience for me."

"I'm glad success has found you again." Julien made a mental note of when she would be in Italy and contemplated whether he should invite himself for a visit and risk rejection or simply surprise her and make it harder for her to turn him away.

Speaking of surprises, he'd been planning one that would be manifesting itself by the time her trip came around in a couple of months. Something he had convinced himself would win her heart forever.

Julien had finally decided he wasn't interested in pursuing anyone else but Blanca. He knew in his heart, she was perfect for him. Their undeniable chemistry, both physical and emotional, and the relentless ache he felt with her absence was all the proof he needed.

His twin sisters had been urging him onward offering their assistance to help him find a wife, but he continued to reject their help. He had Victoria on his side, encouraging him to keep steadfast in his pursuit of Blanca. Julien's baby sister understood how he couldn't casually throw his heart to the wind and expect random dates with their older sisters' acquaintances would amount to someone as intriguing as his American beauty.

Blanca was not only young and beautiful, bursting with liveliness, she also had common sense and sought out the best in everyone—always caring, always supportive. Those were the qualities he wanted in a life partner. Victoria understood Julien's need for someone like that long before he did. Blanca's strong independence drew him into her, but it was also the one admirable quality in her that kept them apart.

"I think you definitely need to plan for extra days," Julien replied, finishing his espresso and checking the time on the watch he'd started to wear. "I am going to have to bid you *adieu, mon chèr ami* (farewell, my sweet friend)."

"*Addio, ti bella bestia* (Farewell, you gorgeous beast)," she purred in Italian.

"What was that?" he asked, gathering his briefcase and rising from the table.

"That's for me to know and you to figure out," she winked and hung up.

She is definitely going to be mine again someday.

***

In the two months that followed, Blanca and Max had managed to work out a new routine of meeting almost every Saturday for yoga and sometimes on Tuesdays to share a quick lunch at À la Vôtre!, the winery's restaurant. The context of their conversations had been kept a mystery to Julien, though he did his best to prod and pry the details from Blanca during their daily FaceTime chats.

Blanca kept insisting her friendship with Max felt like a house of cards, ready to collapse at the slightest disruption, but Julien continued to try his best to assure her that Max was still there for her and only adapting to a new and exciting life with his cousin.

Julien's daily communication with Blanca stayed the course over his early morning tasks and her late-night insomniac activities, and sometimes it was even the other way around. After a long day, he would collapse in bed at night with Blanca on the phone, and she would be begging him to bore her to death so she could finally drift off to sleep in the early morning. Julien knew he was imbedding himself into Blanca's life irrevocably, even if it only wore the modest label, *friend.*

"Have you gotten my present, yet? You haven't said anything to me about it. I'm wondering if it was lost in the mail," Julien asked with a yawn, as he watched her shuffle around her house, packing for her trip to Italy while he tidied up the kitchen.

"Present? Aw, you got me a present?" Blanca's twenty-sixth birthday came and went a couple of days ago. She had celebrated with Maxie and Chase at a local bar with drinks, and it bothered him that he couldn't be there with all of them.

"I haven't picked up my mail for the last few days." A flash of light washed over the screen, and he could tell she was walking down the street to retrieve her mail from the cluster mailbox. "Got it." She held up a large package with a thick stack of envelopes to show him.

"I was worried you wouldn't have it by the time you leave. When is your flight again?"

"Which one?" she drawled, heading back to her house as he headed up stairs on his end of the call.

"All of them. I'm allowed to worry about you flying alone." He crawled into bed and rested his head on a stack of pillows.

"I'm flying out of Sacramento at six o'clock, then, from San Francisco, I head to New York. From there, I go to Heathrow in England, then to Malpensa Airport. I should be in Milan before my fiftieth birthday I hope."

He grinned at her joke. "Promise you'll text me at every terminal?"

"You and Maxie both."

"I'm glad the two of you have reconciled."

It's perfect timing with my surprise you're about to unwrap.

The time had finally come for Julien to unveil the project he had been working on for months—the gift he was certain would nudge their friendship closer towards a solid relationship.

"We're what Americans call BFFs—best friends forever. At least that's what I keep telling myself. I hate that I feel like one wrong move, and she'll ditch me in a hot minute for your cousin once and for all."

"And what about us? Will our friendship last forever?" The words were out of his mouth before he had a chance to weigh their potential effect on her.

She had just torn open her present, though, and his surprise claimed her response.

"*Proprio Come Rayne* (Right as Rayne)," she read, examining the cover. It had a digitally enhanced close-up of a young woman's face with a single curl of golden hair falling across her cheek, and a stormy ocean reflected in her sea-green eyes. Blanca held up the book for Julien to see. The back cover was an iridescent, gradient shade of emerald green to turquoise with a brief summary in white typeface. "You bought me an Italian romance novel. Cool—wait. *Rayne?* Julien, what did you do?"

* * *

Blanca

Blanca sat down on the edge of her bed between her carry-on duffel bag and her suitcase. She flipped the camera around so that it showed the book to Julien. She set the book in her lap and stared at the cover in awe—the author's name, Blanca Grazia, finally registering to her. She opened the front cover—her eyes darting around the page, then, she turned another, and another.

"It's in Italian." Her words tumbled out with garbled excitement.

"Surprise."

"*Right as Rayne?*"

"I'm sorry, but your original title didn't translate well. I hope that is all right?"

"I love it," she gulped. "How? When?" She couldn't believe it. She wasn't sure she wanted to believe it. And yet, she was overwhelmed with excitement to see her name on the cover of an actual book.

Her book.

This amazing gift in her hands that could potentially send Maxie into a ... *rage.*

Oh, crap.

"It's your proof copy. I hired an editor to polish and translate your manuscript into Italian."

"An editor?"

"*Oui.* Her name is Amilianna Rossi. I hope you don't mind, but I gave her permission to create a prologue out of some of the superfluous material in chapter one, so that it introduces three princesses much like the princes in Basille's fairytale. Mademoiselle Rossi said she needed to smooth out the connections to the plot, but, overall, she thinks your story is wonderful. She also included the cover art in her fees. If there is anything about the book or cover you don't like, make note of it, and she'll address the changes. Then, once you approve your proof, I will have as many printed as you want through a print-on-demand company she recommends."

Blanca's jaw went slack as she flipped the screen back around to see him—her guts doing summersaults with excitement and worry. "You did this for me?"

"I've been working on it for a long time. I wanted it to be a surprise. I'm very proud of you for writing a book, and I wanted you to be proud, too. I owe our friendship to this book," he added.

"This novel might be the coolest gift anyone's ever given me, but I've got to tell you that I'm in total shock. My story sucked." Her honeyed cheeks blushed into a rosy glow. "You said that editor cleaned this thing up?"

Blanca started to read through the first paragraph of the prologue.

"That's what she does. She really enjoyed your book. In fact, she was considering pitching it to a publishing company she does editorial work for."

Blanca tore her eyes away from the page and back onto Julien. "No. No, no. No, don't do that. Maxie will never speak to me again if I flaunt this bad boy in her face right now as it is."

Julien tipped his nose and laughed. "Don't panic on me. I would never do anything to jeopardize your friendship, but I think you're worried over nothing."

"Not nothing. All she ever does is whine that she doesn't have enough time to polish her book before she said she'll even try to get an editor to take a look at it."

"So, she, ehm, she is going to try to get her novel traditionally published then?"

"Oh, yeah. Absolutely. If I show her this beautiful book, she'll flip. Maxie doesn't handle jealousy very well." She smirked, holding her book up next to her face, flaunting a cheesy grin for him to see.

Julien flashed her a humored smile then raked his fingers through his shaggy hair and looked away. "We all love you, Blanca. Not even Max could ever hate you, I'm sure of it. You can read it on your trip."

"I love that idea." She stood up and tossed it into her overnight bag. "It'll be excellent practice for me to brush up on my fluency. I can speak Italian, but reading it might take me some time. I love a good challenge like this." Blanca looked at him glassy-eyed and full of joy.

"There you go," Julien said, muffling another yawn as the night waned on for him.

This guy is incredible. Look at me. Not failing behind Maxie's back.

* * *

Julien

I need to call Chase and tell him to keep his mouth shut about that book.

Chapter Twenty-Two

"Disenchantment, whether it is a minor disappointment or a major shock, it is the signal that things are moving into transition in our lives."
~William Throsby Bridges

Blanca

With only a week total to get some wanderlust out of her system, two traveling days included, Blanca was settled into her seat ready for flight *numero uno* from SMF to SFO. She barely had time to take her seatbelt off before she had to put it back on again for touchdown then board her second flight bound for New York.

That flight took almost six hours. Five of which, she'd snoozed through after stumbling over the prologue in her book just after takeoff. Speaking Italian was a breeze, but reading it, not so much.

Though, the challenge of reading *Right as Rayne* excited Blanca, it was still a little overwhelming considering how tired she was. It had been a long night of insomnia with that adrenaline rush that always flooded her body just before her latest travel adventure. Sleeping before the crack of dawn just wasn't her thing anyway, and switching her sleep patterns to adjust to being in Europe seemed like a better plan. At least, that's the story she told herself just before she dozed off on her second flight.

Even though Blanca had been to Italy several times before, she was a virgin to Milan. The thrill of immersing herself in a new part of Italy had her humming with excitement. The opportunity to work under the famed Italian hair stylist, known only as Giuseppe, was an honor she couldn't believe had been granted to her.

She had included the articles on her being the best stylist in Sacramento's magazine and a screenshot of the makeover post on her boss's website in her application to intern, and those accolades were enough to catch Giuseppe's attention for his current project. Blanca was one of two hair stylists along with two make-up artists who would be working with seven runway models.

Opportunities galore!

Blanca kept in touch with her friends as she waited to board her next flight for London, England, lumping Julien, Chase, and Maxie into a group text. She figured, why not knock it out at the same time? Her parents got a separate text just in case she forgot to keep things PG. Julien was chill with the whole shameless flirting thing she had started up with him again a few weeks ago, and nothing pleased her more than to embarrass Maxie even when she was thousands of miles away. The fact that Chase was on the thread, too, was an added bonus.

Blanca: *I survived round one*
and two of coach

Blanca kicked her heels up, crossing her ankles over her duffel bag in front of her as she sat in the terminal of JFK.

Julien: *Glad to hear you're surviving,*
but how were the other passengers
holding up being trapped on a plane
with you?

She shook her head with a big smile. *Julien and his sarcasm. Always good for a laugh.*

Blanca: *Bahaha, they endured my snores*
Maxie: *Don't forget to pick me*
up a souvenir in England
Blanca: *What about a bobby's baton*
Maxie: *I'm afraid to ask why*
Chase: *Do tell*

Blanca: *Every time she says 'spank'...*

Blanca let out a laugh loud enough to cause a few people around her to look her way.

Chase: *LOL, she does say that a lot*

Maxie: *Never mind*

Blanca: *At least you're getting some. Is it wrong I kinda enjoyed getting felt up by the last security guy?*

Julien: *Report him NOW*

Maxie: *Down boy*

Blanca: *OK, Maxie, I'll grab you something at the airport. I'll have some time to kill*

Julien: *When does your next flight take off?*

Blanca: *Speaking of which, gotta board*

Julien: *Take care*

Maxie: *Be safe*

Chase: *Bye*

Much to Blanca's frustration, the flight was packed, and her carry-on had to be crammed in an overhead bin above a snobby businessman's seat. He sneered at her any time she tried to shimmy something out of it, so she just sat still and huffed.

Though, she'd splurged for her last two flights to be first class, the only comforts that came out of it on that particular flight were all the free crystal flutes of Champagne the attendant kept serving her between snacks, meals, more snacks, and a tray full of pastries that tasted like dog food compared to Julien's desserts.

Ah, Julien. The best at everything.

Blanca allowed too much bubbly and sheer boredom to envelop her in another needful nap between all the calories. Champagne, like Julien, had a way of comforting her, and extra sleep seemed like a win all the way around.

When she touched down at Heathrow Airport and had an hour-long wait before she had to board another airplane again for her last stretch to Milan, Blanca shopped. Then, she texted her group chat a picture of two graphic tees she'd snagged in a gift shop—one pink, one yellow—that both read, "If I had a British Accent, I'd Bloody Never Shut Up!"

New yoga tops on fleek. Bam.

Then Maxie, or actually, Chax, texted a picture back.

... Their hands ...

... Fingers entwined ...

... And a big, fat rock weighing down their obnoxiously loving gesture.

Blanca sat upright from her reclined position in a booth at an eatery in the terminal. She brought her phone up to her nose to get a better look at the iceberg parked on top of her bestie's finger.

No f—ing way.

Blanca: *WHAT?*

Maxie: *I said, YES*

Chase: *To be specific, she said, 'Okie-dokie'*

Blanca: *You guys just moved in together!!!!*

Julien: *In all fairness, they've been living together for four months*

Blanca: *No one's asking you ... wait, you knew about this, Jules?*

Blanca jumped to her feet, dismissing the awkward glances thrown at her by her fellow flight-mates who were sitting around her at the other booths and tables.

Chase: *I told him yesterday*

Maxie: *I knew you'd be mad at me*

Blanca: *Shuh*

Blanca eased back down in her seat, glaring at everyone who was giving her the stink-eye.

Julien: *Please see the good in this*

Blanca: *Don't tell me what to do, traitor*

Chase: *Why are you so against us?*

The word *us* made her nostrils flair.

Blanca: *You guys rush into*
everything. Can't you two just
slow it down?

Chase: *Why? I love her*
She loves me. We are happy
together

Blanca: *Maxie? Hello?!*
Why does he have to speak for
you now?

Chase: *She's crying. You made*
her cry

Blanca: *Julien? Sorry I snapped*
at you, I didn't mean to. Have you
abandoned me now, too?

Julien: *Never*

Blanca: *Please tell them to*
slow down! They don't listen to me
... Sorry I made you cry Maxie

Chase: *We are planning on a*
long engagement

Blanca: *Oh. Okay. Whatever.*
What? Like years?

Blanca wiggled out of her seat again and slung her duffel bag strap over her shoulder then headed for her gate.

Maxie: *No, I've always wanted to*
be a June bride

Blanca stopped dead in her tracks and stared at the text. *Mother F— You did not just go there!*

Blanca: *Hey, there she is—again,*
sorry ur crying, my bad

She started walking again, shaking her head in a fury.

I was supposed to be the June bride!

Blanca sidestepped several carry-ons in the waiting area at her gate and sat down in the only seat left as her flight was about to board, and, by the looks of it, once again, it seemed to hint that it would be packed like the last one.

Maxie: *It's fine. You've always been envious of my relationship with Chase. I get it*

Blanca dropped her iPhone in horror. *Oh, damn, girl.* She scrambled to pick it back up off the carpet before someone stepped on it. She checked the text again to see if she'd made a mistake in what she had read. *Nope. Maxie grew some balls. Good for you. Way off on your accusations, but you go on the comebacks.*

Julien: *Are you still there?*

Blanca: *Yep. Dropped my phone in horror*

Julien: *Everything is going to be fine*

Blanca: *You got that right. In about three hours, I'm going to be sipping Frangelico and living it up in Milan with a bucket-load of models*

Julien: *You'll fit right in*

Blanca: *Bahahaha*

Julien: *Max, you still around?*

Chase: *What do you want?*

Maxie: *Yes*

Julien: *I'll talk to her about it*

Blanca: *Heellllooo, I'm right here!!!*

Blanca stood up and stepped in line to board with the other first class flyers.

Maxie: *I'm sorry I was mean earlier*

Blanca: *Don't' be. I'm proud of you U R way off, but congrats on sprouting some gonads – just don't start hating me because I'm mad at you! We'll argue about this later. I'm boarding my flight right now*

Chase: *Take care*

Blanca handed her ticket to the attendant then shuffled along with the others down the carpeted tunnel of weird smells. *If you fly, you understand.*

Maxie: *I'll talk 2 you tomorrow*
Blanca: *It is tomorrow, but sure,*
call me whenever, CIAO

Blanca found her first class seat on the airplane and sat down with a huff. As she was about to turn off her cell phone again in preparation of her final flight, she noticed another message notification pop up.

Julien: *I'm still here, love*
Blanca: *Of course u are,*
you're always here for me
Julien: *Call me when you land*

Blanca leaned her head back on her headrest and whimpered, blinking back the tears threatening her happy feels that she was almost in Milan, hours away from another new journey taking hold of her life.

You know, the one spiraling out of control at the moment.

She swallowed hard and responded to Julien.

Blanca: *I don't want to talk about it*
Julien: *Of course, darling, call me*
anyway. We have a novel to discuss
Blanca: *About that... I haven't had a*
chance to read much of it—but I'll try
again. I have to go now, bye, ciao,
arrivederci, whatever, waah, I hate
how I feel right now!
Julien: *It will be fine, I'll see you soon*

Blanca powered her phone off. Then, it dawned on her what Julien had said.

See me? Soon? FaceTime? Must be FaceTime. But what if?

She powered her phone up again as a steady stream of people flowed by her down the aisle to their seats. She started texting a reply. First it was, *What?* Then, it was, *What do you mean?* Then, it was, *You better not be planning to ...* and finally, she resolved to just shut her phone off again.

She was on overload as it was.

Blanca was exhausted emotionally, spent on dealing with the bomb her bestie had just dropped on her, pissed that everyone knew about it but her, and hurt that they all waited until she was out of strangulating reach of Chax to inform her. As lame as she knew her pathetic reasons to be, she felt like Julien was her only friend left in the world, and the thought of seeing him, as much as it scared her, could only help, at that point.

She was desperate like that.

In fact, screw it. I need my French lover to make everything in my life feel good again. One week in Champagne. One week in Milan. One week somewhere else on some other journey. This is my new ME. To hell with everyone and everything else.

Blanca pulled her novel out of her carry-on and zipped the bag back up, handing it off to a flight attendant who placed it in the overhead compartment for her. The elderly gentleman who had just slipped into the seat next to her nearest the window greeted her in Italian and motioned for her to let him out of his seat again. She obliged and then sat back down as he hobbled to the bathroom.

Blanca cracked open her book and held it to her nose, drawing in a deep breath of all that yummy, fresh paper smell.

Mine. All because of Jules.

Screw you Chax and your perfect life together.

She thumbed past the epilogue she'd already read then began to peruse the first chapter to help get her mind off things.

Things like ...

... that gargantuan, sparkly diamond making her bestie abandon her once and for all.

Stupid, pretty rock.

... and that fabulous June wedding her bestie was going to have.

That was supposed to be me, dammit.

Not to mention the fact that her *fiancé* was a total hottie.

Chase just is. I have no shame.

At least she had Julien to count on.

Jules—my friend, my confidant, my lover, and now my potential rendezvous? Why not? I'll talk him into flying over to see me.

Maybe, she was hurt.

Maybe, she was mad.

Maybe, all she ever wanted ... all she ever fought for ... all she never gained in return was everything life was just handing over to her bestie, one perfect scenario at a time.

Maybe, just maybe, she was ... *JEALOUS.*

Oh, no-no-no-no-no! This can't be happening to me!

Blanca's eyes lost focus on the page that she had been reading, her heart wrenched itself into a bloody, pounding mass of ache, and tears of rage, sorrow, frustration, and grief clouded her vision. She closed the book and shoved it into the seat pocket in front of her. She curled her knees up to her chest and wrapped her arms around them, rocking back and forth, silently cursing at her friends, at herself, at everyone around her who stared at her like she was crazy—because, *let's be real here,* she was.

She was absolutely certifiable, and it showed.

"I need a shot of something strong. Right. Now."

The flight attendant, who had rushed over to her to assess the situation, nodded dutifully, and, within a few seconds, handed her a pungent, golden drink on ice. The elderly man returned from the restroom and nudged past her back into his seat, forcing Blanca to put on a happy face and reciprocate his cordial small talk.

Between, *"Grazie yous (Thank you),"* and *"Pregos (You are welcome),"* she tipped her drink and let the burning liquid flow down her throat.

Preggo. That'll be next on Maxie's 'perfect life' check-off list. Gah!

The captain came on and told everyone to buckle up, to which she did, then slammed her eyes shut in silence, letting the alcohol gurgling in her tummy take over her tiny, size 2 body, sending her into a comfortable, tingly numb.

When the sensation began to wear off and her worries returned mid-flight, she had one more shot of whateverthehellthatwas, enabling her to feel absolutely, irreparably, helplessly *fine* about everything, just like Julien said it would be. All. Of. It.

Jealous? Pft.

Blanca shook her head—an absurd grin spreading across her face as she systematically dismissed all her troubles as if she were doing a countdown to her week long break from reality once she stepped foot in Milan.

Ahh, Julien. Jules. The only one in the world I have left. What a flippin' mess.

Blanca no longer needed attendants to dote on her anymore, lest they still wanted a good laugh. She had prattled on and on about all her plans to make it big as a stylist in the fashion industry for a whole week playing with hair on a bunch of glamorous models. *Pft.* Nothing was going to bother her while on vacation. Nothing. *Niente.* She had to make the most of her time and satiate her wanderlust, sans the mountain of troubles that awaited her at home.

As soon as the flight ended, Blanca bid her elderly travel buddy goodbye. She chose to let everyone else on the airplane pass by her while she waited in her first class seat before she snatched her duffel bag out of the overhead compartment and sashayed out of the terminal like she owned the joint. The booze may have helped bolster her self-confidence a bit because, when she walked right into the middle of an entourage of paparazzi snapping pictures and yelling, "*Bellissimo,*" at *her,* or so she thought for a hot minute, she brandished a saucy smile and thanked them all for welcoming her to Milan.

That was until the drop dead gorgeous object of their desire strolled past her to board the airplane long before anyone else would be allowed to, leaving a floundering pile of lusty, young men in her wake.

"*Chi è lei* (Who is she?)" Blanca asked the nearest twenty-something buffoon, drooling all over himself.

"*Donatella De Luca. Lei è un'attrice nella soap opera solo ama la speranza. Essa reproduce la speranza* (Donatella De Luca. She is an actress in the soap opera, Love's Only Hope. She plays Hope)!" He wept as he clutched his fists to his chin.

Good grief. Have some humility.

Blanca carried on, rocking her hips, clicking her heels, and shaking her troubles away as she abandoned her foolish hopes and dying dreams to the past and immersed herself, once again, into a new adventure called Milan, Italy.

Chapter twenty-three

"Love is composed of a single soul inhabiting two bodies."
~Aristotle

Julien

All Julien could think about was how he was going to handle Blanca's outrage when he told her he wouldn't take *no* for an answer in wanting to visit her. She needed him. After the way she'd handled the news of his cousin's proposal to her best friend, he had to be there for her, whether she wanted him to be or not. He owed it to her. He owed it to himself.

***Julien:** What hotel are you staying in?*

***Blanca:** The pretty one*

***Julien:** S'il vous plaît?*

***Blanca:** Begging me now, are we?*

A few seconds later, Blanca sent him a picture of the hotel's welcoming booklet that included the address.

***Julien:** Can I FaceTime you?*

***Blanca:** Sure, but I'm Headachy, so I might still be snippy. I made a drunkass fool out of myself on the plane.*

I'm no better than Skyler being
wasted at my job –
Julien: *We all make mistakes*
Blanca: *You have no idea*
Julien: *I'm FaceTiming you now*
Blanca: *Ok, but I don't want*
2 talk about it ... them ...
u know what I mean?!

Julien FaceTime'd Blanca and waited for her to answer the call. When she finally did, she was tucked in bed, peeking out from under a bright white sheet, groggy and every bit of beautiful.

She quirked up the corner of her mouth and smiled at him. "Hey, sexy."

"*Bonsoir.* Are you all right?" He returned the smile as he sat down at his desk and began searching on his computer for flights to Milan.

"I am A-Okay. I'm in a fancy hotel, talking to a hot guy, even if you're an idiot to be wasting your time with me. But, you're gorgeous, so I don't mind. Don't mind at all."

"You don't sound okay."

"I'm hung over, *capish?*"

"Ah, *je comprends* (I understand)," he grinned half-heartedly. "I'm sorry about—"

"Shhh. Don't say it. Don't say anything about *them.* I'm on vacation. I've got plans to live the good life for a whole week. I've decided to leave all my woes behind me in America like a bad Skeeter Dee song."

He leaned his iPhone up against a container of pens and pencils so that he could type faster, locking in a flight that would arrive the following afternoon. "I have to say one thing. I am sorry I didn't tell you as soon as I knew. I didn't think it was my place to share something that should come directly from your best friend."

"If you would have told me, then it would have come from my best friend."

He froze and shifted his eyes to hers. It's one thing to be navigating the friend-zone, but it's an entirely other to be elevated to the status of being her *best* friend. "Come again?"

"You heard me. You're all I have now, Jules." She closed her eyes and moaned. "Even though I have no idea what to do with you right now."

"I'm coming to see you tomorrow."

Her eyes flew open. "You're what?"

"I just booked my flight. You can be upset if you like, but, ehm, I need to see you. I miss you."

Blanca studied Julien's face for a moment with no particular expression, just a point-blank stare on his iPhone screen. Then she smiled. "I miss you, too, Jules. Come to me baaa-by."

That was far too easy.

"I'm planning on staying with you," he continued, testing the waters with more details as his worry for her increased.

"Sounds good."

Huh?

"You're seriously all right with this?"

"*Sì*, but I start my training first thing in the morning, so you'll have to take a cab to the hotel. I'll let the concierge on duty know that my sexy, French lover will be arriving later and that you'll be needing a room key."

Julien couldn't tell if Blanca was abiding by his plan out of a place of passive aggressive defiance or docile defeat. Would she tear into him when he arrived or embrace him and pick up where they'd left off in Champagne? Either way, his mind raced with plans to extricate himself from the status of friendship and restore his rightful title as her lover.

He had done everything he could to seduce her with his acts of kindness, tending to her emotional wants, helping her feel accomplished, and conducting himself as a gentleman throughout their conversations, but it was time to take hold of his own wants once again. Blanca had become the purpose behind his ambition for success and his drive towards completing his own dreams. He needed only to close the deal and solidify their commitment to one another. Then Blanca would be his bride someday the way Chase had finally found his.

"I don't know what to say. I, ehm, I thought you'd be upset with me." He picked up his iPhone and powered off his computer then headed out of his office.

"Yesterday, I would've been outraged. Right now not so much. I need you. There, I said it. I have to have something for me, and that would be you, in Milan, with All. The. Feels. It's the only way I'm going to survive this mess." Blanca closed her eyes again.

"I need you too, my love," Julien replied, as he headed up stairs for bed.

"But only for the week." She yawned really big, moaning in protest at the sleep overcoming her without a quiet goodbye.

Ah, there it is. The condition. One week is all I need, my petit vixen, and then you'll see ...

***

When Julien finally arrived at Blanca's hotel and obtained his own key to her room, she had already met all the models and had given one of them a custom, multi-colored dye job and a cut. Blanca had kept Julien filled in on every single detail of her day via dozens of brief texts and pictures of the model she had preened. Giuseppe had instructed her on the style as he stood at Blanca's elbow rattling off his likes and dislikes while the other understudies *oohed* and *aahed* over Blanca's use of blended vibrant colors.

As Julien awaited her return, he made phone calls in between his quick responses to her. He managed a few things with the tasting room in Épernay, but he mostly delegated tasks all day to his brother-in-law, Everett, Lillie's husband, who had taken on a more prominent role in the family business.

When Blanca finally walked through the door of their hotel room, she threw her arms around Julien's shoulders, stretching up to hug him even though her stilettos had to have been at least four inches high. "I'm so happy that you're here! Look at you! Dang, you look different. More ripped? And the messy man-bun! Sexy! Your hair has gotten so long!"

"Nice to see you, too." He laughed, sliding his hands around her waist and lifting her feather-light body up off the ground.

Just the sight of her again and the feel of her in his arms throttled him with excitement.

"I'm starving! I haven't eaten all day."

"I'll take you to dinner," he offered, as he eased her back down.

"I need to rinse off first. I reek like chemicals."

Julien stepped out of Blanca's way as she rushed around, grabbing a few things out of her suitcase—no trace of sorrow on her face. If anything, she looked like she had just come back from having the time of her life. As she disappeared into the bathroom, he sat down on a wingback chair in the corner. The room was large but sparsely furnished with only a small table with two chairs, and a desk. The bed took up most of the room.

That's really all Julien needed as far as he was concerned. It was only a matter of dinner and some heart to heart, and he would have the woman he had fallen so deeply in love with back in his arms again for good if all his plans could succeed.

When Blanca emerged from the shower, draped in a towel and rambling on about the techniques she had learned that day, Julien felt something permanent anchor itself in his heart with her. The moment was sublime—simplistic in that she was getting ready to go to dinner, and he was patiently waiting for her, as if they had been married for years, and this was their routine.

Everything about it felt perfect.

Blanca's sudden contentment had him scrambling on the inside to figure out what had gone wrong for everything to suddenly be so right given his past history of failing at pretty much everything.

"Can you help me with the zipper?" Blanca asked, shimmying her dress up under her towel then letting the towel fall to the ground. A slick move because, if Julien had seen her naked, they wouldn't be dining out any time soon.

"Of course, beautiful," he cooed, running his fingers along her spine as he tugged the zipper up—the feel of her dewy skin igniting his body with desire.

Once he'd secured her dress, she turned around, barely coming up to his chest without her shoes on. "I just need to add a little makeup then I'll be ready to go."

"Even without it, you know I think you are gorgeous," he added, as she stepped around him.

"Thank you."

Thank you? No comeback. No warning. No playful insult?

"Julien, you should know one thing, though," she continued.

Ah, here it comes.

She wiggled her feet into a new pair of high heels and walked back over to him, unfastening the clamp in her hair and fluffing up her thick tresses that she'd avoided getting wet in the shower. "I don't plan on getting much sleep tonight."

Unbelievable.

Julien pulled Blanca into a kiss—his tongue thrusting into her mouth, claiming what was his. He had yearned for her taste, her touch, her scent for too long. He had no idea where her sudden need for him was coming from, but it didn't matter. All that he cared about was their present and their future. The life he fantasized about with her would be riddled with random outbursts of passion. Just like that one. He was living the dream.

Blanca tugged at his bottom lip, caught between her teeth as she made little moaning sounds. His arms wound around her, tugging her into his firm body—her tongue flickering and teasing his mouth. He pulled back then lunged at her neck, leaving a trail of reddened bites as he let out a low, agonized groan—his blood pumping fierce and hard.

She pressed against his shoulders, trying to catch her breath. "I think we, ohh, we better head out. We have all night to finish what we've started. But. Whoa. Dude!" she added, sliding her arms around his biceps over his shirt, you feel bigger, harder. I'm definitely exploring all this manly-man tonight."

Julien pulled back and searched Blanca's eyes. She meant it from what he could tell. He would have all night—it wasn't a moment of weakness in her. He kissed her once more on the corner of her lips then excused himself to the restroom for a moment. When he returned, she had applied a faint amount of makeup from her cosmetics case that she had set up on the table. She had transformed from gorgeous to stunningly glamorous in an instant and stole his heart all over again.

* * *

Blanca

Much like most of Europe from start to finish dinner was at least three hours long, if not more. As they both nursed another glass of wine and picked at a plate of cheese, rounding out their seven-course meal, Julien finally brought up the inevitable again.

"I have to say that I was certain you were going to put up an argument about me visiting." His heavy-lidded eyes searched hers over the candlelight.

"I guess I just figured my heart is shattered into a million pieces anyway. Saying goodbye to you in France broke me once, and it'll happen again by Saturday, but this," Blanca put her hand over her heart, "this pain from losing Maxie is so much worse. I can handle us."

May as well call it like it is.

"It doesn't have to be."

"I can't help how I feel. Maxie and I have been friends too long to let a guy get in the way. I know I'm being selfish, though, so I have to let her go. Hand her over to your cousin. Get my sorry ass out of the way. She texted me today and said we can deal with everything when I get back. That's it. No, 'Hey, how's it going in Milan?' Nothing. She doesn't even want to talk to me anymore. She doesn't care."

"Max is not abandoning you. She's only entering a different stage in her life—one that I hope to experience with you someday. I want us to have a life together."

Uh, that was bold.

Julien didn't even bat an eye when he said it, too. He waited for

Blanca's response as though he were expecting her to freak out. She was so far gone in the free-falling stage of freak-outs that all she could do was come to her own defense of what she wanted. Interestingly enough, it wasn't too far off from his dream of them being a couple, the more she thought about it.

Blanca tilted her head and smiled. "So, here's the deal about our life together, as you put it. Having you here. This moment right now. *Us.* This is what I want. You've been the only thing consistent in my world for the past year. Besides, what happened in France was the best and worst thing that's ever happened to me. I keep thinking, if I got over you once, I can do it again."

Julien looked off to the side—his jaw ticking. "Why do you have to get over me?"

"See, that's the thing. I've got it all wrong. I'm diving headfirst into us again because I realized last night that I don't actually have to get over you. Why can't we just do this?" She motioned around her. "Wherever I go, you'll find me. This can be our life together. No *goodbyes,* only *see you later,* so that way neither of us ever gets hurt again."

"Random, transcontinental hook-ups?"

She scrunched her face up. "Eck. No. We don't hook-up. We're way more classy than that."

Julien bowed his head and sighed then looked up at Blanca. He reached across the table, covering her hand with his. "I will follow you wherever you go, Blanca, my love, but I want something in return."

She leaned in, maneuvering her hand so that her fingers laced with his. She didn't reply. She just stared, waiting for him to continue. Julien had tried so hard to help her, only to flounder and flail. She had thrown herself at him, pushed him away, pounced at him again, back and forth, like a yo-yo on a string about to snap.

She had to hear him out. She owed it to him. He needed her.

Blanca could see his Adam's apple working his throat—the words a breath away from being spoken. She knew what was coming, and she knew she had to say *yes* to him.

"I want you to be mine. No one else's. Commit to me. To us."

Mine, huh? Sexy in an alpha-male-in-a-tacky-romance-novel-kinda-way, if I do say so myself. Rawr.

"Fine. I'm all yours. Have your way with me. You've ruined me in that department anyway. No one is ever going to compare."

Julien laughed—warm and easy—the sound rolling over her in comforting waves. "I'm sorry, not sorry," he drawled in a cheesy American accent.

"I'm not sorry either, so there," she giggled.

"Oh, I wanted to ask, did you get a chance to read your book? The editor would like your approval on her revisions with the translation as soon as possible, so she can wrap up the project."

Aw, crap—the book. Just shoot me now. "Yes, I read it. Thanks again for dragging my nightmare on." She squeezed his hand then let it go.

His eyes clouded with doubt, and it made her guts roiled with shame. "I thought you were excited about it? It's our book baby, remember?"

Julien's desperation to please Blanca plagued her with guilt, when all she wanted to do was be the one to make him happy. *But, nope.* There she was again just making him feel foolish for trying.

Dammit. I need to fix this, too!

"I *am* excited. I think it proves once again what a gentleman you are in what you're trying to do for me. I appreciate all of it, I do, but, I … you … oh, Julien," she sighed, sorting out how to give him the least offensive reply, knowing she was letting him down. "The romance novel thing is Maxie's dream not mine. She won. I lost. Just like everything else. That book could totally destroy our friendship once and for all."

Blanca picked her wine glass up and tipped it, draining the last drop into her mouth. She could see the wheels turning behind Julien's eyes as his fingers fidgeted with his cloth napkin on the table.

"I see," he finally said.

"Please, don't be mad," she whispered, searching his face for a glimmer of forgiveness.

Julien leaned back and graced Blanca with an easy smile. Whatever argument he had just had with her in his head came and went. “I think it’s time to walk back to the hotel. We’ve got a lot of catching up to do.”

And now it’s time for some makeup sex?

“I love that idea!”

She was ready like that.

Chapter twenty-four

"Let the beauty of what you love be what you do."
~Rumi

Julien

While Blanca preened her models during the day, Julien fielded phone calls to and from Everett and Chase from the hotel room, negotiating grapes with one and dictating new packaging for his Blanc de Blanca with the other. He had decided to heed Chase's advice to market a less seasonal look for his most recent ventures and broaden his distribution. In the last six months, his cousin had gone from rebuking him for his new business endeavors to being his most instrumental influencer in seeing that all his plans succeed.

Every evening, Blanca would burst into the hotel room, smack his mouth with a quick kiss, then head for the bathroom, emerging in the most exquisite way—always wearing a new dress and flaunting the new makeup technique that she'd learned that day from her teammates. She would captivate him with her resplendent beauty, night after night.

When they had only two days left, Blanca came *home* completely transformed, and, once again, riveted Julien with feelings of love and lust. Her hair had been changed from a gradient brown and blonde to a deep, silken black with highlights of smoky blue and indigo throughout it.

Julien's breath caught in his throat at the sight of her. Blanca's Italian, Greek, and Sicilian attributes had become more pronounced—the high cut of her cheekbones, the buttery, golden sheen of her skin, her lustrous jade eyes. He was utterly spellbound by her.

"Never in my life have I ever been so captivated as I am right now," he muttered in her ear as she embraced him, like she did each day, in a gentle hug after walking through the door. "You look absolutely amazing. I can't take my eyes off you."

"*Grazie* (Thank you)," she cooed—a delicate bloom spreading on her cheeks as she kissed his lips. "You give the best compliments. You know that?"

They looked at each other in silence for a moment.

He dipped his nose down to hers and nuzzled her cheek. "The only thing I know is that I have never felt like this before."

This is what forever feels like. This is love.

Blanca swayed a little in his arms then let go of him and looked over to the bathroom for a second. "Tell me all about those feels later tonight. I want to make sure I give you my undivided attention."

Julien groaned in response then released Blanca from his embrace. She disappeared, as usual, into the bathroom, emerging gloriously, then refreshed her makeup and took his hand, leading them out the door. The sweet tap dance of their makeshift life all wrapped up in routine gestures over the last few days kept him floating on air.

Their dinner plans that evening included meeting up with the other interns, two of which had significant others with them. One of the models and her husband were to join in, as well. The couple lived locally and seemed to have been the one to spearhead the dinner party, according to Blanca's texts earlier in the day.

Over dinner, everyone spoke in broken English, reveling in excitement about the runway show that would finally come the following morning. Eight designing graduates from fashion institutes around Europe were debuting their collections, and Julien learned that the event promised a decent crowd for a graduation ceremonial event of sorts.

All evening, Julien watched Blanca unfold in her element—a part of her he hadn't witnessed yet, and it moved him to see her so full of joy discussing her passion for styling. She spoke with authority and charm. The others seemed as drawn to her as he was, and it filled him with pride that he could call her his girlfriend.

* * *

When the night came to an end, they stumbled into their hotel room, joined in a passionate kiss, tearing at each other's buttons and zippers.

"Watching you tonight drove me wild," Julien growled, throwing Blanca's dress across the room alongside his shirt that she had just discarded. "Every word out of that luscious mouth of yours—" He nipped on her bottom lip as she struggled to unfasten his belt buckle—the rest of his comment getting lost in his heated lust for her.

Blanca giggled against his mouth and reared back as she tugged down his zipper, letting his slacks fall to the floor. "What was that?"

"You were so … ah … so … ehm, I loved how in command you were at the dinner party. I, uh," he breathed, losing his thoughts to her tongue again as it glided along the rigid swell of his pec, flickering against his skin.

"You like it when I'm in command?" she purred, twisting in his arms so that her back was flush with his abs.

She bent against him—his body following the curve of hers. And he grabbed her hips and nuzzled her against him, looping his thumbs under the thin black strings that barely held the scrap of fabric between her thighs in place.

"Have your way with me, gorgeous," he half-snarled, discarding her panties to the floor then twisting her around in his arms again to face her. "But the heels stay on tonight."

Blanca looked down between them at his bulging boxer briefs. "Like what you see?"

"I love what I see," he countered—his eyes roaming her body, landing on the only other thing she wore besides her stilettos—the tiny Champagne charm.

It dangled off its chain, swaying between her breasts.

Oh, mercy. Just marry me now already.

Julien could honestly say he worshipped Blanca's naked body, lilt and firm—her dark, silky hair flowing past her waist in loose waves. "I love every second I have had with you."

Blanca grabbed the waistband on his briefs and eased them down to the floor then stepped back with a little swagger. "It has been fun, hasn't it?"

He backed away to get a better look at her—his legs bumping into the edge of the bed. "Fun? *Venez ici* (come here), and I'll show you what fun feels like."

She sauntered up to him, bearing a mischievous smile. "Eff yoouu nnn-now. Fun."

"Then, by all means, I need to have fun with you *maintenant* (right now), and in as many positions as you'll let me."

Once Blanca was within reach, having let her play out the little tease and taunt game for as long as he could stand it, Julien slid his hand under her hair and gripped the back of her neck, pulling her into another passionate kiss. He maneuvered her to the bed, and they parted lips just long enough for her to shimmy up onto the blanket. He bowed over her, giving her that time she needed to run her fingers over his chest, nip at his earlobe, whisper into his ear about how much she needed him inside of her.

"Anything for you," he whispered against her mouth.

Blanca arched her back and moaned with delight as Julien began to lave the dip in her neck—his lips searching out her thrumming pulse. He, then, nipped at the tender skin under her ear in the way that always made her mew.

Julien reared up, anchoring his arms at her shoulders and holding the position for her as she roamed his body with her eyes. He always waited—always gave her those few seconds of longing for him that she insisted she needed before he thrust into her, claiming her as his lover.

Blanca delved her fingers into Julien's hair, unraveling the knot he'd tied it into. Then she pulled him into a frenzied kiss. His tongue slid along hers as she raked her fingernails along his spine, locking her ankles around his back, rocking her hips, and igniting his blood with lust as they fell into their perfect rhythm together as they made love.

* * *

When morning came, Julien accompanied Blanca to the fashion show. He sat alone in the third row, amused by the events unfolding before him. He loved knowing the extravagant, sensuous parade of models owed their brilliant, colorful hair to his amazing girlfriend who hid behind the scenes.

The celebration afterward included toasting with L'Angevin Champagne—an endearing surprise that Blanca had coordinated. The small circle of friends she had made during their week in Milan embraced Julien as though they had known him for a long time despite it having only been their second encounter all week. Blanca had been sharing stories about him—about them—talking to the others as though they'd been together for months and not just days.

And, in Julien's heart, they had been.

* * *

Blanca

A whole world of intrigue burst before Blanca in a shimmering parade of all things chiffon and taffeta. The fashion industry pulsed with a heartbeat that she understood. Beauty erupted everywhere in the clothes, the makeup, and the hair—each part coming together to make an artistic whole. It felt surreal to her. One taste, six hurried days, and she was hooked. She wanted to be a personal stylist and work on the road someday. No more booths, no more bosses, no more accountability to anyone but herself.

"Anyone but yourself and *moi,*" Julien added, as he sat upright in bed, flipping through the channels on the television, as she expressed her excitement about her decision to figure out a way to make that lifestyle her new career goal.

"And you? Yes, of course. I'm totally committed to us. Wherever I go, you'll be there, or at least, you'll try to be." Blanca tossed the damp towel through the open bathroom door and slid her naked body into bed next to him.

She leaned her head against his shoulder, dragging the sheet up over her as they settled into bed together once more. They had only a few hours left before they would need to leave their hotel room, having made arrangements for a late check-out as their separate flights didn't depart until later that night.

"I don't even know where to begin, but the good news is Giuseppe agreed to help me with referrals. It's a start. I mean I still have to get ahead at work and save more money. Plus, I can't just flip my house until I've lived in it for at least two years, and I build some equity up in it."

Julien planted a kiss on her head. "Breathe, my love. You have time to figure it all out."

She looked up at him. "So will I see you again in a few months at Chase's birthday party?"

He landed on a soap opera and turned the volume up then put the remote down, giving her his full attention. "*Oui,* I will definitely be there."

"Planning on making me scream my head off soon?" she teased, motioning to the blaring television show, most likely meant to drown out their sounds of passion because she knew he didn't understand a single word of it.

"Absolutely." Blanca nestled into his shoulder as he gripped her tighter. He let out a belabored sigh. "I hate having to say goodbye, but—"

"No *goodbyes*—only *see you later,* remember?"

"Ah, that's right." Julien buried his nose in her neck, sliding his hand along her thigh then nudging her to his side. He wriggled down until he was also on his side, facing her—propping his head up on his hand. "I was so proud of you today."

"Thank you. I was proud of me, too. It's been a long time since I've actually done something for myself that was worth anything."

"That's not true."

"Yeah, it is. I'm pathetic like that," she pouted.

Julien sat up and tugged on Blanca's arm to join him in the middle of the bed. She scooted up to him, and he lifted her up by her bottom, straddling her onto his lap. "I don't think you're pathetic. I think you're perfect," he said, wrapping his arms around her and sliding her against his body. "You've done so much with your life, and yet, you're so young."

"What have I done besides go on vacation a lot to get way more continuing education credits than I'll ever need for my Cosmetology license?" she balked, tilting her head back to receive his kisses as he nommed on her neck.

"What about your book? That's a big accomplishment."

Oh, crap. That dang thing.

Julien tightened his grip on her, hoisting her higher, easing her down, then sliding her up again, as her chin rested on his shoulder.

"It sure did feel like it at the time," Blanca moaned, as she gazed aimlessly at the soap opera flickering behind him.

"You are brilliant, you know." Julien nibbled at her shoulder. "And smart, and sexy, and most of all, you are mine."

"You've got that right. I'm all yours, especially if you keep doing that," she breathed, noticing the actress in the scene, sprawled out on a beach towel like a Roman goddess, looked familiar. She had a novel in one hand and a pink cocktail in the other. An oiled up, muscular, cabana boy made small talk with the beautiful, young woman about the sparkling beach before them.

Blanca finally recognized the actress as the one that she had seen in the airport when she had landed in Milan.

Heh. Cool. Donatella De Luca.

"I've got all kinds of plans for us. This week is only the beginning," Julien mumbled below her ear.

He ran his tongue along her collarbone, sending shivers throughout her body, pebbling her skin with arousal. Her head lulled to the side as he teased her earlobe with his tongue and rocked her hips up again, moaning in her ear.

Blanca let out a gasp—her eyes widening in shock.

How did she? When did I? What the hell?

That book in Donatella De Luca's hand, yeah, you guessed it. She was reading *Right as Rayne.*

Julien hummed in her ear, gathering her tighter in his arms. "I have a secret, but I'm not going to share it with you, not yet." He reared back and took her with him as he tumbled over on his back.

"You and me both." She gasped then succumbed to his fervent kisses in a fury of passion.

Chapter twenty-five

"When you encounter difficulty and contradictions, do not try to break them, but bend them with gentleness and time."
~Saint Francis de Sales

Blanca
Saying, "See you later," to Julien in Milan felt even worse than when she had said, "Goodbye," to him in France, but not for the reasons you'd think. Nothing could've prepared her for the ache that was accompanied by *HOPE*. Hope in seeing him at the end of October. Hope in FaceTiming him every day in between. Hope—that festering, little tickle thrashing around in her heart, confusing her into thinking she had the whole situation under control.

He flies to see you. You fly to see him. We both fly to see each other. My life in a nutshell.

The whole long-distance thing had never been something she thought she'd try to do, let alone even give up her salacious freedoms for one single dude, but the truth was, she didn't want anyone else. Julien was more than enough to tide her over until the next time they'd see each other in person. Being around him all the time would be too overwhelming, like having her favorite dessert all day every day, day in and day out, in and out, in and out ... She'd die of too much *fun* if she didn't get bored with it first.

As far as the distant future was concerned, Blanca figured she had nothing but time to let her relationship with Julien run its course and either go belly-up or become a permanent traveling show. If *see you later* got easier, would it mean they were nearing the end of their feels for each other? But, if separation remained a dread, could they stand the ongoing torture to be apart? Either way, she knew only one thing for sure and that was that they were both in the same place emotionally. And that place looked a lot like being in love.

As hard as it was for Blanca to stomach that she had allowed herself to become so vulnerable, she kept her head in check with her heart, telling herself daily that it was normal to be scared. It was okay to be weak. And, no matter what, it was best to keep things unfolding in the moment. Only because their circumstances—his life in Champagne and her life in Napa Valley—kept the timing of their relationship from ever becoming more than it was turning out to be. That reality, sadly enough, actually comforted her like an old misery she didn't know how to scrape off the bottom of her shoe, so she just shuffled along with it pretending it wasn't there.

They were living for the moment—her mantra in life—but the moment in Milan had gone, taking her feel-goods with it. Having been home in Napa Valley for a whole week, she felt like she was suffering from the *I miss yous* like some sort of malignant disease. She also had come to the conclusion that she must face the next major painful moment in her life. She had to deal with making things right with her bestie—or the person formerly known as her bestie.

You know the one. She now refers to herself as Chase's fiancé.

Blanca had reached out to Maxie with a text earlier in the day, only to be one-upped by a phone call from her instead of a text reply, touting a formal invitation to join the future newlyweds for a get-together later that night.

Blanca agreed, figuring she might as well go and get her big, fat apology about everything over with face to face.

"Hey, Siri, text Jules," Blanca blurted out at her iPhone, as she drove to the vineyard.

A smooth, English male voice purred, "What would you like it to say, You Gorgeous Woman You?" *So, yeah, that's what I programmed Siri to call me, because, you know, he's my cyberspace beotch, and let's face it, I'm hot.*

"Jules, I'm headed over to see Chase and Maxie to straighten things out. Wish me luck. You better call me later. I miss you."

Siri piped up and asked if he could send the message, and Blanca said, "Yes."

As Blanca cruised down the main road cutting through the valley, she passed an illuminated billboard of none other than Maxie's douchebag, cheating ex-boyfriend, Bartholomew Moore.

Oh, good grief! Really? Reeaalllyy? What an asshole.

He stood short in a suit and tie. His meaty arms were crossed over his puffed-up chest, as he sported a smug, toothy grin advertising his new private law practice.

New Private Law Practice? Guess your uncle's Accident and Injury Law Firm gave you the boot. Ba-ha-ha.

That guy, Bart, was as sleazy as they came. Figures he'd park a billboard a few miles from Angel of the Vine Winery so Chase, his family, and now Maxie would have to see him every time they drove into town.

What a sore loser!

Maxie had given Chase's parents so much dirt on that dude, it's a wonder he could even practice law anymore. After Maxie had returned with Chase from France last year, she wrote up a legal statement on how Bart had held her against her will, practically kidnapping her in the way that he tricked her into staying with him. He'd even gotten her to sign a bunch of legal papers to sue the winery for her injury. Although, she wasn't even coherent when she scribbled her name on them. When Maxie snapped out of it, Bart took all her savings as a severance fee then filed her lawsuit anyway. He even got the idiot guy who caused her to fall in the first place to sue the winery for his injuries, too.

Did I mention he was an asshole?

In the end, both lawsuits came to a screeching halt because of her statement, and the insurance company coughed up ten grand each for Maxie and that other guy. Funny how the L'Angevin family was all hunky-dory with Maxie being a part of their family now.

She wins again.

If Blanca had been around, none of it would've happened in the first place.

The memories of that summer still haunted Blanca. As angry as she was at Maxie, her BFF was still the most important person in her life, and seeing that *stunad's* cheesy grin glaring at her from the side of the road after all he had done only fueled the guilt Blanca felt for being jealous.

Gah! I hate that word!

Blanca pulled up to Chase's cabin, which was embedded into the hillside overlooking a portion of the rolling, vine-laced hills and valleys at Angel of the Vine Winery. Chase's parents' sprawling home sat further up the hilltop along the same dusty road, but it was enough of a distance for Maxie to brag about feeling like they were all alone, perched on top of heaven.

I know it's so sweet it makes me want to vomit, too.

The two-story cabin had a glass façade, and, at night, you could see straight into it when the lights were all on inside. Blanca noticed Chase descending the spiral staircase that jutted down from his loft—*their* loft. No legit bedroom, just an upper deck with a wooden railing, so they could gaze out of the massive windows at the magnificent view while canoodling in bed, watching the sunrise.

Blanca glanced around, trying to spot Maxie inside of the cottage, but didn't see her anywhere. As she marched up the steps of the porch, littered with rocking chairs, Maxie opened the door, which meant she was hiding behind the mottled glass inset waiting for her to knock.

Sneaky.

Maxie threw her arms around Blanca's neck the second she stepped into the entryway. "Oh, my goodness! I love your hair! I'm so glad you came!"

"Thanks, and why wouldn't I come? The three of us used to hang out all the time."

Too snippy? I'll scale it back a bit. I'm supposed to be on a mission of repentance, and she's way too chipper. What gives?

Maxie offered up a smug smile and took Blanca's purse from her, looping the strap onto a coat rack in the corner of the entryway.

"Sup, Chase?" Blanca added, as he crossed in front of them and stepped up to the dining room.

"Hello, Blanca. We're so happy that you agreed to come over," he replied, as he walked into the kitchen and began to plate some desserts that would no doubt be joining the two French presses full of steeped coffee parked on the dining room table.

"Need any help?" Blanca offered, growing increasingly suspicious of all the ooey-gooey chitchat about her coming over like it was a major event for her to come see Chax.

Again with the third-wheel routine. Sheesh.

Chase motioned towards the living room. "No, I've got it. Why don't you two ladies just have a seat while I prep everything."

"Isn't he such a gentleman?" Maxie sang out, as Blanca followed her down the steps into the sunken living room.

A wide hardwood walkway framed the deep, carpeted pit of total relaxation. Tiered levels went down to the living room and up to the kitchen and dining room. Off to the side of the kitchen, a full bathroom was tucked away at the end of a short hall, but, other than that, the space was wide open. The sunken living room, which took up most of the ground floor, made the inside of the cabin seem a lot bigger than it actually was because of the high, exposed-beamed ceiling.

Blanca sat down on a section of the leather, u-shaped couch as Maxie grabbed a remote off the coffee table and turned down the television that hung on the brick fireplace. She settled onto the couch next to her and sighed, following Blanca's eyes as they roamed along the walls below the loft. They were blanketed in Grand-mère Mimi's paintings, and a faint ache in Blanca's heart for Julien and Chase's loss whispered to her. On the other side of the chimney, book-filled shelves held her attention next. Funny how Chase loved books so much he found himself someone who now wrote them.

Yet another chapter in their fairy tale romance.

"I see these paintings so differently now," Maxie began, opening up a conversation with Blanca.

"Mimi was most definitely an amazing artist."

"She certainly was. She seemed very spirited, like, she kind of lived a robust life full of—"

"Challenges," Blanca butted in.

Maxie nodded. "And passion."

Blanca picked at a tiny thread poking out on the hem of her black miniskirt. "I wish I could've met her."

"I only visited with her for a few minutes when I was in Champagne last year, but she left quite an impression on me. Julien brought me over to her house after his birthday celebration."

"Ah, that's right. You spent the whole day with Julien and his family."

The whole freakin' day. Then you went back for seconds a few days later, you—gah! Enough with the jealousy already.

Focus. Focus. Focus.

Maxie cocked an eyebrow at her. "You kind of remind me of her in some ways. You love a good challenge, and you do everything with all your heart."

Interesting choice of words.

"That's so polite of you to say."

"It's true," Maxie beamed, craning her neck around Blanca to look at Chase in the dining room.

Blanca shot a glance over her shoulder and caught Chase shrugging. He flashed a quick smile at them and continued to fuss with the table spread.

Either I'm being set up, and they already know about all that's coming in my guilty confession, or they've officially become Disneyfied.

As much as the small talk humored Blanca in a bad horror movie kind of way, she figured it was time to spill her guts and get it over with—rid herself of all the jealousies she harbored in being the worst best friend in the whole world, once and for all.

Here goes nothing.

She took a deep breath and let it out, straightening her spine then reached for Maxie's hand. "I have something to *tell* you," Blanca began.

Maxie's fingers tightened around hers, and she leaned in. "And I have something to *ask* you."

I knew it! "Okay, you go first."

"Ladies, please come join us," Chase interrupted, drawing their attention back to the kitchen.

"Surprise," Julien grinned, as he emerged from the short hallway beside the kitchen and sidled up to Chase.

* * *

Julien

Blanca slow blinked as if she couldn't believe her eyes. The tiny quirk at the corner of her lips let Julien know that the surprise he had hinted at during their last moments in Milan had been a welcome one. Even though she looked like she was about to faint from shock, she seemed all right with him showing up unexpectedly.

He rushed across the kitchen and practically jogged down the handful of steps into the living room, careening around the couch to get to her.

Blanca stood up—her mouth parting but no words coming out.

She didn't have to speak. He knew the instant she spread out her arms to welcome him with a hug that she was pleased to see him.

"I told you I had some secrets in the making," he laughed, cradling Blanca as Maxie stood up and applauded them.

"All right everyone the coffee's getting cold," Chase interrupted.

Maxie headed to the dining room while Julien stole a semi-private second with his love.

Blanca looked at him with tears welling up in her eyes. "You're here? Here! How is this even possible? I was just texting you this morning."

"You caught me on one of my layovers." He squeezed her and planted a kiss on her forehead as she nuzzled into him again.

"You've been scrambling to catch up on work all week. How are you even pulling this off?" Her words came out muffled against his chest.

"That's my other surprise," he said, tipping her chin up with his finger so their eyes could meet again. "I handed my responsibilities over to Everett, Lillie's husband. I'm going to be making our Blanc de Blanca here in America."

Blanca's jaw went slack, and her glossy eyes widened even more. "You're making your Champagne here? Here?" she repeated, releasing her arms around his waist and pointing down with both fingers.

"Ehm, technically, it's considered sparkling wine now, but *oui.* I'm making *our* brand here at Angel of the Vine."

"That's ... that's ... quite a surprise."

Julien searched Blanca's face unable to discern if she was happy about his announcement or terrified as he gripped her shoulders, afraid to release her.

This is not how I'd planned this to go.

* * *

Blanca

Blanca looked up at Julien—blinking back her tears as a tidal wave of excitement, panic, and confusion washed over her. She reached up and grabbed onto his arms as she began to grow weak in the knees, and Julien took it for another hug, embracing her once again.

"Come on, you two," Chase interjected.

"You're happy for us, *non*? I've missed you so much this week that I almost told you everything." Julien slid his hand into Blanca's and led her up the steps into the dining room as he kept explaining himself to her. "My uncle is sharing his different vins of Chardonnay with me to create our own blend, and he's only taking a percentage of the profits for production costs."

"How long will it take?" Julien had pulled a chair out for Blanca, and she eased into it.

"Once it's bottled, it will be at least eighteen months before it hits the market," he replied, sitting down next to her.

She stared at Julien ... at her French lover ... at the man she was falling in love with ... at the very reason why she had been lugging a sorry sack of heartache and guilt around with her all week. "So, does this mean you're moving here?"

"Yes!" Maxie shouted across the table. "Isn't it wonderful, Blanca?" Maxie fluttered her hands in the air, smacking them together ferociously.

Again with the clapping?

"Quit it, or you're going to put an eye out with that thing," Blanca muttered, motioning to the big rock on Maxie's finger.

"Jealous much?" Maxie quipped, wiggling the ring at her.

As a matter of fact ...

"Don't be," Maxie continued. "I'm sure you'll have your own ring by spring. Isn't that right, Julien?"

Says the woman who always wins at everything.

Blanca stared at her dumbstruck and slightly annoyed by the pitchy warbling in her ears thanks to the info-bomb that was just dropped on her about Julien moving to Napa Valley.

Oh, and let's not ignore the whole ring by spring thing. What the hell? I'm barely getting used to the idea that I'm committed to him now!

Julien frowned at Maxie and turned to Blanca, reaching out and tucking a curled ribbon of glossy black and blue hair behind her ear. "Please don't be scared. I'm not asking you to marry me. Not yet, anyway."

Blanca let out a breath she didn't even know she was holding in. "I'm not scared."

Well, maybe a tad. This is all way too fast for me.

"Good. Trust me. Trust *us.* We have all the time in the world to work this out."

"All the time in the world?" she repeated, just to be sure.

"As much time as you need."

Blanca looked across the table at Maxie and Chase again, as they served themselves some colorful macarons and tiny bites of something coated in a chocolaty shellac.

Chase offered Blanca and Julien the tray of desserts, and she plucked up a lavender-colored macaron, setting it on her plate with a shaky hand. "Thank you."

"Are you all right, darling?" Julien asked, noticing her jitters as he took a bright yellow one for himself.

Her eyes darted from Julien's to Maxie's then down at her plate at the too-pretty-to-eat cookie. "It's like you knew I needed you right now, and here you are. I'm fine. Just slightly freaked out by all that's going down tonight."

"I'll always be here for you for as long as you'll have me."

"Aw, that is so sweet," Maxie sighed, watching the two of them as she stirred some cream and sugar into her coffee that Chase had just poured for her.

Blanca let out a soft ripple of nervous laughter, tossing her head back then leveling her eyes on Maxie. "This is crazy. I don't even know where to begin. You helped plan this? Bring him here? Tonight?" Her nervous giggles continued to gain traction so that the others couldn't help themselves but join in the laughter.

Chase tipped his coffee cup at her in a makeshift toast then took a swig. "We all did. We've been working on helping Julien move here for months."

Blanca's laughter died down, and she panned all their faces, landing on Julien's guarded smile. "Wait? Move in here? You're not staying in your uncle's guestroom?"

"No, silly," Maxie huffed. "Either way, I can't have Julien creeping up to the house at night. You can see everything going on in our bedroom because of all the windows."

Maxie leaned over the table with one of the French presses and poured some coffee into Blanca's cup for her—those gianormous boobs of hers spilling out of her neckline right in Julien's face.

Hold up, beotch. Did you just call my boyfriend a creeper?

"So?" Blanca postured.

"So, that's where my favor of you comes in," Maxie quipped, as she picked up the creamer and added a splash to the cup. "Julien's going to be your new roommate."

Julien reached under the table and gripped Blanca's thigh to get her attention. "I didn't think you would mind if I moved in with you? I'm sorry if I'm intruding."

Blanca glanced at him. "Intruding? By moving in with *me*?" She swung her eyes over to Maxie, who was stuffing her face with a pink macaron, then back at Julien again. She leaned into him to whisper, "Did she just imply you'd try to ... to *watch her in bed* in the middle of the night?"

His eyelids flared open in shock. "Come again?"

"Nothing. Never mind. It doesn't matter. Game on," Blanca grumbled, covering Julien's hand on her thigh with her own and giving it a tight squeeze. "Jules, my delicious and oh so sexy boyfriend, I'd love it if you would move in with me."

"*Bien*," he cooed in reply.

Maxie picked up the platter of treats and held it out to Blanca, forcing her to let go of Julien's hand that she had been holding discreetly under the table. "You have to try a chocolate raspberry *petit four*. Here, take one."

Blanca reached out and took two of the bite-sized morsels from the tray, putting one on Julien's plate then popping hers into her mouth. "Thanks. Thanks a lot," she muffled, around the tiny nom of cake.

"Now, what was it you said you needed to tell me?" Maxie asked, as Chase picked up his fiancé's hand and brought her curled knuckles to his lips, then reared back with pride to look at the ring he had given her.

Blanca stared at their loving gesture, not entirely sure they weren't trying to rub it in their faces just how much in love they really were, as Julien's territorial fingers began to climb her thigh under the table again.

Without batting an eye, Blanca replied, "It doesn't matter anymore."

I win.

Chapter Twenty-Six

"There is no charm equal to tenderness of heart."
~Jane Austen

Julien

The late afternoon sun beat down on Julien's sweat-soaked t-shirt as he pushed a lawnmower through the bramble in Blanca's backyard. He had already pulled most of the weeds up and bagged them, piling the bags in the garage to dispose of them the next day. He had cleaned and organized the garage for Blanca and wanted to get the lawn taken care of before nightfall.

Blanca waved hello to Julien through the bay windows of the kitchen nook, letting him know she had gotten home from work. The sight of her sent his heart racing with excitement, just as it did every day. They had fallen into an easy routine over their first week they'd been *roomies,* as she liked to say.

Though, they were so much more.

Julien had gone home with Blanca after that night at Chase and Max's cabin with no formal discussion about the events that had unfolded. They just curled up into bed together and fell asleep. Then, Chase and Max both drove over the next day with the rest of Julien's seven pieces of luggage and left him the keys to Chase's SUV with a warning to take care of it or else.

The rest of the week Blanca and he fell into a lazy pattern of crawling out of bed in the late mornings after long, sleepless nights of lovemaking. Julien would then maximize his time each day cleaning and organizing things around the house while Blanca put in several hours at the salon. When she would come home late in the evenings, he'd give her some downtime alone then finally seek her out when he couldn't stand being away from her another minute.

The routine they had begun to establish felt like *home* to him.

Blanca had only mentioned to Julien once in a brief, middle-of-the-night conversation that making such a massive leap in their relationship did, indeed, scare her, but she also said she wouldn't have it any other way—something about it feeling justified.

Julien wanted to ask Blanca why—to probe her heart and learn what it had been about their relationship that made her agree to welcome him into her home, her heart, and her life, without putting up a fight, but he refrained. Knowing Blanca feared the very kind of commitment Julien was expecting of her, he kept his curiosity to himself.

Julien owed everything to Lillie's husband, Chase, and his aunt and uncle for helping him start his new life with Blanca. The way he chose to perceive things was all that mattered to him. Their almost yearlong friendship had finally culminated into a magnificent, strong, and genuine relationship.

When Julien finally finished mowing the lawn, the sun had melted beyond the ragged trees along the hillside view from the backyard. He stripped his shirt off and tossed it in the laundry room down the hall and went to the master bedroom to shower. Blanca was nowhere to be found which meant she had tucked herself away in her Zen Den. It was her sanctuary of peace where they had spent a few times just lying together in silence on the pile of pillows on the floor, giving into the stillness they both seemed to crave sometimes.

After his shower, Julien dressed in some gym shorts and a t-shirt—his new, casual, American look, Blanca would tease—and rapped on the door to her yoga room, hoping she didn't mind the intrusion. He had missed her so much during the day and wanted to see her and be with her, basking in the joy of knowing she wasn't disappearing on him any time soon.

"Come in," Blanca chirped.

Julien opened the door and found her upside down, balancing on her head with her legs straight up and toes pointed, holding a stiff position.

"I'm impressed," he smiled, stepping around her and walking over to the chaise lounge to have a seat. "Do you mind if I watch?"

She lowered her legs and maneuvered into a sitting position on her shins. "Join me."

Even better.

Julien walked over to Blanca and sat down on the mat in front of her, awaiting her instruction.

"Do you want to try some Acro Yoga with me?"

I have no idea what that means, but my answer will always be absolutely.

"I'm all yours, beautiful."

They hadn't ever exercised together before. Exercise, though, had become something Julien had started incorporating into his lifestyle back in Champagne. Chase had created a routine for him to follow a couple of months ago, and Julien had already spent two mornings with Chase getting in a painful workout at a local gym.

Julien's body, though muscular and firm, lacked precise definition the way Chase's body reflected a fitness obsession, so seeking Chase's help to shape up seemed logical to him. Taking his body from moderately toned to rock hard was something Julien had mentioned to Blanca that he'd wanted to do when he had headed out with Chase at the same time she'd been leaving for the salon a couple of days ago.

Her response once she'd returned home not long after he'd gotten back from the gym, however, came unexpectedly.

Blanca had commented that she didn't want him turning into a meathead like Maxie's ex-boyfriend. She had told Julien that she'd loved that he'd become so muscular but still somewhat soft against her body.

She'd also said she didn't want to compete with a gym for his time or worry that she'd lose him to a *gym skank* someday. Julien had to assure her that he was one-hundred percent devoted to her, and he only wished to continue to refine his physique not change it.

The need to profess what he thought Blanca could already see in his heart caught Julien off guard. It wasn't until mulling it over in his mind all night that it occurred to him that Blanca had been merely projecting Max's and her past problems from their previous relationships onto him. And, though, her ex had ended their relationship a long time ago, he recognized that she hadn't completely gotten over the pain her ex had put her through.

"I've always wanted to try yoga with a partner," Blanca said, breaking into his thoughts with her proclamation.

Julien leaned over and stole a kiss from his beautiful girlfriend, then scanned her hilarious graphic tee. "Namas'tay in Bed," he read and chuckled. "I love our lazy mornings staying in bed."

"So do I," she smiled back and leaned in for another kiss. "Now get on all fours."

"Hey, you're stealing my line from last night."

She gave him a saucy smile.

Julien did as she commanded—his long, blond hair falling in his face. "All right. Doggie style it is."

"Now hold still. I'm going to balance on you." She arched over him until her back was flush with his. Then she hooked her arms around his shoulders, and, though, he couldn't see what she was doing, he had a feeling her legs were straight up in the air again because he no longer felt her against his back, only the pressure of her along his shoulder blades as her ponytail hung past his shoulders.

He supported her weight, holding still and keeping her steady. Pride surged in him that she'd finally included him in her workout routine—another element in their relationship falling into place.

After a few minutes, Blanca rolled off him. "Now lay on your back and bend your knees to your chest."

Again, Julien changed positions groping her tight derrière in the tiny black shorts that she wore as she maneuvered around him.

She giggled at his affectionate gesture. "Okay, now hold me up with your feet."

Blanca bowed over him, centering his feet on her hipbones and motioning for him to hold hands with her.

"Lillie and Colette used to play airplane with Victoria and I when we were children," he reminisced.

"My brother and I used to, too," she smiled—her ponytail tickling him in the face. "That's kind of cool that as kids, even in different countries with different customs and all, we have this in common."

He hoisted her up, light as a feather, and rocked her forward and backward, as she grinned, taking flight. "So, ehm, your love of different languages comes from all your travels?"

"I think it might be the other way around. Once, when I was younger, I visited some relatives in Italy with my family, and it opened my eyes to the whole world, not just the small city I grew up in. I've always spoken Italian because my father insisted we learn it, but with the other languages, I think I was just going with a theme."

"A theme? How?"

"The romance languages. I already had a little bit of Spanish under my belt from high school, and I learned Portuguese because I went to Portugal one summer and made learning it part of my immersion before I even left home. Then, when I went to France last year, Maxie and I made a bet that I'd learn French if she learned Spanish."

"And who won."

"I guess I did."

Her smile dimmed, and she looked away as she wobbled above him.

Julien squeezed her hands. "You were so close to me when you were in Paris. I wish I had met you that summer."

"Well, you didn't. I went home, and you went sightseeing with Maxie."

"And without her, I never would have met you. You see. It was meant to be."

"I guess."

"Blanca," he said, beckoning her to look him in the eyes. "I cannot read your mind right now, but if I could guess, you were worried about something that never existed between Max and me, *non*?"

She looked at him. "I know I'm being a *stunad*. I just haven't done the relationship thing in so long. I forget all the crap that comes with it."

"What crap? What does that mean?"

"Jealousy. Insecurity. The stuff that has kept me single until you … you asked me to commit to you in Milan."

Julien bent his knees then flexed them again, causing her to squeal and teeter. "If I've ever said or done anything to cause you any concern, I apologize. I am completely, irrevocably, madly in love with you, Blanca."

She looked down at him—her eyes searching his face, her bottom lip caught in between her teeth as she processed his words. "I love you, too, Julien. I really do. I am sorry that what I said made you feel like you had to apologize to me. I'm the one who has to work through my emotional hang-ups."

"I am not going anywhere, unless, of course, you want to bring me along on your vacation again. Wherever you lead, I'll follow, *oui*?"

"Yes. Oh, that reminds me, Giuseppe sent me an email today and said he wants me to work with him again next summer on whatever new fashion recruit the institute tosses at him."

"*Très bien.* That's wonderful! So you're going to Italy again?"

"Yes, only this time I'll have several months to plan and save for a longer trip."

"And, you are inviting me, *oui*? We can travel together like we had planned, *non*?"

She closed her eyes and tilted her chin up. "If we're still together this time next year, then, yes."

If? I'm hoping to be married by then.

He spread her arms apart, causing her eyes to pop open as she swayed and giggled again. "Of course, we'll be together, my love. So, ehm, is Italy your favorite place you've traveled to?"

"My favorite? I don't know. Everywhere I go is so intriguing. Italy is like home base."

"So you were pleased with your Italian novel then, *non?* It was a pleasant surprise?"

"My Italian? Oh, that. Yep. I was definitely surprised, and now it's time for me to fly. Let go of my hands," she commanded, then spread her arms out at her sides, balancing her body above him without any support.

Julien started making rumbling sounds, blowing raspberries like an airplane flying through the air causing Blanca to laugh and screech as she wobbled on top of his feet, flapping her arms to keep from falling. She held the position a couple of minutes then dropped her arms and wriggled off his feet. "All righty, Jules, did you want to try it?"

"I'd crush you, darling."

She laughed. "You might, but I love the weight of you on top of me. You're the best human blanket in the world."

Julien sat up and crossed his legs mimicking the position she had just curled up into. She reached out and took his hands in hers. Julien looked down at her delicate fingers contrasted against his large, roughed-up hands from all the yard work he had done that day.

"How did things go today at the spa?"

Blanca smiled at him, kneading his knuckles with her thumbs. "I'm almost booked solid through the next three months. I refuse to work more than eight hours a day, though. How was your day at home?"

Home. I love the sound of that.

"I cleaned and sorted your garage and also, as you saw, knocked down the grass in the back a bit."

"Thank you for doing those chores for me. You know, you don't have to."

"I want to. I want to do everything for you. I'll take a load to the local trash receptacle as soon as I can figure out where it is?"

"You mean the dump," she smiled. "Chase is going to love you filling up his vehicle with trash bags." She tossed her head back and laughed. "You know what else we need to do, we need to get you set up with a driver's license once your work visa clears, just in case you get pulled over sometime."

"Right. Laws. I should buy my own vehicle at some point, as well." He leaned over and kissed her lips.

She inhaled and exhaled on a smirk. "This is getting pretty real between us with this kind of talk."

"As real as it can get, love. Is there anything specific you would like me to tackle next around the house?"

She shook her head. "I can't think of anything. You're still going to let me help you with the taste testing for the Blanc de Blanca, right?"

"Of course. All we need to do is pick a day to go to the winery and start blending the different Chardonnays together until we find what we're looking for."

"You know, everything you say sounds so damn sexy with that accent of yours. You could be talking about scrubbing the toilets, and I'd be swooning all over you."

Julien shook his head and laughed. "Are you hinting that you want me to clean the bathrooms tomorrow?"

Blanca gasped with laughter. "No, don't. Please, don't do that for me. I'll take care of that chore. Is there anything I can do for you?"

"Besides love me forever? I have *une petite requite* (one small request)."

"Lay it on me."

"Let me take you to a nice dinner tomorrow. Show you off on my arm. It will be your gift to me."

"You taking me to dinner is more like a gift for *moi*," she purred. "What's the occasion?"

"I'm getting older."

She scrunched her nose at him. "Wait? Tomorrow is your birthday?"

"*Oui*. I'll be thirty-one."

"Why didn't you say something sooner?"

"We have all the time in the world to discover the little details about each other."

Julien could only assume that the expression on Blanca's face was one of embarrassment. They hadn't spent a great deal of time delving into deep conversations about themselves. Their calls and texts over the year had been full of lighthearted banter—nothing too personal—unless it was about Max.

He looked down at her tiny hands covering his, gently rubbing his knuckles with her thumbs as she tending to him with care.

"We haven't really discussed me coming here either," he added, hoping to open up the conversation.

"What's there to talk about?"

"How are you doing? Ehm, I mean, are you still fine with me being here? We're coming up on our second week, and we've never been around each other longer than this. I feel I need to check in with you and make sure we are still good."

Blanca tilted her head to the side and let out a sigh. "Can I tell you something that might make you uncomfortable?"

"Talk to me, *s'il vous plait* (please)?"

"It's about my ex."

I know.

Julien waited, gazing at her.

She took another deep breath and looked down at their hands joined together.

"Blanca, talk to me. You will not make me uncomfortable."

She looked up at him and nodded. "Okay. Okay, I can do this," Blanca began. "So, uh, when I got engaged before, I moved into this crappy, little apartment with him, like, a week later. I thought I was done. I thought that I had found the one, and we would live happily-ever-after. I was so in love with him, and Maxie was still with this boyfriend of hers she had been dating since our freshman year of high school. Everybody thought they'd get married, you know?" She sighed and squeezed Julien's hands. "Then, when I met my ex, and we got serious, I thought, 'this is it,' and Maxie and I would eventually buy houses on the same street, and our babies would grow up to be best friends, just like we were."

Julien threaded his fingers with hers. "That sounds like a reasonable circumstance to hope for."

Blanca offered him a pitiful smile then shook her head. "I trusted him completely. He meant everything to me. Stupid, twenty-year-old, ignorant me. So, when he broke off our engagement out of nowhere and told me to move out, it crushed me. Then, he started dating this eighteen-year-old cheerleader a week later. I guess, from what I heard, he had his eye on her for a while. I was devastated. He would parade her around in front of me on campus, too, like he was deliberately trying to hurt me even more. This person who was supposed to care about me—who had been planning our wedding with me—became my worst enemy, all because he didn't want to be with me anymore. He couldn't just break up with me and move on. He stuck around to rub it in my face that he'd left me for this other girl."

"I'm so sorry someone could be so cruel to you—someone you trusted with your heart."

Someone I will, no doubt, kill if I ever have to meet the evil, little bastard.

"I know I made it seem like that part of my past was no big deal when we talked about our ugly break-ups that week I stayed with you during Christmas, but it's why I'm scared to death to believe that what we have is going to last."

"You don't have to be afraid, Blanca. Our relationship is solid."

Blanca pulled his hands up to her lips and kissed his scuffed knuckles. "I love that you're here, and every night with you has been amazing, but I can't help but think it's only a matter of time before everything falls apart. As much as I can honestly say that I'm falling in love with you, I'm also just living in the moment with you, quietly wondering when it's all going to end."

Julien wiggled his hands out of hers and cupped her face. "I am not *him*, Blanca. What he did to you, how he could break your heart then continue to cause you even more pain, he deserves a lifetime of suffering for it. I will never hurt you. You mean everything to me. I can't imagine my life without you, Blanca. I love you. *Je t'aime. Je t'aime pour toujours* (I love you. I love you forever)."

Tears began to cloud Blanca's eyes. Whether she believed him or not, she had certainly heard him.

"I love you, too, Julien," she replied through quivering lips, tugging his hands away from her face. "I do. I wouldn't be this scared if I wasn't really in love."

"You'll see some day. You'll see me for who I am and what you mean to me, and when you do, you will know what real, everlasting love is," Julien assured her, tugging her into his arms where she belonged. "And I'll never let you down. I promise."

"Oh, Jules," she moaned against his chest. "Where does all your hope come from?"

Chapter Twenty-Seven

"The secret of humor is surprise."
~Aristotle

Blanca

On Tuesday, Blanca joined Julien at Angel of the Vine Winery to taste test several Chardonnays. Though the same type of grapes sat in the giant vats surrounding them, the crushed fruit had been churned and aged at different intervals creating unique spice racks per batch.

Not sure what that meant, but the resident sommelier who accompanied us and talked our ears off said it was important.

They all worked together to craft a blend of three of the varietals, determining which cuvée would become Blanc de Blanca.

"Fruity with a subtle note of oak and butterscotch," Julien had described their final blend once they were done.

Blanca had thought it tasted more like, "A gentle nibble followed up by a firm smack on the ass." That may have had more to do with where her mind was considering how scintillating the whole wine tasting experience felt to her.

The sommelier, on the other hand, thought they were both nuts and laughed off their apparent disregard for his presence as Blanca mauled Julien in front of him shamelessly throughout the day.

Afterwards, Blanca and Julien perused a catalogue for the perfect bottle to package their brand, settling on of all things ... *wait for it* ... a bubble. Yep, a tiny glass globe that had a flat bottom and held ten ounces of liquid—the perfect size for a twosome to enjoy a little bit of sparkling wine together. The bottling would require renting some special equipment to maneuver the odd shape, but Julien's uncle, who popped in on them while they ate lunch at the winery's restaurant, assured them it would be no problem.

By the time Julien and Blanca had finally called it a night and headed home, they had drafted a logo to stamp onto their cork tops. They had also agreed to leave it to a professional to pilfer their brains for a sense of what they were looking for in a design for the label. They agreed that they wanted to make their label into a tag that would hang off the bottle's snub neck instead of a sticker slapped onto the side of the glass like a traditional bottle sported.

From the L' Angevin Champagne crossing over to sparkling wine, to the brand and even the shape of the vessel, everything about their Blanc de Blanca reflected elements of their journey together.

Sappy, I know. But, hey, bubbles!

On Saturday, Blanca joined Maxie for an afternoon of Aerial Yoga. They spent an hour twirling, swinging, and laughing while being suspended from a warehouse ceiling by fabric bands. Their weekly routine had slowed down to only one wacky yoga class a month, but if that's all her bestie was giving of her time, Blanca seized it with grabby hands.

It was on their yoga play date that Maxie asked Blanca to be her maid of honor via black and white, graphic, workout tank tops that read, you guessed it, "Bride," and, "Bride's Bitch."

Well, maybe you didn't see that one coming, but that's fine.

They swapped out their other tops for the new ones just before class started and laughed, and laughed, and laughed. It was kinda mean, but deep down inside Blanca knew she deserved it.

She was humble like that.

Two weeks later, Julien was tossing *I love you* around like a four-letter word on YouTube. Blanca tossed it back just as liberally without reserve. She did love him. She was even *in love* with him.

Julien never brought up the future, though—sticking to the whole here and now mantra like a champ. Likely because of Blanca's rant about living in the moment that one night in the Zen Den. A rant she still stood by because their whole love affair resonated with a sticky-sweet feeling of being too good to be true. A tell tale sign that one prick of disappointment from either of them and their bubble would burst. As much as Julien assured Blanca on a daily basis that his love for her was legit, she couldn't escape the dreadful mentality her damn ex had plagued her with.

When Chase's birthday slash Halloween bash rolled around again, the four of them were every bit the bells and beaus of the ball. The happy couples even coordinated their costumes thanks to Maxie.

Was there any doubt?

Sandy and Danny and Rizzo and Kenickie.

Blanca just went with it. The days of pretending to be good versus evil angels were long-gone and replaced by the reality of those charades anyway.

Julien had no clue what Grease even was, and, when Chase tried to summarize the plot over a late lunch before the droves of twenty-somethings started arriving for the celebration, Julien pretended to doze off—obnoxious snore sounds included. At that point, Blanca didn't feel much like explaining the dynamics of their characters' relationship.

And why would I? Movie love is a volatile mess. Their love? Yep. Still perfect.

Blanca didn't need that kind of negative in her life. The whole living for the moment mantra she had clung to like a buoy in a turbulent sea of future what if's had her all kinds of coo-coo lately. She even started wondering if Julien would ever pop the question, and if so, whether she was brave enough to say, *yes.*

I know, I know. This is the scary crap in my head that keeps me up at night. Bear with me.

When the holiday season was upon them, Julien's parents flew to America to see him, staying at Chase's parents' house. They embraced

Blanca like she was part of the family, just as they had done a year ago. Even Chase's parents insisted that she come around more with Julien.

He had been spending hours at the vineyard each week, meddling in that end of the L'Angevin family empire. He even started working alongside the chef of À la Vôtre! to help prepare all kinds of pastries for the holiday crowds that visited the winery's tasting room by the droves that time of year.

Unfortunately, or maybe fortunately, Julien's parents' visit came and went the week before Christmas. The situation left Blanca with an in to ask Julien to spend Christmas with her family in the Bay Area instead of with Chase's family at the winery, and she took it.

She was ready like that.

Blanca was going to bring her boyfriend home to meet her family.

Though Blanca's parents lived in Sacramento, her Nonna Alba on her pop's side, aunts and uncles, and several cousins that lived all over the Bay Area all convened at her nonna's in San Francisco every year. Grand-pop Sal, had already passed away a long time ago, and her other grand-mom and grand-pop lived outside of Los Angeles and hosted their own soirée full of family.

"So, next year," she gulped, terrified to be plotting their life a whole year in advance, "We can go to my other grandparents' party, unless we don't." She peeked at Julien next to her as he pulled into Nonna Alba's slanted driveway in his relatively new SUV.

"*Très bon.* I like that plan," he replied, throwing on the emergency brake.

The sudden relief in Blanca almost made her dizzy.

"Really? *Eccellente,*" she eeped. "You'll have so much fun. Los Angeles is so crazy."

Julien smiled and shook his head. "We still need to enjoy this Christmas, too, love."

Oh, right. The moment. Dammit.

Lately, the epic battle of *Team Fear of Failure* versus *Team True Love* played out in Blanca's head non-stop. Hoping for a future with Julien had become her dirty, little secret—well, maybe *one* of them anyway—

and wanting him to do more than just tell her he loved her was driving her nuts.

She didn't just want to hear it, she wanted him to show it, *you know, like with a ... different kind of sparkling thingy besides that glass bubble of wine they'd made together.*

The truth was getting an engagement ring had consumed her every thought since ... *since Maxie had gotten hers. Gah!*

Blanca's evenings for the last few months had consisted of helping Maxie via texts, calls, and FaceTime chats to create a spectacular wedding venue. Their wedding was going to be all any blushing bride could ever dream of. One Maxie and Chase deserved. Maxie had set aside all her novel writing adventures to hone in on the wedding of the century, and, like the BFF Blanca tried to be, she was helping Maxie orchestrate it one Pinterest pin at a time.

Being the French gentleman he was, Julien told Blanca to stay put as he eased out of the car then walked around to open her door. The drizzling rain had slowed up for a few minutes as if God had cut them some slack, giving them a chance to grab a few things out of the car and head for the house.

Never in a million years did Blanca ever think she'd be bringing another boyfriend home for Christmas again. At least, not any time soon. Not after the only other guy to ever make it past her nonna's front door had been her ex fiancé.

The opportunity to show Julien a deeper, more personal side of her life felt like a blessing and a curse. On the one hand, she wanted him to meet everyone, show him off, and let her whole family know that she'd managed to succumb to an actual relationship that, for what it was worth, was working. On the other hand, she thought she could put him to the test and see if he really was as all-in as he had claimed to be by diving headfirst into a frenzied houseful of Grazias.

Blanca didn't know if she was excited or scared to death knowing some of her snoopy relatives were bound to dig him for his intentions with her. Intentions she hoped reflected them moving from living in the moment to something more ... permanent. Like her bestie.

Double gah!

* * *

Julien

Julien's eyes lit up at the sight of the clunky Victorian house—bright yellow and white and bursting with character. Through the front windows to his left a large, shimmering Christmas tree flocked with hundreds of ornaments could be seen and on the right the windows revealed a living area with several people walking about with wine glasses, mugs, and small plates of food.

They walked up the steps to the front door and rang the bell. The first person to greet Julien was Blanca's brother, somewhat short, but not quite as short as his pint-sized beloved. He had thick arms threaded with veins and stood tall like a young man who would take on anyone who dared to mess with his baby sister.

"Lucas meet Julien, Julien—Lucas. He's all bark and no bite, Jules." Blanca hoisted her Strasbourg souvenir canvas bag, loaded with presents and a couple bottles of L'Angevin house red and white, back up on her shoulder. Julien carried a matching bag twice as heavy and had tried to wrestle the other bag from Blanca, but she insisted on carrying it herself.

"Hey, how are ya?" Lucas asked, shoving a hand out to Julien.

Julien clutched the young man's hand and shook it with vigor, unsure of who was actually dictating the aggression. "It's a pleasure to meet you."

"Come in. Come in. We're all anxious to meet the mystery man in person. We've heard so much about you. It's nice to finally put a face to the name."

The smile on Lucas' face let Julien know that he was under scrutiny and welcome all at once. The family resemblance in both his cheeky personality and those jade green eyes had him chuckling to himself as he stepped through the threshold into Blanca's grandmother's home.

He hadn't gotten more than three steps into the foyer before he was absconded by a bevy of young women—Blanca's pre-teen and teenage cousins—who fawned, pawed, and cooed over him with multiple greetings.

"You can slobber all over my boyfriend later, girls," Blanca chirped, slapping her cousin's hand away as it had tried to take a walk through Julien's loose waves of golden hair.

Boyfriend? I'd prefer love of her life, soulmate, her one true love, but it will do for now.

It flattered Julien to see Blanca garner so much attention because of him, hoping it further solidified his permanency in her life. She had been reciprocating his overt attempts to proclaim his steadfast love for quite some time. Her *I love you* had always followed his, and her affection had been ever passionate. Her caring ways enveloped him each day. He appreciated knowing that his status in her life had obviously become the family gossip.

"I demand details later about how all of you already know so much about him," Blanca said to her adorable entourage of starry-eyed cousins as they scattered away.

"Very cute," Julien replied, smiling sheepishly at her.

Blanca motioned with her head towards the kitchen. "Follow me."

Another group of people flocked around them, taking their totes and throwing their arms around his neck and hers—a swarm of names and relations rising above them in an uproar. Then, someone shoved a plate of assorted fish, shrimp, crab, salmon pâté, rolled red meats, olives, sliced bread, and a stack of crisps at him to eat.

Julien felt right at home instantly.

"I love calamari," he said, plucking a battered ring up that dripped with marinara and popped it into his mouth.

"It's *calamad.*" She winked at him then pointed at a rolled piece of meat. "And we call that capicola, *gabagul.*"

"Gabagoo?"

"Close enough," she giggled. "*'Iamo* (let's go)." She led him out of the kitchen down the hallway.

They joined several others towards the back end of the first floor in the family room. Blanca's parents rose to greet him, hugging him with grunts and vigorous handshakes, all the while exclaiming how happy they were to finally meet the man who was capable of wrestling their daughter's heart away from her.

In the corner of the room, another Christmas tree with colorful blinking lights and clumps of silver tinsel hanging off it had several gifts piled under it. Someone had snatched the tote off his shoulder in the kitchen only moments ago and must've helped themselves to the contents because he also spied the two gifts they had brought for each other.

The sight of them suddenly struck a little fear in him.

They had discussed keeping their gift exchange as benign as possible financially, so they vowed to make them less monetary and more personable. Little did Blanca know that her idea to do that was the perfect segue he needed for the first part of his latest surprise that had been brewing since Milan.

As he panned the room packed full of her family members, it occurred to him that Blanca might not appreciate his sentiment if she had to open his gift to her in front of all her fawning relatives.

Oh, no. What have I gotten myself into?

Everyone began to fill up the room, sitting on furniture or folding chairs, or standing around as the adults raved about the Feast of Seven Fishes—an Italian tradition of serving seven types of seafood on Christmas Eve. Blanca explained the tradition to Julien as he set aside their empty plates on an end table.

As they waited together, hand in hand, on the couch, they began to take questions left and right.

"How did you meet?" ... "What part of France are you from?" ... "How long have you been dating?" ... "How in the world did you get Blanca to settle down?"

"Just look at him, dear." The wife of the gentleman who asked the last question replied, answering for her husband.

Julien tried his best to answer as many questions as he could without dominating the conversations with his boring life in France.

What sounded like a majestic vacation to someone—life atop a hill surrounded by grapes in a lush land miles away from a café or boulangerie—was just the other L'Angevin estate, a place he no longer identified as his home. For Julien, Champagne was lonely, isolated, and only meant for a sojourn with Blanca again someday to visit his own relatives.

As the fellowship waned on, everyone ate before eating then ate afterwards before declaring it time to open presents from each other. A couple of the teenagers handed out the gifts from under the tree, and everyone began unwrapping them and showing any and everybody what they had been given in a chaotic uproar.

Blanca and Julien had brought tin containers of cookies they had fashioned together the day before as their gifts to everyone. Looking around, many of the tins were already open and circulating thanks to the mystery relative who had emptied the contents of their canvas bags when they had first arrived.

The only other gift they had brought was a PlayStation game for Lucas to go with the gaming system Blanca's parents had said they had bought for him. Her brother shouted out his *thank you* out to them. Julien and Blanca nodded back as they suddenly found themselves on the receiving end of several presents that were intended for making their home more pleasant.

A crystal candelabra. Pewter serving dishes. Picture frames.

Gifts that reflected a distinct knowledge that they were living together.

Gifts that looked an awful lot like household items better suited for an engagement party instead of Christmas.

It surprised Julien how Blanca's relatives embraced him like he was already part of the family. It seemed neither of them fully grasped just how much her entire brood had been in on the details of their relationship until that evening. Blanca kept swearing she had only mentioned minor tidbits about him to her immediate family and a couple of cousins when it became apparent she was missing at last year's

Grazia Christmas festivities. But, as far as everyone in attendance was concerned, they were already as good as married and needed help decorating their home.

Marriage.

It weighed heavily on Julien's mind all the time. What he would give to be able to walk down the aisle towards Blanca immediately and be done with it. Live their lives out in pure bliss. No more abiding by her restrictions to keep to the present. Never to question, or wonder, or even doubt if one day the moment would come to an end.

Julien lived with an element of fear that she would find fault with him, and that would be enough for her to move on. Much like that dark cloud of doubt that rained on her all the time.

He also feared her need to compete with Max on a romantic level. He didn't want her succumbing to an interest in their future together primarily because his cousin had taken the next step with her best friend.

Julien had a plan, though. One Chase, the ultimate expert at planning, had begun to help him concoct. A plan that would take several months to completely manifest and perhaps accelerate them past Blanca's fascination with competing with Max. The first part was helping him to move to America and move in with her. The second part she had casually dismissed away six months earlier was about to unfold in a rebirth whether he wanted it to now in front of everyone or not.

I should've planned this through more. What was I thinking?

The anticipation had Julien's hands feeling clammy as he second-guessed if he should've gone with a more generic gift instead of what he had wrapped up to hand to her on Christmas Eve.

"Open our present, Blanca," her mother urged her, motioning to a young boy to bring her daughter a large, shimmering gift bag billowing with red tissue paper. Blanca took the gift bag from her cousin and pulled out a beautiful, brightly colored crocheted blanket with the initials J & B on it. It was large enough to cover their queen-sized bed. A few giggles erupted out of the teen girls when they saw it, only furthering Blanca's need to fan the blanket out over both of them, staking her claim to Julien with a smirk.

Blanca leaned in to whisper in his ear. "Are you comfortable with all this attention?"

"I'm fine," he assured her, though his knee bounced, betraying his nerves.

I only want you to need me, love me, and be willing to spend the rest of your life with me. That is all.

Julien wrapped his hand around her thigh under the blanket anchoring himself to her as they watched her father give her mother ruby earrings, and her mother give him ruby cufflinks in return. A planned exchange that had them laughing with everyone else at their distaste for surprises in the form of unwanted presents.

Unwanted presents. Now there's a terrifying thought.

Blanca wanted to give Julien his gift first, insisting to anyone paying attention that it was no big deal.

Unlike mine, perhaps.

"I hope you're not offended by it," Blanca said, handing him a small box wrapped in silver paper, flaunting a red ribbon bow.

He tore the paper open and lifted the lid to the box uncovering a handwritten piece of stationary. "I hereby entitle the sexiest man alive to an afternoon of girly pampering at Beauty Defined Day Spa," he began, smiling at her loopy handwriting. "Your luxury package spa treatment includes a new hair style by the most awesome stylist from Italy to America, a facial that will leave your face as smooth as a baby's butt, and your choice of dining pleasures at one of the many fine restaurants nearby as long as they serve garlic French fries." He leaned over and kissed her cheek. "I love it. What a thoughtful gift."

"If you don't want to get—"

"It's perfect. I could use a haircut and some garlic French fries. I don't know how Chase can stand his hair this long. I tried to be fashionable and lump it into a bun, but, as you know, my hair doesn't always cooperate," he said, fisting his big wavy curls that sprawled down to his shoulders.

"We'll come up with something you'll be happy with, but I warn you, I'm plastering the before and after pictures all over my social media. You have a face that could sell anything."

Blanca's compliment warmed his heart and detonated a bombardment of *awws* from her family.

Julien gave her a medium sized box, wrapped in the same silver paper his had been adorned with. "I hope you aren't upset about your gift. I wasn't expecting an audience like this. Please, don't be angry."

"As long as it's not a sex toy, I'm good," she teased under her breath.

Blanca peeled the paper off and popped open the tape sealing the flaps together and peeped inside. "My ... my book?" She pulled her novel out of the box and flipped it around. The paperback bore a striking resemblance to the previous cover she had seen before except the back cover had an additional accent of royal blue to it and now had a marbled, oceanic pattern. On the front cover, the title, *Right as Rayne,* had been transformed with gradient orange and yellow hues reflected in a silver, iridescent color.

"I wanted to surprise you with the completed version," Julien pleaded. "I didn't know everyone would be watching."

Blanc gave him a stunned look in reply.

"Show us what you got, sweetie," one of her aunts called out.

Blanca, expressionless and quiet, turned the book towards everyone.

Nonna leaned over in her chair across the room from them and squinted. "*Right as Rayne, si?* Oh, look, honey, it's your name. You wrote a book? You wrote a book!"

Suddenly, as many relatives applauded Blanca as did ask a torrent of questions about the novel. Saying Blanca was surprised was an understatement. Her jaw went slack—her eyes wide and unblinking—as her attention careened back onto the book in her hands. Blanca's family members tried to answer their own questions with assumptions until finally pleading with Julien to tell them what was going on since Blanca had suddenly lost her voice.

Chapter Twenty-Eight

"It is difficult to know at what moment love begins; it is less difficult to know that it has begun."
~Henry Wadsworth Longfellow

Julien

Julien glanced around at everyone in the room—eager faces expecting an answer staring right back at him. "Blanca wrote a novel a year ago, and I had it translated into Italian and printed for her as a gift last summer for her birthday. This copy is the final edited version."

"Uhahuhm," was all Blanca could utter.

Blanca's mother stood up and snatched the book out of her daughter's hand for a closer look. You wrote a book? You didn't tell me this?" She turned on her heels, keeping the book with her, and sat back down next to Blanca's father as everyone else continued to murmur and unwrap more gifts.

Blanca snapped out of her stupor with an attitude. "Yes, I did. Remember I told you about the workshop Maxie and I went to last year? I sat at your kitchen table for a week trying to finish it before December."

"Ah, that's right. I think I remember that now. Wasn't Maxine writing one with you, too?"

Blanca gasped and turned her attention back to Julien. "Maxie. Oh, no. She's going to kill me. She was planning on trying to get her book published as soon as all the wedding stuff was behind her."

Julien draped his arm around her shoulder. "She's going to just have to deal with the fact that you are the one who gets to claim being a success first. Our book baby is complete. You're a romance author, my love."

"I'm not— I don't— This isn't who I am. It was just a bet. She won. I mean, It's sweet that you went to all this trouble for me but—"

"That's so romantic," Blanca's mother shrilled, passing the novel off to someone asking to see it then fisting her hands together and waving them in the air victoriously.

Blanca's parents stood up and applauded their daughter, garnering the full attention of the room, causing everyone to burst into cheers.

Julien buried his nose in Blanca's ear as she tried to shimmy the blanket up to her chin and hide. "I'm so sorry this has become such a public spectacle. I didn't mean for you to be overwhelmed. There's more, but I'll tell you later in private."

"More? More!" Blanca inhaled and exhaled, still processing the information. "I thought I told you not to bother with it?"

"I took that as you only not wanting to worry about any of the responsibilities of it. You approved of the proof, remember? I've been working with the editor off and on for months to create the paperback."

What have I done?

Blanca parted her lips to speak but her father approached them. He leaned down and kissed her cheeks, gripping her shoulders. "I am so proud of you, Blanca. You were always such a smart girl, speaking so many languages and traveling the world. Julien, you cannot clip her wings when the two of you get married, you hear me? You have to let her fly, let her be free to be all that she can be."

"Married?" Blanca uttered. "We're not ... we haven't even talked about ... I didn't—"

Oh, no. No. No. No. Don't panic. Don't leave me.

"What she means to say is that we're so caught up in the joy of Christmas with all of you, we don't want to take away from it concerning our relationship."

Lucas piped up with a smirk. "Valentine's Day. You should propose on Valentine's Day. That's the day reserved for love. Maybe you guys could put some lead in it and beat Max to the punch this summer with your own wedding."

"I can't … this isn't … I need to catch my breath. If you'll excuse me." Blanca threw their blanket off them and tossed it at Julien then rushed out of the living room.

As Blanca's relatives continued their discussion on the best time for Julien to propose to her, as well as when and where they should hold their wedding venue, Julien uttered his apologies for needing to leave the room and trailed in a panic after his beloved.

Blanca locked herself in the bathroom, and Julien could hear her hyperventilating through the door. "Please, darling, let me in. Talk to me. I love you, please," he pleaded.

Blanca swung the door open and grabbed his sweater in her fist, dragging him inside the bathroom with her. "I don't know what to do?"

"You don't have to do anything. They are only excited for you. It's a grand accomplishment to write a novel. They want to include me in all that joy. Don't let them affect us, *s'il vous plaît?*"

"You … you weren't going to propose to me, too? That's not your other surprise?"

"*Non, non.* I have to, ehm, I need to still speak with your father about my intentions, but I, ehm—"

She covered her face with her hands. "Okay, okay. Stop. You're doing that nervous thing again with your voice. Please don't freak out on me when I'm already freaking out."

Julien pulled her hands away to look at her. "Don't you think we should talk about our future before we make any announcements to your whole family? Our relationship is only getting stronger. It would seem we would naturally, ehm, I, eh, I think we definitely need to talk."

"Yasss! Talking. Good. Very good, the talking," she nodded.

"So, you're not panicking on me, then?"

"Oh, I'm flipping out." She swallowed hard—her eyes darting between his. "You're really serious about us, aren't you?"

"I've never been more serious about anyone or anything before in my life, Blanca. I love you, and I will marry you someday, if you'll have me. I would like to ask your father for your hand first before I propose, though."

Blanca's jade eyes grew wide and glossy. "You would do that for me?"

"I would do anything for you."

"Yeah, no kidding," she mumbled under her breath. "Does Maxie know about my book, yet?"

"*Non,* you asked me not to tell her, but I have a confession to make."

Blanca furrowed her brow. "What?"

Please don't hate me for keeping secrets from you.

"Chase has known about me having it translated from the beginning, but I asked him not to share that with her and respect that you would like to tell her yourself someday. You *are* going to tell her about all this eventually, *oui?*"

"Yeah, sure. Someday. Just not any time soon. I doubt dropping this bomb on her before her wedding of the century is going to bode well for my friendship right now. She's not doing anything to her book until after she gets married." Blanca blew out a breath, causing the ribbon of curl dangling in front of her eye to flutter.

"She'll be fine."

Especially when I tell you the second part of the surprise.

Blanca shook her head and worried her lip between her teeth. "Nope. She's gonna kill me if she finds out."

Or not.

"Only if we decide we should get married on the same day as them and hand out your novel as our party favors," Julien jested.

Blanca released a nervous laugh. "My family hasn't scared you away by planning our whole lives for us, have they?"

"Not at all. I've been worried all night about them frightening you."

"Okay, wow, we really do need to talk when we get home. If you're not scared then I'm not scared. At least, I'm trying not to be."

"Everything will be all right, darling. We know what we are. We know what our love is made of. No one can dictate the pace we want our relationship to take." He pressed his lips to hers for a brief moment then hugged her. "Let's get through this evening and tomorrow celebrating Christmas. Then we can worry about everything else when we are not on display like we've been all night."

"I'm in," she whimpered, nodding once.

When they emerged from the bathroom together, everyone had already begun to gather their things and get their coats on to head to church for Midnight Mass. The order of events on Christmas Eve had been a little different than Julien was used to, but, overall, he felt very much like he was at home with his own family.

The food. The fellowship. The laughter. Even the crazy mishaps. Through it all, Julien felt like he belonged. And in that comfort, he decided he still had plenty of time to keep Blanca in the dark about the rest of her surprise.

At least until Max's wedding had finally passed.

Julien felt he had no choice but to.

I screwed up again.

It would absolutely devastate Julien if Blanca ended their relationship when he finally had the courage to tell her. All because of a frenzied hype surrounding the novel debuting on some Italian soap opera several months ago. Amilianna Rossi had taken the liberty to pitch *Right as Rayne* to a publisher she did editorial work for unbeknownst to him until recently. And that phantom novel every young woman in all of Italy saw on TV then immediately had to have was going to make its actual publication debut come summer right after his cousin tied the knot.

* * *

Blanca

When the church service was over, most of Blanca's aunts, uncles, and cousins went home. Only Blanca's immediate family prepared to spend the night with her nonna. Julien grabbed their joint suitcase out of the trunk and set it in the bedroom they intended to share, according to Nonna Alba.

Two twin beds.

That's Nonna for you.

When Christmas morning came, Julien convinced Nonna and Blanca's ma to allow him in the kitchen with them to help cook while Blanca sat at the bar counter, sipping coffee and quietly reminiscing about their dessert-making adventures in Champagne the year before.

He worked alongside the two women prepping the crusts on some breakfast tomato pies they were making, looking ever so sexy in his dark blue plaid pajama bottoms and wrinkled t-shirt.

This guy has no clue how tragically beautiful he is. And he's mine. Mine. Maybe even forever. OMG.

Blanca wondered if Julien had been second-guessing their life together for the long haul since all the chaos the night before with her nosy family. He didn't utter another word about their future or plans to get married for the rest of the night. And that thought prompted a flutter of nerves and doubt in her tummy. She wondered if their conversation in the bathroom had more to do with saying what he needed to just to appease her during her major spaz.

One thing Blanca knew for sure was that Julien had no intention of just coming right out and proposing to her like she had hoped for. He was going to ask her pop first.

Even better. Squee!

All Blanca wanted to do was wrap up the holidays and get home to talk about *it.*

Get engaged. Have a wedding. Be married.

Just. Like. Maxie.

Gah! Maxie!

"Wouldn't you say so, love?" Julien asked, breaking into her mental meltdown with his sexy French drawl.

"I'm sorry, what was that, hotness?"

"I was telling these charming, young ladies here," (*Insert caddy giggles from my nonna and my ma*), "That we are nearing our six month anniversary."

Only six months? We've been together for—no, wait. We've known each other for over a year. Stats on being a couple, half that. Hmph. No wonder he hasn't proposed yet. We haven't been an actual couple for very long.

"Yes, we've only been dating for a few months."

Boo.

Blanca's ma patted Julien on the back. "Well, I sure do hope the two of you can both enjoy your lives while you're young. It sounds like you've already been on some exciting trips together. Blanca has always had a wild hair in her for travel. And, with you having family in France, that will give her a reason to never have to give it up."

"Ah, Mrs. Grazia, I may have to steal your reason when the time comes for me to convince her of something I still need to speak to your husband about." Julien slid two pie pans lined with fresh dough crust over to her nonna and wiped his floured hands on a towel he had slung over his shoulder.

Did he really just say that out loud? To my ma. And Nonna?

"Oh, you'll get our blessing. We've been waiting for you for a long time."

"Momma!"

Julien shot Blanca a worried look. "One thing we know for sure, and that is Max and Chase's wedding needs to come first, right Blanca?"

What? Why? Oh, yeah. Another reason for her to kill me ... if I get married first.

"Yep, sucks to be me."

Chapter Twenty-Nine

"Love, whether newly born, or aroused from a deathlike slumber, must always create sunshine, filling the heart so full of radiance, that it overflows upon the outward world."
~Nathaniel Hawthorne

Blanca
When Blanca and Julien finally came home after their Christmas adventures in Grazialand, they waited until they were both curled around each other in bed to bring up the M-word.

"I think it's important that I seek out your father's blessing formally, even though I know your parents approve of me asking for your hand in marriage," he began, as if they'd been talking about *it* for hours.

Blanca propped her head up in her hand as she draped her leg over Julien's thigh while he rested against several pillows. "I think that's kind of cool, to be honest."

"As long as you're being honest, how do you feel about us getting married? Do you ever think about our future? I know we agreed to keep our conversations in the present and live for the moment, but can you see us taking that next step in our relationship? If I ask, will you say, *yes? Oui? Si?* Any language will do."

Blanca hesitated for a second—the past rearing its ugly head up, as usual, to mock her with a sickly haunting of too-good-to-be-true. "I'll say *yes* if you promise me you'll mean it when you ask."

"I promise I won't ask until I know we're both ready."

Blanca looked away from him—her lips pressing together as if to keep from blurting out something stupid.

Julien lifted her chin with his finger. "Hey, I see you. I know what you're thinking, and you're wrong. We belong together. That's why we've gotten along so well."

Blanca slid her hand over his smooth chest and sighed. "Can you see through me all the time or just when I need you to?"

Insert blubbering confession in three ... two ... one.

"I do have one concern," he began, smoothing her unruly hair down.

Uh, never mind.

Blanca wrinkled her nose. "I'm sorry I keep leaving the cap off the toothpaste. It won't happen again."

Julien smiled at her attempt to add some humor to soften his blow.

She sat up and pulled the blanket over her chest to combat the sudden tremors she felt. "Okay, lay it on me. What you probably meant to say is you have lots and lots of concerns."

"*Non,* just the one."

By now, Blanca's stomach had rivaled an Olympic gymnast in its acrobatic feats.

"Whatever it is, it's not a deal breaker if I don't give you the right answer, is it?"

Julien looked away, pulling his bottom lip between his teeth as if holding back something he feared speaking out loud. The awkward pause between them stretched on for a few seconds longer than Blanca could stand. She was about to say something else when he continued.

"I need you to know that I'm committed to you completely. I think having open communication is important. We need to be able to talk through our problems, not pretend they'll simply vanish if we ignore them."

Yep. That's never worked well as a strategy for me no matter how many times I try.

"Is that it? That I have been avoiding discussing our future? Because I'm under the impression that this moment we're living in right now kind of puts an end to my rule."

Julien nodded thoughtfully. "True, but what concerns me is that you're sudden interest in wanting to marry me has something to do with my cousin's future wife and her big day."

Busted.

Blanca drew in a ragged breath. "Maybe, at first. It's hard to plan Maxie's wedding and not get caught up in wanting to be the center of attention myself. I was supposed to be a June bride, and here she is stealing my dream."

He nodded. "I know you love me."

"I do—"

"Remember that line later."

Laughter rippled out of Blanca. "Just be there when I'm going to say it."

"Deal," he replied, roughing up her hair playfully after he had just combed out the tangles. "I only want you to say it, though, if you're really ready. It's a lifetime commitment that I'm asking of you when I propose. You need to be sure. You have to accept me for all my faults and shortcomings, for every dirty secret I confess, and all the ones I keep from you. You have to love me as I am."

They looked at each other in silence. A stillness settling on them as Blanca hesitated to completely spill her guts about her beef with Maxie or just let the conversation stand as it was.

She reached out and stroked his cheek. "I won't let Maxie's perfect life cloud my judgment. Not anymore. Not when our life is even better."

Julien leaned into her hand. "I love you. No matter what."

No matter what? I guess only time will tell.

* * *

On New Years Eve, Blanca treated Julien to a hair makeover at the spa, as he cashed in his Christmas present to be pampered and poke his nose into where she worked. An hour later, Julien rocked a shorter hair style, sprawling out in chunky waves at the tops of his ears with huge curls tumbling over his forehead to his eyebrows.

Slap a suit on him and you'd think he belonged on a runway modeling for Armani. My boyfriend is beyond hot.

* * *

Valentine's Day came and went. No ring. Nothing. Well, not *nothing*. Blanca and Julien did go on another hot air balloon ride—just the two of them. No Maxie and Chase that second time around. It couldn't have been a more perfect opportunity to pop the question. *But no.* It was fun, though. Scary fun. *Like cling to my sexy, future husband fun.*

The day before Easter had them running all over a grassy meadow at Angel of the Vine Winery's annual Egg Hunt chasing after Blanca's little cousins as they scooped up eggs. It meant the world to Blanca that so many of her relatives would drive all the way to Napa Valley for the event. It was a huge affair that required tickets and vended wine and food.

Naturally, when Julien presented her with a plastic egg at the end of the day, as her family was about to leave for Sacramento and the Bay Area again, she was sure the time had come. *But, nah.* She cracked it open to find a silver charm in the shape of a cluster of grapes. It went perfectly with the silver Champagne charm dangling from the necklace he had given her forever ago that she wore everyday. It was pretty, shiny, sweet, and kind, but what it wasn't was a ring.

In between the holidays, Blanca continued to work hard at her job at the spa. Her regular customers multiplied by the week, and she even had several styling jobs she did on the side for a local theatre production and a few country singers in town that Skeeter Dee had referred to her.

The independent route of being an on-call stylist a half-a-dozen times a month was beginning to look mighty tempting as the pay almost equaled a full week's work at the spa. With summer coming and her three-week-long trip to Italy along with it, she had some options about continuing at Beauty Defined Day Spa.

Julien insisted that they extend their trip from one week in Milan to two additional weeks in Rome. Blanca agreed full-heartedly to the plan.

Wanderlusting as a couple? Yes, please.

Julien had been splitting everything down the middle as far as bills and the mortgage payment went, and even if he did up and disappear out of her life one day, she was in a place financially where she could handle everything on her own anyway.

As any woman should be.

Emotionally, on the other hand, she needed him like the air she gulped during Hot House Yoga yesterday with Maxie.

By the time the big day for her bestie and his cousin rolled around, Blanca had come to expect that their cozy, above-average relationship in all its sexy glory was just going to keep cruising along at a snail's pace. Marriage was bound to happen. Just not in the next decade if Julien didn't get on with the asking.

The thought of proposing herself popped in her head all the time. What if she came right out and did it? Got on one knee, said the words no man ever gets to hear. She was a strong, independent, forward-thinking woman. She could do it. She could upstage him. Unless, dare she think it, he wasn't ready or had secretly changed his mind. Again with the old seesaw of emotions.

She was insecure like that.

I really need to stop. I'm annoying myself as much as you.

Maxie and Chase's wedding had to have been the turning point. It finally made sense to be giving her BFF all the attention she deserved. No more excuses in her mind about upstaging her bestie's day with her own fanfare like Julien had worried about—the conclusion Blanca had come to as to why she was still just a girlfriend.

The wedding event of the century included hundreds of family members, friends, and neighboring vintners. Julien's parents even flew in for the event, staying the entire week before and dining out with Julien and Blanca twice in that time frame. Even Blanca's parents and brother had come to the wedding, having known Maxie since she and her were barely teenagers.

When Blanca and Julien's parents met, they all instantly bonded with back slaps and lots of kisses. Left cheek. Right cheek. Left cheek. Right. They even asked other guests if they could trade seats so they could all sit together at the same circular table at the reception. It was quite a sight from the long table that they sat at from a distance. All of them, including Lucas, laughed and carried on like they all knew each other for years as Blanca and Julien looked on at them.

Everything about Maxie and Chase's wedding, from the French inspired pink, black, and white theme, to the man who played songs on an accordion while walking around all the tables inside the big white tent, was perfection.

Their ceremony had been outdoors in the courtyard under an arch draped in panels of white tulle. The perimeter of the courtyard was lined with the LED trees, shimmering in all white, creating an ethereal feel to the event. The angelic creature in the middle of the fountain had been adorned with garlands of multi-colored daisies, and the folding chairs each had crisp, white covers and black tulle bows protruding from the back. Chic yet elegant were the only words that came to mind when taking in all the nuances surrounding them.

Watching Maxie and Chase say their vows while standing by her side felt right. Everything about the love those two shared felt tried and true. Her bestie really had found the one. Chase was going to love her and treat her with respect and fulfill his vows as promised because they were meant to be, and Blanca had come to terms with that.

From the first dance to the last, Blanca felt nothing but joy, peace, and happiness for the bride and groom. No more jealousy. No more self-pity. Just a bundle of love in her heart for them.

And speaking of love, Julien finally managed to nudge their relationship along, sans a ring, though, as the night waned on.

Almost everyone had left once Chase and Maxie headed off to the airport to get an immediate start on their honeymoon in Santorini, Greece. A crew had even come in to start breaking down the contents of the tent. One feature still remained, though, and Julien asked Blanca if she would join him in experiencing it before they headed home.

Two rows of grapes had been strung with white lights, and the dirt and rock pathway between the plants had been sprinkled with silk rose pedals. Maxie had called it a lover's lane meant to facilitate a romantic stroll for any takers. Julien, proving himself the most romantic man on earth once again, took Blanca's arm in his and sauntered down the lane with her, raining professions of his love to her every step of the way.

"I have never been more in love with you than I am today—from your hair, your eyes, your dress, your smile—you glow in perfection. You are the most exquisite woman I have ever seen, and you're not too shabby on the inside either," Julien teased.

Ooh, sweet talk, my favorite.

Blanca's hair had a fringe of bangs—*don't ask, it was a major emotional faux pas one day*— with a French twist. Several tendrils fell down from her crown, still black as silk with ribbons of blue and indigo throughout it. Her eyes—smoky, smoldering, and rockin' some thick falsies—looked gorgeous. Her dress—a black silk slip with embroidered pink roses climbing up from the hem and a plunging back—fit her like a glove. Her smile—a matte, kissable lipstick that begged for him to taste them. Her heart—loaded and pulsing with an ever-present awareness of the future yearned to move forward with him.

I do look super hot tonight.

Blanca swayed into him as they pivoted and walked back through the lover's lane. The ambiance hummed of so much romance.

"And you, Jules. I haven't been able to take my eyes off you. That whole tight swell you've got going on with your biceps in that tux, *whoa,* forget everything I ever said about you working out too much."

"Well, ehm, I'm all yours. You have made me so happy. I never thought I'd be in love with an American beauty, but you have stolen my heart completely."

Blanca stopped them and turned to face Julien, looking up at his glassy eyes full of tender longing. "If your heart belongs to me, then you can have mine, too. In fact, you can keep it forever."

Did I just propose?

He leaned down and kissed her lips softly and slowly then held her gaze. "I intend to when the time comes, but I'll share one, little secret with you in the meantime."

She gave him an *I'm waiting* pout.

Waiting on a lot of things.

"Your father gives his consent."

"You asked? You asked!" Blanca lunged up and threw her arms around Julien's neck.

"When you were dancing with Chase."

Italy! Her mind exploded with possible scenarios. *He's going to propose in Italy. Of course, he is! That's where our relationship began! That's why he wanted to extend our trip and head to Rome!*

"As far as the best man goes, isn't it traditional for you to be doing bad things to the maid-of-honor by the end of the night?"

Julien bent down and scooped Blanca up in his arms. "Then we better go home now." He took off with her, laughing and screaming, carrying on like two lovers should, without a care in the world down Lover's Lane.

Chapter thirty

"The beauty of a woman must be seen in her eyes, because that is the doorway to her heart, the place where love resides."
~Aubrey Hepburn

Blanca

There just weren't enough synonyms in the world to adequately describe the rush of round two in Milan styling hair for fashion models. A new rookie designer and two new interns that Giuseppe put Blanca in charge of plus the same models as last year made for a recipe of epic excitement. Their little unit of awesome was becoming *a thing.*

Julien spent the week in Champagne visiting his family while Blanca filled her time busting her butt making fabulous hair happen. Being apart from him the first few days were heart wrenching, but it also showed her she was still an independent, driven woman at her core who didn't *need* someone else to complete her life.

Life was feeling exceptionally complete as it were in her career ambitions, but, boy, oh boy, did she *want* him. It became clear to Blanca how essential to her heart Julien had become, and it had nothing to do with snagging a ring in some petty, jealous way to be like Maxie.

Two halves making a whole? A plus-one to her life? *Nope.*

That kind of logic didn't work in Blanca's head. She was already whole. She was already one with herself. So was Julien. Together, they'd still be one but in a multiplicative kind of way. She was ready to be a wife, and that resounding mental break-through kept her from going nuts while they were apart for a few days.

As far as accepting the new era of her friendship with her bestie, Blanca was so over with the whole woe-is-me kind of thinking. Gone was the childish Chax mindset. Maxine Novaline-L'Angevin would always be her BFF. Not even marriage could put a strain on it. Even if the time they spent together had to find a way to fit into the cracks of that new era of their busy lives, at least Blanca knew their friendship was back to being solid. Or, at least that's what she kept telling herself.

* * *

Blanca climbed into bed with her cell phone, pulling the covers up over herself.

Blanca: *Can't get warm, need my*
human blanket at night

The only glow in the hotel room emanated from her screen.

Julien: *Miss you, how was your day?*

Blanca: *Wonderful, draining, missed*
you 2. How was yours?

Julien: *Busy, tiresome. Everyone*
sends their love and wishes you
could've come to see them but
understands how busy this trip
will be for you

Blanca: *Aww, I miss them too,*
give my love to everyone

Blanca's heart hummed with familial warmth. A sensation she embraced with happiness. It was almost hard to believe that she once harbored a fear of attachment to Julien's wonderful family.

Julien: *Have you heard from Maxie?*

Blanca: *Just keeping up with all the*
pics she posts on Facebook.
She won't reply to my nagging about

when they're starting a family.
I need auntie status pronto!
Julien: *It's their honeymoon, lol*
Blanca: *What a perfect time to*
fool around recklessly and get
knocked up!... BTW, when will you
be here? I need some recklessness
in my life right about now
Julien: *I'll be there the day after*
tomorrow, ready and willing. I better
let you get some sleep. Talk to you in
the morning
Blanca: *Buona note (goodnight),*
love you, forever
Julien: *Bonne nuit, (goodnight),*
love you, always

Blanca rolled over on her side and set the iPhone on the nightstand. A comforting peace enveloped her like a thick fog, and she drifted off to sleep.

About five hours later, Blanca's alarm warbled out into the hazy hotel room, and she jabbed at the screen until it stopped its annoying but ever-so-effective purpose. She glanced at her texts to see if she had missed any from Julien.

None.

Noticing that Julien hadn't texted her, Blanca fired off a text to start their day together. A mild nostalgia bubbled up in her as she was reminded of the several months they'd spent texting each morning and or night before they became roomies.

Blanca: *Wake up, wake up,*
wake up. I miss you!
Julien: *Just opened my eyes,*
About to text you, too, I'm up
in more ways than one
Blanca: *Make me miss you*
even more, why don't you?!
Julien: *I forgot to mention*

I was at grand-maman's last
night, cleaning and packing some
things into storage—Didn't even
make it to the bedroom,
I fell asleep on the couch after
talking to you

Blanca sat up and stretched, shaking off the groggy slump that came with still managing a time change on only a few hours of sleep.

Blanca: *Sorry, bet you're really*
stiff, bahahahaha
Julien: *... Definitely, I'm laughing*
out loud, or LOLing as you goofy
Americans would say
Blanca: *Ha, lol! What's your*
plan for today?

Blanca slid out of bed and headed to the bathroom. She cranked on the faucet in the shower and waited as she continued to read Julien's texts.

Julien: *Keep working here mostly.*
Then head over to the house to see if
Victoria needs any more help
moving in— she has redecorated the
house in all purple PURPLE
Blanca: *Your house is purple now?*
Julien: *Her house now, love*
Blanca: *How long is she staying there?*
Julien: *She'll be headed to Cairo*
this winter, putting in six weeks
at a time
Blanca: *WOW!!! We have to visit her*
one of the weeks she's there!

Blanca waved her hand through the trickling water to see if it had warmed up then started shimmying out of her panties.

Julien: *She would love that,*
let's do it
Blanca: *My shower water is hot, I*

better jump in. Call me later,
I need to hear your voice or
FaceTime so I can see that sexy face
Julien: *You took the words*
right out of my mouth – I'll call
you again around noon
Blanca: *love you, always*
Julien: *love you, forever*

Blanca put her phone on the bathroom counter and stepped into the shower. Another day in Milan. Next stop, in a few more days, Rome. Planning a trip to Cairo instantly made it on her To-Do List. She knew, too, that Julien meant it about traveling to Egypt. They would head to Cairo sometime in the fall to see his sister, to see more of the world. Just. Like. That. Then another adventure would manifest, and they'd start planning again. This lifestyle was their future.

The world continued to get even broader for them as other advantages to travel presented themselves by the end of the week. The opportunity to participate in Giuseppe's program again the following year became apparent. He seemed to be sizing her up all week like it was a hands-on job interview to become a regular fixture in his entourage each year in July like the models had become.

Making the trip to Europe to participate in the week long event was a no-brainer. Blanca could indulge in her wanderlust, and Julien could visit his family and assist where needed with the business. Extend the trip, and they could go and do and be all that they wanted together. The lifestyle suited them especially since Julien had been saying he'd begun to crave traveling, as well.

Being an English speaking American fluent in Italian and also able to converse fairly enough in Portuguese, French, and Spanish made her a hot commodity in the fashion industry. Blanca had learned that week that her networking had already begun without her—her name being tossed around among the other designers, stylists, and industry peeps since last summer.

She had become the, "Spirited American with vibrant style and a handbag of languages skills to boot." Her career path had begun to take a distinct turn away from being in a salon environment day after day. A position she no longer felt suited someone as lively as her.

Julien and Blanca's time apart, though difficult, felt right, and they realized their relationship could handle the strain of being apart as hard as it had been. Both of them knew that there would be times when they couldn't always accompany each other on their travels, but they were learning that everything would be fine and dandy during those moments in their lives.

The plan, though, had been to never have to be apart.

* * *

As Julien let himself into Blanca's hotel room with the key she had told him to snag from the concierge in a quick call before he boarded his flight to Milan, Blanca surprised him with yet another hair color scheme. She posed on the bed in an emerald green nightie with her thick, long locks dyed a reddish, chestnut brown. Her softly curled mane glistened like burning coals.

"You are the most exquisite beauty I've ever seen," Julien commented, hustling out of his clothes and climbing up over her body on the bed.

"So you like redheads? *Gabarusses?*" she replied, sliding off her elbows onto her back and threading her fingers through his hair.

"Only you." He dipped down and kissed her slowly, teasing her lips apart with flicks of his tongue.

Blanca wrapped her legs around him, hooking her feet together and giving into his tender kisses. He trailed little nips down her neck then along her shoulder as his breath became ragged.

"I'm not letting you go," she whispered, tightening her grip on him with her thighs.

"So you want me forever?" he breathed into her neck.

"And always," she giggled, arching her back as sensational waves of swoon ebbed and flowed throughout her body.

Her new hair color had cranked the level of vibrant on her jade green eyes way up, causing Julien to rear back and gaze at them repeatedly, muttering all kinds of naughty French phrases at her as he hovered over her body.

"Ahh, I love this man. We survived the week apart. We've got this." She smiled against his collarbone, as she nuzzled his warm skin—her heart complete and full just like her life.

* * *

The following day, the runway show proceeded flawlessly. Blanca walked away with a fistful of business cards and a copy of her contract with Giuseppe to rinse and repeat the following summer with an option to make it a regular gig. She had even secured a mid-year venue with a different fashion designer, Alexandre Amaral, who had been introduced to her by the designer who was part of Giuseppe's team.

Alexandre was the daughter of a woman who had been a longtime fashion designer out of Brazil. Her mother had paraded her collections at Fashion Week in São Paulo for many years. Blanca had helped Alexandre with translating her Portuguese into Italian when she needed an interpreter because the young lady spoke no other language except a tad bit of broken English.

At the end of the show, Alexandre had approached Blanca about working with her on a small venue in Paris that she had been accepted into as an up-and-coming designer. Alexandre had asked Blanca to translate for her, as well as be her models' hair stylist. Given Blanca's limited French skills, she had been apprehensive to accept the offer, but Julien had pulled her aside and offered to help in translating French. Blanca then agreed and plans were set in motion. France was added to their traveling To-Do list.

Total power couple, if you ask me.

Blanca knew right then, Julien was in her life to stay. To bend to her whims of traveling, to tend to her heart's desires, to follow her wherever she went, and lead wherever she would go. A new lifestyle of flying off on short-term journeys had starting taking shape, and her styling career was pushing it into full throttle.

Always and forever had become the new them.

Chapter Thirty-One

"Nothing is more wretched than the mind of a man conscious of guilt."
~Plautus

Julien
Convincing Blanca that they needed to head to Rome after her workshop was easy. He covered his true intentions up with touring all the major landmarks in one exhaustive day. Coming up with a way to convince her that she now needed to bust out a pen and start signing autographs because she was a fully-fledged author now, not so easy.

Julien had screwed up again. He had waited too long to tell her about what the editor had done over the holidays, and the time had come for Blanca to take center stage because *Right as Rayne* had become an instant success according to Ms. Rossi's text to him last week. A text reminding him as Blanca's agent that they had a schedule to keep to.

Julien looked across the table at Blanca—an amber glow from the candlelight flickering over her dewy face. Her heart shown in her eyes—full and expectant—as if she knew at some point in Rome he'd be handing her a ring. In fact, he worried that she probably thought that tonight was going to be it. But, instead of a ring tucked away in the pocket of his jacket, he had something far more life changing to give her.

Julien looked around at the other couples in the outdoor eating area of the restaurant assessing their proximity. Safety in numbers. She'd be less likely to cause a scene just in case his news infuriated her. After spending hours sight-seeing in Rome, Julien had asked that they end their day dining out—a perfect scenario to tell her what he couldn't for so long.

I shouldn't be so fearful. Chase and Max are married. Blanca has nothing to worry about anymore.

Blanca cocked her head to the side. "Whatcha thinking?"

Julien reached into the inner breast pocket of his black sports jacket and pulled out a wrinkled envelope putting it on the table and covering it with his hand as Blanca grinned at him.

"I have been keeping something from you for a long time. Something that I thought would've made you the happiest person alive, but, when I tried to tell you at Christmas, I realized that it was only going to upset you then. I should've told you sooner, but it's perfect timing now, I hope. Everything between Max and you has been resolved, *oui?*"

Blanca set her wine glass down. "Jules? What's going on?" She brandished a coy smile at him. "And what's that about Christmas? What is it with that season and so many secrets? Okay, spill it. What did you do? Is that envelope full of immigration documents? Are you being deported? Is that going to be your angle to get me to say, *yes?*" She offered him a lazy laugh.

He shook his head. "These two weeks that I've insisted we stay in Italy, specifically, Rome, ehm—it's because of your book."

The twinkle in her eyes dimmed. "My book? What? You mean, *Right as Rayne?*"

"*Oui.* You know I only have the purist of intentions with you and helping you to see all the wonderful things in yourself that I do. You are an incredible stylist, and you are also a talented writer. Your story was lighthearted and fun, just like you. It's only right that you share it with others."

Blanca's smile dissolved into a frown. "What's in the envelope?"

Julien handed it to Blanca then tented his fingers together, resting his elbows on the table as he waited for her to open it. "Read it to me. Amilianna texted me a few days ago to verify our first appointment."

"Appointment? Amilianna, the editor? Julien, what's going on?"

He tipped his nose to the envelope she held with both hands. She stared at his address indicating Champagne with a postal mark from November and a publisher's logo tucked in the corner.

Blanca tugged the letter out and unfolded it—her eyes growing wide with guarded curiosity as she began to read it out loud to him.

"Dear Ms. Blanca Grazia,

It has been such a pleasure to work with you and your agent, Mr. L'Angevin, on *Right as Rayne*. The release date for your novel will be May 14th. In accordance with your contract, your twelve signing appearances will fall consecutively from the 9th through the 19th of July. Transportation and accommodations to each event will be provided for the two of you. In honoring your agent's request to limit your time for touring and maintain that all signings occur in Rome, you will be required to appear on, "*Buongiorno, Italia,*" concluding the promotion of your new release. We look forward to working with you this coming summer.

Sincerely,
Amilianna Rossi
Freelance Editor
Premiere Prodigy Publishing"

The letter began to quiver. "I'm published?"

"*Oui,* darling. Apparently, an actress found your novel on one of your flights last summer to Milan. She showed off the book while filming a scene on a soap opera."

"Love's Only Hope." Blanca uttered the television show's name more to herself than to Julien as she put the letter down and snatched up her

Chianti, taking a gulp.

"You knew that your novel was on television?"

"I saw the scene," she confessed, finishing off her wine.

Julien threw his hands up and burst into laughter. "Why didn't you say something?"

"Tell you what? That I ditched the book on a plane," she began then recoiled, shifting in her seat.

"You didn't lose it?" Julien's joy dissipated into a scowl as her abrupt confession stung him.

"No. I—I didn't *lose* it," she sighed and covered her face, parking her elbows on the table. "So now I'm published, and I'm supposed to go on a book tour this week? What the hell, Julien? How did this even happen?"

Her tone cut through him, slicing him down to a mere oaf floundering once again from another mistake. He leaned back—anger welling up in him as it began to sink in that the book they'd created together meant nothing to her the whole time if she was quick to toss it away as soon as he'd given it to her.

Blanca slapped her hands down on the table and looked up at him. "Start explaining now."

Julien folded his arms over his chest and stared at her. "When you threw your *birthday gift* away on the airplane and that actress found it, all her fans decided that they had to have the novel after they saw her reading it on her show. Ms. Rossi's contact information is on the inside cover, so the actress's agent got in touch with her. Ms. Rossi then pitched it to one of the publishers she works with to get it on the market before she even told me what she planned on doing with the manuscript. The deal was done before I had a chance to talk to you about it."

Blanca's eyes drifted down to the envelope. Her finger tapped against the postal stamp. "But you've known since November?"

"I didn't ask for the book to be pitched to a publisher. Ms. Rossi did that, all on her own. I only agreed to the publishing contract on your behalf. I didn't say anything to you because I knew that you wouldn't agree to any of it as long as Max and you were still fighting. But, that's all over now that she's married, *non*? Perhaps, she can finish whatever it is she needs done to her own book and try to get it published like you, *oui*? Why is being published such a horrible thing to you? *Je ne comprends pas* (I don't understand)."

"No, you don't," she groaned, shaking her head, fighting back tears. "What the hell is, 'Good Morning, Italy?' Am I going on a talk show, too?"

He nodded. "*Oui.* I'm sorry, but *Right as Rayne* has become a phenomenon—the mystery novel everyone couldn't buy last summer. Now, they can."

Blanca whimpered—a desperate look in her eyes growing wilder by the second.

Julien shook his head—his anger unfolding into fear. "I shouldn't have snapped at you. Forgive me, *s'il vous plait* (please)? I had no idea that you hated that I had your novel translated so much you would try to get rid of it and hide that from me."

Blanca looked at Julien, wiping away the tears that had escaped her eyes. "I don't hate it. Your intention behind it is the sweetest, nicest, most romantic thing any man has ever done for me. It's all my fault if Maxie wants to kill me when she finds out."

Julien unfolded his arms and leaned over the table, grabbing her hands in his. "*Non.* I still don't understand why you see any of this as a terrible thing. You and Max have worked everything out. She supports you completely. She isn't jealous of your book at all."

"Wait. How would she know? Does she know? Julien?" Blanca shrilled. "Oh, no!"

"Chase told her last week. He knew about the book being translated but kept his promise to me to stay silent until you were ready to tell her, but you never did. They asked us to join them in Santorini, but I told him that we couldn't. I told him we were going to be here, in Rome, and everything else kind of poured out of me. He told Max immediately."

"They both know about all of this, and no one said anything

to me? I've sent her, like, dozens of texts all week. She never said a word."

"Oh, Blanca, everyone knows. I invited my whole family to come to the talk show to support you."

"You what?" Blanca yanked her hands away from his and stood up then reeled a few steps in her stilettos.

Julien sprung out of his seat and rushed to her aid. He steered her towards her chair again and helped her sit down.

"Everything will be all right, love. It's exciting. You're published. Young women everywhere are celebrating you. It's because of your novel that we have been a part of each other's lives now for two years. Without it, you wouldn't have reached out to me after I went back to France."

"It's because of that novel my whole world is going to fall apart." Her voice trailed off as she slumped in her seat.

"Nonsense, darling. Everything is perfect, just like it has always been. We are going to start your book tour first thing tomorrow. All you have to do is smile and sign autographs for ten days then appear on the talk show. Everyone will be there to cheer you on even though no one will be able to understand a word of it." He offered a mediocre laugh.

Blanca's eyes cut to his. "Everything will be in Italian?"

"Just like your book, love. I wish you had told me the truth about it upsetting you. I only wanted to celebrate all that makes you so beautiful and exotic to me by having it translated into Italian in the first place."

He watched her work down a lump in her throat—her glossy eyes gaining focus. "I don't hate what you did. I think it's endearing actually," she repeated.

"So you forgive me?"

"Only if you forgive me, too."

"There's nothing to forgive. I never should have kept any of this from you. I was selfish in thinking that I would lose you over my mistake. I am not losing you, am I?"

"No. I brought this whole mess on myself." She sighed and tipped her chin up. "The book is only published in Italy? I just have to sign my name on a few copies then we can go home, and Max gets to be the author in America, and I'm back to being a traveling stylist everywhere else?"

"*Oui,* but you both can be anything your hearts desire."

"Believe me with all my heart on this one, Jules, I am just a stylist. And that is all I want to be."

"Except one more thing—"

Blanca pulled in a breath, as if awaiting the rest of his sentence in fear.

"My wife someday? You still want that, as well, *non?*"

"If you just proposed to me, I'm going to kill you. This is not a good time."

"*Non, non.* I will do it when the moment is perfect. I need you to say *yes,* remember? Now, let's get you back to the hotel. You look like you're about to pass out from shock."

Chapter thirty-two

"But what if I fail of my purpose here? It is but to keep the nerves at strain, to dry one's eyes and laugh at a fall, and baffled, get up and begin again."
~Robert Browning

Blanca

Clammy hands, rose-tinged cheeks, breathless words —the amount of stress Blanca lugged around with her felt almost unbearable. She paced in one of the green rooms that she and Julien waited in. They were to meet with the hostess of, "*Buongiorno, Italia*," any second before stepping out on stage in a few minutes.

After hanging out in Roman bookstores yapping it up with teenagers about a twenty-year-old mermaid named Rayne for the last several days, Blanca had thought she'd gotten over the whole insta-published author bit.

But, nooooo.

She was a hot mess that even Julien couldn't manage to calm down.

"Is it because it's a live show?" Julien asked, as he sat on a worn couch, watching Blanca cross back and forth in front of him wringing her hands.

Live. No do-overs. No chance to hop in a time machine and get it right the first time.

"No. It's not that."

"Is it because I told you that the show is sold out?"

Standing room only. All eyes on me. And then there's the bazillions watching me from home.

She shook her head. "No. Not that either."

"Is it because the producer said Donatella De Luca is going to be making a surprise appearance to meet you during the show?"

Meh, I already kinda met her. At least I got out of her way at the airport in Milan last year.

"Nope."

"Is it, ehm, because you didn't know how famous you'd become as an author until the tour?"

Famous? I'm famous. Famous for writing a kissing book about ... a fish woman.

"It's because everyone is here, isn't it?"

She stopped pacing and stared at him for a beat. "Yeah, that's it. That's the one."

Not really. I don't know. Maybe? Meh, that's my story, and I'm sticking to it.

The look on Julien's face was a cross between mortification and fear, like he knew he screwed up big time. He just didn't know how or why ... *unless ...unless this is it.*

Everyone is here, and I'm freaking out. And its scaring him. Him! Oh, no. This can't be happening right now!

A lanky girl with neon blue, horn-rimmed glasses holding a clipboard swung the door open prompting Julien to stand up next to Blanca. The peculiar girl had been the same assistant to bring them to the green room over an hour ago. "Blanca, Julien, I'd like to introduce you to Pia."

A gorgeous woman in her mid forties with a head full of fluffy, permed, dyed red hair stepped into the room.

Pia shook Julien's hand first. "It is a-uh pleasure to meet-uh both of you-uh. You will-uh be my first guests." Her accent was so thick she may as well have spoken Italian—at least Blanca would've understood her.

"Thank you for having us," Julien said, as Blanca just nodded—complete terror over all that was about to go down ripping through her body like a flash flood.

Pia pulled her hand away from Blanca's handshake and scowled at the nervous sweat Blanca had just transferred to the woman's palm.

I know. I'm gross. I'm sorry.

Pia resumed her professional, toothy grin and waved her hand in the air. "Showtime-uh in a-uh few minutes. My *assistente,* she will-uh *preparare* you in the wing for-uh your cue to come on-uh the stage. She will-uh take it from here-uh. *Scusami,* I need-uh to wash-uh my hands."

"I'm nervous," Blanca offered, but the woman just motioned at her dismissing any concern and turned on her heels proceeding out the door.

"Come with me. You're the first ten minutes of the show," the assistant added, motioning with her head to follow suit.

Just shoot me now.

* * *

Julien

Julien grabbed Blanca's trembling hands and brought them to his lips hoping to calm her as the assistant peered at both of them out of the corner of her eye. They were all waiting in the wing. Ahead of them, they could see a row of empty chairs on stage but could only hear Pia belting out something in Italian to the crowd. The audience members erupted into loud cheers at whatever Pia had just concluded in her monologue.

Blanca's eyes widened. Then their focus drifted off to the side.

"What did she say?" Julien asked, wishing he could speak Italian.

"She is really hyping up the whole celebrity angle with Donatella De Luca finding the book on the airplane. She says it's destiny."

"I believe it was—even if you tried to throw it away." Julien flashed her a pitiful smile, but it fell flat on her.

Blanca drew in a deep breath and furrowed her brow, prompting him to lean in to hear what she wanted to say to him. "Oh, Jules, I have to tell you something."

He looked down at her—her jade eyes ablaze with worry—and wrapped his arms around her shoulders, pulling her into his chest.

"I have something to tell you, as well, my love."

"You go first," she gulped. Her eyes grew wider as Pia continued to address the audience, taking questions and dropping both Julien's and Blanca's names intermittently.

"You're good with Max?"

"Yes?" she wheezed—the tone of her voice betraying her certainty.

Julien let go of Blanca's hands and cupped her face to get her to look at him. "It's going to be fine, darling. All you have to do is tell the audience that you left the proof copy on the plane on accident. They don't need to know the truth. Then, answer a few questions about the book tour."

"Okay, I guess." She worried her bottom lip between her teeth.

"Then tell me why you're so afraid?"

Tell me that you know what I'm going to do. Tell me that you're mad at me. Tell me that we'll talk later. But, please, just go on stage with me and shine.

Blanca groaned. "I did something—or, actually, I didn't do something. Either way, I betrayed the only two people in this world that I love as much as my family. By pretending if I just ignored it then my problem would just go away. But it didn't, and now you love me, and I love you."

"*Je ne comprends pas* (I don't understand). Of course, we love each other. You're panicking from stage fright. It's all right. Everything will be perfect."

Blanca looked terrified, like she somehow knew what he was going to do, and didn't want him to do it. Once again, he screwed up. He was putting his love for her on display for all to see just like he had done at Christmas with her book. She deserved a more intimate, a less showmanship display of his profession of everlasting love.

Julien shifted on his feet, his stomach lurching with nerves as he let go of her face and shoved his hands into his pockets. He had to come clean and let her know that he'd done it again. He'd made another mess of everything.

Pia's was in on it.

His whole family came to watch him do it.

He was about to put their love to the test with the grandest of all marriage proposals.

Julien's grand-maman's wedding ring he'd gotten while in Champagne was burning a hole in his pocket next to his wallet, cell phone, a scrap of paper he'd written his proposal on that he'd been memorizing, and the car keys. He felt he was left with no other choice but to give his beloved the benefit of the doubt and tell her what was about to happen in front of his entire family and all of Italy.

Blanca stared at him, mouth agape—her eyes losing focus with each blink. "You're going to break up with me."

He let go of the box in his pocket and slipped his hands out of his pockets again. "What?" He gripped her shoulders. "No, I, ehm, I'm going to—"

"Showtime," the assistant interrupted.

She was in on it, too, and apparently not about to let Julien ruin his own surprise.

The assistant pushed her way between them and stood next to the curtain, motioning for them to come to her. "Walk on, smile and wave, then take a seat. The show will cut to commercial, and someone will outfit you both with microphones."

Julien took Blanca's hand and led her out onto the stage. The audience erupted with excitement, and they both smiled and waved right on cue. Julien's whole family filled up the second row—Maxie and Chase sandwiched in the middle among them. Pia said a few words to everyone, and then the teleprompters on each end of the stage, obscured from the audience by big, potted, fake plants, revealed that they had cut to a commercial break.

Two male stagehands rushed out from the wing holding clip-on microphones and small battery operated power boxes with antennas flopping off the end of them. The young men stepped up in front of both of them and quickly clipped one microphone onto the pocket of Julien's maroon dress shirt and another onto the collar of Blanca's deep teal blouse. Then they tucked the battery packs behind them on the seat out of sight from the audience and rushed back off stage.

Julien wanted to tell Blanca he loved her no matter what. He wanted to plead his case and beg her to forgive him for flaunting their relationship and for turning her dedication to him into a spectacle for all to see.

All the words pressed at him to come rolling off his tongue in a steady confession. But he could not say them, not with the microphones already picking up on their murmuring hearts and their shortness of breath.

"*Tre, due, uno,*" someone behind one of the cameras shouted.

Julien and Blanca looked at each other—desperation in both their eyes—then turned their sights onto the sea of smiling faces.

* * *

Blanca

Blanca panned the faces of Julien's family members one by one—her smile softening at the sight of them, then her heart about damn near stopped. There was Maxie. Right smack dab in the middle of her BFF"s new extended family—the one Blanca wanted to call her own. Maxie L'Angevin—her best friend in the entire universe, her biggest cheerleader of all time—sitting there smacking her hands together. A cheesy smile spread from ear to ear. Knowing she would be there was one thing, seeing her there an entirely other.

A screen behind them flashed a picture of the front cover of *Right as Rayne*—the young woman's face, a golden curl falling across her cheek, the turbulent ocean reflected in her eyes, Blanca's name as big as the title itself, shiny and colorful. The audience *oohed* and *aahed*, then the uproar died down, and Pia began the interview, asking her first question of how it all began.

Blanca thought for a minute, a lunatic grin turning the corners of her mouth as she replied in Italian. She reminisced that her best friend had always wanted to be a romance novelist and how they had made a bet to finish their books in a month. She even motioned to Maxie in the audience. A camera pivoted around and zoomed in on her—all bright-eyed and blushing.

It sunk in to Blanca that everyone who came to support her couldn't understand a word of what was going on, and that little saving grace seemed to be enough to help her relax a little bit.

Then Pia asked her about the book's humble beginnings in Italy.

The humiliation of Blanca's atomic failure as a writer rose up in her again as she thought of what a mess her manuscript had been and how harsh the Amazon reviewers were to her.

Blanca shared with Pia how her first version of the book was awful, and she had given up as a writer—a dream she never wanted for herself anyway. She even tried to explain how Maxie was the true writer between the two of them.

But, no sooner was Blanca feeling like she had gained some control over her composure, the interview shifted onto Julien, and Pia started speaking in both Italian and broken English.

Nooooo!

Pia countered Blanca's comment with a question for Julien, asking him how he had played a part in the success of the novel.

"I helped her by having her novel translated into Italian."

Pia rattled off an interpretation, and the audience cheered.

"And that-uh book-uh, what happened to it-uh?" Pia followed up her question in Italian.

"I gave it to Blanca, and she brought it with her to Milan where we were going to be meeting up together."

Every female in the audience squealed at his answer.

He's mine. Grr. For now anyway.

"Blanca, you-uh somehow lost-uh the book-uh? Tell us-uh how?" Again, she followed up her question with an Italian translation.

Blanca squirmed in her seat as she lied about how absent-minded she must have been to leave the book in the seat back on the airplane.

Pia paced in front of them then stopped on the far left end of the stage. "And-uh, Julien, your love-uh for this-uh woman, it is-uh like a fairytale."

No, no, no, no, no.

"Blanca is the most beautiful woman I have ever known. She is compassionate, caring, and always putting others first. She has my heart completely. I love her." Julien reached over and covered her hand with his.

Pia recounted his compliment, word for word, as everyone in the audience cooed over them.

"We have a-uh special guest-uh who would like to-uh meet you."

To their right, Donatella De Luca, in all her sexy glory, came gliding onto the stage as the audience stood up and detonated into a frenzy of whoops and shrills while applauding her. She waved at all of them and walked over to the row of chairs, situating herself next to Blanca and throwing her arms around her neck.

The teleprompter cut to another commercial, and a stagehand hurried out, clamping a mic onto the spaghetti strap of Donatella's sundress and dropping the battery powered antenna box behind her. The actress turned to Blanca and squeezed her knee, breathing in Italian how happy she was to finally meet her and how much she loved her book.

Julien leaned over Blanca's lap and extended his hand—Donatella quickly grabbing onto it then letting go—as Blanca sat between them shifting her eyes to Maxie in the audience, who was chatting it up with Victoria down the row.

"Tre, due, uno."

Pia welcomed everyone back to the show and, in Italian, asked Donatella a few questions about how she had stumbled upon the book.

Donatella confessed that, after she had found it in the seat back on the airplane and had begun to read it, she couldn't put it down. She said she felt guilty for keeping it instead of giving it to a flight attendant for the lost and found.

The actress also said, when she had been filming the following day, she'd asked if she could switch out the prop book that she was supposed to be reading in the scene for the copy of *Right as Rayne* because she was on the last chapter. She said she had finished reading it on camera, and her reaction in the final scene after the cabana boy left had been true to her feelings about the book's happily-ever-after ending.

An ending that happened to be a proposal.

"And this-uh love story. It is-uh a lot-uh like yours, Julien and Blanca, *si*? Only it is a-uh mermaid's tale."

The audience laughed at the double entendre as Blanca noticed Maxie's brow furrow in confusion.

Rut-roh.

"Blanca," Julien began, standing and taking her hand, pulling her up with him.

It's really happening.

Julien dropped to one knee, and Blanca covered her gaping mouth with both hands.

"I love you, Blanca." He pulled out a tiny, scuffed box from his pocket and plucked a beautiful ring from its faded, velvet cushion, stuffing the centuries-old looking box back into his pocket again as the audience rumbled with a hushed excitement. "I have loved you for so long I can't even remember the first day that I knew. You are so much a part of me. I cannot imagine spending the rest of my life without you. In the words of Rayne's true love, Marlon, 'I will forever be yours, if you'll only be mine. I will forever love you 'til the end of time.' Blanca Grazia, will you marry me?"

Blanca dropped her hands from her mouth—her shoulder's slumping, a fiery heat clawing up from her toes to her neck, as the sound of sirens blared in her ears.

"You bitch!" Maxie screamed out, rising up in the audience. "How could you do this to me?"

Blanca turned to look at Maxie—the words she still couldn't come right out and say stuck in her throat choking her to death. Words that were bound by her petty jealousy. A confession she should've owned up to a long, long time ago.

That the stupid, famous mermaid book ... wasn't *hers.*

Right as Rayne was Maxie's book.

Julien had accidentally downloaded the wrong manuscript.

Chapter thirty-three

"Doubt thou the stars are fire, / Doubt that the sun doth move. / Doubt truth to be a liar, / But never doubt I love.
~William Shakespeare

Blanca

As Maxie nudged her way down the aisle and bolted for the double doors out into the lobby, Chase scampered after her. Blanca stared at both of them, frozen stiff and speechless. The audience escalated into an uproar, so Pia announced a commercial break.

"Blanca, what's happening?" she heard Julien ask. "Blanca?"

She felt his fingers grip her elbow as she snapped out of the trance of total humiliation. Reality smacked her right in the face as she looked up at Julien who had stepped into her line of sight. "What's going on?"

His words echoed throughout the studio, and, in one flailing swipe, Blanca plucked off their mics and tossed them onto the ground. "Come with me," she pleaded and grabbed his hand, tugging him along as she fled off the stage and down the aisle towards the lobby.

Pia shouted at their backs. "*Ritorno. Cosa sta succedendo? Non puoi partire da ora* (Come back! What is going on? You can't leave now)!"

But, leave they did, right in the middle of the show, like maniacs chasing down crazy, and it was all Blanca's fault.

Once they burst through a set of double doors out into the lobby, Blanca stopped dead in her tracks and panned the expansive space of employees scurrying around. Maxie and Chase were nowhere in sight.

"Why is Max so angry with you?"

"There she is!" Blanca spied Maxie through the glass, running to a vehicle across the street in the parking lot with Chase following after her. He threw his hands in the air like he was trying to make sense of it all. Just like Julien was scrambling to do on his end. "We have to talk to her!"

Before Julien had a chance to question her again, Blanca was out the glass doors and jogging down the steps of the studio.

"Maxie, stop! Wait! I can explain!" She halted her momentum as a few cars passed in front of her.

Chase and Maxie both whipped their heads around as Chase opened the car door for her. Then, she disappeared out of sight into the vehicle. A growl emanated from across the parking lot out of Chase as he closed the car door and jogged around the other side. He shrugged at Blanca indicating he still had no clue what was happening then slipped into the car and started it. Julien grabbed Blanca by the arm to stop her from lunging herself in front of another car as they both watched Chase and Maxie drive away.

A flood of camera operators came pouring out of the building with Pia on their heels rattling off a battery of commands as they surrounded Blanca and Julien. "What-uh is happening? Tell us-uh why your best-uh friend-uh ran out on-uh you?"

Blanca stared at the microphone then panned the cameras in her face completely losing sight of Julien who somehow escaped through the mob.

"My friend, Maxine Novaline L'Angevin is the one who wrote *Right as Rayne.* It was all a big mistake. I didn't mean for it to get this out of control. I had no idea it was going to end up published." She craned her neck around a cameraman trying to find Julien, but Pia stepped up closer to her and shoved the microphone back into her face. "Julien?

Juuulliiieeennn!"

"Are you-uh saying that-uh Julien and you-uh conspired to steal-uh your best friend's novel?"

"No! It's not a conspiracy. It's just a horrible mistake. I didn't even know it had been published until a week ago! I thought … it wasn't … Juulliieeen?"

"But-uh you have-uh been on tour, *no?*" Pia insisted. "You have-uh pretended like-uh you did-uh write de story."

Gah! I'm the worst person ever!

Blanca stumbled backwards then turned and shoved her way in between two of the film crew. She ran across the street and started heading for her rental car in the parking lot. As she approached the empty parking space, Julien sped around and pulled up next to her in their car.

He reached over the seat and threw her door open. "I was coming to get you. Get in and buckle up."

Blanca hopped in and slammed the door as one of the cameramen and Pia starting charging towards the car waving their hands in the air frantically. Julien switched the vehicle into reverse and then stopped abruptly, and finally surged forward and merged onto the busy street that ran alongside the studio lot.

Once they were a mile or so away, Julien finally broke the awkward silence between them filled only by Blanca's heavy breathing.

"What is going on?" he asked, infuriated.

Here goes the end of all my hopes and dreams.

"It's hers."

"What is? My grand-maman's wedding ring? It was my inheritance. Chase knew that I would be giving it to you. He had Max's ring custom made from one of his mother's heirlooms. She has no right to be angry with you."

The ring? The ring! I didn't say yes. I didn't say anything. I ruined another engagement for him!

Blanca shook her head—her face scrunched up in agony. "Not the ring. The book."

"What?"

"You downloaded the wrong file when I was with you in Champagne for Christmas forever ago." She gulped and cleared her throat.

Julien reared his head back as if he had smashed into an invisible wall that had jutted up between them out of nowhere. "I did?"

"Yes! I should've told you as soon as I figured it out when I was reading the book on that flight."

"But, the book, it was yours. Rayne's story, *non*?"

"We *both* named our characters Rayne. In my book, she's just a woman who loves dolphins and lives by the sea. Maxie's Rayne is a mermaid who swims with dolphins."

Julien nodded slowly—his temple ticking with silent rage as he stared at the road before them—unchartered and wide open with no destination in mind.

Just like our future now. Gah!

She was terrified like that.

* * *

Julien

It was happening all over again—another proposal gone to waste. And it was his entire fault.

"I'm so sorry I did this to you," he uttered, as he kept his eyes on the road.

"No. *I* did this to me. I should've said something to you a long time ago."

He glanced over at her briefly. "Is that why you left the book on the flight?" She nodded in shame. "Whatever happened to the copy I gave you at Christmas?"

"That one is still at my nonna's house. My ma says she has it on display in the guest bathroom because it's decorated with a beachy theme and fits right in."

Crapper reading material? That's almost funny.

"Oh, Blanca, why didn't you tell me what I had done?" His accent dripped of sorrow.

"You didn't do anything wrong. It's all me. I'm the *boombots* (idiot) who got jealous."

"Why would you be jealous of her book?"

"No, not the book. I'm jealous of you … and … and Maxie," she groaned. "You loved that novel so much. You kept going on and on about how my story meant everything to you and how it's the reason we're even together. Then you go and have it translated into the best gift in the whole world because you loved it so much. When I figured out it was Maxie's, I didn't want to tell you."

"Why not?"

"You did everything for her. *Her!* All of it. And, like a *stunad* (idiot), I tried to throw the book away, but it ended up getting published, and the next thing you know I'm on a talk show in Italy wondering what the hell happened!"

"I did everything for *you*. Only you."

A frustrated growl escaped Blanca as she doubled over in her seat, clutching her stomach—her thick, reddish hair tumbling forward and hiding her face.

"I ruined everything by being jealous—stupid, freakin' *jealous*." Her words came out muffled and breathless as she began to cry.

Everything? Your friendship, probably. Our engagement, definitely.

Julien reached over and began to rub her back. "We'll get through this together."

Blanca lifted her head up and peered at him prompting him to retract his hand. "You still want to be with me?"

"Of course, darling," he replied, although his heart was crumbling into a million pieces. "I am upset, but we'll work through this. That's what couples do."

"Huh? Really? You don't hate me?"

"*Non.*"

"I hate me." The words came out of her soured and pithy. "Where are we going anyway? We have to go back to the hotel. I need my purse. Do you have your phone on you? I have to talk to Maxie."

"Here." Julien stretched back and pulled a fistful of things out of his pocket, including his cell phone and the ring box. He dropped the engagement ring into the console and handed his iPhone to Blanca keeping his eyes straight ahead as he turned down the street to their hotel.

"Thank you." She powered his cell phone on and stared at the ring box in front of her. "I'm so sorry that I screwed up your proposal."

Not as sorry as I am.

"It's fine."

She sucked in air between sighs as Julien's iPhone sparked to life. "You probably don't even want to marry me now knowing what a horrible person I am."

That makes two of us in everyone's eyes.

"We can talk about all of this when we get to the hotel."

Blanca's voice—so small and weak—came out in a whisper. "Okay."

"Find out from them what, ehm, everyone is going to do now. We were all supposed to go out to lunch after the show to celebrate our engagement before we fly home this afternoon."

"Oh." Her tears continued to flow. "You have seven messages," she added, as she pulled up his contacts.

"That doesn't surprise me," he frowned, as she dialed Maxie's number. "Actually, don't ask. I'm sure everyone's figured out by now that we're not celebrating anything today."

"I'm sorry I ruined everything—of course, it's going to voicemail. Dammit." Blanca waited a few seconds then left a message for Maxie to call her as soon as possible so she could explain. "Do you want me to play all your messages for you on speaker?"

"No. Just power it off. I'll deal with everyone's questions later. I'm sure Chase has filled my family in by now."

Julien glanced at Blanca out of the corner of his eye as she powered down his cell phone and set it next to the ring box in the console. She sat silently, staring at the worn box, tears still sliding down her cheeks and mottling the silken blouse she wore with drops like rain.

How could so many things go wrong in an instant? What did I do to deserve this? Just once, I'd like to have something go right in my life.

Julien gathered his breath and reached over, snatching up the ring box then maneuvering to tuck it back into his pants pocket again as Blanca turned her attention towards the side window.

"I'll try again someday," he groaned.

At least I hope to.

Chapter thirty-four

"There is no love without forgiveness, and there is no forgiveness without love."
~Bryant H. McGill

Julien

While Blanca sat on the end of the bed in the hotel room crying to Maxie on her cell phone, Julien paced the floor pleading with Chase. Both of them were arguing that neither Blanca nor he had been conspiring to ruin their perfect, happily-ever-after lives. Their conversations dragged on for barely ten minutes before Julien was the first to get hung up on. A few seconds later, Blanca threw herself back on the bed and tossed her iPhone onto the night table and hid her face in her hands.

Julien groaned, "I take it your call didn't go well either?"

"When do we need to head to the airport? I just want to get out of here. You are coming with me, aren't you? You aren't abandoning me, too? Please wait until I'm home first before you dump me."

Julien sat down on the edge of the bed beside Blanca and pulled her hands away from her face.

"You should've told me what I had done, but you didn't. I shouldn't have taken so many liberties with your—Max's—book, but I did. We are both guilty of creating this mess. They will forgive us eventually, but what we need to do right now is forgive each other and ourselves and move forward. I am not going to leave you. I love you. The real question is if you still love me."

Blanca sat up and threw her arms around his shoulders. "Yasss! Yes, I do!"

If only you'd said that a couple of hours ago when I had proposed.

"Then let's gather everything up and wait at the airport for our flight."

Blanca gave Julien a tight squeeze then pulled away from him. "Does your family hate me?"

"*Non.* They are only angry with me. They are having a hard time believing that I didn't do all of this to razz Chase on purpose by coming after his new wife with my antics. I've spent the last two years building everyone an impressive case against me."

"I'll tell them what I did. It's all on me."

"I already explained everything to them. I think its best we, ehm, let things cool off and sink in for them. "

"All righty. We'll wait." Blanca stood up and started rushing around the hotel room packing her suitcase as Julien watched her quietly. "So we'll go to the airport and wait there, too. And us getting engaged?" She turned her eyes to him. "*We* can wait, right?"

I really don't have much of a choice.

"Of course."

"I owe you a perfect proposal opportunity after all you've been through."

Julien only shook his head with a pitiful smile.

At this point I don't even care anymore. I just want to skip to the marriage.

* * *

Blanca

Maxie said she hated me. Hated me! She said she never wants to talk to me again. She said she should've taken Julien up on his offer to fool around that summer. She said she's getting even. What the hell?

"Thank you," Blanca mustered a smile, taking the mocha Julien had gotten for her as she sat in the terminal mulling over her argument with Maxie. "Lemme ask you something."

Julien sat down beside her. "All right."

"What exactly happened in France when you were with Maxie? Did you try to hook up with her?"

Julien drew in a deep breath and exhaled shaking his head. "I may have threatened Chase with something like that. I can't remember. I did try to kiss her. I thought I had explained that to you when we first met. I never had any real feelings for her, but she was a beautiful woman staying with me, and my cousin wasn't doing a very good job at convincing me that he actually had any genuine feelings for her until after she left. You aren't siding with my family now, are you?"

"Maxie said some things."

"And did they hurt your feelings? Make you doubt my love for you? Work you up into a jealous mess again?"

"No—maybe." *Ouch.*

"Max has a right to be mad at me. I did not know you then. I hardly knew her. I had every intention of making Chase angry that summer, but it backfired on me. Max is a wonderful person, and I recognized that and wanted to get to know her better. Instead of driving them apart, my razzing only pushed them together. Now, they are happily married, and I'm to blame."

I get that you're trying to joke about it. But double ouch.

Blanca offered him a fake laugh then took a sip of her mocha and gazed through the wall of windows looking out over the airplanes taxiing in. "She said she's going to get revenge."

"Really? I doubt she would try to include me in anything. She's my cousin's wife now, remember?"

Gah! You're all family now, and I'm the stunad on the outside looking in!

"I know. I know. I'm just—I don't know. I'm my own worst nightmare. I bet this entire country is talking crap about me right now."

"The editor did leave a message to say the studio would like to have all of us on again. Apparently, we were quite a ratings boost this morning."

Blanca smirked at that.

Julien bowed his head. "She's also looking into the legal ramifications of plagiarism. She said Max called her but wouldn't go into any details."

And there it is. Revenge at its finest.

"She's going to sue me. Just you watch."

* * *

Julien

That first week back in Napa Valley proved to be as awkward as it was stressful. Awkward because they'd fallen into a stagnant routine of trying to stay out of each other's way. Stressful because Chase and Max were still stewing over what their next move would be. Blanca plunged right back into work at the spa, and Julien moped around the house fixing things that weren't broken because he wasn't welcome at Angel of the Vine Winery anymore.

Neither of them engaged in anything other than small talk. And speaking of being engaged, that sore topic went to the wayside along with any mention of their future together. They were living in the moment once again, and it was tearing them apart.

When Ms. Rossi finally called Julien in the middle of the night to address the legal consequences of what Blanca had done, they listened in together on speakerphone as they lay in bed. When the phone call concluded, Julien pulled Blanca into his arms and cradled her as she wept.

Blanca whimpered, "So that's it. They're pulling all the copies from all the stores, and they've lawyered up against me in case they get sued too."

Julien smoothed Blanca's hair and held her tighter. Just having her in his arms again fed his soul the nourishment it needed. "They won't do anything else, not unless Max strikes back. They're only going through the motions."

"So it's over?"

"*Non.* She said they've relinquished their rights to the novel."

"What does that mean?"

"You own the book again."

"I can't get rid of that dang thing, no matter what I do!"

Julien couldn't help but chuckle. "We'll figure something out."

Blanca wiggled her leg underneath Julien's thigh and draped her other leg over him, nuzzling into his neck. "I miss this. I miss us."

"So do I, love."

"What's next?"

"I'll go over to Chase's tomorrow and force him to talk to me. At least I'll be able to come to him with the good news. I don't know much about the legal matters of publishing, but there must be something positive about the rights to the book no longer belonging to that publishing company. Ms. Rossi said that she emailed me copies of all the legal documents the publisher filed to severe your deal. The hardcopies will take a few weeks to arrive."

"I meant you and me."

Julien kissed her temple. "If we can survive this, we can survive anything."

And we will, my little devil. We will.

* * *

As Julien drove towards Angel of the Vine Winery, he pondered all the information that he knew. He had virtually signed countless papers through the process of publication, but he had never paid much attention to the details. He feared that confronting Chase unarmed with questionable facts was a wrong move. It occurred to him, as his attention veered along the side of the main road, that he needed to contact a lawyer and go over the documents that he'd been emailed. He realized that he ought to better understand how to approach his cousin and face the rest of his family about the matter legally.

Julien turned around and headed back home. After a phone call and a quick trip into town to print some documents off his laptop, he only needed to meet with a lawyer he'd booked a consultation with, catching up with the man at a sports bar nearby that next afternoon. It wasn't even going to cost him—the lawyer couldn't wait to meet him and learn about all the details of what they'd inadvertently done to his cousin's wife, and he said he'd help out as best he could.

* * *

Blanca

"What the hell, Julien! Bart Moore! You called Bart freakin' Moore to help us? That's Maxie's ex who sued your aunt and uncle twice!"

Julien raked his fingers through the top of his hair as he paced the floor in the living room. Blanca set her purse down on the kitchen table having just walked through the door after a long day at work only to be handed that info bomb.

"How was I supposed to know that? It was a long time ago. I'd probably only heard his name once in passing back then. My life in Champagne was too reclusive."

"How did this even happen?" She stomped back into the living room—arms crossed and lips pursed.

"I saw his ad along the main road. It was so obnoxious and eye-catching I figured he must know what he's doing to have the biggest billboard I've ever seen."

"He put that there to taunt your family! He's not even in Napa—he's in Sacramento. He didn't say anything about knowing who you were related to?"

"*Non,* ehm, I guess he did make a weird noise and laughed it off after I gave him my full name. Then he said he wanted to meet me for beers and talk about what we'd done tomorrow evening."

"Ugh. This is bad. So, so bad. What is he doing? How is that buffoon even practicing anymore?"

"He said he's working on a class action suit about some diet pill that's catching in people's throats and choking them to death. Deciphering contracts is something else he also does. He claims he's somewhat of a handyman lawyer."

"What a *chooch* (jackass)!" Blanca let out a slow groan.

"I can't believe I screwed up again. No matter what I do, I just can't get it right with us."

Blanca tipped her nose in the air and closed her eyes, drawing in a deep breath. "You didn't know. Keep the appointment. I'm coming with you. I have some things I'd love to say to him face to face."

Julien stopped pacing and stood in front of her. "Blanca?"

She opened her eyes. "What?"

"Are we still all right?"

"If relationships have to go through hard times to test their survival, we're looking at a lifetime sentence together after of all of this."

Gah! Love is messy!

Chapter Thirty-five

"True friends stab you in the front."
~Oscar Wilde

Blanca

The sports bar was crowded for a Tuesday evening. Julien led Blanca through all the jovial, warm bodies slurping their beers and getting their game on. The fleeting thought of her life before this wrecking ball of a man came along and swept her off her stilettos whooshing away with her slunk past her mind.

She didn't miss it one bit.

Not the thrill of being pursued.

Nor the zing of being caught.

Nope.

The angst of pleading her emotionally unavailable status when her partners wanted more—those days of dread were long gone.

She was all content, and satisfied, and full of genuine feels, although she was a wreck scrambling to keep up with wanting it all with Julien.

Her love for the man who, one minute was her calm in the storm then the next minute *the actual storm*, grew even stronger the more complicated their relationship became. Julien L'Angevin was her perfect mess, and all she wanted to do was fix everything, including herself—an even bigger disaster—so she could get on with being married to him and face the crazy world together as one.

She was determined like that.

As they nestled up to the bar without a single available stool to sit on, Blanca panned the area for Bart while Julien flagged the bartender down.

"I don't see him, yet," she quipped.

Julien looped his arm around her waist.

Oh, I miss this affection. Purrr.

"We are a few minutes early."

"Let's get a couple of drinks and hit the pool table or some darts or something." She winked at him in an attempt to lighten the mood.

Blanca had stewed all night long over what she had wanted to say to that human equivalent of toe jam, Bart Moore. What she'd managed to come up with was a simple rant. Short and not at all sweet. Then she planned on leaving with Julien. That was it.

Easy, am I right?

Blanca was hoping after their encounter they'd head over to Chase and Maxie's and wing it through all their limited knowledge of the publishing business to try to come up with a plan together. Whether she would walk away with a bestie again or not, she couldn't foresee. All she knew was she'd had about all she could take of living in limbo—living for the moment—and was determined to take charge of her future.

The bartender handed them their beers, and they weaved their way through the crowd over to the pool tables and dartboards. All the tables were in play, so they decided on a round of darts while they waited. Blanca couldn't remember when they had last gone out and had some fun together, and tossing some darts at a target, as ordinary at it was, felt incredible.

As soon as Bart walked in, he locked eyes with Blanca from across the room. His dopey, cheesecake smile fizzled into a stone cold sneer as he made his way towards them. She elbowed Julien and motioned at the stocky, meathead-of-a-buffoon waddling like a penguin because of his steroid-induced bulk.

Julien laughed. He actually guffawed at the sight of Maxie's ex. "That billboard didn't do him justice. This guy is a freak show of all things pompous."

"I couldn't have said it better myself, babe," Blanca laughed with him. She clutched a fistful of darts then thrust one at their dartboard on the far wall that already had three of Julien's darts poking out of it.

Their mutual amusement over the sight of Bart united them instantly. That snake didn't stand a chance in wreaking any more havoc in their topsy-turvy lives as it was.

"Hello, Blanca," Bart oozed, sticking out his hand to greet her.

Would it be wrong if I just stabbed him in the throat with all these darts and ran?

"Hello, pond scum." She only reached over and grabbed her beer off a narrow counter along the wall, taking a swig while staring his pudgy, extended hand down.

"Now, now. I wasn't the one who set up this whole *soirée.*" Bart shifted his attention over to Julien and tried to shake his hand, as well, but Julien wasn't having it either.

That's my guy.

Julien approached him forcing Bart to look up at him. "I made a mistake in calling you. I won't be needing your service, but Blanca, here, has some things she'd like to say to you."

Bart raised both of his hands in a defense gesture and backed off, flashing a toothy grin. "Hold up, I'm going to need a drink for this."

He pivoted and waddled over to a waitress who had been working the pool tables and gave her his order then he returned to them.

Blanca set her beer down and tossed another dart at the board. "You have a lot of nerve, you know that? I can't believe you're still practicing law. And what's with that hideous billboard?"

"Funny how it came in handy, didn't it? So, you're on the outs with Maximus now? You're—what are you?" He shifted his attention over to Julien. "Her friend? Her latest conquest? Don't tell me you're actually dating this tramp? Five months of dating her friend and not once did I ever see her with the same dude twice."

The waitress that took Bart's order came up to him and handed him a beer off her loaded tray.

Julien reared over him. "Roids have you moody, little man? Say another disrespectful word about Blanca, and I will end you."

"Easy, buddy. I'm just here because you wanted to meet with me. Remember?" Bart dropped a fistful of crumbled dollars he had pulled from his jean shorts onto the waitress's tray then shushed her away to grab him another beer as he started pounding the one he had been given. "So, eh, you two stole some literary property in the form of plagiarism? A novel, was it? And you want to give it back? There is a quick and easy way off the top of my head, but it's going to cost you."

Julien finished his beer and set the bottle down. "We're not giving you a dime."

Blanca thrust another dart at the board in the distance. "Do you know what you are, Bart? You're a predator. I hate you for verbally abusing Maxie all those months. You can try to insult me all you want, but your words mean nothing. You are a heartless, hell-bound, evil piece of shit. You don't deserve love. No woman should ever have to tolerate you."

Bart's eyes shifted between Julien and Blanca as both of them stood side by side, and he bowed his head. "Fine. Yes. I'm a horrible person. Are we done here? I came all the way out here for some free entertainment, and you've both been so accommodating. Now, if you'll excuse me, I have better things to do than offer my help to the both of you."

As Bart pivoted, the waitress he'd sent to fetch him another beer sidled up behind him. He bumped into her loaded tray of various drinks and toppled it over. Bottles and wine glasses shattered onto the ground at their feet causing Bart to reel backward and fall flat on his back in the sloshy pool of stinky booze and broken glass.

The waitress was all apologies saying she'd grab a broom and some towels as she rushed back to the bar. Blanca and Julien burst out into laughter at the sight of Bart wallowing in the foamy puddle. Julien reached out with an extended hand to help Bart up off the floor, but the humiliated *gagoots* (moron) grappled at Blanca's feet instead and curled his fingers around her shin in an attempt to use her leg to help himself sit up.

In one fail swoop, he knocked Blanca off her feet. Her hands flew up and so did the remaining dart she was holding. But, in three ... two ... one ... beats of everyone's hearts that frilly, little, red dart barreled down at Bart and landed right smack dab between his legs ... and popped his nut.

* * *

Julien

"Karma, ain't she sweet?" Blanca rasped between bouts of laughter, as Julien grabbed her up off the floor then began raking his hands over her body ensuring that no broken glass had gotten on her. He could care less if he cut himself in the process.

"Are you all right, love?"

"Never better."

"Call 911! Call 911! Please!" Bart squealed back. He curled up into a fetal position and yanked out the dart and tossed it aside. No one seemed to notice him or care that he was writhing all over the floor.

"It's going to cost you," Blanca retorted, stepping around him.

"A pseudonym. Just use Max's name as a pseudonym, and the book is theoretically hers. Now get me some help!"

"That's it? That's all you've got? Lame." Blanca wheezed between giggles as Bart eased onto all fours like the dog that he was, refusing Julien's extended hand a second time.

Suit yourself.

The waitress and the manager returned with a broom, dustpan, and several hand towels. "We called 911 for you, sir. Are you okay?"

"I should sue you for this!" he growled at all of them.

And, on that note, Julien draped his arm around Blanca's shoulders and ushered her away.

* * *

Rolling up to Chase's cabin, they could see inside where Max was tending to something in the kitchen. It was a bold move for both of them to simply show up uninvited and demand all of them work things out peaceably, assuming his cousin and his cousin's wife would even be home. Neither Julien nor Blanca would have it any other way, though. Julien was willing to do anything to help Blanca mend her friendship with Max if it provided an open door for him to pull Blanca into the family fold once and for all, taking her as his bride.

They'd been spotted because Max stormed out of the kitchen and rushed over to the front door, throwing it open and waiting in the threshold. She looked furious and eager. Chase appeared behind her brandishing a sneer all of his own. Their meeting was not going to go down smoothly by any means.

Julien and Blanca climbed out of the vehicle and took each other's hand as they stepped up onto the porch. No one broke eye contact, and everyone stayed silent. It was an epic standoff of dominance. They weren't leaving until a resolution had been set in motion, even if it had to happen right there on the porch.

"I just turned Bart into a eunuch—maybe," Blanca blurted out.

All eyes careened to her, and Max's jaw literally dropped. "Huh?"

Blanca postured on her. "Let us in, and I'll explain."

Brilliant. Bait her with curiosity. I love this woman.

Max looked over her shoulder at Chase who shrugged and moved aside, and she huffed, "Fine. Come in."

Blanca ducked in first slinking past Max. She marched right up to the dining room table and took a seat. Julien scrambled after her mumbling his *pardons* as he slipped by Max and avoided Chase altogether.

The unsuspecting hosts followed behind and took seats across from them. Then, the staring contest resumed for a few more seconds before

Blanca finally spoke up. "I let Julien think your book was mine. He's totally innocent in this whole freakin' nightmare, so stop hating on him. I take the blame for everything."

But I love you enough to let it all go.

"This is true. I was not being vindictive by any means," Julien added, but his stomach sank with grief at the unfortunate reality that it was, indeed, her fault from the beginning. "I made a terrible mistake. I did not know that Blanca and you had both named your characters Rayne. When I saw the name in the document title of her most recent files, I had no idea I was downloading your book, Max. I did not do any of this maliciously to razz you or Chase. You have to know that I wish you both only the best."

Max's face softened towards Julien, and Chase covered her hand with his, halting the slight thrumming of her fingertips on the lacy tablecloth.

Blanca leaned forward in her chair. "Believe me when I say I didn't know he had your book published until a couple of weeks ago. I only knew about the Italian paperback he had created for me for my birthday. I should've told him he had mistaken your book for mine, but I didn't."

Max rolled her eyes then glared. "Why not? Why keep living a lie? That's not a healthy way to conduct yourself in a relationship."

Julien shifted in his seat as he held his tongue against Max's criticism.

Blanca looked between Max and Julien. "You had just told me you were getting married, and I was angry at you."

"So? What does that have to do with Julien?"

"You want me to spell it out for you? Fine. I was jealous. I was jealous that you let another boyfriend come between us." Blanca tipped her head to Chase. "No offense, dude. I think you're awesome, and I really am happy that she married you."

Chase gave Blanca an expressionless nod. Then she continued to address Max. "And it was right after you had told me that you had gotten engaged when I noticed that the novel was yours and not mine. I was so jealous of it that I ditched it on that flight."

"I don't get it. You already read my book when we all flew to France. Why would you be jealous of it all of a sudden? Writing's not even your thing."

Julien cleared his throat and lowered his eyes. "I, ehm, I may have made a bigger deal about how wonderful the book was than I should have."

Blanca took Julien's hand under the table and cupped it with both of hers, flooding his heart with warmth as she continued her confession. "I was jealous of *you*—not your book. I was jealous of all the attention Julien was giving *you* when he thought it was mine. I was afraid if I told him that he screwed up and went through all that trouble to translate *your* book—well, you'd have that connection between you two, not me. I wouldn't even be with Julien if we didn't bond over my stupid story in the first place. I couldn't have him feeling like he had let me down, and then run to you with this incredible, loving gift."

Julien lifted his eyes to Chase, and Max made a small noise like she'd been holding her breath but finally let it go. "Like I said to you on the phone after the show, Chase, I didn't tell Blanca that the editor had gotten it published until we were in Rome."

Blanca added, "And I didn't say anything when he told me because I was afraid. He signed a contract. I had to be at the first bookstore the next day. Besides, how do you tell someone you love they may have ruined someone else's life because of you? I kept thinking all week, 'What if he feels so humiliated and embarrassed that he dumps me and takes the train back home to Champagne?' Just like that when we were finally in a place in our relationship where I wanted to marry him."

Julien squeezed Blanca's hand under the table and whispered, "I wouldn't have left you. This is my home, here, with you."

"I know," she whispered back, as Max and Chase exchanged peculiar looks.

Blanca piped in again, "I swear I was going to confess everything to you and Julien as soon as we came home from Europe. I thought no one would know what was going on because everything was in Italian, then all hell broke loose."

Max shook her head in frustration. "Did you know that I've had agents out of New York calling me everyday wanting to pitch my book to the big five because of that talk show? They aired it that afternoon with all kinds of extra footage. The entire country wants the book that was so good the author's best friend tried to steal it!"

Blanca squinted at her. "Is The Big Five another talk show? Because if it is, I don't want anything to do with it."

"No! The top five trade publishers. Don't you know anything about—nope, never mind. I give up. So, am I going to have to hire a lawyer to sue your publisher to get them to pull *my* novel with *your name on it* off the market?"

"It's already done. They gave me the rights to it again, too, so help me figure out a way to hand it over to you. Bart said—"

"What the hell, Blanca? Bart is as good as dead to me."

"Actually, he might be wishing he was after what I did to him."

Max cocked her head to the side. "I don't even know if I want to ask."

Julien let out a small laugh. "Let's just say I made another mistake."

Blanca shrugged. "I may or may not have rendered his ability to procreate thanks to a dart."

And, for the first time since they arrived, Max smiled.

Chapter Thirty-Six

"True love stories never have endings."
~Richard Bach

Blanca
Thank God she's finally cracking a smile, sheesh.

Julien let go of Blanca's hand under the table and tented his fingers together on the table. "We'll do whatever we need to, but all I ask is that you don't sue her for plagiarism. There must be a way to switch the copyright without a legal battle. The publishing rights have been restored to her, so I would assume she could then sign them over to you somehow."

"*No,* I'm not going to sue you. Hate you for a while, *maybe.*"

"I'd hate me, too."

I own it. I'm a total turd on this one.

"I'll contact the copyright office first thing tomorrow," Julien interjected.

Chase offered a weak smile. "I'm relieved to know that you weren't trying to come between us again."

Gah! He's in love with meeeee!

"I would never dream of taking advantage of my sister-in-law or you. Those vindictive days are behind me. I only want to spend the rest of my life supporting Blanca as best I can."

Aw! Mine, all mine, all mine. He was never really into her.

"Just make sure you both communicate better," Chase added.

"Agreed."

Blanca pressed her lips into an awkward smile and looked between Julien and Maxie. "I promise."

She was remorseful like that.

* * *

The following morning, true to his word, Julien contacted the copyright office through an email, which landed him a phone call only a couple of hours later. Apparently, the guy Julien laughed with for a solid thirty minutes had heard all about what had happened and couldn't wait to get the inside scoop. Since Maxie wasn't going to sue Blanca to get her novel back, the process to reinstate the manuscript's rightful author would be an easy transition but with loads of legal paperwork.

So be it.

That afternoon, just before Blanca headed to the salon, she reached out to Maxie in a text with the good news and was met with a simple reply of, *thank you.*

It took another month for Blanca to hear from Maxie again even though Julien had been polishing up production on Blanc de Blanca at Angel of the Vine Winery almost every day. Their vin was set to debut at Christmas time which was only a few months away.

Maxie: *Congratulations*

Blanca: *Thx*

Maxie: *When's the big day?*

Blanca: *Not for a few weeks*

Maxie: *Well, I hope you enjoy the adventure. Stay out of trouble*

Blanca: *I'll do my best but you know how it goes with me*

Blanca couldn't help but do a little happy dance. Trouble had become her badge of honor. She had quit working at the salon just when the fall season was about to bring in droves of holiday customers. That didn't go over too well with the owners, but it wasn't like the news was a surprise. Her calendar for the next solid year was booked with different gigs all over the world thanks to her connections she'd established in Milan.

The *big day*, the day Blanca would embark on yet another adventure with Julien, was coming up soon. They were going to run off to Cairo and hang out with Victoria for a week. Then the following week, her new career as a personal stylist would have them in Los Angeles preening a band for a charity event that Skeeter Dee had connected her with. The traveling would be endless. The adventures—all to come.

Maxie: *I hope you two*
come back finally engaged

Blanca looked over at Julien who had his nose in a newspaper. An actual newspaper. How the heck he found one was beyond her scope of interest, but there he was sitting on the couch in the living room reading it. His feet, crossed at the ankles, wiggled on the coffee table as if he were anxious to be relaxing.

Blanca thought about how she should respond to Maxie's comment but then settled on letting her have the last word. It was the least she could do for her bestie. *Bestie.* Their relationship was fractured but not broken, and Blanca counted on time and Maxie's success as an author to mend their friendship someday. If she were ever going to get married, she'd need her BFF by her side all the way.

Blanca stood up from the dining room table and walked over to Julien, tugging the newspaper down to see his face. "Hi," she grinned.

"*Bonjour.*" He folded the paper and set it on the table then tugged her onto his lap. "What can I do for you?"

"Maxie is talking to me again."

"Max? Wonderful. Chase did mention to me the other day that her agent keeps telling her you were the best thing to ever happen to her writing career."

"I'm probably her new cuss word. Instead of, *Oh, spank*! she's probably like, *Oh, flibberdeblanca!'*

A gentle laugh rolled deep from within Julien's chest. "I can see that."

"You know what I can see?"

He tilted his head and gave her a quizzical look. "What?"

"*You.*"

She pressed her lips against his, looping her arms around his shoulders as she kicked her legs up into the air, pulling him down over her. She nestled into the couch on her back as he shifted his weight and leaned over her, nipping at her lips again then veering to her neck.

"I love you, Jules."

"I know," he responded, muffling the words in her ear as he dove into the tender flesh just below her thrumming pulse.

"So this trip of ours to Cairo—any major events going down I should pack for, or will it all be khakis and sunscreen?" she squeaked out, as he settled in between her legs.

Julien covered Blanca's mouth with his, slipping his tongue along hers, provoking a small moan out of her. His heart clamored in his chest thumping against hers as he maneuvered on top of her in a slow rocking rhythm. She held onto him like her life depended on it, like everything she could ever hope for was right there in her arms for the keeping.

And, by the time Julien was done devouring Blanca with kisses, she knew the answer to her question.

* * *

"I'm not joking. How in the world it could be raining in the middle of the desert is proof nothing ever works out right for me." Julien raised his hands up to the sky, marred with gray clouds hammering both of them in a sudden downpour, as he knelt before Blanca in the sand.

Nope. This is perfect. Absolutely, positively perfect.

"It's okay. I'm used to it," she laughed, doubled over holding her side as she gasped for breath. "Now, what were you saying?"

A flash of lightning shattered above them followed by a crack of thunder. The fury made Blanca jump and squee with delight. From a distance, their tour guide looked as though he were growing impatient as he held onto the reins of their camels, all the while Victoria shook with silent laughter, trying to hold her iPhone steady as she filmed them.

"I was saying how much I enjoy our random adventures together," Julien chuckled, as he dug into a pocket of his cargo shorts.

Blanca tossed her head back and closed her eyes for a moment, letting the rain patter against her smiling face—her hair a sopping mess of bedraggled, amber tendrils—yet another color change to suit the autumnal season. "We do know how to have *fun*, don't we?"

"Ah, *oui.*" Julien reached out and took her hand. "Blanca Grazia," he continued.

She opened her eyes and looked down at him—soaking wet and grinning from ear to ear—little rivets of water streaming off the brim of his Indiana Jones inspired leather fedora.

Julien held up a platinum ring between his fingers—a crest of emerald cut diamonds arching along its curve—his Grand-mère Mimi's treasured wedding band. "Will you marry me?"

"Yes! Yes! Yasss!" Blanca added a little hop to her apparent enthusiasm as he slid the ring onto her finger.

That man kneeling before her, who'd taught her what commitment was, who'd suffered through her chronic mishaps and indiscretions, who'd given up his life to help define hers—he was all she ever wanted and all she ever needed. He was the one who filled her with hope that true love could be hers.

Julien stood up and draped his arms around her looking down at her glistening face with so much love in his eyes it could fill an ocean. "Love you always, Blanca."

She grinned up at him—giving him a soft peck on the lips before answering as her heart bubbled over with joy.

Bubbles!

"Love you forever, Jules."

And she would.
She was in love like that.

Epilogue

"Sit in reverie and watch the changing color of the waves that break upon the idle seashore of the mind."
~Henry Wadsworth Longfellow

Blanca

"Aunt B? No. Auntie Ba-Ba? Nah. Auntie B. That's it! I'm going to be Auntie B from now on."

"You'll have plenty of time to decide. You might even want Stirfry to come up with his or her own name for you," Maxie suggested.

"Stirfry?"

"The baby looks like a little shrimp on the ultrasound," Maxie shrugged.

"Yep. That's gross. Why not go with something sweeter like Jellybean until you know if you're having a boy or a girl?"

Chase and Julien shook their heads muffling their laughter as they all sat in a row on bar stools looking at the raging sea through the massive windows before them. Silver storm clouds maneuvered across the hazy sky, bursting with heavy rain.

The sound of the raindrops pummeling the wooden deck in front of them was more enticing to Blanca that the eclectic renditions of wordless Christmas songs that filled the enormous, crowded coffee house. The joint hummed with a muffled chatter as, once again, it felt like all of California had come to join them for the afternoon.

Blanca fiddled with her half-empty cup of nutty, maple, mocha something-or-other that the flannel-wearing barista had handcrafted for her. It might've been the best-tasting espresso drink ever, second to the one she remembered from two years ago when she came to Fabrewlicious Coffee & Tea with Maxie while on their writer's retreat.

"Jellybean *is* cute. Maybe I'll steal your idea," Maxie jested.

"What's mine is yours. Mind if I don't reciprocate?" Blanca chided in return.

An earthy hint of pine and spruce swirled about them emanating from the enormous Christmas trees studding the crowded coffee house. White lights shimmered through the handmade, seashell ornaments and metallic blue and silver bulbs—or bubbles—as Blanca liked to call them, giving the trees an oceanic touch to their Christmas cheer. And, speaking of bubbles, Julien's Blanc de Blanca had already been retailing for a week, holding its own among other wines in the holiday market.

"This view is incredible. We'll have to come back to Sea Sprite in the spring when the weather changes again," Julien commented, as he watched the foam-capped waves tumble onto the shore in the distance far beyond the deck.

"I love that idea," Blanca replied.

"It has been nice for all of us to get out of the valley for the weekend. This town is pretty cool," Chase added. "But what's with all these people? It's like Abercrombie & Fitch threw up in here, and why do I feel like we're the only couples that are married?"

"*Almost* married," Blanca chirped in. "It was like this when we came here a long time ago. I guess it's a thing."

"When does everyone start arriving for the wedding?" Maxie asked, then downed the last of her licorice spiced herbal tea.

Julien leaned over past Blanca and addressed Maxie's question. "My parents will be in town next Friday, but everyone else will start trickling in the week after."

Maxie continued, "I think it's great that you're having your wedding so close to Christmas. It brings everyone together on both sides of your family."

"*Our* family," Blanca added, looking between Julien and Chase who were seated on either side of her and her bestie.

Bestie? No. Soon-to-be-sister-in-law? Nah. Sister. That's it! Maxie will be my Sis now. Squee!

"Oh, spank! We're about to be legally related, huh? That's so cool."

Blanca blushed a little. "I think so, too."

"Can I call you my sista?"

"Yasss!"

"I still can't believe that you pulled everything off in under six weeks. Your wedding coordinator must be a rock star."

"She is—a very expensive one, but you've been a huge help with all the little details these past two weeks. Thank you for being willing to help me."

"Aw, of course. I want your wedding day to be all you've ever wanted it to be. I always have."

"You know what I want it to be? Already behind me. I just want to be married to this sexy, French beast-of-a-man. I want to be his wife, that's all."

Maxie gave Chase a coy smile as she replied, "I know what you mean."

"I did suggest eloping," Julien added. "But my sisters would kill me."

"Yes, they would," Chase replied with a laugh. "Except Tori. I could see her showing up one day married, not a word about it to anyone, but, then again, I wonder if she'll ever settle down."

"Actually," Maxie perked up. "She mentioned to me a few weeks ago that helping you two finally get engaged was so exciting that she was actually contemplating how much fun she could have if she had a serious boyfriend to travel with on her excavations."

"Maybe the next time we come back to Sea Sprite we should bring her," Blanca pondered, elbowing Julien as she waved her hand over her shoulder at the noisy crowd of hotties behind her. "We should bring her here to do some shopping."

"Here?" Maxie cocked her head. "Nah, she needs a city boy to balance her out—a suit-and-tie kinda guy."

"You think? Meh. I bet she'd be happier with a bearded beach bum."

Maxie cocked an eyebrow at her. "Oh, really. You bet me, huh? You're on."

Blanca crossed her arms. "Deal. We see who can find Tori the love of her life by—"

"No!" Julien and Chase both shrilled in unison.

Blanca threw her hands up in the air. "Oh, come on. Really? What could possibly go wrong?"

On second thought ...

The End

Acknowledgments

In 2015, a few months after I had completed the rough draft of my first novel, *Whine with Cheese (Vineyard Pleasures Series, #1)*, someone turned my attention to NaNoWriMo. Yep, it's a real thing: National Novel Writing Month. Having never heard of the event before, I was immediately intrigued.

A worldwide novel writing challenge. Local and virtual write-ins. Support across every social media platform known to humanity. How did I not know about this mysterious and wonderful word, NaNoWriMo?

The challenge is to complete a 50,000 word manuscript in one month starting on November 1st. It didn't take long for the self-doubt to sink in. Write a novel in thirty days? *Pft.* Yeah, right. My first novel, *Whine with Cheese,* took me a long and tiresome nine months to write. A literal, darling book-baby, if you ask me. I had taken my sweet time crafting that novel, writing only when the mood struck until I had finished the rough draft. I wasn't convinced I'd even want to try to knock out another novel without polishing that one first, let alone, write it in a month alongside thousands of others.

Then I got to thinking ... but I could use the accountability ... and I could use the community encouragement. I bet I could knock out 50,000 words in 30 days if I forced myself to sit down and write everyday. I've got this.

And by November 30th another novel was born. It was done. A total disaster, but yeah, finished it, hit submit, and earned my badge on the event website. It was so messy and word-driven that I still have yet to revisit it to see if I could resuscitate any charm out of the drab thing to tweak it into something I'd be proud of. I was so focused on reaching my word count each day (1,665) that the story suffered for it. Needless to say, the following year, I skipped out on writing another NaNoWriMo book.

But, whoa, what an impression the experience had on me.
I spent the following couple of years getting *Whine with Cheese* ready for publication—did I mention that I liked to take my time when I write? I also drafted a plan for two five-book series while I mulled over that first book, and I marinated on the plot of *Love the Wine You're With* the whole time.

I came to the conclusion that I absolutely just had to make the kink in Blanca and Maxie's competitiveness a NaNoWriMo competition. Considering I had so much personal angst to draw from, the subplot was born. Then, on top of that, my husband, Joel, tossed me the idea of the plot twist. All him. He's a treasure trove of fodder. On YouTube, he's known as **Philly.500**. I'll just leave it at that. Go discover. Go laugh ... a lot.

Then the next thing I knew, synchronicity reared her silly head, and the time to write *Love the Wine You're With* had come. Summer of 2017, I sat down and wrote it. Ten weeks. Almost 100,000 words. Done. There I was pecking away at my laptop, creating another RomCom while I was basically following the write everyday model that the NaNoWriMo event promotes. At the end of summer, I had basically done the equivalent of the challenge twice. I allowed myself to ignore my daily word count and just let the story unfold. And, most importantly, I allowed myself to go back and preen as needed so that I could keep moving forward.

With *Love the Wine You're With (Vineyard Pleasures, #2)* coming out on November 1st in honor of NaNoWriMo and just in time for the holidays, I thought it would only seem right if I challenged myself to join the event again and adhere to my new approach of quality not quantity when writing everyday instead of earning the badge. So I registered for the event again, I hunted down my local peeps on social media, and I found myself in a coffee shop talking to a local newspaper about what I was about to do …

* * *

First and foremost, I thank my husband and children for their love, patience, encouragement, and teamwork in helping me write this novel. You are all so amazing and wonderful. I am so blessed! I love you, family!

Thank you Robin Woods for the use of your story prompt. It worked perfectly in that scene! Prompt Me and Prompt Me More can be purchased on **Amazon**. Thank you, as well Robin, for vetting through the first fifteen chapters of my rough draft with your super-human hole picking skills.

Thank you Anette B. and my mom, Doris, for beta reading my book and finding all the oopsies with your eyes for detail.

Thank you Maria M. and Rayenne H. for letting me tab into your brain about your reading experience as you joined Blanca and Julien on their worldly adventure.

And thank you to all my readers. I love making you smile!

About the Author

BROOKE E. WAYNE is a Contemporary Romantic Comedy novelist who lives the RomCom dream in California. She is married to a South Philly, Eagles-obsessed Italian who she met online before it was cool. They have two young daughters who flood their happily-ever-after lives with girly giggles and immeasurable love.

When she is not dribbling sticky sweet/sensual romance with a lighthearted, witty twist all over the pages of a RomCom manuscript, she teaches English Language Arts.

Brooke E. Wayne
ROMANCE WITH A KISS OF HUMOR

http://www.brookeewayne.com

http://www.facebook.com/authorbrookeewayne

http://www.twitter.com/brookeewayne

Vineyard Pleasures Series

Whine with Cheese
Love the Wine You're With
Wine Not? (Coming Soon)

www.ingramcontent.com/pod-product-compliance
Lightning Source LLC
Chambersburg PA
CBHW060512180626
46817CB00002B/347
* 9 7 8 0 6 9 2 9 7 7 5 2 1 *